Inverted

Surviving The Upsidedown World

Craig Matthews

Inverted

What The Eye Beholds Series— Book II

By Craig Matthews

Craig Matthews Media

Inverted

Published by Craig Matthews Media, Port Huron, MI

ISBN: print 978-1-7355017-8-9

Permissions for quotations or use may be sent to:

Craig@CraigMatthewsMedia.com

INVERTED

Visit for news and information on this and other exciting titles.

This book is a work of fiction and in no way describes any particular person living or dead.

Editing: Larry Giroux

Cover: CMCreations

Formatting: Nancy Kuykendall

Proofreading: Joy Neal Kidney. Arlene Jacobucci.

Inverted

Surviving The Upsidedown World

By Craig Matthews

Surviving upsidedown.

Up is down. Back is forward. Last is first. Weak is strong.

Twenty-five years after surviving the collision of worlds in Charity's Fire, the next generation has been trained to lead the underground. Then, the eldest runs away to Mars to escape the demands of leadership, and the second in command turns into a selfish rebel—bent on destruction.

Is everything always falling toward chaos?

As millions on earth flee the grip of the tyrannical Global Union, who will lead the outcasts to freedom? Who will rescue the downtrodden? Who will stand in the gap for the persecuted? Where will they run?

Short-sighted human ambitions must fall to the ground and die before the real plan can emerge from the fertile soil of impossibility.

Are the Rebel and the Runaway really cowards?

Was their preparation another divine distraction?

Or have they suffered enough to be in the perfect position from which the underground can launch an exodus of Biblical proportions.

Inverted

Strong is weak. First is last. Forward is back. Down is up.

Survive upsidedown. #invertedthe book #surviveupsidedown

Inverted

What The Eye Beholds Series—Book II

by Craig Matthews

ACKNOWLEDGEMENTS

THANK YOU

No book is created in a vacuum. Life is swirling all around us as we authors create. I began planning this story before the first book in the series was published. Writing commenced in the winter of 2024. At that time, my wife Connie feared I would do something to one of our grandkids in this story. She was so nervous. I only laughed and planned on reading it to her just before publication. That was our thing— I would read my books out loud to her to check how the book sounded and to let her experience the story firsthand. She knew the three main protagonists were loosely based on a few of our grandchildren and did not want me to kill them off like I had done to two people in the first book of this series, Charity's Fire. When I read that book to her, she had difficulty sleeping one night because she could not figure out how that book could end on a positive note. As I tell everyone, you must read to the final page to understand my crazy brain.

Then, in November of 2024, the unbelievable happened— my wife of forty-three years, eight months, and eight days suddenly passed away. I had not read her this book. Grief put everything on hold for many months. Every writing project came to a screeching halt— except one. I began journaling six weeks after her funeral. That was the moment I could think enough to process some of my emotions on a page. Another month passed, and I was clear-headed enough to write a novel in six weeks, quicker than ever. That work is not associated with this series and is targeted to be released at the end of 2025.

But this book was still on the shelf for a few more weeks before I had a dear friend read through it for me. I gave it to her on my way out to Kansas City. She is a lifesaver. Joy Neal Kidney carefully and skillfully pointed out all of those silly mistakes I would have caught by reading it aloud to Connie plus many more. Joy has made me a better writer. I sincerely appreciate her input on this work of fiction.

Larry Giroux loves to edit! Who could imagine that was a thing? So grateful for his expertise.

My mom is almost 92, and she is my biggest fan. Although her macular degeneration is an issue, she reads and rereads all of my books with gusto, taking notes for me throughout.

I hope you enjoy this upside-down adventure— I think Connie would have, after catching up on the sleep she missed from all the stress induced by listening to another one of my crazy tales.

Peace,

Craig Matthews

Introduction to Terms

Some Unique Terms to Inverted.

EVO: The Exterior Environmentally Versatile Operation Suit, affectionately called Evo, the standard LIFT employee dress for outside operations on the surface of Mars.

Bubble: The Emergency Personal Atmospheric Containment Units (EPACU) that can be deployed on top of the head to provide breathable air. When deployed they snap into position and are twice as large as a human head and transparent.

Betts Calendar: This calendar is based on the first landing— which we know happened on the Earth date of 20 June 2027, which was 28 days before the Martian summer solstice in the northern hemisphere— Betts decided that the Martian calendar should begin on the vernal equinox of the same year, meaning the first landing by humans on the Martian surface was 139 sols into the new martian year, which would hence and forever more be called, Year 1. It's why the 5th of Navi is celebrated as arrival day every MY.

SOL: Martian Day (24 hours 39 minutes and 35 seconds)

MY: Martian Year (687 Sols— nearly two Earth years.)

LIFT INC: The transportation company based in the Bahama's responsible for all movement of all non-military supplies and materials to and from the surface of Mars, Luna, and Earth.

MEF: Mars Expeditionary Force, United States Marines Battalion stationed on Mars.

F.P.: Federal Police (American).

Warriors: also called Angel Warriors.

Reaper: Top Demonic Warriors covered in black and carry razor sharp scythes as weapons.

Leech: Anchor setting demon worker slugs.

Cube: (Cube-omnium) A tiny Martian apartment.

Shimmer Blanket: A specialized blanket that camouflages biological life heat signatures hiding beneath it from satellites and electronic surveillance. On satellite readouts, it appears like a shimmering heat signature that is indistinguishable from its surroundings.

G.U.: Global Union is a one world government approach to global governance on Earth led by the Chinese Communist Party and has replaced the United Nations.

C.S.A.: Compliant States of America.

Niner Mike: Rebel group working in the Western North Carolina mountains.

Biological-Digital Storage (BDS): An electronic storage area in an inactive brain space that had been surgically segmented to store mission-critical information.

E-stols: Laser Pistols.

LOS: Line of Sight

F.E.: Is the acronym Warriors used for the term Flicker Envier. These people hang around flickers because they saw something different in their lives and hoped their strength would rub off on them.

MGA: Martian Global Authority is basically the United Nations of Mars.

Hum: A nuclear powered Martian work truck (land system vehicle) meant to be lived in for a week at a time.

CMP: Central Martian Power— a power creation and distribution company near Shepard.

Rocker: An automated launch vehicle used to carry scientific experiments to orbit.

Revolver: Twelve massive cargo ships that run on a continuous loop between Earth and Mars without slowing. Revolver are spaced about a month apart and unload and reload while passing by each planet. Revolvers are a simple ship. A fifteen hundred foot spine with a Quad Ion Pulse Drive engines on the back, the CP stuck on the front end with a CM docked out front of the CP. Everything else is clamped onto the rails of the spine. An access shaft runs up the center of the spine.

GL-2: The most powerful rocket ever built by LIFT.

S/F: Spray foam reinforced with carbon nanotube technology.

Atmo: Breathable air.

120E: is an electromagnetic pulse weapon based in a mortar round.

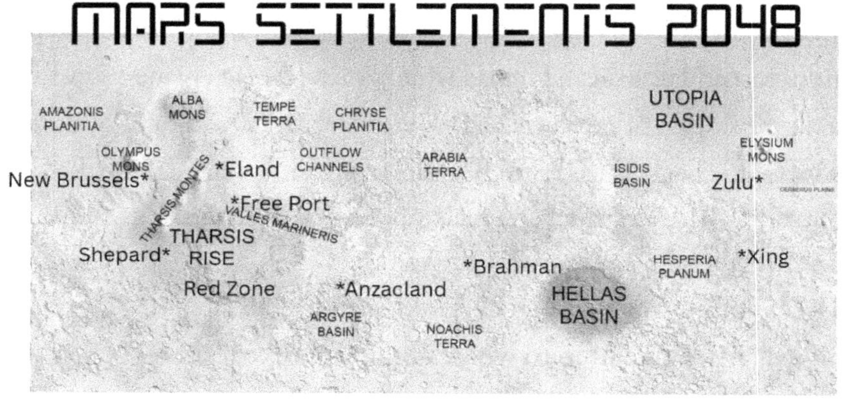
MARS SETTLEMENTS 2048
AMAZONIS
PLANITIA
ALBA
MONS
TEMPE
TERRA
CHRYSE
PLANITIA
UTOPIA
BASIN
ELYSIUM
MONS
OLYMPUS
MONS
OUTFLOW
CHANNELS
ARABIA
TERRA
ISIDIS
BASIN
New Brussels*
*Eland
Zulu*
THARSIS MONTES
*Free Port
VALLES MARINERIS
THARSIS
RISE
Shepard*
HESPERIA
PLANUM
*Xing
*Brahman
Red Zone
*Anzacland
HELLAS
BASIN
ARGYRE
BASIN
NOACHIS
TERRA

INVERTED

CONTENTS

ONE

Sol 7618

He stood camouflaged in the crowd—buried in the everyday sameness while white-knuckling the righteous judge in his left hand.

"These capitalist slaves need an awakening," he thought. One corner of his mouth raised in a smirk, knowing his three pounds of plastic explosives would launch a glorious new day of enlightenment. He believed his act of bravery, and those of his brothers, would introduce enough chaos all over the planet that the city-state democracies ran by oligarchs and corporations would crumble as people demanded order.

In his periphery, he noticed a guy in a uniform separated from everyone else. He tried not to turn his head and stare, but he could not stop himself. A bead of sweat formed on his forehead and rolled down behind his dark sunglasses. Pulling his hat down, he tried to melt back into the gathering.

As Kars watched dust dance across the tops of his boots, the ache returned to his gut. He did not notice the eyes boring into him from the man with sunglasses in the middle of the group of people behind him to his right. Kars waited for the sun and the train to arrive when the longing inside his heart showed up instead— blinding him to everything else. This was his favorite time of day when the world paused to catch its breath before the sun broke over the distant horizon. Today's peaceful moment triggered a longing for the same emotions he had when fishing back home.

Hundreds of mornings he had watched the sunrise while casting his line to the zipping reel, the plop of the lure, and a cool breeze on his face. Buried deep in his heart he longed for that abandoned home and the people he had left behind. Now, all he had was this dust, driven by a distant wind and a sudden desire to feel again. Tears found their way to the corners of his eyes, and he did not look to see if any of the strangers waiting with him were aware. Most of those people were busy nursing steamy cups of one form of mud or another while checking messages or mindlessly searching their comm units for the latest social media rumors. A few folks and Kars anticipated the colorful show in the sky. Still, no one noticed that his loneliness had boiled over— not even the sadistic guy in the sunglasses.

An inch-thick glass wall separated them. Kars touched the side of his helmet, and his face shield sunscreen changed to a shiny gold. Then, his surging emotions forced his head to look up and find the bright blue star. When he located it, his hand naturally stretched toward the place where he had left a large piece of his heart. At this time of year, Earth was brighter than all stars except Jupiter. It felt closer to him than the end of his gloved hand and simultaneously further than the thirty-eight million miles it lay across the solar system. Thirty-eight million miles is as close as the two planets got to each other, but to Kars Dee, it felt like an impossible divide.

A sudden thump against his back caused him to stumble forward.

"What up, D?" came with the shove.

"What's your problem?" Kars' anger piqued.

"Your suit not working?"

"That's why we are waiting for the train outside, you idiot."

"Sorry. I didn't know your PA was out, I thought it was just your comms."

"No, my prox has been in and out, too."

"Sorry man, I would have done something a lot more fun if I'd have known."

"Where's Benz?" Kars asked— not amused. No one answered. He banged the side of his helmet, and a crackling and fuzzy voice came through.

"Can't hear you, Kars."

Two more guys shuffled up in the dust to wait for the train. Benz, along with the kid, Hagus. Benz waved his arms, but Kars could not receive his transmissions. Kars lifted his arms in frustration, and Benz gave him a sympathetic thumbs up.

Colors began radiating on the eastern horizon as thin clouds refracted the arriving sunlight. The particles in the atmosphere gave off an orange glow as shafts shot up through the suspended dust. The sky directly above their heads was still black as night— which made the scene out in front of them more brilliant as distant mountaintops glowed with the arrival of the new day.

None of the four men in space suits noticed the approaching train barreling into the station until the ground shook beneath their feet. The steel rails squawked, and breaking wheels shot tiny sparks in opposition to the mass in motion. All the men with the LIFT logo on their backpacks naturally took a cryptic step away from the tracks. Inside the terminal, the waiting passengers pushed toward the airlock and paused for it to work through its cycle. Once the train stopped it went into its static discharge protocol to remove the dust build-up on its surface. This is accomplished by electrically charging the particles and then reversing the charge on the skin of the train. In so doing, the dust is statically neutralized and simply falls to the ground. The station's retractable airlock shoots jets of air on approach to the side of the train and then magnetically seals itself to the car. The AI checks the seal and then fills the airlock with atmosphere. The doors inside the terminal unlock, and another group of passengers climbs aboard in their shirt sleeves.

This was just another day in the life of all fifty-three passengers boarding the early express train in Free Port, except for the guy holding the oversized gray specimen case. This train was headed north to Eland and scheduled to arrive ninety minutes after departure. The four space-suited figures outside the terminal had walked toward the middle of the train and its manual airlock. The men would have to cycle through independently, which took about a minute for each man to accomplish. The passengers knew they'd be waiting for the LIFT employees to get aboard before the train departed.

All four men moved forward when they entered the train. The LIFT employee car had enough room for the men to remove their suits if they wanted, plus storage lockers for their equipment. They removed their helmet latches and twisted the unit to release it from the bracket.

The air in the car had a distinct iron smell, and the men scrunched their noses in an involuntary response.

"Pew," Benz said. "This place needs cleaning."

"You gotta get that fixed!" the Latino kid, known as Foot, said to Kars. He pointed at Kars' helmet and had pushed his boss with the snarky joke.

"Ya think?" Kars said.

Hagus, the last guy onto the train, struggled to remove his helmet, and Kars stepped over to help him. "Your latch isn't all the way open, Hagus."

"Dang rookie." Benz laughed while working to free his own gloves.

Muffled speech emanated from beneath Hagus' helmet as Kars gently tapped on the latch and worked it open. Removing stuck helmets can be dangerous, as many have lost their lives because, initially, the suit controls were all inside the helmet. After those deaths, LIFT added forearm controls for the life support functions. Still, even these are not always enough— if the dust causes the helmet release to stick while it is sideways on your head, you can not see the controls. You have to operate the life support buttons blind. There have been many who have died with a stuck helmet and no way to dislodge it. They simply ran out of O2 without a buddy to help. The current protocol is to completely cycle the airlock before removing your helmet. Seems simple enough, but people are not always wise.

"Good thing you got a buddy to help you, Hagus," Benz said, pushing the kid's piss-me-off button— again.

"Relax. Almost got it," Kars said to Hagus. "You're going to need to vacuum this track out."

"Come on," Foot said, "I'm not waiting for you to get into the breakfast line." Hagus and Foot had only been on the dust bowl for a MY. Rookies had to have a hand-holding veteran with them on the job at all times. Only after surviving three MYs is anyone considered enough of a veteran to work on their own projects. One vet can have up to six rookies on their team at any one time. Kars thought knew that having two rookies was more than enough ignorance gathered in one place.

Hagus, a Scottish immigrant, came out of his suit cursing the dust and Benz.

"Hey, listen, you made a dumb mistake by not cleaning your helmet latch after you wore it the last time. I'm not going to your funeral for a stupid rookie mistake. Take care of your equipment. You don't understand how many guys have died for dumb shit like this. Stop it! Do your job, or I'm bouncing you." Benz turned away.

Hagus' anger turned silent.

"You guys go get some food, we are going to work on my comms," Kars said.

"Don't forget your PA." Foot flashed his toothy grin.

"Ya."

"Are we going to need to replace that comm unit?" Benz asked Kars sitting down across from him, trying to release anger over his stupid Scottish coworker. Kars sat on the bench at the utility table, still in his Evo suit with the helmet in front of him, while removing and inspecting his gloves.

"I want to, but this will be the third one this year."

"Its gotta be the dust." Benz said.

"The bane of my existence."

"The reality of life on the Bowl," Benz said.

"If I would have been warned about the dust ahead of time, I don't know if I would have rode the wagon." Kars was frustrated.

"I know you would have," Benz said.

"What are you talking about?"

"I was coming— so you were coming along."

"Whatever! I signed up first."

"Only after I talked to you into it."

"You were too afraid," Kars deadpanned.

"Shoot! Fear is the whole reason we are on this rusted rock," Benz said, pushing his best friend's hand off the table.

The two rookies exited the LIFT employee car and headed for breakfast. LIFT offers a hot food selection during morning runs, which is free for employees and tastes decent. The food line had cleared when the pair entered the dining car.

"You should take them guys a peace offering," Foot said as the train lurched forward.

"Screw that," Hagus said.

"Well if you don't, I will."

The unwritten protocol for rookies required them to take food to superiors when the boss kept working before the rookies ate.

"Brown-noser."

"Brown's better than bounced, Esse."

They both understood that being bounced from LIFT meant getting fired, losing company housing, and possibly the prerogative for living in Free Port. The law required every Free Port citizen to have a job to breathe the recycled O2. No job meant you had to catch on in another city or out in a God-forsaken mining camp. There were always jobs available in the mining camps because people got killed all the time. Mining was the most dangerous job in the universe and the last place any sane person on Mars wanted to be.

Foot slid butt-first back into the LIFT employee car with two plates heaped with steaming hot food: scrambled eggs, imitation bacon, and foe-tato cubes with greens. His two fingers on his right hand held a carrier with two hot coffees— known as Martian Mud.

"What? No five fingers of death?" Benz mocked.

"Thank God. They were all out," Foot said. The five fingers of death were the name for old Army MREs of beef franks and beans, which could be found in remote worksite emergency bins. One of them had given Foot a case of the runs for three long days a couple of weeks back.

"Foot, you're alright for a dumb immigrant."

"We're all dumb immigrants on Mars, Boss."

"Some are more imma than others, if you catch my drift." Benz laughed.

"Thanks, kid," Kars said.

"Careful, the mud burned my mouth." Foot waved his hand in front of his open mouth, then left the car in a hurry to get breakfast.

Martian Mud is a poor excuse for coffee. Still, it is the only thing they have been able to grow on the planet with enough volume to support the population's desire for a coffee supplement. The genetically enhanced chicory root is harvested in all the big cities and roasted to look like coffee. Black tea leaves are added for caffeine. The black tea and chicory plants are thriving on Mars, and the grounds created are recycled— they are a healthy soil additive for the farms because they retain so much moisture.

After stuffing breakfast into their pie holes, the two friends replaced Kars' comm unit and his proximity alarm radar sensor, which are also in the helmet. The Exterior Environmentally Versatile Operation Suit, affectionately called Evo, was the standard LIFT employee dress for outside operations on the surface of Mars. Most corporate employees across the planet use some variation of the Evo, but the robust units require daily maintenance and frequent software upgrades to maintain their working status. Every LIFT employee leased a specific Evo to use and care for. When certain maintenance items had to be replaced before the engineering specs called for an upgrade, a pro-rated percentage was deducted from the employee's earnings. A third Comm unit in one Martian year would cost Kars a steep ninety percent of the part's wholesale price. The final piece of the helmet repair for Kars was to tape the seams with 100mph tape to help keep the dust at bay. Fortunately, the off white duct tape, matched the skin of his helmet, and was available without cost to all employees.

After the necessary systems diagnostic checks, the men found their two understudies sitting at a table in the train's dining car, three cars forward from the LIFT airlock.

Both Kars and Benz are naturally quiet men, enjoying the silence contained within their Evo suits. Walking into the raucous atmosphere of the dining car made them want to return to the peaceful work car and wait for their arrival in Eland.

"Wait! These guys will know the answer," Foot said to the whole car, while standing and pointing at his bosses.

Almost everyone was in the middle of a debate, with lines drawn up for each side of the argument.

"I don't need to settle anything." Benz shook his head and waved his hands in surrender.

"Come on, boss, we need your help. We are lowly rookie immigrants to your fair world."

"Shut up, Foot."

"Why do you call, Juan, Foot?" a young Asian woman sitting across from Foot asked Benz.

"Because he's good at soccer and insists we call that sport football. Which we know it is not football, because we," he pointed to Kars and himself, "played football all through high school."

"American Football." Kars revealed a quick mocking smile.

"Yeah. Real football." Benz high-fived Kars.

This action triggered loud objections throughout the car.

"Were you guys any good?"

"I played for twelve years," Kars said.

"That doesn't mean you were any good," she said.

"Our team went to the state championship our senior year," Benz said.

"And I know the guy who scored three touchdowns in that game," Kars said.

"Wait. Wait, this wasn't the argument we needed you guys to settle," Foot said.

"Okay. Okay. What's the question?" Benz asked.

"This guy over here is an Earthie," Hagus pointed to a guy behind him, "and is staying in Shepard."

"So lemme guess—he works for Amazon?"

"Right." Foot looked at the guy and asked him, "Do you?"

The black-haired man gave a thumbs up.

"He lives in Shepard. Rode the wagon up six weeks ago and doesn't want to miss his mom's birthday. We know Earthies don't recognize the Betts calendar."

"The time converter is online. He can access that when he visits Free Port again." Benz started to turn away hoping to short circuit the argument that they had walked into.

"Right, he knows that, but doesn't know how to explain it to her."

"Come on, old timer. Give him the inside scoop on what happened," someone yelled from the front of the dining car.

"Old timer! I got your old timer..." Kars said. "Where are you from?"

"You wouldn't know where it is."

"Try me."

"Calumet."

"Michigan. On the Keweenaw peninsula."

"How'd you know that?"

"Let's say I like maps."

"Wow. No one knows where Calumet is."

"Okay, Benz, give our Michigan brother the scoop," Kars said.

Benz looked around sheepishly at the crowd then cleared his throat. "Alright, children. The Betts calendar. Lesson one," Benz said. Benz was a quiet soul, but he enjoyed the spotlight every once in a while.

"An original Martian explorer on the first mission, while surviving the long Martian winter had spent a few days locked in his cabin along with, as the legend goes, a gallon of homemade moonshine."

Laughter rolled across the car.

"During this time, Dr. John 'Mookie' Betts came up with a calendar from a Martian perspective. Not one imposed on Martians by the bureaucrats on Earth. The calendar was a big hit once discovered by the first settlers."

"I thought they were the first settlers," someone said.

"No, John Betts was part of the team of original explorers from NASA and only stayed a year on the planet."

"Why Mookie?" another guy asked.

"He loved the Dodgers and their second basemen for a long time was a guy named Mookie Betts. So, of course John Betts accepted the nickname."

"Back to the calendar!" someone shouted.

"Okay. The Betts calendar is based on the first landing— which we know happened on the Earth date of 20 June 2027. Since that was 28 days before the Martian summer solstice in the northern hemisphere, Betts and his moonshine, decided that the calendar should begin on the vernal equinox of the same year, which happened 139 days before the landing. So, the first landing by humans on the Martian surface was 139 sols into the new Martian year, which would hence and forever more be called, Year 1. It's why we celebrate the 5th of Navi as arrival day every MY."

"What do you mean by MY?" The Amazon worker asked.

"Martian Year. Today is the 30th Nox MY 11. If you are a science geek, you may prefer Sols, which means Sol 7618 is today. Earth calendar is 28 April 2048.

"That's all fine and dandy but what about the crazy names for months?" The Asian woman across from Foot asked.

"Months on the other hand were more difficult to determine since the moons of Mars are, according to Betts, fast and slippery. It was probably more of his moonshine speaking during this part of his calculations. Turns out, alcohol at .38 gravity has a more powerful effect on the human brain."

The passengers clapped in response to the reminder of why Martian bars were so popular.

"You are a pack of drunks. Anyway, Betts referred to stars, weather observations, and even girlfriends to come up with the names of the months.

Thankfully for many, he used some Latin words to make us Martians appear somewhat intelligent."

A man in dark sunglasses and a cap in the front of the area got up and hurried out of the dining car. Kars noticed and watched him walk away into the next passenger car almost at a run, and then lost him as he exited into the next car. Kars noticed an uneasy feeling rising in his gut.

"Betts decided there would be 20 months and most would be about 34 sols in duration, except the unlucky 13th month. Moonshine was definitely speaking more than the scientist here, because the thirteenth month is kept to only 28 sols, and is known as..."

An explosion filled with soot ripped through the front of the dining car, sending a spray of blood and human parts mixed with former pieces of furniture into the cold Martian morning.

Two

Sol 7618

Free Port, Mars

"Junior, stay out of the sun."

"Roger, captain."

Captain Helek of the Martian First Division had given orders for his Warrior, a Private known to him as Junior, to go stealth and take up an observation post five hundred meters above the four men standing near the train depot. The sun was about to rise, so he reminded his young soldier to stay below the rising sun's rays. Those early morning shards of light had been known to bounce off Warrior's wings and give away position to the enemy. Explaining this to the kid for the third time wore on the Captain.

"Iggy, you take point on the deck fifty meters to their six."

"On it."

Iggy instructed the remaining four soldiers to form their one, two, and one defensive posture behind the four space suits.

"Sarge, where do you want us when they are cycling through."

"Corporal Lu, I want you to stay on the deck unless Junior IDs something. Then, I will give you further instructions."

"Roger that."

"Rookies." Iggy was irritable this morning. Everything had been so quiet in Free Port for the last few days, which was not normal. "Awful quiet, Cap."

"Yeah. I'm burning through the Vanu in the terminal. Nothing but a few Leeches setting anchors or eating." Helek's position was on the roof of the terminal.

After the train arrived, the four suited men cycled through the airlock one at a time. The crowd inside the terminal pushed through the gate and found seats inside the train's passenger cars.

"Iggy, set up your OP on top of the last car. Go stealth."

"Roger. Stealth Observation Post on the caboose."

Helek smiled at the old train word. It brought up ancient memories from a couple hundred turns back while working on a different planet.

"Caboose," Helek said.

"Junior, when the train departs, go one click, remain transparent, and mirror the marks." He didn't want the kid to think he would stay hovering over an empty terminal.

"Roger. One click up, stay over the marks on the train."

"Affirmative." Helek almost clapped in glee like shiner parents watching their child go on the toilet for the first time. He was amazed the kid understood.

As the train began its trip north to Eland, Helek went to the locomotive and took a position on the roof behind the radar unit. At the same time, Iggy's guys gradually made their way forward along the roof, scanning and watching the humans below.

⸺◆○◆⸺

When the methane-based plastic explosive blew, it peeled back the front ceiling of the train's dining car, and all the atmosphere flooded out into the near vacuum of Mars. Twisted metal, insulation, electrical parts, glass fragments, and soot shot through the car, slicing bodies on the way through. Arms, legs, and heads were pierced and mangled in a split second. Some people still had the look of laughter when they were impaled. The blast lifted the train off the track and gravity brought it crashing down, disconnecting it from the rest of the train while missing the rails, rolled onto its side, and skidded to a violent stop.

Both Kars and Benz had been protected from the shrapnel by the bodies of the gathered crowd listening to Benz's presentation and something else. The explosion tossed everyone around and as the dining car ground to a stop all the bodies were thrown forward. The mass of the train pushed across the barren wasteland, and the cars to the rear smashed and twisted into a compressed accordion-like shape. The separated locomotive towing the unaffected cars continued briefly before shutting down.

Both Benz and Kars' suits automatically deployed a Bubble over their heads in response to the violence. The plastic shell began providing life support and atmosphere to the men. The sudden loss of power just before flipping over caused ceiling panels to drop the life saving units, and boxes of Bubbles came flinging out with the spin.

Kars rolled out of the booth in front of where he once stood, ears ringing, eyes out of focus for a split second. Benz was near, so he reached over and shook his arm. Benz moaned in response.

"Come on, Benz— EA! EA! EA!" Signaling an emergency loss of atmosphere."

Kars struggled to reach his feet in the dark shadows of the train's tumbled interior.

"Come on, Benz!" He realized his comms were down when the Bubble deployed, so he intuitively looked for his helmet, which had been in front of him on the table a few seconds earlier. He reached for his forearm control and found the aux comm control. "Benz. Come on, buddy. EA. EA. EA!" His voice came through the auxiliary speaker inside the front of his partner's Evo.

"I hear ya," Benz said.

"Find our helmets." Kars said.

Benz started moving, trying to stand. Blood seeped from his leg, near his calf. "I got hit," Benz said.

"Hit your suit lights."

They both turned on the lights that shone from the shoulders of their Evos. Kars bent over and took a look.

"Your suit is sealing the tear. Find your helmet and get diagnostics on the wound. I'm starting to deploy Bubbles."

"No, I'll help with Bubbles first."

As Kars moved forward his head cleared. Benz hobbled toward a pile of Bubbles on the floor, previously the side of the train.

"I need some!" Kars cried out.

"Here!" Benz tossed Kars a box of a dozen, and he ripped open his own.

The Emergency Personal Atmospheric Containment Units (EPACU) had always been called Bubbles because of their ridiculous look when deployed around a person's head. The unit was placed on the top of the head and tapped twice to deploy. A plastic bubble divided into six sections shot out of the unit, and magnetic clamps sealed the sections around the person's neck to provide breathable air. With the 1% atmosphere on Mars, the Bubbles snapped open with a distinct pop, making the person wearing it look like they had a head twice as big as usual. How the Bubbles deployed tended to cause the wearers to experience sudden ear pain and high-pitched ringing, but when compared with dying— the sudden pressure on the eardrum seemed insignificant. The units were standard safety equipment all across the planet.

Kars slammed three people within reach with Bubbles and handed them a few to give out.

"Got another box?"

Benz found more and tossed him one.

The first minutes of loss of atmosphere was critical because the near vacuum of Mars would cause all liquid to boil off, including the water in the person's blood and skin. Then, the tissue would freeze solid. Without the Bubbles, the eyes bulge and popped after a couple of minutes of exposure.

The men worked furiously to save as many as possible. Even the wounded were given a Bubble. The units could be expanded to cover the person completely, but to fully deploy, a couple of people were needed to pull the rip-stop plastic down and under the feet.

Unconscious bodies had piled up in front of the dining car from the sudden stop of the derailment. Getting to individual heads became more difficult with every passing second. Some bodies were covered in regolith— the loose rock and dust made deploying Bubbles problematic.

Kars began throwing people back to Benz, who Bubbled them and sat them down. The 38% gravity helped tremendously, making Kars appear to have superhuman strength. His everyday job had helped keep him in good shape over the years.

Kars came upon Foot, who was injured and trying to open his eyes when Kars slammed his Bubble down with a crack. Foot was lying on top of another man. Kars pulled out the bottom of the Bubble enveloping Foot before continuing. He rolled him off and slammed another unit over the guy beneath him, then another, except that third guy was already dead.

A few of the Bubbled people began helping. The Asian woman was Bubbled but didn't know what to do.

"Start getting a count of people," Kars told her. She nodded and stood still, her tears falling.

Kars grabbed her by the shoulders. "Take people outside and get the units fully deployed. Have someone help you. Do you understand?"

"Yes."

"Move. Now." She left. Everyone who came to Mars, even visitors, had to pass a "Bubble Class," but it is difficult to get people who are in the middle of a disaster to remember their first priority and then move quickly to help others.

Benz began pulling broken booths and tables off of more people and trying to lift them out so Kars could hit them with the device.

"Almost done here." Benz tossed another male back to Kars. He looked like he was already gone, but Kars deployed the unit in case he was only in shock.

Part of the skin of the train had folded back and then twisted inside. Kars moved over toward the last unexplored section and found Hagus' dead body.

"Crap, the Scott is gone," he whispered into his comm. Benz flashed his lights to signal that he had received the message. Kars put a Bubble on the kid anyway. He had to remove some debris and yank him up out of the mangled metal to free him.

A woman beneath Hagus reached out a blackened hand toward the light on Kars' suit. Within a second, Kars slammed one down on her head. Her lips and side of her face were already turning black from the Martian frostbite. Kars thought she may have a chance to survive. He pulled her up by her armpits to free her from the melee. He then deployed the Bubble fully.

"Don't panic. I am coming right back for you," he said. The insides of the lower part of the Bubbles were made from reflective material designed to keep body heat in.

Benz found another guy behind a twisted wall section. The man sat up, trying to breathe non-existent air, like a fish out of water. Benz hit him with a Bubble, and the unit snapped down to the guy's belt.

"You've got one of those new Mag-Belts!" Benz said as the guy took in a deep breath of good air. "You're gonna be alright."

Captain Helek had a unique view. He rested on the train locomotive while looking back at all the cars, obediently following their locomotive leader. He watched a man run forward through the car in front of the dining car.

"Cap, the guy running armed a bomb beneath his seat!"

"SHIELD WALL." Helek screamed. Lu instantly sight-shifted to surround the Marks with his wings. A half second later, the boom threw everything into instant chaos. The derailment and crash even startled Captain Helek.

The force of the explosion in the physical world on Mars passed through the Angel Warriors with no effect. Of course, they were all surprised by the act of terrorism and scrambled to intervene with the Shiners on board the damaged train. Defensive positions were taken up, swords were ripped out of their sheaths, and they openly scanned for the presence of Cast Warriors, violet eyes blazing in every direction.

"Full alert!" Helek said. "Iggy, report."

"The blast in the front of the dining car has done a lot of damage. Everything is still rolling around. Lots of wounded and debris." The three warriors left at the train's rear had jumped to hover above the wreckage, and their eyes had gone crimson in full search of enemy warriors.

"Junior inform JOCC. Tell them we need the Ready Team to shift, Code Red to us."

"Roger, Captain! Code, code RED!"

"Easy Private. Make the call. Stay calm."

"Sir! Yes, sir."

"Iggy, how's LU?"

"Scorched on his wings, but otherwise, he's fine, sir."

"His Marks?"

Iggy knew Lu was assigned to provide instant protection over the two humans today and had done his job. "They are good. One leg wound, shrapnel."

"Send Lu forward after the running bomb planter."

"Roger. Lu forward. Stealth Captain?"

"No stealth."

"Roger that."

Lu came rushing forward over the top of the train, his massive blackened wings spanning beyond the car's width. He had to shift twenty percent to the flesh side to protect his marks, which was the reason he was singed. Lu could see Helek's position on the engine. The first two boxcars, the robotic transportation carriages, were undamaged. The three passenger units directly behind them were fine— except for the last passenger car, which was missing part of its roof and rear end. The rear wheels had lifted off the tracks but fell back down when the dining car disconnected. As Lu inched forward, a Reaper shot through the second car's roof, trying to gain altitude as fast as possible. Lu was quick and launched toward him— eyes now seething a righteous red. While the Reaper flapped with all its might, he watched Lu gain on his position, and a growing fear overtook the devil. As he turned to look forward toward the brightening sky, Helek's sword appeared and sliced the Reaper in half. Helek phased out of stealth and watched the Reaper fall back to the ground, spinning and oozing its disgusting black goo.

"Finish it," Helek said to Lu.

Lu gladly swooped down after the black-suited enemy had bounced down, slicing its head in half down to the core.

Above Helek, a squad of five more Angelic Warriors popped through their shift and entered the airspace by the Captain.

"Ready Team One reporting, Captain Helek."

"Helek here. You guys got here quick."

"We are based outside Eland now."

"I want you guys stealth and on site," Helek said. "Hook up with Iggy for assignments."

"Roger, Hamms out."

"When did they move you off of Luna?" Iggy asked.

"One week ago," Hamms said as his team swooped down into position above the disabled train.

<hr>

Protocol called for the healthy to get everyone fully deployed into Bubbles and then retrieve the Tram so the survivors could be loaded into a more stable environment. LIFT was specific about its procedures. Kars hadn't noticed any other LIFT employees from the front of the train coming to help. Because he could still move, he decided to fetch the Tram, while Benz remained to organized the rescue effort. This would still fall within the company's emergency guidelines, so he found Benz.

"That's everyone?"

"I think so."

"I'm going after the Tram," Kars said, remembering the injury to Benz's leg.

"Alright I'll get everyone moved outside the wreck." Benz said.

"Take care of that injury."

"I'll have time on the ride back."

Kars's long leaps across the dusty ground got him to the rear of the train within a minute. The derailment had caused the train cars to pile up against each other, and he was not sure if he could unload the vehicle.

Every train on Mars is required to have an emergency tram car. The E-Tram is a wheeled vehicle with a self-unloading crane feature. Each vehicle is designed to hold fifty people in an enclosed space with atmosphere. There are seats with restraints and a small medical bay in the back.

Kars knew laying the wounded survivors out would take up more room than what their Tram had. "We will strap them on the roof if we have to," he thought.

"Benz, you copy?"

"Yeah."

"See if you can find our helmets and gloves."

"On it."

Benz had the Asian lady, Ling, organize all the survivors outside the car. She instructed all the able-bodied people to get the wounded outside, fully deploy their Bubbles, and wait for their ride.

The last car was smashed up against the next. Kars had to figure out how to unload the emergency vehicle from the wrong side on the fly. The train car was off the rails but perched over the twisted steel beneath.

With a jump Kars was on the side of the crane and pressed into the seat. He hit the power controls and tried to remember his most recent training on the E-Trams from a MY ago.

"Come on!" he said out loud, wanting to smack his helmet, but all he had on was a Bubble. The Bubbles Rip-Stop material allowed light in— but was unfiltered Martian light. Looking through the plastic skin was disorienting enough while walking, but seeing the details of the display panel was almost impossible. Using his small motor skills was a huge challenge with the mittens. His Evo had deployed the mittens in response to the rapid loss of Atmo. They were smaller versions of the head Bubble but designed for hands. They had finger slots but not as deep as a regular Evo glove.

"There you are!" Kars said, and the crane sprung to life. He unlatched the Tram and hooked the crane to the rail on the left side. He yanked up and tore the safety railing off the train, then swung wildly around and dropped it on the other side, where it crashed into the next car in line. Kars smiled at the crashing metal and the glass shards that were sent flying with the drop.

He hooked the Tram, released the load pins, and slowly lifted. Within a minute, he went through the start-up procedure inside the Tram to bring the systems online.

"How is it coming back there?" Benz asked.

"Powering up now. Three minutes and I'll be on my way."

"Alright, we got lots of bleeders up here."

"I triggered the emergency beacon— help should be on the way."

"Right."

Five minutes later, as Kars approached the line of Bubbles, streaks of light passed overhead and then flipped around. As Kars stopped, he set the emergency brake on the Tram and jumped to the ground. With the move, two MEF Marines in jet packs swooped in over his head and sounded an alarm. Kars fell to his knees with his hands over his head and face in the dust.

"What are you doing?" Benz asked him over the auxiliary comm.

"I thought they were gonna zap me."

"For what? Helping?"

Kars got up as the Marines exited their jet packs and bounded over to the Tram.

"Whose in charge here?" one Marine asked over the comm.

"Does it matter?" Benz said while lifting a man up into the Tram's entry hatch.

"I'm Sergeant Meyers, MEF. How can we help?"

"These people need to get on the Tram. There are several more who haven't been fully deployed into their Bubbles." Benz pointed.

"We have wounded," Kars said.

"Medic Bugg is less than five minutes out."

"I count more than ten." Benz knew the civilian Buggs only carried ten people.

"I'll get another one coming."

"How about help getting the wounded on the Tram. These have a med bay?" Benz felt dizzy.

Four more MEF Marines landed. The black Medical Bugg, with a white underside and a Red Cross painted in the middle of its belly, came racing overhead, blowing dust and debris with its twelve motors whining. Five Marines climbed out of the Bugg with powered stretchers. One Medic began running triage through all the wounded and assigning each either a Tram ride back to base or a Bugg ride for the more severe.

The medical Bugg blasted off three minutes later, and another replaced it. In the meantime, a hundred marines took up positions around the train while another fifty climbed all over the wreckage and even evacuating people from the front cars of the train, having deployed Bubbles on all of them.

Marine Major LaBelle brought Kars and Benz their helmets and gloves. "I found these. You can put them on in the Bugg." He lifted his chin up to point to the medical unit behind them.

"Thanks," Benz said, and Kars nodded.

"I need to talk with you, ASAP, so get them helmets on and you can help me figure out what happened here."

"Okay." Benz went to turn but collapsed face down.

"Benz!" Kars called out and rushed to his side.

"Medic!" Major LaBelle called over the comms, setting a pin that would show Benz's position to the closest Medic.

"Shrapnel through his leg," Kars said on comms.

"Go, get your helmet on!"

"Sir."

Kars left Benz as the Medic arrived. He banged on the Bugg hatch, which opened.

Under a green airlock light, he depressurized his Bubble by pressing the button on the top until the pressure hissed off, and the clamps became loose.

He glanced at his Evo rails and grabbed the vacuum line to clean it.

Kars returned outside the Bugg in four minutes while Benz headed into the back of the Bugg on a stretcher.

"How is he?"

"Lost some blood but he's alive. I'm having him flown in to the military hospital."

Kars just hung his head.

"What's your name, son?"

"Kars Dee." Looking downcast inside his helmet he wondered what had happened.

"I see you've been here awhile?" The major pointed to his '05 patch on his shoulder.

"Yeah. Maybe too long."

"Been with LIFT the whole time?"

"Yep."

"What's your job?"

"Robotics tech."

"Which means nothing to me."

"I am certified to work on all LIFT systems."

"All?"

"Yes."

"You have access to the entire LIFT map?"

"I've been on every inch of the rails— many times."

"What did you have to do with this?"

"We were in the dining car, when it blew."

"What blew?"

"It was a bomb."

"How do you know?"

"Seen all kinds of pressure explosions since I've been here, and this had fire and ball bearings flying out of it. I think it came from under a bench seat."

"Could it been a wheel bearing that overheated and ripped a hole through the floor and burned off O2?"

"No way. That would be the first time ever."

"But it's possible?"

"No. It's not."

"Why?"

"Because you can hear wheel bearings going bad for a hundred klicks, plus all the vibration will shake your teeth lose. None of that happened before the blast."

"I need to know if this was an accident or something different."

"It was something different. I saw a guy run out of the dining car seconds before it blew."

"What did he look like?"

"Only saw his backside. Dark hair. Stocky build. Wearing a black hat. I think I saw sunglasses."

"Are you saying this is an act of terrorism?"

"Yes. One hundred percent."

The Major stood silent for a few moments, watching over the recovery.

"You and your buddy saved a lot of lives today, Mr. Dee."

THREE

28 April 2048

Teapot Key, Florida

It was another warm and sunny day. A teal cabin with a vaulted thatched roof, surrounded by exotic tropical flowers, sits fifty feet off the shore and is cocooned by brilliant white coral sand. The house is tucked below several coconut palms with two beige hammocks stretched through the trees as the wind gently shuffled the fronds. The coconuts in the trees were green and tender on the idyllic Florida island.

Two sisters adorned in their latest swimsuits were nestled under the trees in Adirondack chairs, waiting for the noonday sun to give them a proper warm-up. It's already eighty degrees, but their Florida blood doesn't fully warm until it's ninety. The fire ring, stack of wood, and two picnic tables are off to the left behind them. Sitting in the structure's shadow, a man with mirrored sunglasses, a beige floppy-brimmed sunhat, and a Glock sidearm is Dennis— one of the bodyguards living on the island.

Every chance Connie got, she sat out in the sun, warming herself. The activity always triggered fond memories of simple times when she enjoyed family, ate homemade wood-fired pizza, all while gathering around her pool in the woods. Back before the war began, she lived in Michigan with her husband. Of course, both Craig and her sister's husband, Bruce, were killed in the opening days of that conflict.

"I didn't even know there was a war," she thought. "Now I can't get away from it," she mumbled. Connie was tired from fighting for twenty-five years, and she knew it would continue until the Good Lord took her home. This was her calling, and many days, it was exhausting.

The sisters had relocated to the Florida Keys. Nan, the eldest, was 85, and her younger sister Connie was a few weeks away from 84. They had lived together since surviving the attack on Charity Island. Both women have never been able to shake off the nightmares, no matter how much they prayed, fasted, and begged God to remove them. The darkest of the reoccurring dreams is the one in which they had died on the island along with their husbands, not from the demonic storm that had claimed their spouses but from the hands of the two derelict drug addicts who had attacked them. Both women say they cannot remember exactly what happens next in the dream, but they recall a deafening gunshot and wake up covered in sweat. Living close to Charity Island in Au Gres had proved too difficult to overcome, so less than a year after the incident, they relocated south to a different kind of island.

Their island Key is distinct from an island only in how it was formed. Both are surrounded by water, but a Key is formed through biology, the growth of coral. Teapot Key is surrounded by an aqua-colored sea and white sand. The sand had been imported from Miami ten years before they arrived, and so were the coconut palms that covered the island paradise. After selling each of their homes, they and their mom bought a dilapidated cottage on the northern tip of the island to spend the rest of their days enjoying the private beach while organizing and teaching their grandchildren how to survive and fight in the war.

Little did they know that Bob, the owner of their Key, had watched them for years to see if they were for real or just another group of cheats and losers trying to take advantage of people's pain. They passed the decades-long test but never knew that Bob had believed in their cause. When he died childless, he left them the entire estate— including all of the forty-acre island paradise, along with the main house and cabins.

The grandmothers became the Queen Bees to their grandkids, and the Key was known in certain underground circles as the Hive. They kept their humility and remained living in the three-room cabin even after their beloved mother passed. The main house on the Key was transformed into a training center for the secret network. The other cabins housed various leaders over the years.

———◦———

Soaring a kilometer above the women and their bodyguard, a Select Guardian Squadron circled in formation. As another warm and calm day formed Colonel Amadan grew nervous that complacency had settled into his warriors' routine. Of course, this had always been a concern for him, and he often planned unique exercises to keep his warriors engaged.

"Alright warriors we are going to war-game today."

"Sir!" Master Sergeant Gilboa responded.

"I appreciate your enthusiasm, Gills," Amadan said.

"Just need to break up the routine, sir."

"I hear that. April in Florida is tough duty." Amadan smiled, teasing his friend and compatriot.

"Colonel," said a voice into their in-ear communicators.

"Go."

"Colonel, are we expecting anyone today?"

"Not that I know of."

"We've got a speeder in bound."

"A speeder?"

"Affirmative."

Amadan looked to Gilboa for an explanation.

Gilboa moved to his ear and whispered, "The kid means a fast hydrofoil boat."

"Heading and speed, Private," Amadan asked.

"Southeast at forty knots, six minutes out."

"Copy. Go two, stealth."

"Roger. Two klicks Elle and maintain stealth."

Amadan gave Gilboa another look, and the sergeant knew he had to send out two of his underlings to investigate the approaching boat.

"Tic, take the new kid and check that boat. Approach from their six, stealth, at twenty.

"On it. With me Spaz." The two warriors broke formation, dove east, and disappeared into the wind.

"Send Adams in, above the marks, real slow and quiet." Gilboa turned to tell the remaining squad member the instructions when Amadan waved him over.

"No, I've changed my mind. I want you down there, Gills. Adams can stay with me."

"You sure?"

"Yes."

"Roger that."

"Sergeant Gilboa broke ranks, dove down toward the cabin, and pulled up a hundred meters above the sisters, using his massive wings to brake. He scanned the area for threats and then went stealth. "Over cautious," he thought about his Colonel and grinned.

"Colonel, they've got a Shimmer over the boat and are leaving no wake."

"Roger on the Shimmer," Amadan said.

"Plus the hull is transparent, sir," Tic said.

"What?"

"Yeah, you can see right through it."

"Tic, I need to know who is on board."

"Three Shiners, sir."

"Move Spaz to the 2-7-0 and work on getting their ID. You go minus two klicks, up three on their six. Let's make sure they don't have a tail."

"Roger. Spaz to the nine o'clock maintain 20 ID. I'm going vert to three klicks on six, two klicks rear."

"Copy," Amadan said. He knew Tic loved those three-kilometer vertical climbs as much as anyone else.

"Report, Gills."

"Clear scan. Up ten."

"Have you ever seen a transparent hull?"

"Negative, Colonel."

"Me either."

⸻ ◆ ⸻

A jeep covered with a digital white and tan camouflage pattern came racing through the trees, carrying three armed guards and a driver. The guards jumped off while the jeep turned and departed— headed back to the main house. Upon arrival, one of the guards whispered into Dennis's ear. As the head security officer Dennis gave instruction for his men using hand signals. The four of them took up positions around the women.

"Ladies, we have a fast incoming boat," Dennis said.

"Breathe gentlemen." Nan slid on a shirt over her swimsuit.

"Father, we ask for your protection, which we know you already have in place. This isn't surprising you one bit. I pray for these folks on this boat that you would pour out your mercy on them," Connie prayed. "And bring them here in peace."

"Amen," everyone said.

Five minutes later, the see-through boat appeared fifty yards offshore in front of the women. It was hard to make out and almost silent as it approached the beach. A familiar-looking man waved from behind the pilot's wheel. The boat slowed and climbed up onto the beach, its hydrofoil folding up to reveal bulbous tires. The hum of an electric motor followed the boat, as did a soft rattle of the Shimmer blanket above its deck.

The guards on the beach were on high alert with their black AR-15s pulled into their shoulders.

"Easy boys. This is an old friend," Nan said while getting to her feet. The guards lowered the barrels of their guns.

"Ladies!"

"Larry Shields! Where have you been hiding?" Connie said.

"He's been hiding in a transparent boat!" Nan said as her eyes adjusted to take in the sight.

Larry climbed down from the boat, now a beach transport vehicle, and helped a beautiful woman down the ladder. She wore a floppy sun hat and was followed by a gentleman of about thirty years old.

"Diana, Connie, you remember my daughter Megan, and this is her husband, Taylor."

"Come here, let's have a look at you," Nan said, extending her arms. "Megan, you are stunning! Oh my goodness! You are beautiful in every way possible!"

"Taylor sure is a handsome fella," Connie said.

"Thank you both," Megan said. "So kind of you to have us on your beautiful island."

"Thank you." Taylor nodded.

"Larry Shields, get over here and give us old sisters a hug!"

After the warm greeting, a wave of calm washed over the entire group.

"That's quite a boat Larry," Nan said, flashes of her long-lost red boat dancing through her mind.

"New gift from Uncle Doc."

"No kidding?" Nan asked.

"He had five delivered, no questions asked."

"Wow. I'm so impressed," Nan said.

"It's fast and stealthy. Even climbs up onto the shore," Larry said. "Good for getting around in the Keys."

"Can you boys fetch up some lemonade for our guests?" Connie asked Dennis, the head of security. She forgot who was supposed to do what on the island, as the faces serving the women constantly changed.

"Yes ma'am." Dennis smiled.

"Hey Dennis!" Larry embraced his son-in-law.

"Mary will be thrilled you guys are here," Dennis said after the hug.

"I wanted to surprise her."

"I won't say a word. I'll have her bring the drinks from the big house. I'll tell her one of the Bee's wants to see her."

"Perfect."

Dennis keyed up his mic and asked for Mary while the group settled around one of the picnic tables in the shade.

"It's still so beautiful here." Larry looked out over the teal water, his midnight blue Tigers baseball cap shading his eyes. He took a long, cleansing breath to release the stress from the ride.

"How long has it been?" Connie asked.

"Well, it was after Wendy went home, so ten or twelve years."

"That's right," Nan said. "Now you're taking over as head of security for Florida?"

"No, just south Florida including the Keys."

"Any word on Melissa?" Connie asked.

"Not getting much news from the west. I think they must be okay since people are still coming over the pass. I figured you'd have better intel than I do," Larry said.

"It's tough getting anything out of California these days," Nan said.

"Right."

"But like you said, the refugees are still coming, so they must be okay," Connie said.

"I'm glad she is with your grandkids on this mission."

"The Quads are doing good work... I meant that the whole team is," Connie said.

"I know you did. And they are doing good, important work," Larry said.

"I think her and Ry have become a thing," Connie said.

"I knew there was someone on the team she was close with. I'm glad it's him."

Megan and Taylor smiled with the news.

"So, when did you two tie the knot?" Nan asked.

"A month ago!"

"How exciting," Nan said.

The talk turned to their wedding.

When Mary arrived with the lemonade, she almost dropped the drink cooler upon seeing her father and hastily left it in the sand.

"Dad!"

"Dennis, you're such a jerk!" she said to Dennis as she ran by. He only smiled at her. Mary fell into her father's embrace.

"I missed you, girl!"

"Missed you too, daddy. I'm glad you came. We've got news." Dennis drew close.

"Oh yeah?" Larry asked.

"Yes, Grandpa we do."

"Really? Grandpa!"

"Yes. Just confirmed two days ago."

"Congratulations, Larry!" Nan and Connie stood. When Nan hugged Larry, her double-barbed hook and anchor tattoo shone out from the sleeve of her UV shirt. Taylor recognized the logo.

When the congratulatory hugs were completed, everyone except the four guards was seated at the table or in the beach chairs pulled over from the fire ring. Connie looked at Larry. "So what brings you sneaking up in here, Larry?"

"We've got news on two fronts."

"Really?"

"Yes. Its important and I didn't want to chance sending an encrypted message."

"They tell me the encryption we use is state of the art."

"It is. But they all have their weaknesses. I wanted to show you personally."

"Dennis, let's put up a Shimmer," Nan said to their main security guard.

"Yes ma'am."

The four poles were already in place to hang the specially coated rip-stop Mylar sheet. The specialized camouflaged blanket hid everything beneath it from satellites and electronic surveillance. On satellite readouts, it looked like a shimmering heat signature, just like the rest of the surrounding sand.

"Okay, let's have it."

Larry pulled out a laptop from his backpack. "There are two reasons we came today."

"Yes?"

"First, is this one." He opened the lid of the thick black unit, scanned his retina, twisted the computer around, and set it in front of the sisters.

"Where is this footage taken?" Nan looked at the motionless screen.

"This is from Free Port."

"The Bahamas?" Nan asked.

"No." Larry looked into Connie's eyes.

"He means Free Port, Mars." Connie's heart skipped a beat.

"Yes. This was taken a few hours ago." Larry stood and hit play. A grainy image from a train began to move. He sat back down across from the sisters.

"This video was filmed from a security camera located at the front of the train looking toward the caboose."

"Where is the train headed?"

"North from Free Port to Eland."

"Is he on board?" Connie asked while gripping her sister's arm.

"Yes."

"How do you know?" Nan asked.

"I cannot say, for security reasons."

"Okay," Nan said.

"Plausible deniability," Connie said.

"Right."

Fifteen seconds into the video, a violent explosion sends a train car up into the air as its roof is ripped open from the inside out. The sisters yelp as the video shows the car slam to the ground and rolls on its side while the rest of the train acts like a folding accordion, and a dust cloud billows up in front of the camera.

"A missile?" Nan asked.

"No. The explosion happened from the inside."

"A bomb," Nan said.

"Is he?" Connie asked, tears pushing into her eyes.

"Gone? We don't know yet. As soon as I got this news I wanted you to know."

"Are you sure he was on the train?"

"Yes. His name is in the electronic manifest. Plus he communicated with a friend that he was working up in Eland today and had to take the sunrise train."

The reality became heavy inside the girl's heart.

"Oh Lord!" Nan said. "Is he listed with the injured?"

"No. Not yet. We don't have any list. We know a couple hundred Marines are on site. The military has shut down the scene so they can investigate."

"How long is the delay?"

"Right now Mars is close— so its only five or six minutes. I told my guys to keep me informed."

The sisters nodded.

"We need to pray." Nan began speaking out her adoration toward the King of the universe. Everyone bowed their heads, while most spread their hands, palms out, like they were waiting for a gift from God himself.

Five minutes in, Larry stood up, pulled his phone from his pocket, and pressed it to his ear. "Yes," he whispered, turned, and walked away.

When he disconnected, all eyes were on him as he moved back to the circle. He took Connie's hand into his own. "He's alive!"

"Oh, thank you, God!" Connie said, and tears burst from her eyes.

"In fact he wasn't injured. Benz got wounded with shrapnel in the leg but both he and Kars managed to save a lot of lives."

"How good is the intel?"

"Rock solid."

"Oh, thank God!"

"I'm having the video sent over."

"Is that safe?"

"Yes. The video is going viral. No one will be the wiser."

"Viral?"

"They are saying the two LIFT employees are genuine heroes."

"Wow. Thank you, Lord!"

Five minutes later, another dark and grainy video showed two beige-suited lift employees bounding between people while deploying Bubbles among the wreckage. Then, there were different views from other people who had been rescued.

The group watched the feed again.

"Yes, we thank you, Lord!" Connie said. Everyone clapped.

"I knew he would show up sooner or later," Connie said.

"I knew he would too, Con," Nan said.

After the tears and relief washed over the group, Connie took a long iced tea drink and looked intently at Larry. "You said that you came here for two reasons."

"Yes. You have a good memory."

Connie's smile was her only response.

"I don't know how to say this."

"Just say it, Larry," Connie said.

"It's that granddaughter of yours. She's causing trouble again."

Nan and Con offered disgusted facial expressions, which everyone noticed.

"What do you want us to do with her?" Larry lifted his cap and combed his fingers through his hair as if he had run out of ideas.

"She's gonna have to figure out her own crap," Nan said.

"Connie?" Larry asked.

"She's right. Bry has to get it together before it's too late."

Within the hour, the two eighty-year-olds took Larry inside their cabin. They gave him a sealed correspondence for their contact in Bonita Springs.

"They'll know what to do," Connie said.

"Have him memorize and destroy before he heads out."

"Okay. What do you really want me to do for 3?" Larry whispered to the women.

"Nothing. She's gotta figure her crap out on her own," Nan said.

<hr>

"Gills, I've been thinking," Amadan said.

"Scary, Colonel," he says and laughs at himself.

"Right. I think I need you to go on a special mission."

"Sir?"

"I want you to go find Bry and report back through command."

"Isn't she the rebel child?"

"I don't know about that, but I think she may need our protection."

"When?"

"Now."

"On it, Cap."

"With all discretion, Sergeant-Major."

"On it. Stealth all the way."

"You know where I'm headed?"

"Yeah. Follow that correspondence. Report back when you put eyes on her."

"Roger that. You guys have fun without me," Gilboa said.

"Don't be taking any side trips, Gilboa," Amadan snickered.

"Yes sir."

With that, Sergeant-Major Gilboa popped out of sight and into stealth.

Four

Sol 7619

Free Port, Mars

The metal walls on Kars' Cube felt cool to the touch. He had been in bed for five hours and was unable to sleep. The soft blue light beneath his bed normally comforted him. On this particular night the glow annoyed him. Visions from the explosion pounded at his skull. The blood and gore visited him like an unwanted guest showing up at an inconvenient time. The shrapnel and dust cloud covered and obscured his thoughts. He felt dirty— even after a shower. The damn dust was a part of him now, flaking and falling off of his skin.

The monitor on his wall at the foot of his bed called to him. He had watched the video feed from the wreck and accounts from some survivors at least five times through. Everyday Martians called him and Benz heroes, which made him smile. News shows all over the planet were still investigating the matter before they offered their opinion on the apparent act of terrorism and the response.

What had kept him awake was the realization of how close he had come to dying— like Hagus had. It was unsettling to think about the nine people who had lost their lives while he was somehow spared. It was like he had been shielded from harm, just like his grandmother had taught him many years ago. The more he tried to shake the images, the more fear took control.

Fear, of course, had been Kars' hidden companion for as long as he could remember. The grip had tightened when his grandfather and great-uncle had been killed a lifetime ago on that infernal island. Of course, fear had always played a role in his life, from the fear of looking weird to his peers to the fear of disappointing his parents and even a common fear of being perceived as an outcast. Fear had been his lifelong companion and constant nemesis.

Now he understood that his fear had been the reason he had left Earth thirteen years ago. That was when all the death, destruction, and leadership demands, attacked him and pushed him to seek an adventure on Mars instead. Once others had paved the way, he was not afraid of physical challenges like skiing, backpacking, racing dirt bikes, or even riding a rocket to a new world. So, after living almost twelve years on Teapot Key, Kars and his best friend got jobs with LIFT and were accepted onto one of the transports during the Great Migration of 2035. They boarded a Starship on a hot day in the middle of July, and after enduring the ten minutes of terror during liftoff, the boredom of the four-month journey set in.

Then, as the ground from the Red Planet raced toward them for the final two minutes of their journey, the rocket engines fired and kicked up a massive dust cloud, setting them softly down on a new planet. They had relocated to Mars. He ran away, and he knew it. His Gigi told him as much— but then prayed for him anyway. She watched the launch from the grandstands with a gnawing sadness as her eldest grandson rode a pillar of fire and left Earth behind. She did not understand her grandson or God's plan at all.

2035 was the year that Earth and Mars were closer than they had been in many decades. The natural twenty-six-month cycle brings the planets close. Their elliptical orbits are not perfect, so the only constant in the distance between the bodies is the variation of distances. '35 was when many governments and corporations planned for the migration, with over three thousand launches taking place.

The lure of a new opportunities in the face of the deterioration of the prospects of life on Earth was marketed to the younger masses. Kars ran toward the new and away from the pain of the known. He convinced himself if he could just put the past behind him, then all of the challenges of his old life would fade into history. He figured he had left his biggest problems sitting on Earth. He knew living on another planet would have difficulties. Still, he thought he would exchange one massive set of issues for another, smaller set.

When they landed the words, "Welcome to your future," played throughout the ships to great applause.

"Leave you worries behind," they promised. "Ride a rocket to the stars and have all of your dreams come true." The propaganda was thick.

"Connection, community, shared dreams and goals. When humans work together in peace and unity there is nothing that cannot be accomplished!"

"Peace, fulfillment, wealth, and the freedom to pursue the life that you have always dreamed of!" The marketing effort was unprecedented.

It hadn't taken Kars long to discover that people carry their issues wherever they go. The technological paradise promised to all who took up the adventure of a lifetime still came down to a lot of hard work in crappy conditions. People were still people, broken bits and all, no matter the location.

Now, in his bunk, a door of understanding had been opened with the bombing, and he did not like what he had witnessed. All the gadgets in the universe couldn't change his fundamental flaws. Being on Mars had not brought out the best in people, it had brought out the petty and the selfish. The disconnect for many on Mars was discovered a few years after humans arrived— the pettiness and brokenness did not create resilient people who thrive in harsh environments. Learning that lesson caused many to bury their emotions and dive into fantasy thinking to cope with the pressure of always facing death right outside their window. The suicide rate in the Martian utopia is four times as high as on Earth. Nobody talks about it— while the cemeteries continue to grow.

To thrive on the Red Planet, people must remember that life anywhere is filled with danger around every corner. People can adapt to danger.

After the bombing, all these unexpected thoughts whipped through Kars' mind in a loop and into a blender. So, he tried to put his thoughts on something else. He considered about the intricate details of his home. The exterior walls are skinned in aluminum. Every Cube in this part of Free Port measures the same four meters in the three directions that define volume— length, width, and height. They are designed to stack on each other and connect on five sides. Each unit has only one sliding door located in the front. Engineers designed gaps between the Cubes, so special foam insulation was sprayed between the connected surfaces after setup to deaden sound and retain heat. Even the ventilation system is standard for all the Cubes and is controlled by the atmospheric AI.

"Yes, but you almost died!" The unwanted voice interrupted again, and another wave of fear crashed into his comfortable home. "You ran away from your calling!" said another.

The extended forays into meaningless facts could not break off the racing thoughts. He got up well before the sun, and since Benz was shacked up with another woman somewhere in the city, Kars climbed out of his loft. The headspace in the loft area is not quite six feet, which allows the lower area to have higher ceilings.

Kars slid down the ladder between his loft and Benz's, slumping on the couch with his water bottle as his only companion.

⚊⚊◆⚊⚊

"He's still awake," said the Leech with the wrench to his two identical coworkers.

"I know that. He's also so tired anyone can just waltz in here," said the second to the third.

"I can't wait to get the big drill going and set another anchor!" The third smiled.

"Just help me tighten this one first." The first pushed against his over-sized open-end wrench.

"You've got it," said Three.

"That fear anchor is so old it'll probably break," said Two.

"The fine threads make them last longer," One said.

"Last longer! Ha! The only thing those threads do is take way longer to tighten."

"Those threads are what makes these old anchors so strong," said One as he shook the chain to check for tightness while flexing one of his scrawny arms.

"So strong. NOT!"

"I feel like the new anchor models are better at capturing more of the heart."

"And the drills are so much better at getting the anchor buried deeper."

"New, phew! That's what I say to you two." One smiled at his rhyme.

"You'll see how awesome this new drill and anchor system are just as soon as he experiences another traumatic event."

"How much worse can it get than almost getting blown up?"

"Something bad is coming, I can smell it."

"You're weird!"

"Weird is relative."

"You have relatives?"

"Your relatives are weird?"

"My coworkers are stuuuupid."

"Don't forget weird!"

"Yeah, that too."

"I mean how weird is it that we get to do such important work?" One said.

"Who would have figured that I was grown in a pool of sludge on Apollyon and now I'm here on another planet doing His work!"

"And the benefits are spectacular!"

"Stop dreaming about food and get ready to run that drill!"

"Yeah, yeah. You steal the fun out of everything."

⸺◆⸺

Kars was half awake on his couch when his door was knocked off its bottom slide and thrown open. Benz's body crashed into Kars on the couch with a grunt.

"What the."

Two brawny, black-shirted men charged in, picked Kars off the couch and held him by the armpits with his feet off the ground.

"Hey Kars, the Gestapo wants to have a chat." Benz wore half a smile and a swollen eye. He rubbed his chin as he spoke.

"Mr. Dees, I presume," said the last man entering the Cube. Several people hurried by in the corridor, trying not to watch. The interrogator's hard-heeled boots clanged against the metal floor.

"I am Lieutenant Ridge from the Free Port Federal Police."

Kars immediately thought the man looked like a mole— a large mole dressed in all black, with a red armband and a black F.P. logo inside a white circle.

"Mr. Benz has been cooperating with us on a new investigation."

"I see that," Kars said. Benz remained quiet.

One of the Goons slapped Kars' face. "Respect the Lieutenant."

"I've still got U.S. constitutional rights," Kars said.

"You ain't got nothing we don't give you," said the other Goon who punched him in the stomach. Kars fell to the floor as all his air had been forced from his lungs with the violence.

While on the floor, they searched Kars for weapons and began throwing things in the Cube around, looking for anything incriminating. Goon number two, the one with the black baseball hat, climbed up into the loft and tossed Benz's bedroom, then Kars. He smacked his head on the header and nearly fell off the catwalk between the rooms. He grabbed the ladder as his hat dropped to the floor below, cursed, and climbed down. When he turned, he had a trickle of blood running out of a horizontal cut on his forehead.

Kars and Benz made eye contact and knew what each other was thinking.

"Mr. Dees, we just need you to answer a few questions," the Mole said.

"What the hell is this about?" Kars said.

"What were you doing on the train, Mr. Dees?"

"My job."

Goon number one, the guy with the slicked-back hair, yanked Kars up and slammed him on the couch.

"Enough." Ridge said to the enforcer.

"We have video evidence no one else has."

"Okay."

"All the way from outside this door, to the depot, and the entire ride. We have video through the explosion and during your destruction of the LIFT Company's Tram car."

"What are you talking about?" Kars asked.

"You used the crane to rip parts of the Tram car off and then used those pieces as a weapon to break into another car."

"You're full of shit. I had to remove the railing in order to unload the Tram from the wrong side of the train. People would have died if I hadn't hurried. In my rush I dropped the railing over the far side of the Tram and it crashed into the adjacent car, which was already damaged in the crash."

Kars stood but the Goon with the bloody cut pressed him back down into the couch.

"Why did you stay in the LIFT employee car when your cohorts went to eat breakfast."

"If you have video evidence, you already know why we stayed." Kars said A Goon inched closer.

"Stop!" Ridge ordered his soldier.

"My comms unit was on the fritz all week. It's in my reports. I knew I would have the time on the ride to Eland to fix it."

"That wasn't the only thing you repaired, was it?"

"No, my Proximity Alarm was busted as well."

"And?"

"And what? We fixed it."

"Why did you wear your Evo suits into the train, Mr. Dees?"

"It was just easier."

"Easier for what?"

"For the situation. To fix them. Then, when we finished, we were almost to Eland."

"Convenient excuse, don't you think?"

"What?" Kars stood again.

"How you two were the only people wearing Evo suits in the dining car that was bombed?"

"I'm not following your logic."

"Facts, Mr. Dees. We follow the facts wherever they lead."

"Sounds like I need a lawyer."

"We are just having a conversation here. We can bring you in for formal questioning if you feel guilty or need legal counsel." Ridge used his many years of interrogation experience to leverage the situation. "I was letting you know what I already knew."

"I am supposed to believe that you are here as a favor to me?"

Ridge said nothing.

"If we were deliberately trying to blow people up why would we help them out of the wreckage?" Benz asked.

"To cover your real crimes," Ridge said.

"That's stupid," Kars said.

One of the Goons hit Kars in the face, knocking him down to one knee. The other lifted him back up as Ridge moved in to get in Kars' face.

"I'm going to be looking into every aspect of your life, Kars Dee. I'm going to turn your world upside down. I'll find out if you ever farted inappropriately," Ridge said.

"They are very inappropriate, officer." Benz laughed out loud, mocking the stupidity of the entire day.

Kars only stared, eyes wide. He was incapacitated by a raging torrent of fear.

"I'm reaching all the way back to Earth to turn over every rock that you ever crawled under with your pathetic little life. If I find anything, anything, I will personally get you run out of LIFT for good. You'll be scurrying off to an Indian mining camp just to eat or to prison on Luna. You breathin' my air?"

"No," Kars said, and one of the big guys hit him again.

"He doesn't understand the reference." Benz stood and one of the Goons moved over to him.

"It means do you understand what I am saying?" Ridge said.

"Yes," Kars said. "Of course."

"I'm going to need you to stay in the city until I get this all cleared up."

"My job takes me out of Free Port everyday."

"I'll be talking to your boss."

"Whatever," Kars said.

"We aren't done talking about this," Ridge gave the place one last look before leaving. One bully knocked Kars back toward the couch. He slammed the door on his way out, causing the bottom to swing wildly out of its frame.

"You breathing my air, is a saying," Benz said. "I hear it in the bars all the time."

"It's a stupid saying. When did they pick you up?"

"Last night I went to a club over in the Depot District."

"What's her name?"

"Lulu." He waited for a wisecrack that never came. Kars' head spun off somewhere else.

"People bought me drinks, slapped me on the back, then Ridge walks in with his two lovers."

"What?"

"The two guys that were with him. Anyway, he watches us from a booth like a stalker and waits for me and Lulu to leave."

"Did they grab her too?"

"No. Just me. They stuffed me in a van and began to discuss the explosion. I got lippy with them and they smacked me around."

"Why? We saved a lot of lives."

"I don't know. Something crazy is going on," Benz said.

FIVE

Sol 7619

Free Port, Mars

Fifteen minutes after Ridge and his Goons left Kars and Benz's cube, Mr. Brady from LIFT messaged both men to report immediately to the corporate office. He wanted them there as soon as possible.

"What do you think this is about?" Kars asked his buddy as they walked into the LIFT corporate headquarters. The building was a gleaming glass structure in the middle of Free Port's Central City District. Central was the oldest dome in the American development. A massive 3D printed facility, the largest 3D dome on Mars, had connections to every district in the city via a state-of-the-art subway system with fifty-two connecting tunnels.

Mr. Brady waited for the pair outside his office door. He had them pose for a picture of them shaking hands and a congratulatory video segment for corporate recruitment use on Earth.

"Congratulations on a job well done! You guys saved a lot of lives. Everyone here at LIFT is proud of you boys."

The video segment was done.

"Okay we need a debrief." Brady motioned with his head to move inside his office.

Kars and Benz settled into cushioned chairs across the desk from Brady.

"Well, I do appreciate you guys risking your neck to save lives. It sure makes LIFT look good and we treasure the positive vibes that go along with it."

It was the first time Brady actually looked at his two employees. "What happened to your face?" He asked Benz and then followed up with another question. "You must have been tossed around in the wreck?"

"Something like that." Kars remained silent.

"What was the problem you had with your Comm unit, Mr. Dees?"

"It was in my report from a few days earlier. It had been on the fritz all week. I thought it was just dust in a connector, so I took the unit apart to clean it but ended up replacing it and the harness."

"Wait— you worked on your own helmet?"

"Yes."

"That's not normal."

"It is for me, I'm certified in all LIFT systems."

"All?"

"Yes. Check my record."

"I just don't hear of many employees working on their own Evo's."

"Most don't say anything and do it themselves, or hire someone like me."

"Why?"

"Because you guys charge way too much money to fix our equipment."

"I'll take that into consideration." Brady stared through the man knowing he would get push back from corporate HQ on Earth.

"Thanks." Kars was skeptical.

"I have a burning question that I need you guys to answer."

Both men waited for the question in silence.

"You were within thirty feet of the explosion, according to the accident report."

"We were halfway back into the dining car," Benz said.

"So, that's about thirty feet," Brady said, looking to Kars for confirmation.

Kars shrugged.

"Why doesn't your Evo's have any evidence of scorching?"

"I don't know," Benz said.

"No idea," Kars said.

"Security tells me that methane PE bombs blow up very dirty on Mars. Yet, your suits are not covered with soot. Corporate is wondering why? Actually they're are wondering how it is possible. Most everyone else has methane soot on their clothing."

"Maybe it stuck to the material of the clothes but not the Evo material?"

"There is video feed from multiple angles available," Benz said. He was irritated at the direction of the questions.

"You guys and the Gestapo both have more video of this than anyone. Why are you hassling us?"

"We aren't hassling you, we are just asking."

"How do you think we got bruised up, Mr. Brady?" Benz asked.

"What do you mean?"

"The Gestapo Goons and Lieutenant Ridge just paid us a visit. They knocked us around trying to get at something we know nothing about."

"Really? Lieutenant Ridge has always been reasonable whenever I have spoken to him."

"That's not how I describe my encounter," Benz said.

"What about you?" Brady looked to Kars.

"They aren't real friendly types."

"Listen, I want you guys to take some time off. Relax. We're gonna get you both brand new Evo's. State of the art— fresh off the assembly line. A couple of heroes deserve new equipment."

"Wow," Kars said without emotion.

"Yeah, wow. I'm sure our suits are beat to crap and couldn't be certified if we tried," Benz said.

"The Evo's will be ready by the end of the day!"

"Very thoughtful, Mr. Brady." Sarcasm dripped from Kars's swollen lips.

"Thanks for coming in, boys! Oh yeah, here are a couple of credits for a real nice dinner at Angelo's. Enjoy. Thanks again for coming in." Brady waved his security man inside the office. He ushered the men out.

"How long are we on vacation?"

"I'll be in touch, or HR will be."

The abrupt end of the meeting felt forced to both Kars and Benz, like most everything on the dust ball these days. They waited until they were outside the facility to speak. The two men looked at each other as they walked toward the Tube.

"New suits?"

"Yeah. I think we need to get our old suits so we can salvage them," Benz said.

Kars wasn't following.

"We get our old suit and stash them somewhere, in case the new suits are too new, if you know what I mean."

"Too new?"

"Yeah, like these guys might be trying to get rid of the heroes or something. Who knows after the night I've had," Benz said.

"We can check them out. Take them apart," Kars said. "Take the GPS and bio-metrics out of them. Make sure there is nothing fishy."

When they had walked a couple of blocks, they both lifted their heads from their whispering, noticing one of Ridge's Goons shadowing them across the street.

"Let's lose this guy," Benz said.

They turned down an alley and skipped through an equipment tunnel before the big Goon came around the corner. Descending two floors, the pair doubled back beneath the square and took the narrow lane to the next Tube stop, a half mile away. The advantageous part of the subterranean levels in Free Port was it had far less surveillance apparatus and was dimly lit. The men exchanged knit hats and activated their Faraday devices before entering the Tube gangway, and then they separated. Keeping their eyes lowered when entering the train made it more difficult for the cameras to identify them as their Faraday device scrambled their bio-chip signals. They both knew the blind spots on Tube trains and slid over into those spaces.

Exiting the Tube car beneath the Depot District, they walked in different directions and took separate stairways down one level.

The seedy dive bar was only a kilometer down tunnel 226E. It was originally carved out of the rock as a place to service a massive boring machine in place. An opportunistic entrepreneur known only as Harry built a front wall out of old shipping containers and started serving booze to paying customers on the down low after the tunnel was completed.

There are no windows, address, or surveillance, but everyone who works the tunnels or pounds the dust knows how to get to Harry's Dive. Harry's is behind the red door with the diagonal white stripe, like that found on a scuba diver's Surface Marker Buoy. The best part of this particular bar is that there is no biometric surveillance equipment. The boys entered the club and turned off their Faraday scramblers.

Sitting at the far corner of the shadowy speakeasy, the pair whispered into their drinks as they planned how to deal with Brady, LIFT, and Ridge's Goon squad following them. Within ten minutes, two different LIFT employees coming off the midnight shift unwittingly sat near the pair.

"Hey, ain't you those two famous Martians?"

Benz and Kars only stared at the men who looked like they were in their late twenties.

"You know the bombing?" the other guy said just above a whisper, trying to elicit a reaction.

"Why?"

The two men looked around and slid over a couple of stools, sitting next to Benz as Kars was next to the rock wall.

"You guys made us look good!" The heavier guy had a Brooklyn accent.

"Real corporate heroes," Benz said.

"So, any idea on who did it?" Kars whispered as the bartender brought four more drinks over at the behest of the guests.

"Cheers to you guys! You're freaking heroes in my book," whispered the second guy with the blonde hair.

"Thanks," Benz lifted his glass in appreciation.

"You heard the wrinkle coming out now?"

"No."

The pair shared intel on the bombing. Looks like someone is trying to pin it on some religious nutjobs. But there is no way."

"Why?"

"Because they would not have used a dirty methane based bomb."

"Why not?"

"Getting methane is a real bitch unless you own a rocket or a rocket company."

"So who?"

"If you're asking me, I think its the freaking Commies," Brooklyn said.

"I thought the Commies were killed off, right?" Benz looked at each of them in succession.

"We were led to believe that they were killed off, but who really knows?"

"We were in Xing right after the coup went down," Benz said. "They had Communists hanging from every street corner. I think they were thorough when they cleaned house."

"No, I think the CCP from Earth has sent up new infiltrators to cause trouble and nobody on Earth wants to push China's button to start another war down there."

"What makes you think that?" Kars asked.

"We will call it a good friend in Xing who operates in some inner circles."

"The damn Commies are messing with the trains again?" Benz shook his head.

"They want to control them and everything else."

"Before the revolution in Xing the CCP operatives were well known to pay off high officials to look the other way, at just the right times, if you know what I mean," Brooklyn whispered.

"Well the Gestapo paid us a visit last night."

"No comp?"

"Had to escape some prying eyes on the way down here."

"Gestapo is following you?"

"You guys better watch your backs."

"Anything we can do?" Brooklyn asked. "Name it, we'll get it done."

"Thanks. We might take you up on that one day," Benz said.

Three hours later, Kars and Benz made their way back home, but they took a detour to pick up some of their personal tools from their work locker and tried to figure out how to get their old suits back home.

"Wait. We don't have to take them home. We hide them here and get them when we need them."

"What are we going to say happened to them? And what about the cameras?" Kars said.

"Who cares? We can do the mirror trick to get in."

"Yeah, that could work. We can't log in we'll have to wait until someone is walking out to enter."

"The exterior camera by the entry way we'll use a hat on."

"Lets go in through the back, we can kill the lights and then cover the camera. We'll just have to tie a line to the hat and yank it off when we are past."

Neither of those things happened since they ran into Brooklyn and his blonde-headed friend, Rick, and asked them to block the feeds for a few seconds as they passed.

They were able to get their suits out into the warehouse and store them high up on a parts rack that could not be spotted from the ground.

Then, they waltzed through the employee entry and claimed their new Evos, checking them out for an initial shake-down run, which was required. They asked about their old suits, claiming they were not at their locker, which they weren't and no one had an answer.

After returning home with their suits, they fixed the slides on their door. Then they reinforced the hinges, floor mounts, and the lock to slow down the Goon squad the next time they wanted to break down their door. They used their plasma welder to set two more guides in place in the upper and lower tracks and a plate to the back of the door.

The only thing ruined beyond repair was the seal on the bottom of the door— which was ripped off when the Goon squad kicked it in. They'd have to buy another one and adapt it to their new setup. Each Cube unit was sealed from the rest of the dome in case there was a sudden pressure release so people wouldn't suffocate in their sleep under a total power outage, a lesson learned the hard way when the entire population of a mining village dome was killed ten MYs back.

While sitting at their dining table, which folded up into the wall next to the fridge, Kars turned on some loud music while they whispered ideas and plans to each other.

——◆◇◆——

"High-lo, high-lo, it's off to work we grow."

"High-lo, high-lo, high-lo, high-lo, high low! High low!"

"That's not the right words to the song!" protested one Leech.

"Who cares!"

The line of five Leech whistled at the prospects for a good night's work. Each carried a piece of equipment necessary for their job.

The seal was off the entry door, making access to the Cube as simple as walking down an unoccupied tunnel. They made their way up to the loft on the right and found their way inside Benz's mind.

"Alright. First things first." The smiling Leech found a spot to relieve himself and was immediately copied by the other four.

"And as we gather for this somber occasion..."

"Shut up!"

"Don't you mean as we gather for the loyal order of water buffalo meeting?"

"You've been on a cartoon binge again?"

"Well, maybe!"

"Attention! The first order of business is to tighten the fear anchor. That should be located three back and four to the right." He pointed, and one Leech went to look.

"Here it is!" he said. "It's so loose, we can get six or seven turns on this one!"

"Great!"

"This could be an early night!"

"Don't forget we have a work order for the roommate too."

"Oh, no!"

"What?"

"Yep. We pulled duty for both of them."

"Crap!"

"How about you two go tighten the crap out of the fear anchor and well get drilling the new insecurity anchor?"

"Team work makes the dream work!"

"And it fills my belly!"

<hr>

The door's seal was breached for a second time on the same night. At 4:30 a.m., a figure covered in a Shimmer blanket went down the corridor to Cube 2938. The second level walkway was empty, as was the first level below and the two levels above. Using expanded metal for hallway floors allowed residents to see through all four levels of this "Cube-omnium" in Free Port. Since the cameras on each level only pointed down the hallways, none looked up through the floors above them and under the electronic covering. The figure in the Shimmer blanket was aware, moving steadily but with caution.

The doorway to Cube 2938 had a boot print and dent from a forced entry. It appeared to have been burned, no welded, in a few places where the metal became dark under the intense heat of the process. The seal on the bottom was off, which made sliding the envelope under the door easy. It was so easy, in fact, that it slid all the way under the couch, unbeknownst to the stealthy delivery guy in the hallway. The word "Bombing" on the outside of the envelope was face up— per his instructions. Still, only the corner of the tan envelope was visible above the couch.

65

Six

29 April 2048

Wilderness of western North Carolina

A slender woman sits beneath a mature pine tree outside a cave, looking out over mist-shrouded mountains. She is tired and dirty as one leg dangles over a cliff face while the other is folded beneath her. She is drinking a hot mug of tea cupped between cold hands. Her layered clothes are tattered, but her boots are relatively new and sturdy. As she grips her mug, she notices her dirt-encrusted thumbs, which sparks a memory. Setting the mug aside momentarily, she tries to clean the dirt from her hands. She holds her palms together, lining up the creases on her thumbs, and connects what looks like a seven on her left thumb with the semicircle of a backward "c" on her right. With the connection the tattoo flashes into a number three on the infrared light scale. Tapping the side of her sunglasses, she changes the lenses to infrared mode. It reconnects the tattoo, which makes the resulting number "3" glow bright red. This brings a smile to her weary and weathered face.

The memory is a primal connection for her, like charging up a device running low on power. She leans back into the pine tree to support her head while it swims with vivid pictures from her past. Moments later, she taps off the micro-switch on the right side of her glasses to power down the infrared option to protect from signal bleed and conserve power. Not that she was concerned, but if her mountain hideout in western North Carolina was under surveillance, she would have been warned. Her concern for the safety of her team was first and foremost in her mind. They all understood that you can never be too safe when hiding from the known world.

"Bry, chow's online," a muted male voice spoke from the darkness of the cave entrance behind her.

Another cold batch of porridge awaited as her hunger hid behind a veil of fatigue.

"K. Thanks," she said just above a whisper, returning an appreciative but tight-lipped smile toward the dark portal.

Bry was exhausted. Tired from all the running. Weary from sleeping in caves, under bridges, in dilapidated barns, and holes in the ground. Her irrational fear of spiders still drove her nuts, as did the crinkling of Mylar blankets. She wanted to curl up with a thick blanket and a good book next to a fire for a couple weeks to rest and regain her motivation. Still, their circumstances were not going to allow it. Living the outlaw life in a surveillance culture was next to impossible. If they didn't have help from on high, she knew they would have been snatched up a year ago. Even with all the assistance, it seemed like their luck was drying up. The initial luster had been washed off their cause, and the real mission involved a ton of unappreciated hard work.

Her group had lost a member last week to desertion, and two others had been wounded and captured ten days before that. Some of her superiors blamed her for the losses. Now that their cadre was down to four she was certain the Bees would hear about her "unfocused efforts," as she was described when her commander chewed her out after the desertion. Their operational orders had been changed from surveillance to interdiction because another team had been captured three days ago. She wondered if their leader was described as unfocused. What the leadership failed to recognize in her estimation was that their area of operation had become much more active with the arrival of a Battalion of Global Union Peace-keepers. The missions that week were diverted where it made sense, but not all activity was controlled. Now, Bry and her team would search for, and escort, refugees. These new orders would make them more vulnerable to capture.

"Sissies," Bry whispered, downing the rest of her spruce tea with a grimace, knowing she needed the vitamin C, even though it tasted like a dead pine tree. She double-blinked while looking at the index button inside her digital glasses. She used her eyes to scroll and find the archived image. It popped up on both lenses, a semi-transparent interruption to the trees in front of their cave. The picture was of a nine-year-old girl with her arms wrapped around the neck of a bearded man while laying her head on his shoulder as they smiled at the camera. On the other side of the man in the image was a dark-haired boy leaning into the man and smiling. The three people enjoyed a moment in front of a window during Christmas time. The girl's shirt is adorned with printed Christmas lights. It was apparent they all enjoyed posing for the picture. "Miss you, pops," she thought while choking back some rising emotions.

"I must be tired." Bry knew she couldn't put a indicator marker on the picture, or someone could hack her preferences and figure some things out. Things she didn't want to be figured out by anyone outside. The real reason for looking at the picture was in case she was captured. Before the mission, the team leader was obligated to isolate their storage units. That storage system contained all the information they had gathered during their recon mission which had not been uploaded. Under normal circumstances, the intel was uploaded and erased before a team engaged in a mission. However, since the current situation did not allow her to return to base before engaging, isolation was necessary.

The storage units were located in a segment of her brain. It was a Biological-Digital Storage (BDS) area in an inactive brain space that had been surgically segmented to store mission-critical information. The access portal was located beneath the skin, behind the ear, where a micro-magnetic connection synced with special Smart Spec glasses. Everyone on the teams wore Smart Specs, but only she had the BDS tool.

The advantage of being able to carry encrypted messages inside the head of the operators without anyone having direct knowledge of the message was critical to maintaining an Underground advantage over the constant intrusion of the controlling surveillance state.

As Bry stood, the sun hung low on the distant horizon, fighting to glow through the clouds. The foggy mist between the rises hid the valleys in twilight and mystery. With the cascading orange hues, it appeared as if she stood inside a painting as birds sang their goodbye to the day. "Thanks," she whispered then blew a kiss toward heaven.

Passing through the black entry curtain, Bry slid inside the cave to find her compatriots gathered around a makeshift table with an LED lantern giving off a sterile white light.

"What? Where did we get Mac and Cheese!?"

"It's a surprise. Dylan got a couple boxes at that trail town north of the Smokies," Chase said.

"Hot Springs? And you've been hiding it from us?" Bry asked.

"Saving it for a day we needed it."

"It's a nice surprise. I was dreading another bowl of oatmeal."

"Me, too."

"Dylan and kind aren't two words you often hear in the same sentence," Chase said.

"I didn't realize that you knew what a sentence was." Oliver laughed.

"Chase, do you have any of those hot sauce packets left?" Bry asked, stirred by a renewed hunger.

"I've got one to split."

"A couple drips is all I need," Bry said. "I'm a lightweight on spicy."

"We getting orders tonight?" Dylan asked Bry.

"Supposed to. What time is it?"

"19-58."

"Hopefully we get a resupply," Oliver said.

"No doubt. The food stores are low," Chase said.

"How low?" Bry asked.

"4k."

"Only four thousand calories left?"

"Yes, that's all we have in the bag. Plus personal stores."

"Looks like you're going to be losing some of that baby fat, O," Dylan said.

"I will squish you like bug, little boy-man."

"You've gotta catch me first."

"I'll just hang out next to Bry."

The cave erupted in laughter and catcalls at Oliver's insinuation that Dylan hung around Bry for reasons beyond the mission. The noise immediately died as the team remembered noise protocols. It was good to laugh and better to laugh over a good meal. Bry had no reason to remind the men of their mission in that lighthearted moment, even though she was blushing.

Bry exited the cave an hour later, letting her eyes adjust to the deepening darkness.

She clicked the power button on the black satellite phone, holding it to her ear. After a few moments, a gentle click prompted her to input a numeric code, which she did with symbols, dashes, and numbers in all the right places. She listened while the phone cycled through its encryption protocol.

"Go," said the deep male voice.

"Three. The bear in the hill has green eyes. The bear in the hill has green eyes."

"Roger, Three. Sister's Bald has no water. Repeat. Sister's Bald has no water."

"Confirm."

"You guys ready to go?"

"Roger that."

"Damascus road has a Gooch Gap."

"Affirmative. Damascus road has a Gooch Gap," Bry repeated.

Fifteen minutes later, the team members were ready to leave the cave and the mountain. All four had their Night Vision Goggles, or NVGs turned up on their black helmets and AR-15s at the ready in a front sling. Gear was stowed in their rucksacks, packed for stealth. They cross-checked their suits before exiting the safety of the cave. The flowing cape they used was the newest version of a T-400 Shimmer. The suits allowed them to move out in the open without being detected by Low Earth Orbit (LEO) surveillance satellites. The newest ideation of the cape attached to their helmet covered their backpacks and hung to the ground behind them.

Under active surveillance operators crouched down so the satellite sensors could not distinguish them from their surroundings. Of course, the suits worked the best while operating under cover of foliage and darkness. The units dispersed the heat signatures from biological entities, making them invisible to orbital scanners. Of course, knowing the cadence of the satellites in the area of operation was vital. The cape communicated via a blue icon on their Smart Specs. The warning gave them thirty seconds to stop moving and ensure their capes were in the best position to cover themselves.

Rogue drones used by the enemy were much more difficult to combat, and teams would be forced to hole up and wait for the mobile units to move out of the area. The Shimmer capes had limited effect on ground-based scanning systems mounted on mobile platforms or hand-held units used by soldiers and the Federal Police. But they gave small teams a distinct advantage over detection systems employed by both the Federal and Global Union. The most significant advantage was that the government did not know they existed— yet.

Bry's team's, official call sign Niner-Mike, were headed north to gather a few packages. Getting places was the easy part of the job. The team had worked together for over a year and understood each other's tendencies, quirks, strengths, and weaknesses.

While out on a mission, the teams set up a diamond. The point-man would use their NVGs and operate twenty yards out in front of the group, clearing the path. The side-by-sides were next, followed by the rear guard. Intel had indicated an all-clear path for at least twenty klicks. Bry had reviewed the satellite images before exiting their cave, which was identified on their map as C-22.

The most challenging aspect of today's mission was traversing through the woods silently while descending the mountain. Once they connected with the established trail, their auto-pilot kicked in. Two hundred trips up and down the same stretch of backcountry trail over the last four hundred days, and the biggest fight was against complacency. Bry sent a message to the team across their comms: "Don't get fat." This reminded them to engage their brains and not go through the motions lazily. It was one of many Niner-Mike sayings.

The underlying mission of Niner-Mike now was to interdict refugees headed south and aid with transportation. They sought to bring the willing under protection for the journey to freedom. Of course, Niner-Mike's area of operation was a hundred miles from safety, and many refugees would not complete the trip. One thing Niner-Mike understood with clarity was the boundaries of their new mission— safely assist refugees to a mobile processing facility. That was it. If they did their jobs and handed off their refugee packages, more could be saved from certain prison and possible death. It was how they helped the cause.

During the last four months, the refugees returning south had been arriving more destitute than ever. The people who escaped left desperate situations and then walked for five or six months. Whole families with little children left the Compliant States. Some had buried several members of their own household, lost to starvation and disease along the way. The situation become bleak since the passing of the Domestic Religious Terrorist Act in 2045. Three years later, the infrastructure for an enforcement apparatus had been built and brought online as the effects of the law began taking hold.

If a panel of judges deemed your chosen religious affiliation hostile to the ordinary operation and freedoms afforded by global civil society, then the members of said religion willingly gave up their Global Union citizenship and rights. Thirty states have passed G.U. compliance measures, many forced due to economic pressures. Six states are near compliance, and fourteen have outright rejected any association with the Global Union.

When the arrests began in the Compliance States, panic ensued. Still, the media actively covered up the growing atrocities against the religious minority, choosing instead to report on the vast benefits of belonging to the G.U. Voices of dissent were quickly silenced— "For the good of the growing Global Union."

Vigilante groups actively hunted the members of banned religions. They were paid large bounties for delivering the deplorable people to the corporate collection centers for processing.

Companies were hired to reopen mothballed prisons and used them to house non-compliant families.

Then, the Child Restoration Act was passed through individual state legislatures to reeducate dispossessed children. Those States stepped in to foster parent millions of children they deemed "abused" by religious indoctrination. Lawsuits were filed on behalf of the imprisoned and made their way to the twenty-one judges on the full United States Supreme Court. The court sided with the state to protect the children from their non-compliant parents. Deeply religious parents wondered how could you fight from a prison cell when you've been declared a terrorist? The Global Union was all about peace, after all.

Free people fought back. Shooting wars erupted across the country, and large swatches of territory were declared free, in direct rebellion against the tyranny of each compliant state. In response to the uprising, Global Union forces, led primarily by Communist China, were brought in to settle the violence, restore peace, and reincorporate the farmlands. When the G.U. conquered an area, a puppet government was installed and then declared to be in compliance with global dictates. They could not care less about who governed over a region because that governance was required to be in agreement with the will of the Global Union's peace initiative.

"Sat," Bry said.

All four operators stopped, took a knee, tucked their rifles, fluffed their capes out behind them, and then looked to the ground. During the break, most sipped at their water tube from the reservoir inside their backpack.

Twenty seconds later, the "all-clear" was called, and they rose to continue.

"Hold!"

"Movement. Twenty yards," Oliver whispered into his comms.

<hr>

Flying while in stealth mode is slow unless you gain altitude and use the height to dive to gain airspeed. Flying stealth meant no stepping through a shift portal. Angel Warriors sent on stealth missions were required to travel like biological life, constrained by time and space because they did not want to give off their heat and spatial distortion signals to the enemy. Master Sergeant Gilboa had traveled through the night to put himself in a position to locate his mark the next day. Exhausted from his travels, he rested on a steel gangplank of a billboard sign for a local Mexican restaurant in northern Georgia. The mission required him to maintain operational stealth mode for the duration. His wings were sore from the 1,100 klicks he flew. He was asleep seconds after his prayers ended.

<hr>

Every member of Niner-Mike silently flipped their NVGs down into position and slid off the trail into the surrounding darkness.

"Six," was whispered into their comm earpiece by Oliver, who was currently operating as the mission point man.

The two members in the center position of the diamond, Bry and Dylan, knew to wait for six bodies to pass them to see if the group had been given an I.R. beacon.

"Beacon confirmed." Dylan was on the opposite side of the trail from Bry.

Bry understood the action following contact was the trickiest. She had to initiate communication with the six bogies without giving herself and her team up. They each drew down on one of the six stumbling people before she spoke.

"Good night for a walk," Bry said.

"Yes it is!" said one of the females in the group.

"Good night for a walk," Bry said again as Niner-Mike clicked their safeties off their guns.

"I'm sorry. If you're a water buffalo," another person said.

"Sit," Bry commanded, All six people sat down on the trail.

"I need the beacon. Toss it behind you onto the trail," Bry said.

"We are looking for the Firefox."

"Silence."

"But they said we'd hook up with you forty miles back."

"If you don't want to get shot as G.U. scum, you had better put a sock in it."

"I don't understand. You're supposed to help us," the voice continued. Then, the talker was slapped on the face by someone in front of her, and she was followed by, "Shut up! You're going to get us killed!" There was a whimper and then silence.

"Confirmed. We are your escort. We have discretion to abandon you if you will not follow orders. Do you understand?"

"Yes. Sorry. She is tired from the trip," said a male voice.

"When's the last time you've had any food?" Bry asked.

"Three days ago we caught a fish."

"Roger that."

"A half click further there is a good spot to pull over to get some calories in you. But you have to be quiet. We could hear you coming for a few hundred meters. Walk on your toes, spread out. We don't get this right and we are disconnecting. Do you understand?"

"Yes."

"Silence protocol from here on out. Copy?"

"Yes," the male voice said.

"Two of you will follow one of us in a single file line. You must spread out by a couple meters each. No lights. We have someone bringing up the rear behind us, he will stay back to check for bogies. If we say "stop" everyone stops immediately. If we say "down" you get your face into the dirt. If you cannot follow orders or refuse to follow orders we will disconnect from you and you will have to fend for yourselves." Bry said.

"Okay. We understand."

"Lets go. Now."

Niner-Mike and the six packages made their way through the darkness. Their progress was painfully slow on purpose. The team knew they had to lower their package's expectations. Niner Mike was not going to save them. Niner Mike was going to assist them in making their way to freedom.

＊＊＊

Gilboa was above the group of ten as they walked through the woods of North Carolina. He had sent his encrypted message to H.Q. and received confirmation. He decided to gain some altitude to guard against potential threats, and that is when he caught sight of the circling Reapers. It was a glint of moonlight off their black wings that got his attention. Gills knew they were looking for a group of ten, and he was trying to determine their squad strength.

"Three unlucky bastards," Gilboa thought to himself and moved to get above them.

During his climb, he reported in and received permission for the sneak attack if there were only three.

Gilboa was directly above their circle. He wanted them to draw closer to each other before he struck.

"Arrived," Oliver said over his comm.

"Roger on arrival," Bry said.

"Stop," Bry whispered. "Down." Everyone took a knee.

"Two by two we are moving right. A hundred meters in we are going to eat and get resupplied. Silence."

"Yes," said one man.

Ten minutes later, the six sat on the ground below a tree as Niner Mike took up a perimeter. The last four thousand calories of food were given to the starving group, with the promise of more to come.

"Four of them look pretty bad," Dylan said to Bry over the comm.

"Chase, separate the two and find out their story after they are done eating," Bry said. "O, set up comms."

"Roger that."

"Dylan, teach them satellite protocol."

"Roger."

Fifteen minutes later, a drone buzzed through the night air, searching for a signal. Circling above the mountains, the three Reapers understood that the resupply vehicle wanted to connect with a ground team signal. So they dove fifty meters above the eight-bladed rotary device and matched its speed and direction. They flew side by side when the green light flashed from above them, and their severed heads fell into the trees. Their winged bodies continued on their course for the briefest of a second before collapsing and falling to the ground.

⸺◆⸺

"I think we have a problem," Chase said.

"What?"

"I think one of our packages is a bogey."

"G.U? How do you know?" Bry asked.

"His story about coming through Kentucky doesn't match. He said he came through Lewis and Carter County in western Kentucky and met up with the rest of these guys shortly after."

"Lewis County is in eastern Kentucky," Bry said.

"Right and he insisted he came from the Chicago area and went south. It just sounds scripted."

"This was one of the two healthy packages?"

"Yes."

"We're not taking a chance. We are leaving him."

"SOP?"

"Yep, tie him to a tree with the light weight rope. Tag his pants. What's his trail name?"

"Zorba."

"I'll let the others know."

"Everyone is loaded up," Dylan said to Bry.

"Unload Zorba. We don't feed G.U.," she whispered.

"Really?" Dylan was verifying the information he thought he heard.

"Chase confirmed it," Bry said.

"That's the fourth plant this month."

"Yeah, they are taking more risks."

"Fox? Are we taking the tag?" Chase asked.

"Yes."

The group heard Zorba's scream as they walked away while the eastern sky brightened.

Thirty minutes later, another satellite passed overhead as the nine people huddled under Niner Mike's four Shimmer coats. No one noticed as one hand was held out from beneath the blanket.

SEVEN

Sol 7620 (30 April 2048)
Central City District, Free Port, Mars

The tunnels of Free Port were quiet as Kars and Benz returned to Mr. Brady's office. Except for the two men, their subway car was empty. As the train rolled into the Central City dome and before the doors opened, Benz moved toward his best friend.

"I'll stay back for a few seconds to watch who is exiting the other cars," Benz whispered, waiting for Kars to exit onto the platform. Kars walked across the open loading area, lit by broad-spectrum lights. He continued up the stairs, looking around the subway station entry before checking the empty streets through the tall windows.

Benz waited to leave the train car until the last possible moment to see if they had been followed. Only two other people were riding this early. They followed Kars up the stairs and passed him to exit onto the sidewalk.

"All clear," Benz said to Kars.

"I don't see anything up here, either."

Both men pushed through the doors and headed toward the glass LIFT building. Kars slowed his pace to match Benz' limp and grimace.

LIFT only had a few employees wandering in for work. When Kars and Benz arrived at the security checkpoint, the female officer smiled as she recognized the men.

"You guys are heroes in my book," she whispered, smiling.

Both men nodded as they swiped their right hands under the scanner. A green light sent them on their way to Brady's office.

"Wonder if Ridge and his Goons are still sleeping?"

"Maybe they are on another case?" Kars said.

"What case right now is bigger than the bombing of a LIFT train?"

"Beats me."

Brady's secretary making coffee, waved both men to the boss's office. "He's expecting you!"

The windows, which had been crystal clear the day before for making the promotional video, had been made opaque for this morning's meeting. As the men approached the door, it slid open so they could enter the room. Brady was seated behind his desk, talking with none other than Lieutenant Ridge. As soon as the door closed, Ridge's pair of Goons sidled up alongside Kars and Benz from the shadows. They bumped into the pair just as Brady told them to have a seat. Ridge silently glared at his famous suspects.

"Thanks for coming in on such short notice. I'm certain we can get this cleared up and get you guys back out on the rails doing what you do best." Brady said.

As he sat, Kars acknowledged that his body was sore from the wreck and getting tossed around by the Goons standing behind them. Benz's eye was black and blue from his meeting with the F.P., and his leg throbbed from his wound. Neither man responded verbally to Brady, but inside, they seethed with anger toward their boss, who was willing to throw their rights under the bus.

"We received some footage from a camera recovered in the wreckage," Brady said.

"From the crime scene," Ridge interjected.

"Right. Crime scene."

"The footage you are about to see raises more questions for me, and by me, I mean the Federal Police of Free Port," Ridge stared at them.

"Boys, this is serious," Brady said.

"Don't you have anything to say for yourselves?" Ridge demanded.

"About a video, we haven't seen?" Benz said, pointing out the apparent contradiction.

Ridge glanced up at his Goons, who were ready to enforce their zero-tolerance policy, but understood the message their boss sent for cooler heads in front of the cooperative Mr. Brady.

Brady's desktop came to life with a paused video. The image was from a comm from one of the passengers on the ill-fated train to Eland.

"This video is from a man seated in front of you two on the train. He was seated facing toward the rear of the train, which means his back was to the explosion," Brady said.

Ridge jumped in, "We believe this man's body protected his comm from the explosion and preserved for us to see a piece of the truth of what happened inside that train. We have identified the man. Before the detonation Mr. Win Lu was a filmmaker, who was here on Mars with a work visa to shoot a Sci-Fi movie. His personal comm unit was specialized to capture high speed footage. It is believed that he used this camera mode whenever he was inspired to capture images that could be used in his productions."

Kars watched Ridge press his tongue against his bottom lip.

"In this first frame we can clearly identify both of you," Ridge said.

The scene brought swirling flashes back into Kars' mind, unsettling him further.

Both the employees remained silent, seated in front of Brady's desk. They sat up toward the edge of their chair with both hands on the glass, trying to get a good view of the video. They did not know that Ridge performed a complete diagnostic review on each of the men through Brady's smart desk. He stole the information, including their employee files and personal chip data, through a program embedded in his comm unit that sat innocently on the edge of the desk, right next to him. He wagered a guess that Brady's work desk would not be protected from intrusion in the same manner as the company mainframe. "These people are so dumb," Ridge thought.

"Play it," Ridge said.

Brady touched the triangle in the middle of his screen. The AI used the desktop monitor to subdivide its surface so each man surrounding it would have his own image to watch.

The scene was silent and surreal to Kars and Benz. With the explosion, the video was blown to take pictures of the ceiling for a brief flash, then went dark. The whole segment was cut to five seconds.

"Yeah? So what?" Benz said out of frustration.

"So what, indeed," Ridge said. "Play it again Mr Brady, this time frame by frame."

As the first frame switched to the second to the third, a flash across the screen happened five milliseconds before the flash of the detonation. Upon explosion, something in front of Benz and Kars could barely be made out, clearly deflecting the blast around the men. The blast shield looked like wings. Their eyes expanded in disbelief. Ridge now knows they had never seen this image before, but he could not let on that he knows the truth about their reactions. "Maybe they don't know, but whoever they are working for knows for certain," he thought.

"What the hell is that?" Benz asked. "You wrote that into the video, using AI or something."

"That video was not altered in any way," Ridge declared.

"Then what is that... that thing?"

"We brought you in here to ask you what you knew about it," Brady said.

"Nothing!" Kars said, his voice had gone up an octave higher.

"It appears to me that you knew you would be protected in the explosion so you could look like heroes when actually you were sent to target someone on that train!"

"I'm getting a lawyer! I will not answer any more of your ridiculous questions," Benz announced.

At that second, the image on the partitioned screens, the four segments of Brady's desk, paused with a different arm or wing embracing each of the men, appeared to melt— like an old film melting against a hot projector bulb.

"What happened?" Ridge demanded.

"I don't know. Let me do a hard restart on my computer." Brady reached for the power button.

Ten seconds later, the desk unit had rebooted, but he found no video on the drive. He accessed the mainframe and found no trace of a video. Ridge looked at his comm unit to download another copy to Brady's desk, but his file was corrupted. He stood in frustration and began to search the F.P. mainframe. Within a minute, Ridge knew that no record of the video was ever being stored on it. It was wiped clean. He wondered if someone hacked in or if it was all just a gotcha joke.

Ridge asked his Goons, "Do we still have Mr. Lu's comm?"

The Goon behind Benz produced the unit from his pocket and passed it to his boss.

When he pressed the power switch on the side of the unit, it sparked and began to smoke.

Benz and Kars looked at each other as Ridge erupted in anger and threw the unit against the glass wall, breaking it into several pieces upon impact.

"I know you two are behind this!" Ridge accused Kars and Benz.

"We're just sitting here with nothing in our hands, Ridge." Benz stood to face the Goon behind him. Kars joined him, staring the Goons down. As the enforcers tossed aside the chairs that Kars and Benz had abandoned, four LIFT security men entered the office with their E-stols drawn. Mr. Brady stood up behind his desk.

"Lieutenant Ridge, I believe this interview is over, sir. If you and your men kindly leave the premises, we can continue this discussion when cooler heads prevail."

"Mr. Brady, you cannot shield these criminals forever. If I find out that you are behind the destruction of that video, I will come for you and prosecute you to the fullest extent of Martian law." Ridge was so angry that he was spitting by the end of his speech. He turned and left the office followed by his Goons who had become compliant with the arrival of the E-stols.

"Listen, I don't know what in the hell is going on here." Brady looked down at his desk, "But I want you guys to take a couple of weeks off while this blows over."

"What?" Benz said.

"We didn't do anything wrong!" Kars said.

"Listen, I don't know what happened. I am moving ahead with the idea that you two are heroes and you just need time to recover from the blast. I'll make sure you get paid."

"I'm not using up my vacation time for this," Benz said.

"We will figure this out," Brady said. "I need you guys to lay low and let this pass. Okay?"

"Yep," Benz said. Kars nodded his response.

"Alright. We will talk soon. Go somewhere to get away."

They walked out of Brady's office and noticed his secretary was crying. As soon as they got out of the building, they paused to look for one of the Goons.

"Let's split up and meet at Harry's," Benz said.

"I think we should go to Oceanside."

"Good thinking."

They bro hugged and headed in opposite directions.

⸺⬦⸺

In a dark and distant command center, a pair of spindly hands glided over a custom keyboard shaped like a round tower. The keys looked like windows on the side of a scale model of a black high-rise building as the fingers flashed over them with a certain poetic motion.

Rising above the dark tower keyboard, the skinny man swiped his index finger at an image on one of the five screens in front of him. The image of angel wings protecting two men in their Evos appeared to melt into the back of the monitor and then disappear.

The six people on Mars in Brady's office could not understand what happened to the feed. Someone mocked them. A slight, ever-so-slight uptick in one side of Kars's mouth went unnoticed by the panicked humans in the room. But the shadowy figure with the distinct keyboard millions of miles away began to laugh out loud in his darkness. He was tapped into an office camera feed, with separate images covering each participant around the desk.

"Got you, sucker!" He pumped his fist in the air.

⸺⬦⸺

Outside, in the vacuum of deep space and above the skinny man laughing at the quirky command center, a squad of four Angel Warriors circled in complete stealth mode above a black space station. Their massive wings were fully displayed to cover the operation center at the front of the space-craft.

The ship's rotating arms stopped their one-G gravitational spin, then retracted. The high-gain antennas folded down, and both arms moved back along the hull for flight. At the rear of the ship, two separate and powerful nuclear pulse drive engines spring to life. Its distinct blue circle of light pushed the craft forward. As it maneuvers away, its unique conical V shape is revealed to the warriors who grabbed on for a ride around the Red Planet.

⋯◆⋯

After their confab at Oceanside Bar, Benz visited a girl he knew near the train station while Kars went home. Upon entering his Cube, Kars' mind was occupied by the strange events of the last couple of days. He was washed out and wanted nothing more than to crash on the couch and sleep for a few hours. As he unlocked the entry portal from outside the corridor, an Amazon package hung on the handle. It was the door seal. He dropped it on the table and turned to secure the refurbished door. He slid the four deadbolts closed, then fell onto the couch. He pulled a blanket out of one of the three drawers on the front of the couch and mindlessly watched the drawer automatically shut.

What seemed like just a few minutes later, Kars was stirred when a group of screaming kids ran past his Cube, laughing in perpetual chaos. Drool had wet his cheek and the cushion. He realized he had been out for longer than he thought. It felt like he just dozed. Checking his comm, three hours had passed.

Kars stretched and let out a long and loud response to the sleep. He decided to get washed up but still had his boots on, so sitting up to unstrap them and reaching to untie his boots he noticed a piece of paper under the couch and grabbed it. He and Benz had just discussed coded language to communicate hidden things in plain sight.

"Dinner is in the freezer," Kars said into his comm, then sent the message to Benz and waited.

Within a minute, his comm chirped with the programmed Star Trek Communicator sound.

"I'm still full from breakfast," Benz had replied.

"Just saying."

"K."

Twenty-five minutes later, Benz knocked on the door with three taps. Kars unlocked the new deadbolts and slid the door to the side. The door opened with a whooshing sound. Benz knew the seal had been replaced but looked down to confirm.

"Just got done fixing it." Kars closed the door and reset the deadbolts on the four corners. They both knew Ridge would have to cut his way in the next time.

"What's up?" Benz asked.

"I was untying my boots and I saw this under the couch."

The tan envelope had yet to be opened. Benz saw the front and looked at Kars. "Bombing?"

"I don't know." Kars chewed at one of his fingernails.

Benz slid his finger inside along the flap, tearing it open. When he tipped the envelope over into his hand a micro-flash drive spilled out.

Kars opened a drawer under the couch and pulled out a laptop. "This is an indy," he said. Benz knew the computer was set up so that it would not be connected to any outside networks.

After the white laptop, which was covered in stickers, booted up, Kars connected to the microdrive with an auxiliary cord.

The bombing video from Brady's office, the one that had disappeared, played automatically. It showed the wings protecting Kars and Benz. Then a message scrolled: "We need to talk. Six hours after this video has been played, three tunnels east of the place you go to dive, on the left, watch for the infrared marker on the ceiling. Come alone."

"This disc will self-destruct in five seconds— remove from your computer."

The screen went black, and then the disc began to glow red.

Kars yanked the cord out and threw it on the floor. It snapped and then popped into tiny shards.

"Holy crap!" Kars said.

"This keeps getting weirder." Benz rubbed his head.

"What do you think they mean by come alone? Like you alone? Or me alone? Or the two of us alone?" Kars asked.

"I don't know. How did they get a video that was destroyed?"

"Who are these people? They must be the people who destroyed it?"

"Yeah. It can't be Ridge. I think he would be taking us downtown for questioning." Benz rubbed his face as he thought.

"Can't be Brady, could it?"

"No way," Benz said. "I think he'd destroy it. They want this case to disappear."

"Are we going?" Kars interlaced his fingers behind his head.

"I think we have to, don't you?"

"I don't know." Kars glanced at the door and the relative safety of the deadbolts.

"They can still get in if they want, Kars."

"Yeah, I guess. Too bad we don't have an E-stol."

"Those would get you ten years of hard time on Luna." Benz' eyes flashed a serious glint.

"I thought there was a case before the court that might change it."

"There was and they said the second amendment does not apply to outer space colonies because of the inherent danger involved," Benz said.

"Stupid. Our God-given rights taken away."

"I know."

"We gotta go meet the tunnel serial killer in some dark cave with no protection?"

"I'm the protection." Benz flexed and laughed.

"Yeah. Your eye is shining with a green and blue bruise. You look like you got half a raccoon head."

"I'm Joe Louis."

They both smiled for the first time all day.

"We could beat them to the tunnel and watch to see who they are and how they are setting up," Benz said.

"You think?

"Let's go."

⸺⬦⸺

Two angel warriors followed the men who made their way to the secret meeting place. As they hurried through the Central City dome's heavy traffic, people walked through the warriors' essence without realizing what had happened. The humans on Mars could experience euphoria for a brief second, which usually played out on their faces with a smile. Captain Helek had a smile of his own with a passing memory. "I remember the first time a human walked through me; it almost made me puke, if I could."

"Yeah, I had a similar response back in the day," Iggy said.

"When was that?" Helek asked.

"Well, I am in my seventh iteration and if my memory serves me I think the first time was in a crowded market in Egypt."

"I loved being stationed in Egypt!"

"When were you there?"

"Been stationed there four times. I'm in my sixth iteration."

"No kidding?"

"Yep. First time was back in Joseph's day. Had guard duty while he was imprisoned."

"Cool memories?"

"Boring memories. But spending my down time in and around the Nile was fantastic."

"I wasn't near the Med. I was in south-central Egypt a few centuries later. Guard duty at a monastery. They hosted a farmers market every Tuesday," Iggy said with a particular fondness.

"You ever had one walk through and become terrified?"

"All the time."

"Crazy, right?"

"How was working out of a monastery?"

"It was a good duty station," Iggy said while watching the guys. "Cap, are you seeing this? These guys are putting on their Faraday hats."

"Let's go stealth," Helek said.

"Roger, Stealth. We got someone on the other side?" Iggy asked before his transformation.

"Yes. Should be Biggs. He's our contact." Helek went invisible.

EIGHT

Sol 7621 (01 May 2048)
Free Port, Mars

Showing up early to the tunnel meeting produced nothing advantageous for Kars and Benz. The infrared marker, activated remotely, pointing them to another tunnel on the opposite side of the city, which ended in a farming cave. Cycling through the airlock, the men noticed the farming bots were busy at work caring for the genetically engineered wheat crop, which was grown in vertical trays since the stalks were only ten centimeters tall. The farm was long, as the rows of immature grain stretched back several hundred meters and was half as wide and smelled of life.

"It smells like heaven in here," Kars said.

"Fresh grass! They should pump this smell through the cubes!"

"That's a great idea. It's wheat, though."

"How do you know that?"

"It said Wheat Farm on the air lock, genius."

"Oh."

They stopped to take it all in. Long support columns reached from the floor to the ceiling, holding a labyrinth of interlocking steel beams topped with corrugated metal. This steel roof was protection against parts and pieces of the cave roof being shaken free given the remote chance of a quake. But the green hues from the wheat plants reflected an aura of life and vitality even onto the cold metal ceiling.

Their instructions from the mysterious people were clear— they were to meet at the south end of the complex. That area was not bathed in artificial grow light but was cast in thick shadows and used to park worn-out equipment. They could see their breath and feel the condensation dripping from the roof like an intermittent rain. Both men wore knitted Faraday hats to electronically shield their faces from facial recognition cameras and thin black signal-blocking gloves to cover the digital output of their LIFT employee chip embedded into the back of their right hands.

Upon arrival at the meeting place, Kars switched his flashlight to infrared mode, to locate the beacon. The marker appeared to be a blotch on the rock a couple of meters above the floor. Then, bursting from a crag in the rock, three bodies all dressed in black, two brandishing E-stols and holding fingers over their mouths to remain silent. After patting Kars and Benz down for weapons, they put a hood over each of them and led them away.

The escorts were careful not to abuse their guests, covering their heads to prevent them from hitting themselves on the tunnel ceiling. Eighty-seven paces later, they stopped, and a door closed behind them. Kars was led another hundred and fifty paces with many twists and turns. Another door was opened, and they walked through. The metal portal clanked shut behind him. Kar's hood smelled of must and grain. When it was removed he blinked his eyes to refocus on a dimly lit room carved from the Martian mantle. There were three identical metal doors along one wall. Kars was not sure which door they had come through. The lone light above them swung from a wire— back and forth, making the room feel like it moved beneath their feet.

"Thanks for coming."

"You kind of got my attention with the whole video thing," Kars said. He tried to focus his eyes and gather his bearings. There was only one man with a sidearm now. Kars figured the other was watching over Benz. When the armed man stepped back from him, another dark figure approached.

"Kars, do you know where we are right now?" The new person was a woman.

"Got no idea," Kars lied.

"You have been in the dust bowl for thirteen years working on the trains and you have no idea where you are right now? The only way this works is if you are honest with me."

"I don't know what this is, so how would I know if I even want this to work. I'm flying by the seat of my pants here."

"Do you know where you are? Think about it," she said.

"I know that we are meeting in the back of the farming cave 236. We never climbed or descended and traveled about one hundred and eighty meters into a hidden tunnel. So yeah, I guess I'm still able to think."

"Right. Good."

"Where is Benz?"

"He is safe and not too far. I needed to talk to you."

"Why me? You know my name, what's yours?"

"I'm Ally."

She stepped out of the shadows and removed her hat. Her blonde hair hung just below her shoulder. She held out her hand to shake, locking their eyes, her blue with his brown. Her hand was small but solid and calloused.

"Happy to meet you, Kars."

"This is a little weird. I'm not sure why you'd want to talk to me?"

"For normal people in everyday circumstances, yes it would be weird. But we are not living a normal world anymore, in many ways this world has been inverted from what we were used to, but this isn't out of the ordinary for my life."

"You must have an interesting way of living."

"I'm not sure I would define it that way, but I can see how some might," she stepped around him, and he turned with her.

"So, you regularly meet strange men in dark places with armed guards?"

"More than you'd think."

"What are you a spy or something?"

"Or something."

"What?"

"Given just those two choices I would say that I am a, 'or something.'"

"Oh, okay. What is the reason behind this clandestine meeting? It can't be just because I'm good with directions and you need someone to show you around."

"Ooo, I like the word! Clandestine. You must read a lot," she said.

"I read. What do you do?"

"Let's say, for a minute, that my job is to open eyes." She extended her fingers on both hands, palms toward Kars.

"Open eyes? Like a doctor, helping the blind or something?"

"No, more metaphorically speaking. I show people a new reality. Or better said, I help people embrace a new reality."

"Hmm. Sounds like the vacation pods in Eland."

"You mean the VR beds where you lay around for a week while an AI inputs images into your brain?"

"When you put it like that it sounds dirty."

Ally laughed. "Dirty and lazy." She laughed more.

Kars laughed along with her.

"Those places have nothing to do with reality." She stared off into space, thinking about the contradiction.

"So, your new reality?" Kars asked.

"Yes!"

"What is it?"

"I'll have to show you. I don't have the words to accurately describe all of it."

"Is it illegal?"

"It's becoming more and more illegal, but that's the wrong question."

"What do you mean?" Kars said.

"You asked the wrong question."

"How's that?"

"I really need to show you. Then you will ask the right questions."

"Oh. What if I don't like what I see?"

"Then you walk away and go on with the rest of your life."

"Really?"

"Yes. Absolutely."

"You can understand some of my skepticism, right? You're going to show me something amazing and if I don't like it then you're gonna just let me walk away and trust that I would never say anything to anyone after you enticed me here with a video that disappeared from the Federal Police mainframe?"

"Well, when you put it like that."

"What if I exposed it all to authorities or a reporter?"

"No one believes reporters anyway. Listen we know we are taking a risk when we show people what we are about, but we have always lived with a risk. This is nothing more than a calculated risk on our part."

"Did you find out about what you are involved with in the same way that I am finding out?"

"Not really, but I would say that many people these days find out about what I am involved with exactly how you are."

"Did you pick me?"

"I don't make those decisions."

"But was I chosen by someone?"

"Yes."

"Okay, why was I selected to get this once in a lifetime opportunity?"

"You're funny, Kars."

"But seriously?"

"I know why you have been selected. I will tell you why after I show you what I need to show you."

"I think your group sends out pretty women to recruit unmarried men."

"I don't get to pick who to contact."

"But you know that it's hard to say no to someone..." Kars trailed off not wanting to continue.

"Someone what?"

"As pretty as you are." Kars thought he must have been hit on the head during the train explosion harder than he knew.

"Thank you. Can't say anyone has come right out and said that on one of these interviews before."

"Wait, this is an interview? Like for a job?"

"Yes. What else would it be? We don't know you, so this is a vetting process.

"For a job then? With the armed guard and all the secrecy surrounding the meeting, I would not have used the word 'interview' to describe this." Kars used his finger to draw an imaginary circle around the concept.

"On this side of seeing, I can understand your feelings of uncertainty."

"Uncertainty? I thought I was going to be blackmailed, or kidnapped, or something."

"No. Wait." Ally brought her fingers to her temples and looked at the ground, gathering her thoughts. "Okay let's start over. I know you have been through some pretty traumatic things during the last few days. I understand how you could think that this is connected to that chaos, but I can assure you, it is not. Or it's not in the way that you are thinking. You were selected before any of that stuff happened."

"Well, now I feel so much better!"

"Relax. You can walk away anytime you want."

"What about Benz?"

"What about him?'

"Where is he?"

"This wasn't for him, Kars. This meeting was for you alone."

"Oh. I thought the message after the video meant both of us come alone. Because we were both in that video."

"No. You are the one we needed to talk too. Cool video, by the way," Ally said.

"Confusing video, you mean."

"No I don't. It's a really cool video."

"You've watched it right?"

"Every single frame."

"So what do you think is shown guarding us during the explosion?"

"An angel."

"A what?"

"An angel."

"Just like that. An angel... here on Mars?"

"Yes."

"And you believe that?" he said.

"Yep. And those wings that are shown protecting you during the bombing kinda proves my point."

"I've seen the video. I just don't know. I mean I was there and I didn't see an angel. I didn't feel an angel holding me. No angel talked to me before, during, or after the explosion."

"I think God has a purpose for your life and that angel helped you identify what it is."

"What? Now you sound like my eighty-four-year-old grandma."

"She sounds like a wise lady!"

Silence interrupted the discussion for a few seconds.

"So, where is this thing you want to show me?" Kars said.

"Who said it was a thing?"

"What?"

"There are things about what I want to show you— but it is not primarily, a thing."

"Now you got me all kinds of mixed up."

"Sorry. I understand. And you will understand after I show you."

"Will I?"

"Yes. Promise."

"Are you selling used cars, or crypto, or time share condos in Brahman?"

"With the Hindus?"

"Yeah and all the Krishnas at their train station."

"You've met?"

"Too many times. Spent six months up there a few years back."

"To answer your question, no. I'm not selling anything."

"It's a job interview?"

"No. It's a life interview."

"A life interview... I can walk away if I want?"

"One hundred percent."

"Alive, I mean."

Ally laughed out loud again and then paused to realize Kars was serious. "Someone has really been screwing with your head." She leaned in closer to the man noting the stress lines on his face.

"Yeah. I thought I would visit one of those special clinics in Zulu."

"That's funny."

"What about Benz? Why can't he come along?" Kars' voice had lowered.

"I need to show you first, then you can decide if you think it would be something that he'd be interested in."

"You're gonna let me decide that?"

"For the most part, yes."

"Are you guys selling drugs?"

"Not selling."

"Taking drugs, then?"

"Oh, yeah."

"What are you going to tell Benz to get him to leave without me?"

"Nothing."

"What do you mean?"

"Benz is going to wake up in his bed."

"So he's not going to know that I am gone or was gone."

"Not unless you decide to tell him."

"Ally," said the armed man in the shadows. "We gotta wrap."

"Okay," she answered. "We need a decision, Kars. Your window of opportunity is closing."

"Alright."

"So?"

"So, alright. I'll have a look as long as you are going with me and showing me this mysterious inverted life interview, not a thing, thing."

"Hmm, you need to work on the whole rhyme thing but, yeah. I'll go with and show you everything I promised."

"When?"

"Now. But the hood has to go back on."

The man was already behind Kars and slid the hood over his head. The silky material smelled different, and then Kars collapsed.

<hr>

"F.E.'s are frustrating," Iggy thought about his Flicker's buddy the F.E. Technically, F.E. was the acronym Warriors used for the term Flicker Envier. These people who hung around Flickers because they saw something different in their lives, hoping their strength would rub off on them.

Iggy followed the friends as they made their way through the deepening darkness of another Martian tunnel. This tunnel had been bored by a mining machine processing iron ore. The walls were smooth but irregular. The tunnels could unexpectedly open up into caverns depending on how the veins of iron ran. Or the tunnel could double in width and drop off hundreds of feet in a side tunnel or up at a forty-five-degree angle, depending on how the ore veins ran.

These were also the places on Mars where people got lost, ran out of O2, and sat down to die. Human comms were awful in these deep recesses of the planet, and the GPS compasses never worked. Even Angel Warrior communication was scrambled. What was never in question was their objective and rules of engagement— those ROEs were locked down before every mission.

Moving in stealth meant they were comm silent. Since Captain Helek had gone ahead with his Flicker, Sergeant Igor was left standing behind his F.E. mark, waiting in a hood and being watched by an armed guard.

<hr>

"Helek?"

"Biggs! How are you doing?"

"Captain Helek now, I see," Biggs said.

"Yes. Made the career move," the warriors embraced.

"Nice. It's good to see you again!"

"It is. It's been awhile," Helek said.

"So, what's up with your mark?" Biggs asked.

"He's afraid. He'll probably run home and hide for the next two weeks."

"Kind of his M.O., right?"

"Yes. You've done your homework."

"I've seen him around. How long has he been yours?" Biggs asked.

"It's all new to me. Some other kid had him until a week ago and I got shipped out to this crap assignment."

"Mars isn't too bad. Cold as deepest hell itself, and dustier than anything, but the Situ is pretty casual."

"You've been here for a while?"

"Yes. I've watched her grow up from a pup." Biggs nodded to his mark in front of them.

"I wonder what's cooking?"

"Something big. It must be huge if they brought a Captain up to replace a private."

"Hmm. Yeah my orders are vague," Helek said.

"Sounds about right," Biggs said.

"Why are they drugging him?"

"They don't know if they can trust them yet. I'm sure they are going to do the same to the other one."

"That's Iggy's mark."

"Iggy from Charity?"

"One and the same," Helek said. "We stayed together for a bit, after."

"I wondered what happen to him. I mean I knew he was still around, not off to Para for another G/T."

"Right. G/T is tough, but we've all been there."

"Except Captain perfect, that is."

"It's Colonel perfect now!"

"That's right. Good for him. Amadan is one of a kind."

"Not too many originals left."

"Maybe a couple hundred?"

"Maybe."

"Where are we headed?"

NINE

Sol 7621 (01 May 2048)
Mars Unknown

Kars woke up inside an Evo. The face shield was blacked out. His vitals blinked at the bottom of his mask display, but no other information was available. He started to panic.

"I shouldn't have trusted her! You are such an idiot," he thought.

His respiratory rate increased with the thought, as did his anxiety. He reached for the exterior buttons on the face shield. Those controls were fail-safe and would override the internal commands that were given through eye movement. Engaging the buttons made no difference.

"They overrode the fail-safes?"

"These people must have incredible power," he thought. In Free Port, overriding mission-critical safety hardware is punishable by banishment. He knew most of the guys in prison for that crime ended up taking a long Martian shower.

"We are headed out to the site I promised to show you." It was Ally's voice through his comms. "Take a nap. Relax."

"You've shut out the face shield commands!"

"We temporarily suspended them," she said.

"That's a crime!"

"Only if you were outside. You're not. Relax and breathe, Kars. We have another hour to go."

"Oh, okay."

He tried to steady himself mentally.

"What do I know?" he thought, remembering his distant training.

He was on a train. He could feel the rhythm of the tracks pulsing beneath him. He felt around; he was lying on thin foam. He heard the squeak of his rubberized finger-tipped gloves grabbing at the material. Reaching out, he detected a wall on each side and a hard covering above him. But there was something about the texture of the walls. He discerned the distinct crunch of Mylar, like the emergency blankets.

"Wait. If I can hear it, then there must be Atmo," Kars knew sound waves did not travel in a vacuum.

He reached for his helmet release and found a ziptie in the lockout holes. He began working the metal against the plastic back and forth against the ziptie's weakness.

Within a minute the tie snapped and Kars swung the first lever to a slight hiss.

"You're not gonna..." Ally's voice went silent as Kars lifted his helmet off.

The space smelled like flowers, but there was breathable air. He banged the helmet against a wall above his head. It was close. So close, in fact, he had to scooch his butt down until his feet pressed against another solid wall to entirely remove the helmet. Fumbling for the suit lights, he found the switch. The interior shone like the sun in response to the bright LEDs on the Evo.

Reality hit him in the face. He was surrounded by a Shimmer blanket in a casket! He began to panic and press out against the metal skin of the death box. Muffled words came out of his helmet speakers as he disassociated from his surroundings. He frantically searched for a lever or internal handle to open the box. There are none.

He kicked and pounded with his fists and began hyperventilating. Kars passed out with voices emanating from his helmet.

—◆○◆—

"Don't remove your helmet, Kars!" Ally said.

"There will be a problem if he rips the blanket," someone said to her.

"I know!"

"Relax. We don't want to draw attention."

"Right."

"Remember if he is discovered we just walk away."

"Yes. Of course. I am trying to save the mission."

"Yeah." He smiled with the suspicious thought that mission success wasn't the only thing she tried to save.

"Sounds like he passed out. His breathing has normalized," the second man said to Ally.

"Good. Now we need him to put his helmet back on."

—◆○◆—

Kars woke with a headache and an instant feeling of strangulation due to a resurrected panic. He heard the speakers inside his helmet come to life and decided to put the unit back on. Getting turned over and scrunched down to be able to maneuver the helmet was difficult causing his claustrophobic feelings to deepen. His breathing was too fast when he snapped the final ring closed.

"Hey listen. You need to simmer down. You are being transported to our meeting place."

"I'm in a freaking casket!"

"No one looks inside caskets. You're safe."

"I can't open it."

"Right. It locks from the outside, like all caskets do."

"I hate this."

"Less than an hour left."

"You must be traveling along with me, but you're on the train and I'm in the cargo hold with the dead people."

"Yes. Control your breathing. Obviously we didn't give you a large enough dose of those sleepy time meds."

"Sleepy time. Yeah. That sucks."

"It's gonna be worth it."

"I have no choice here. I am forced to trust you."

"You made that choice in the cave."

Kars settled in and fell asleep after he turned on some music from Earth. He did not like the new songs being produced by AI on Mars. It was as if everything was being recycled in weird disco vibes, and those songs ran for an hour. He put on his country hits list and forced himself to sing along with a classic about being a long-haired son of a sinner.

An hour and fifteen minutes later, Kars felt his casket move and figured he needed to remain still, but a growing anxious wave built just off shore of his heart. He did not know how long he could last. His metal delivery box was set down with a bang, and then he was transported again. The lid opened above him, and someone plugged a cord into his suit.

"Hold on a second. I'm reprogramming the Evo to function normally," a male voice said over his comm.

"Yeah, okay."

A burst of light flooded his face. Kars fought to sit up.

"Sorry about the meds, Mate. I got that one wrong. Always better to err on this side of the equation. The other side could have put you in that box for good."

"That's one way to look at it." Kars stood on wobbly legs. He banged his head on the low roof of a vehicle.

"You're in a van," Ally said. "Come on, step down out of that box." She offered him a hand. Wearing an Evo, shesmiled at him. "It's not usually this bad," she said.

"Just a cherry on the top of my crap sundae of a week." Kars noticed her blue eyes sparkled at him, which tempered his anger and embarrassment.

"We should only be another fifteen minutes until we transfer."

"Transfer?"

"Yeah. We gotta walk through an old lava tube to get where we are going."

"Okay."

He finished the calculations in his head that he had started earlier and determined they were somewhere outside of Eland. He knew they were headed to Eland while in the casket.

Ally plugged a hose into his feed port and bled it off. "Try this. I think you'll like it."

Kars looked at her distrustful but then sipped at the concoction. "What is it?"

"A secret," she said.

"That figures coming from you. It's good. Kinda reminds me of a protein drink. It's not more sleepy meds is it?"

"No and yuck. Protein drink. That's not very nice of you!"

"What?"

"It's imported hot chocolate mix."

"Just because its imported doesn't automatically mean that it's good."

"Well, I think I should cut you off because you're wrong. Imported chocolate is always good. Always!"

"No, it's pretty good. It grows on you. Plus, you owe me after the whole casket fiasco."

"Fiasco?" Ally said.

"Yeah, if you wanted me to go to Eland you could have just asked."

"How? I mean, why, would you think that?" She tried to regain her composure.

Kars leaned forward as if to whisper into her ear without the suit, as if it would not be heard by others. "The rails from Free Port to Eland are five meters each and ten meters everywhere else on the planet. It's a different cadence on the wheels. I know we came to Eland, and then I was loaded in this van heading east."

"Ah. Okay. Good to know." Ally avoided eye contact.

"And thanks for the luke-warm hot cocoa." It had revived him.

"You're welcome." Ally had not expected Kars to be... she wasn't sure of the word, but she was surprised by him.

When the van stopped, the guards climbed out and signaled the all-clear for Ally and Kars.

"We've gotta put you on dark mode for the next part of the walk. Safety protocols. Take my hand."

When Kars went dark, it felt like they walked him in circles. His Evo compass readout spun like it was searching for a signal.

"We have a transponder override on your Evo so no one can follow Demetrius Colonicov."

"Who is Demetrius Colonicov?"

"You. You are Demetrius. Well it's the suit's ID you projected. But it changes when it's able."

"Weird."

"Ingenious, I'd say."

"If I'm thinking right, we are headed somewhere near the reactor. It makes perfect sense, now."

"Stop it. You're no fun. I bet people hate playing board games with you. And besides, you're wrong," Ally said.

"Well, if I wanted to hide something, I would do it in a restricted zone. A place that would not be believable. We know, well, the people who work out in the Atmo understand that the red zones surrounding the city's reactors have a ban on human activity due to the high levels of radiation leakage from the power plants," Kars said. "We also know Martian reactors aren't particularly clean because they don't need to be. Increasing radioactive pollution in an area irradiated for millennia is not the real issue— the magnetosphere collapsing is. All city reactors have one-kilometer red zones to protect people. That is where I'd try to hide something important."

Ally looked at the man hidden by darkened mask and shook her head and silently stuck out her tongue in his direction. She could only respond after showing him what he needed to see.

"So, you must use the Bio codes off of dead people as a way to hide in plain site. I considered using the codes off of other people's Evo's, but never a dead guy. But you work with caskets so maybe you are in the funeral home business as a cover?"

"You think you are so smart."

"Am I actually smart, is the real question."

"Here to think Kars Dee was only a humble rail worker."

"Robotics is my real craft," he interjected.

"Here to think the humble robotic specialist, Kars Dee, from Free Port is really a genius in hiding," Ally said.

Twenty minutes later, the group stopped as a door closed behind them.

Kar's visor returned to transparent, while his eyes worked to adjust to the room.

He was in a Control Room with panels of switches and numerous monitors glowing blue.

"Where are we?" Kars asked.

"Not the right question, because I can't confirm where."

"What is this place?"

"If you were going to hide a city, Kars Dee, where would you do it?"

"Why would you want to hide a city in the first place, might be the better question."

"What if there were a sudden, overwhelming need to house more people?"

"I think the MGA is severely limiting the number of immigrants now."

"They are, but not everything the MGA says, actually happens," Ally said.

"True, it's more of a desired outcome. But they enforce it under the threat of death."

"The reality is, there are going to be a lot more people coming to Mars and we need places for them to live in peace."

"How can you hide a city?" Kars mocked.

Ally invited Kars over to an opaque window. Pressing the transparent mode switch revealed a massive cave, where hundreds of domes were in various stages of being printed in 3D.

"What the hell?"

"No, not hell. We're going more for the heavenly alternative."

Kars's mouth was open as he looked across the vast area.

"I..." He did not know how to continue.

"This cave is sealed. It has been tested to three Atmo."

"Three?"

"Yes. Certified to sustain three times an earth-level atmosphere without bleeding. It held for seventy-two hours."

Kars had previously worked on HVAC systems and knew 3X was the gold standard against the Martian near vacuum of one percent of Earth's atmospheric pressure containing ninety-eight percent carbon dioxide.

"Hmm." His head spun, not knowing what to say. He put his gloves on the windows like he was trying to touch a model of a city.

"So, any residual thermals are written off due to the reactor's heat signature?" he asked.

"Yes. Plus, the heat transfer to the cave wall is almost nil."

"Yes and?" he wanted to know more.

"We are also borrowing the excess heat from the reactor through a heat exchange system to warm the cave to 20 degrees C."

"Shirtsleeve living?" Kars says.

"Yes. This cave has a membrane."

"How did you do that?"

"Spray-foam."

"You've got to be kidding?"

"Nope. Carbon nano-tube reinforced spray foam. It's a game changer because we no longer need a one-piece membrane to ensure the seal.

"Yeah, I'll say."

"Plus a heat loop absorbs ninety six percent of any thermal loss."

"Wow. Sounds like you guys have solved a lot of real problems."

"Another benefit is the complete electronic signature reduction to the outside world because of the nanotubes. Almost a perfect Faraday cage."

"Okay, Ally. I am officially impressed."

"I figured you would be."

"How many cities do you need?"

"Depends on how many people we can get up here."

Kars's mind raced. The thought hit him that this cave was not repeatable. "That's fine here. But you know this is a unique situation. This cave near a reactor is probably the only place on the entire planet where this is found. How are the new caves going to be powered? You will need a lot of power."

"We are going to bury reactors near each one. Engineered reactors to siphon off all the heat benefits. Actually, we already have enough reactors."

"What? How? Plus, everyone on the planet will be able to detect the power."

"Yes, but we will not care by then."

"What? Why?"

"Because it will be too late to do anything about returning thousands of refugees to Earth."

"So, you are going to build these cities in the dark, populate them, flip the switch, and hope to hell the Mars authority doesn't kick you off the planet, or force you into corporate slavery?"

"Something like that."

"Balls."

"Balls?"

"You've got some big ones."

"I'd prefer to use the term, dreams," Ally said with a snicker.

"Your dream's got big balls," Kars said.

A stifled laugh spread through the group.

"This city will house a couple thousand refugees when completed. We need more. A lot more and we need your help."

TEN

Sol 7622 (2 May 2048)

Free Port, Mars, Cube-omnium #2938

"Benz?" Kars's head throbbed, like he drank way too much the previous night. Rolling out of bed with the clothes on from the day before—at least, he thought it was the day before. "Wait, what is today?" he asked the wall while rubbing his head.

The clock on his monitor displayed 08:40 in response to his verbal request.

Kars sat on the side of his bed, trying to think. He rubbed at his eyes and forehead.

"Ally." He stood up and grabbed for the wall. When he stepped out of his loft, he bypassed the ladder and stepped onto the three-foot-long catwalk to Benz's loft.

"Hey, are you here?"

He stuck his head into Benz's room but could not see anything through the darkness. "Light," he said to activate the ceiling lights, but they refused to recognize his voice in his friend's room.

"Benz lights on," was the override, and they snapped to life.

"Hey are you alive?" He shook his friend's leg.

"What?" Benz said.

"Hey are you awake?"

"Where are we?"

"What?"

"I was waiting for you with a hood over my head."

"Yeah, now you're in your bed."

"Why? Wait, how?" Benz sat up.

"I don't know anything more than you. I need some water." Kars said before leaving.

"Okay, thanks." Benz grabbed his pounding head.

When Kars took hold of the ladder rails, he noticed writing on their metal wall.

"I'll reach out soon, Ally." There was a giant heart drawn around her name.

"P.S. Then you'll have my number. Erase this."

Kars read it again, wiped the dry-erase marker off the wall with his hand, and climbed down the ladder seeking hydration. He tried to process what happened as he drank from a reusable bottle filled with reclaimed water from their mini fridge.

━━◄O►━━

2 May 2048 (Sol 7622)

Wilderness of Northern Georgia

"We've rested for an entire day. We have to push on," Bry said. A couple more hard days and we'll see how far we can get you down the road."

"We appreciate you guys and all the help you've given us," the man with the trail name of Fitness said to the commander.

A couple more of the group of five refugees agreed.

"Just doing our jobs, Fit."

"Still not clear why we left Zorba behind," a haggard woman nicknamed Blue said.

"We cannot reveal those reasons, Blue. You are just going to have to trust us."

"I don't trust anyone these days." Blue stuffed her few belongings into her pack.

"Like I said before, your issues aren't mine."

"But you caused them."

"Hardly. My grandfather taught me a long time ago that my stuff is my stuff. You own yours," Bry said. "He used to say life is ten percent what happens to you and ninety percent how you respond to it."

Blue remained silent as she stuffed her pack.

"Two minutes we're moving out," Chase told the group.

"Make that three because we have a sat inbound," Bry said.

"Protocol, now!" Dylan barked.

After the "all clear," the group finished silently preparing. They stepped onto the trail from beneath their pine tree rest area and began a long day of hiking through northern Georgia's rugged mountainous terrain, always south.

***

Master Sergeant Gilboa had just sent his daily encrypted message to H.Q. while resting in the pine tree above the group of nine travelers. He paused to check the area for movement and found none in any direction. He thought this excursion was going along in good order as he glanced back to ensure nothing unusual happened. The group climbed around a rock face while he followed, swooping low over the trees.

The sudden pain was overwhelming as a Scythe out of nowhere cut through his left wing, severing it at the shoulder joint. Gilboa turned over and fell toward the canyon below. Several more strikes from other Reapers who had just appeared out of thin air and encircled him as he fell. Cutting, chopping, and hacking away at the battled-tested Warrior. He managed to get his sword out and began swinging with fury as they all plunged toward the ground. A couple of swings found their mark, and Reapers screamed and fell away. Gilboa noticed a strange appendage on the heads of each of the four remaining Reapers as they tore him limb from limb. After crashing, the four remaining Reapers ate the Master Sergeant with loud shrieks of victory. At the same time, his essence auto-shifted back to the nearest transport for his return trip to Para as soon as they opened his head. The Reapers debated keeping the head for a trophy but knew the enemy could use it against them. The tough old sergeant was off to experience his fourteenth iteration and a year-long journey back to combat.

◆○◆

Descending with a backpack can be more demanding on the body than ascending. Bry felt pain in her knees as the group worked down and around another mountain. She knew they approached a road crossing the trail and sent Chase ahead to put eyes on. Bry was on point, Dylan babysat the group, and Oliver brought up the rear. She knew it would be tight for satellite fly-bys, so she drew in both points to compensate. What she most feared was a random drone crossing their path. They would have to shoot it down and change course if it took up a station.

"Eyes, copy?"

No response.

"Niner Mike, eyes?"

No response.

She stopped the group with her hand and took up a firing position, using her scope to search. They traveled during the day because the protocol allowed for it after exiting North Carolina. Northern Georgia was much less active G.U. territory. Commanding this ragtag group of five refugees was coming to an end, and Bry needed a few days of downtime. Maybe that was why she forgot to warn O, who was hydrating when the attack came.

A missile from behind them streaked over the head of the group and exploded forty meters in front. An attack drone dropped out of the sky on top of them. The five refugees froze and put up their hands when they realized they had red laser dots on their chests. Twenty G.U. Special Forces troops emerged from the woods behind them and directed them all to lie down, drop their weapons, and surrender.

"Surrender! "No need for today, you to die," was said in broken English.

All three of Niner Mike escorts tossed their rifles and then, per orders, pulled the self-destruct cord located in their sleeves, which brought their Shimmer blankets to demise. The blankets melted into a pile of goo, much to the disdain of the Chinese Major leading the assault.

Both Oliver and Dylan were struck with the butt of a gun to their heads in response, knocking them unconscious.

"What do we have here?" the Major asked, walking over to Bry, who was on her knees.

The officer knocked off her helmet and grabbed her face. Defiance was in her heart, and fire in her eyes. She wanted to spit. "What have you done with my man, Major?"

"Ah, you think that you have military rights protected by Geneva convention. No such rights are given to terrorists. Those men are outlaws and you have brought them to me!"

The major grabbed Bry and brought her to her feet and hugged her. "Thank you! Thank you! A great honor you have bestowed upon me! Let me carry your pack." He took it off Bry's back. They walked away down the trail together the Major resting his right arm over her shoulder.

⚊⚊⚊◆⚊⚊⚊

Sol 7622 (2 May 2048)

Free Port, Mars, Cube-omnium #2938

Benz and Kars moped around the Cube, trying to drink enough water to flush the remnants of poison that could still be in their system. Kars had yet to tell Benz a word about the meeting with Ally. He was still trying to determine what to believe and whether telling his best friend would help the cause. Even that kind of thinking made Kars afraid. He understood that Ridge could beat it out of him if he told him. So he thought he was protecting his friend on the one hand, but being a coward on the other.

He climbed up to his loft to hide and turned on his monitor. Someone rambled on one of the Free Port channels. The story was about a growing dust storm in the southern hemisphere. Kars leaned back and began to think about Ally. She was beautiful, and he needed to remember that fact because it tainted how he felt. In his mind, she was a once-in-a-lifetime type of woman. That is, if everything she said was true; if it turned out to be nothing more than lies, she was just like the rest, just a more attractive version of deceit. He wanted to believe her and thought she was genuine. She pushed him and brought out something good in him. Being so conflicted about everything, his feeling of peace with her contradicted everything else swirling around them, although the hangover from the drugging had him a little miffed.

Kars mindlessly cycled through some Earth channels. The programs were only behind by a few moments in lag right now, so it was like watching it live. It only happened once a MY.

"News out of Georgia today," was the lead story.

"G.U. forces at the invitation of the Compliant States of America have scored a big win with the capture of a well known terrorist. Johnny James has the story from our Atlanta affiliate, Johnny."

The scene switched from inside a studio to a scene out in nature. It was a thick green setting when Johnny James began speaking into a microphone with a circled number seven on it. "Global Union forces at the request of the Compliant States of America captured what they are referring to as a valuable target today in woods just like these. Northeast of Atlanta, operating in thick forested area, these terrorist cells have been running clandestine operations for several years. Today, the G.U. says they have scored a big victory in the battle against tyranny. They call her the Terrorist Princess. Claiming she has carried out hundreds of crimes over the last few years has earned her the moniker of being one of the most wanted people in the C.S.A. Even though Georgia is considered a non-compliant state in G.U. circles, the governor of Georgia said he thought this capture by G.U. forces operating just over the North Carolina border in Georgian territory was a way to build bridges of trust with our more compliant neighbors."

Kars could not believe his eyes. He rewound the footage and listened again. He captured a pic of the screen when a small picture of the terrorist Princess was shown in the corner of the monitor.

"You've got to be kidding me!"

Johnny James finished his report, saying that "sources inside the G. U. military are telling me this Terrorist Princess is cooperating with authorities, naming names and providing intelligence to the valiant G.U. Peacekeepers as they continue their recently named, Freedom campaign.

Reporting from somewhere out in the mosquito infested woods, this is Johnny James. Back to you guys in the studio."

"Thanks Johnny, stay safe out there!"

Kars began looking through his contacts in his comm. Then he remembered the file on the white computer, jumped up, slid down the ladder, grabbed the laptop from the drawer below the couch, and retreated to his loft. Kars gently slid his door shut and powered up the unit.

Deep inside the operating system files were several sub-files where he found his list of contacts from Earth. His Gigi insisted he hid it somewhere he could see it if he ever had reason to need it. He sat and stared at the address as the old feelings of fear crept back inside his heart. He knew for sure what he should do. He could pretend he never saw the report, and no one would know. He had left Earth to leave this kind of stuff behind him, but now more than ever, he could not deny his connections and escape who he was. Trouble had found him, and the tidal wave broke just above his head.

"Are you all right in there?" Benz tapped the knuckle of his index finger on the loft door.

Right then, Kars Dee knew his life would never return to the anonymous fantasy he desired when he first came to Mars. That dream had just been destroyed.

"No. I need your help," Kars said through the closed door to his best friend.

<hr>

Bry determined that she was in the basement of an ancient stone building. The dripping water in the darkness before her supported her conclusion. Her ringing ears along with the scurrying rats enforced this as they kept her awake. The stale, musty air filled her lungs, as much as a couple broken ribs would allow. Her right eye was swollen shut, and her upper lip was split and still oozing. Her left hand inspected her face as her right arm hung above her head from a chain affixed to the wall. The echoes of heavy metal music that had been silenced for ten minutes.

Bry began to doze off when the metal door, fifteen feet in front of her, was kicked open, and an imposing figure filled its frame. Dull yellow light flooded past him into the seedy basement, highlighting his massive shoulders.

"What do you want? Haven't you taken everything already?" Bry was still enraged by the brutality of the assault. Intellectually, she knew the torture was to dehumanize her so they could break her. Emotionally, she was devastated by what the men had done to her.

Bry had not noticed the bucket at the feet of the hulking brute. She fully expected him to turn the searing white lights on again, but he did not. The figure picked up his bucket and walked into the cell. Two more men followed him, carrying some things she could not identify at first. When the leader got to the middle of the room, he stopped while his assistants hastily assembled their next torture regimen.

One end of a battered and stained eight-foot plank was placed on a low bench while the other was dropped to the concrete. Bry's wrist was unlocked, and she was dragged by her arm across the filthy floor to the contraption. She was slammed down and inverted onto the plank. One man slapped her face, breaking her lip wide open again. The other man chained her feet to the board, double-wrapping them and binding the chain with a carabiner, while the other cuffed both of her hands together beneath the board and put his hand over her mouth, attempting to suffocate her.

Bry was waiting for the relentless questions to start, but the men remained silent with business-like efficiency. The man who had slapped her reached down and ripped a piece of her black T-shirt off, then balled it up and grabbed her bloody and bruised face, forcing her mouth open where he stuffed the rag from her shirt into her mouth. Bry bit down hard on his thumb. He groaned and backhanded her so hard she saw flashes of light.

They began pouring the contents of the bucket over her face watching her struggle to suck air through the putrid liquid. She bucked and pulled against the restraints as her vision narrowed, and the raunchy smell of human waste covered her. One of the torturers held a knee on her stomach to keep her on the plank.

"Help me God!" Bry prayed and blacked out.

The torture continued for another half an hour. When they were done, they kicked her over while still connected to the board and left her in darkness and total isolation. Four minutes later, the lights and ear-piercing heavy metal music returned.

Outside in the hallway, the three men watched their Terrorist Princess work her way off of the board, which allowed her hands to reach the carabiner and free her legs. Then she crumpled on top of the plank in a fetal position.

"She'll break by tomorrow," Major Wong said. The G.U. soldiers walked away to go get breakfast.

⸺◆⸺

"What's going on, brother?" Benz sat next to his friend.

Pausing, Kars looked at Benz. After a deep breath, he unloaded everything he had hidden— the bombing and Hagus' death. His fear of Ridge and the investigation. The confusion over the angel wings. The Underground meeting he had with Ally and his attraction to her. Their desire to use him to find places to hide people on Mars. His decision to include Benz in the search for more caves.

"Listen, I know I act like an idiot sometimes. Okay, a lot of the time, but if you are all in on this thing with your girlfriend."

"She's not my girlfriend." Kars interrupted.

"Yet," Benz predicted. They stared at each other.

"I don't even know if it's possible, with her."

"That doesn't matter. I think we need to come up with our own escape plan anyway. Ridge wants to come down on us for helping people. Think about that."

"It's nuts. I agree. I'd like to start looking on my own. You know, see what I can see," Kars said.

"Instead of with Ally's group?"

"I like them guys— I just want to nose around in a few places I've seen over the years, without having an anchor or another boss looking over my shoulder."

"Kars the loner." Benz smiled.

"Maybe."

"I think it could be good to check out a few spots. Maybe we could find a place to hole up if we needed to for a while."

"Yeah. I will need your help to pull it off. You got any side work you can pick up in Shepard or Zulu City?"

"Yeah, people are always reaching out for off-book tech hardware work, why?"

"We need a cover story."

"Someone just blew up my comms the other day from Shepard. Something to do with their new solar array," Benz said.

"We'd need to modify our suits."

"The bios?"

"Yeah. But we have to be able to toggle it."

"That's a huge fine for doing that."

"If they catch me."

"Right. Who are you?"

Kars ignored the comment. "No biggie. I can modify it with an internal software reprogram, along with an external signal distorter."

"You've been thinking about this for a minute."

"Yeah, I have to finish rewriting the bio-codes for the Evo's."

"You know, if you get that wrong you could get dead in a hurry, right?"

"Yeah. I'm installing it on both of our suits today."

"What?"

The men checked the four deadbolts before dragging their Evo's down from their lofts. They had to disassemble the two onboard computers to solder in new motherboard parts to bypass a few less essential but intrusive built-in safety protocols. This would allow them to turn off and on the ability of the Martian satellite network to track them out in the field and the ground-based system near each of the cities. So they could explore without any governments or corporations tracking their location.

Kars assembled the parts for his remote signal generator, which would project his bio-metric signature anywhere on the planet. This would allow him to appear to be working in a location he was nowhere near, and using it in conjunction with his new Evo's ability to toggle its bio-metric signal would render him invisible to Ridge's prying eyes.

Eleven

4 May 2048 (Sol 7624)

G.U. Detention Facility, West of Bryson City, North Carolina

"I would like to thank my gracious Global Union hosts who have welcomed me with open arms. Through extensive collaborative efforts they have freed more refugee hostages from the grips of the tyrannical religious terrorist group known as TJU. The TJU is a secretive world-wide organization who brutally violates human rights. Their ranks are filled with known eco-terrorists and far-right fundamentalist Christians who routinely deny science and undermine global peace initiatives. I know this because I was part of that organization since its beginning. I rose through the ranks of leadership. I was blind to the truth and now I have seen the light of hope the Global Union is bringing to our planet. I only hope that I can make amends for my crimes against humanity. The G.U. is the way forward." Bry gave the scripted speech from the basement dungeon in a slow and deliberate manner, finishing with the one finger pointing forward salute, common for the G.U. community.

Her captors set up a television studio in a basement office with a wooden desk. The green screen behind Bry showed scenes of valiant Global Union soldiers helping people according to the population metrics in each targeted area while she spoke. Bry was forced to read the speech several times into the camera even though her eyes were nearly swollen shut and her lip dripped blood. She had been given honey water before the taping and a thorough cleansing, including brushing her hair and teeth. She requested that her hair be parted in the middle, as was all the rage in the Compliant States media. Her slight eye tremor appeared involuntary and was ignored by the soldiers who dreamed of long vacations home.

The major and his men celebrated breaking the Terrorist Princess, knowing it would be looked on favorably in the coming round of home visitations back in China. They were surprised she broke so quickly, thinking that it was due to her poor health upon arrival. "The tough American girl persona must have been a facade used to recruit more rebels," they decided. Forty-eight hours of brutal torture had been enough. Now, their plan was to release her to the general population, who would certainly see her as a traitor, and they would let the savages finish her off.

—◦—

"Colonel Amadan."

"Copy Tic, Amadan here."

"Sir, private channel?"

"Roger."

One second later: "What is it?"

"Just received some sobering news, sir."

"Source?"

"JOCC."

"Go ahead." Amadan braced himself.

"Master Sergeant Gilboa's essence was just transferred to the Galaxy Rose for transportation to the reiteration hospital on Para, sir."

Tic felt the weight pulling on the Colonel's heart through the comm and in the silence.

"I'm sorry, Sir. I know you were close."

"Everyone was close to Gills. It's a significant loss for the good guys. Let the Warriors know. I need a few minutes. No comms."

"Roger, Colonel, comm block engaged."

Colonel Amadan wanted a few minutes to grieve his good friend without receiving comments over the comm units from everyone and their brother. Turning off his comm would send the comments to a file he could review and answer in good time.

Amadan pumped his massive wings against the pull of wind and gravity, climbing straight into the stratosphere. At apogee, he howled long and hard into the darkness beyond the sphere of the Earth. Pulling his sword, he pointed it skyward. He declared to the universe— "Farewell and following winds, my old and faithful friend. You have given your all to the cause of Him who rules over all! May your journey be a blessing and our reunion sweet!"

Amadan rolled over and dove headlong toward the Florida Key. Pulling his wings in tight, he sped straight down as his emotions bubbled raw.

⸺◆⸺

Sol 7624 (4 May 2048)

The surface of Mars, East of Shepard

"Hold." The message scrolled across the inside of Kars' visor. He paused beneath the Shimmer blanket and waited for the Low Martian Orbit (LMO) mapping satellite to pass. It was a beautiful day to search for possible caves in the foothills a hundred clicks east of Shepard. This was one of the areas he noticed from his early days of working the rails. He wondered about the hills leading up to the western edge of the central Tharsis Rise, with over a kilometer gain in altitude.

Having spent half the day searching, Kars did not feel optimistic about the prospects in this area. However, he had a satellite image of a couple more possible openings in rocks suspected to be remnants of ancient lava tubes.

"Clear for an hour," the message read.

"Thanks."

"Hey Benz, how's the cover girl going?" Kars asked.

"I'm covering my girl, which is you. I can work all day out here— they've got so many things screwed up."

"Just think of all that money we are making."

"Funny, since I am doing all of the work I think I get all the money."

"Only if you can steal it from my bank account. It sure looks like I am working right alongside you according to my current bio-metric readout!"

"Yeah, that's genius. I've got to hand it to you."

"See, now we can agree on something."

"Donut."

"Roger." Kars knew that when Benz said, 'donut,' it meant he had to talk to one of the guys he worked with and had to switch away from their private network discussion.

Kars began storing his Shimmer when a command came, "Swarm. Ten seconds!" His rapid re-deployment was not smooth, and he left his boot exposed to the passing drone swarm. It was a good thing his boot was covered in dust so it would not stand out in the digital imagery the Swarm collected as it flew.

"That was close!"

"Too close. I missed that one. Sorry, I'll get better at this," said the mysterious messenger.

"That will wake a guy up. Better than mud."

"Martian Mud. I've never have had the concoction."

"Oh, you don't know what you are missing!"

"I've got a resupply scheduled in a few weeks maybe I'll have them send me some."

"I recommend you use your weight for some real Colombian coffee and then drop some down to me."

"Not good, I take it?"

"Nope."

"Thanks for the heads up. You never know when a thirsty Martian babe might drop by."

"Make her the Colombian coffee and you'll have a friend for life."

"Life is a long time in a spaceship."

"It could feel like a prison sentence," Kars said.

Fifteen minutes later, Kars wanted to know how they would communicate when he entered the cave."

"It will be tricky but I have a flock coming your way and if we both remain in line of sight it will work."

"They won't get picked up on satellite?"

"Not these babies. Oh crap."

"What?" Kars was in speak-to-text mode on a PCN or private comm network, and the messages were automatically sent at the end of the sentence.

"You need to see this. It's video. Not good. Just came through the net. I'm sorry."

Kars watched the statement from the bloodied and bruised woman in the G. U. North Carolina Detention Facility. His face went pale and his stomach turned over the soup he had just had for lunch. Kars was speechless and infuriated. He sat down on a boulder, pulled his Shimmer over himself, and went silent as he wept.

Snot inside a space suit is not good. It was one reason everyone on Mars who worked in the atmosphere wore Evos. Inside an Evo, you could pull your arms back into the torso of the suit through an arm lock-out mechanism. The special mode locked the joints on the arms away from the body so the worker could pull back through and address things like sweaty forehead, runny nose, and other inconvenient body issues that happen throughout a day's work.

Kars knew his time ticked away as he sat on the rock but needed the pause. He had to get going to the next cave. He stood and mindlessly followed the map on his display. His Perf cameras had gotten dusty, and when he toggled off the map mode on his visor, the two side-panel screens showed that the cameras were covered with statically charged sand-like Martian regolith— which blocked the lens on the sides of his helmet.

The Evo's helmet did not turn; yet to compensate for the loss of motion, there are cameras mounted on each side of the helmet offering a combined three hundred sixty degrees view, far superior to normal vision, right on the visor. Most workers loved the enhanced Perf vision and fought to keep the lens clean. The Evo helmet was large enough for workers to have full rotation of their head inside the unit, which was a design change by the teams on the ground four years ago to combat rising neck issues.

Evos also had a robust anti-static function, in which charged particles were neutralized by reversing the electrical charge on the skin of the suit and sending the charge to the ground, causing most of the dust to simply fall away. Every airlock on the planet employed the same technology. However, airlocks also had a vacuum feature to shoot the dust and debris back outside.

The next hole in the rock led to a cave. Before he entered, his mysterious messenger returned with a question rolling across his visor: "Are you okay? Your heart rate is elevated."

"No."

"I'm trying to find out more details."

"Thanks. Going inside. Comms update?"

"Flock got stalled by a passing ground crew. Ten more minutes. Be careful."

"Roger."

"How goes it?" Benz asked through his comm speakers.

"Just going in another. It hasn't been a lucrative day," Kars said.

"Bummer. One more place checked off though."

"Right. Out."

"Copy."

—◦—

The G. U. Detention Facility was coed. Bry was paraded from the intake dungeon across the yard to the door of a bunkroom. The crowd grew silent as she limped past, carrying a blanket, between two riot-clad GU troopers. They pointed at the dorm . "You're in here." They turned around and left.

Bry walked into a hundred set of eyes locked onto her. Whenever she drew close to what appeared to be an unused bunk, someone stepped in front of her and told her to move along. Twenty-five sets of bunks were on each side of the dormitory, and not one was available. Bry hobbled past the last set, collapsed next to the end wall by the emergency exit doors, and fell asleep. Within an hour, four men threw her outside through those doors and told her they would kill her if she came back.

"Traitors shouldn't live."

Bry lay in the dirt next to the building until it began to rain. She rolled beneath the porch which she had been tossed onto and fell asleep wrapped in her prickly wool cover.

After a dinner of a chunk of hard bread and a ladle of potato soup, Bry returned to her place under the porch. Two GU guards noticed her and chased her back into the dorm to sleep. After the guards left, four men surrounded her, announcing they would make her pay if she did not get out of the bunkhouse. An older woman pushed through the brutes and yelled at them to move along.

"Don't pay you no never mind to them," she said.

Bry just looked at her.

"You need some rest, girl. Those GU Goons looked like they raked you over the coals. I tell you what, you come over and sleep beneath my bunk and I'll make sure those men don't bother you."

"Why?" Bry throat was raw from screaming.

"No one deserves to be treated like an animal. We are all image bearers no matter what."

Bry didn't answer. She followed her to the bunk, slipped underneath the woman's bed, and fell off the edge of the world.

⚬

"Lieutenant Ridge, there has been no activity at the Cube in question."

"I want you to slip in and investigate."

"Warrant?"

"It's on my authority in an ongoing investigation of the bombing. It's a Homeland Security terrorist issue and no warrants are necessary."

"I just don't want this coming back to bite me."

"There's nothing to bite!"

"On your authority, Lieutenant."

Five minutes later, the Goon returned to the comm.

"I will need a torch to gain entry, Lieutenant."

"What?"

"They have reinforced their door, sir. Now the neighbors want to know what is going on, so I left. I asked but no one wanted to talk about where the pair has gone. One said they were probably back at work."

"Okay. No reason to arouse the suspicions of the nosy neighbors. Check with LIFT. Track them down!"

"Yes, sir. And gaining entry to their Cube?"

"Leave it for now, Ridge, out."

* * *

The night sky was crystal clear. Kars was parked next to a cliff— the only obstruction to his view of the stars. He finished placing the final Shimmer over the Hum, securing it with the last stake. All that was left was for him to zip the final seam, and he would be secure from peering eyes. One last glance at the stars gave him a glimmer of hope after a day filled with discouragement.

The orange halo around the orbital foundry shone brightly on this night as its hundred-square kilometer solar reflector system could melt iron and other precious metals. Kars noticed that Jupiter looked enormous. Earth was behind the cliff and out of sight, exactly how his heart felt.

After cycling the airlock for the second time to remove the particles and dust better, Kars entered the Hum. The unit was a top-of-the-line land system vehicle. He wanted to figure out how he had ended up with the best one on the lot, but more than that, he wanted something hot to eat.

As the microwave hummed he thought through the precautions they had taken. The two of them had disabled the Star-Link connection, grounding a Faraday hat over the cluster, rendering it inoperable. The company that ran the contractor work crews for Shepard did not care as long as no one made written complaints about the vehicle, stayed out of the Red Zone, and away from all military bases.

Benz and Kars had signed up for the off-book solar field installation repairs, which the manual said needed a week to complete. Benz knew he could finish the job in a couple of long days, which offered Kars plenty of time to search. Working below solar panels all day offered enough concealment for Benz. They both understood the only thing that could screw this up was an on-site visit by a supervisor. In that case, Benz would have to make up an excuse for Kars' absence and send out an emergency return code.

The likelihood of a supervisor visit was minimal if there were no unique issues. Still, they were worried that if Ridge caught up with them, he could blow the whole deception wide open.

There were several challenges to overcome and inconveniences to solve to pull this plan off. Benz had to solo camp but make it appear that two Hums were parked beside each other in the middle of a boulder field. They used a tent frame the same size as the Hum and hung flex solar panels to reflect energy back like the vehicle naturally does. The friends counted on the idea that no one from the company would be watching them close enough to notify authorities. Any passing satellite or high-elevation drone would think two guys were working in the field like every other day on the planet. They both understood that Ridge could disrupt their plans.

"This Hum is nice," Kars thought as his dinner finished warming in the microwave. He flipped through another row of storage drawers, seeing what he had available to him to eat for dessert. The Hum was the size of a recreational vehicle and had Murphy bunks for two. Those beds were connected to the driver's side wall. The bed frames were lined with drawers holding supplies a couple of Martian grunts could need for a week-long journey into the fray. When the beds were chained in the up position onto the wall, the open area was another workspace with a workbench folding out from the bottom of the bed and tons of storage options.

Usually, teams only get one Hum for every two workers without exception. Benz had complained to an old friend that Kars snored so loud he would not be able to get any sleep, and the job would take longer to complete. The company, Central Martian Power, was desperate for reliable workers and eager to help and Benz agreed to the compromise to get the job done. Because they had spare units on the lot, they gave them each their own Hum.

Of course, no one wanted to spend more than a week straight working out of Hum because that was about the limit the shielding offered to protect humans from overexposure to the amount of rads bombarding people on the surface. The safety protocols would not allow them to work longer in the atmo unless there were additional shielding options, like parking the Hums in a cave or in the shadow of a mountain. There were a few portable shield solutions available, too.

"You good?" Benz texted.

"Just finished dinner. Ready for bed. You?"

"Same."

"Night."

Kars slipped on his oversized helmet from his Evo and powered it on. He had received several more encoded messages. Each had pictures of Bry, battered, bruised, and sleeping under a porch. Close-ups were taken when she slept which showed the extent of her abuse. All the messages disappeared after Kars closed them.

"Please, God, protect her."

———◦O◦———

"Captain Helek, you copy?"

"Go, Iggy."

"Snug as a bug."

"Roger that."

"Your guy, good?"

"He will be in another minute.

<hr>

Three Leech attached to Kars Dee had been trying to tighten the anchors that kept shaking loose inside his brain.

"Get on that primary fear anchor!" yelled one Leech to another.

But the fat little bug needed to be quicker.

The prayer uttered through Kars's heart blew everything up for the Leech. They scrambled around, throwing themselves at their controls. Wrenches twisted in vain. Captain Helek reached inside Kars' heart and plucked the angry chub nuggets free. He popped each of them like a grape.

"Good night, Mr. Dee," Helek whispered as he smiled.

<hr>

Beneath Dora's bed, Bry breathed deep and rhythmically.

"Poor thing," Dora whispered to her bunk mate for the evening. There were fifty bunks in K dorm, but over a hundred people. Most beds were shared, with the floor covered in the bodies of the newer inmates. It was truly a miserable place.

"I didn't think she'd last very long," whispered the other woman in Dora's bed.

"I thought she was supposed to be so tough?"

"Well those animals can break anyone given enough time."

"You think she's working for them now?"

"I don't know, but it sure appears that way. No one will be trusting her anytime soon."

"Did she do that?"

"How could she? She was broken. She'll be helping us real soon."

"Hope so. We need to get moved out. I hate this assignment."

"Almost got enough info to move us back north."

Bry had her ear pressed against the bottom of the thin mattress, listening to every word while keeping up the facade of rhythmic breathing. In the shadow of that bed, a slight smile formed on her face. Operation Insider had been breached. The two women would be marked as traitors to the refugee cause.

TWELVE

Sol 7632 (12 May 2048)

Mars Red Zone, Southeast of Shepard City

You can see Larry, Moe, and Curly if you fly high above the Tharsis Rise. The three gigantic and dead volcanoes are on the northern edge of the massive lava field. The Rise was formed from those three monsters spewing lava for a couple thousand years, resulting in an elevated plain nearly three thousand klicks across. Indignant Martian settlers decided to name the three volcanoes for the slapstick comedians from the early twentieth century, and the Three Stooges Range is the official Martian title. Early on, Kars struggled to remember which was Moe and which was Curly. Larry was easy— he was the tallest and in the middle.

When a huge retail slash cargo company invested in building their city on Mars, they chose to build a couple of hundred klicks south of Moe, which Earth scientists still call Arisa Mons. The company chose the Arisa area as the location for their Martian operations. The area is flat and at the southwestern edge of the Tharsis Rise. This position allowed the city to receive constant cargo drops from Revolvers. It is nearer to the equator and was low enough in altitude on the Rise, so the atmosphere could still be used for passive braking advantages with parachutes. Every gain in altitude reduces the effectiveness of those air braking systems, resulting in more use of chemical thrusters. Passive air braking systems are cheap and effective— mainly because they can be used a few hundred times before being replaced. Cargo ships do not have the same safety concerns as a human-rated systems, and cargo chutes are used until destroyed.

Kars worked the rails out of Shepard for a few years when the new line was being built to Anzacland. That line skirts the southern edge of the Tharsis Rise, running for eighteen hundred kilometers to the southeast before turning due east for the final thirty-four hundred kilometers to the official cave cities of Australia, New Zealand, and Canada. Anzacland is the newest and most isolated city on the planet. Mars may be the second smallest planet in the solar system, but the land mass is about the same size as the land mass on Earth. This reality makes for rail lines that are long, boring, and colder than Siberia.

Robot crews build all the rail lines on the planet. Kars and Benz's team and many other crews kept those bots working around the clock. It was during the construction of the initial line coming southwest into Shepard from Free Port, which lies to the northeast, when they spent a few weeks camping out just south of the Moe volcano. A different season brought him closer to the Stooges when he was on the team for the bullet Train System between Shepard and Eland. Those trains were designed to cut the trip from fourteen hours to four between the two cities at each end of the Three Stooges Range. Kars treasured hundreds of fond memories, many of them pictures of dramatic sunsets bouncing off the extinct volcano— one immortalized as the background of his comm units interface.

It was also where Kars met Kady. She was a team manager for the Bullet Train project and lived in Eland. Their romance lasted the entire ten months of the build, resulting in a hasty marriage. They also fell in love with an overlook condo on the southern side of Free Port, which looked out over a western branch of the Valles Marineris. After the marriage, Kady took a job in Free Port managing teams that trained the incoming astronauts to acclimate to the red planet. Astronauts and cosmonauts. The Russians hired Kady's company to train their team.

All of Kars's fond memories remain north of Shepard. To the south is where Kars' darkest days were spent. The Russians made a significant discovery of a lava tube cave system on the southern rim of the Tharsis Rise. They landed their cosmonauts in Free Port for their initial training. That's where Kady met her Russian lover and Kars' life went into free fall. Kady moved out of their condo after the Russian team was trained and immediately filed for an E-Vorce. The electronic divorces in Free Port made it quick and easy for people to get legal protections after a marriage ended. Kars was devastated and took an extended contract on the line to Anzacland. He had been doing a month-by-month agreement but switched to a contract that lasted until the project was completed, which meant he made more money but would only go home once the line was finished. He sold their beautiful condominium virtually and sent half the proceeds to Kady without comment. He never saw her again.

Meanwhile, the eager Russians moved into their new lava tube home without completing the necessary safety and reliability studies. They were in the middle of setting up their colony when disaster struck in the form of a Mars quake, and parts of the cavern collapsed on the team. Everyone was killed, and their reactor was compromised. Now, the entire area has been designated as a "Red Zone" due to the radiation spilling from the ruined reactor. Twenty bodies are still trapped in that cave. That no-go zone runs north of the rail line to Ansacland, just after it turns due east, a hundred klicks up onto the Rise and two hundred kilometers long. Marian Global authority maintains a monitoring system to warn people of the risks. Anytime Kars has had to work in the area, he relives the death and devastation.

Avoiding the Anzacland line was his highest priority after the collapse. He signed an extended contract to work on the construction of a rail line between New Brussels and Shepard. That line runs on the west side of Moe up to the foot of Olympus Mons. The European Union and United Kingdom occupy arguably the most beautiful location of all the cities on the planet, as the largest volcano in the solar system looms to the north. The Europeans opened an enclosed ski lodge at the base of the mountain in a valley that never receives direct sunlight. They call it the Alps of Mars, attracting people from every corner of the planet. Kars seriously considered relocating to New Brussels but did not want to deal with its governmental restrictions. He liked his freedom too much, and besides, LIFT is headquartered in Free Port.

These memories swirled through Kars's mind as he searched for locations for cities that could be built. In the past, he would not have been able to disassociate from his pain. A new sense of peace allowed him to search with a clear head. It was also with a clear head that he entered into the Red Zone. He had reached out to his mystery man in the sky before proceeding. His "Angel" could remotely turn off the old monitors, allowing Kars to drive his Hum into no-mans-land. Since the active security measures are located only along the border of the Red Zone facing out, the man in the dark spaceship turned the monitoring system back on when Kars was far enough inside the territory. The temporary system outage looked like a typical glitch with aging equipment. Without the system being triggered through movement, no one would be looking for a strange vehicle in the Red Zone or actively searching for anything at all.

"Do you remember the result of the last play of our last game?" was the message Kars sent to Benz after his initial search. Benz did not respond before Kars crawled back inside the cave system, where there was no connection. The flock of eight pocket-sized communication drones had arrived from his Angel. He planned to drop them along his path inside to maintain a line-of-sight connection.

After he sent the message to Benz and resupplied at the Hum, Kars climbed back into the labyrinth of tubes and caves, freeing his communication drones along the way. The shaft he had found and marked earlier was a tunnel on the far side of the Russian cave. That tunnel must have been revealed by the quake that had killed the Russian team and his ex-wife, or a subsequent tremor.

Traversing the graveyard was disturbing as he kept an eye on his radiation detector. The story was told that the Russians had placed their reactor on a tram as they readied it for burial outside the main cave. The reactor must have been moved into an adjacent tunnel when the calamity occurred, sealing off the tube from the main cavern. Kars's radiation meter never got anywhere close to the levels he experienced on the surface. He was not sure why the Red Zone was, in fact, a no-mans-land. Something was fishy. He knew the rock above him was the best filter against the ever-present surface radiation and was the main reason that any cave was such a desirous location for a city. The Russian deaths brought the testing of that theory to a screeching halt for the Tharsis Rise area.

Setting another comm drone at the edge of the newest tube on the far side of the Russian cavern, he entered the dark passageway. He descended deeper beneath the southern ridge of the Tharsis Rise.

Scientists had theorized for years that this entire area would be a great location to find suitable caves for humans to occupy. The final leading edge of volcanic activity left a three-hundred-meter-high plateau above him. From this point, the Tharsis Rise continued north for two thousand kilometers and reached several thousand meters in height. It was the largest volcanic field in the solar system. It brought untold teams of geologists to Mars to study the phenomenon.

Kars pushed in. An hour later, the tube leveled off, and he entered a gigantic cave formed from trapped air during the eruptions. Climbing boulders near the tube opening inside the newly discovered cave, Kars launched a starburst flare and could not make out the cavern's edge; it was too large. He removed his mapping drone from its sleeve on his right thigh and sent it flying off to map the cave. Kars recorded the information directly onto his personal hard drive, which he had loaded onto the drone he called Trippy. He did not want his information to get out to anyone. He set up the sixth comm drone at the intersection where the tube connected to the new cave he called Alpha. The seventh comm drone he sent up to a point near the center of the Alpha, which would still allow him to communicate with his spaceship angel.

From the scan Trippy brought back to Kars, he could make out three more lava tunnels connecting to the Alpha cave and sent Trippy to map them. The final tube showed that it was attached to yet another cave. Trippy crashed, was caught between rocks, and sent out its distress code, then shut down to wait for rescue as programmed. Kars had to take a long hike in the dark to retrieve it. Before he entered the tube, he set up his final comm drone near the entrance, directly across the Alpha cave from where he had entered. However, because of the large boulders in the middle of the cave, there was no direct line of sight. So he had to use the drone in the center as a relay from the far side of the cavern, but this was the end of his connection. After the final drone's laser lost sight of him in the tunnel, he was cut off from the communications and rescue.

When reaching Trippy, he inspected the drone and replaced one of its damaged blades. Climbing up on top of a rise, Kars recharged the battery and released his little bird to scan further. The drone took off and flashed through the cave before returning to its owner ten minutes later, filled with brand-spanking new data. As Kars accessed the latest information, the mountain began to shake and settle. He dove between two boulders grabbing for his head as rocks pelted his Evo. Basketball-sized boulders smashed around him as he pressed his distress button right before getting knocked unconscious.

The distress signal from Kars's Evo was beamed by laser at light speed between the eight drones and then up into outer space, bouncing off a toaster-sized boosting satellite toward the black spaceship in the form of a V. The ship was in geosynchronous orbit, just a tad over twenty-one thousand kilometers above the Tharsis Rise— its gravitational arms extended and circling the craft in the silence of a complete vacuum. Enjoying the gravity inside the ship, a spindly man ran on an inclined treadmill while he dreamed of swimming in a lake. The Earth cravings had hit him hard this morning so he decided to go for a treadmill run through a virtual Yosemite National Park tour for as long as he was able.

The red LED indicator light flashing on his comm worked as designed. Still, it was left lying on the bed, waiting for the man's exercise session to be completed.

—◦—

"Listen I don't know who you are or how you know what we are doing out here," Benz said.

"Let's just say I am an advocate."

"For what?"

"For what you are doing."

"I am fixing a solar array that was screwed up by inferior and mis-programmed installation bots."

"And you are watching out for your roommate."

"I'm going end this comm and finish my work."

"You can't. I've lost comm with him and have had no contact for over twelve hours."

"You've had communications with Kars?"

"We're not supposed to use his name on this channel. I cannot guarantee the security."

"So, our mutual friend has not reported in in over twelve hours?"

"Yes. I think you need to go after him. The window is closing on how long his Evo can hold out."

"How do I know that you aren't screwing with me, like one of Ridge's Goons?"

"You don't. But I know what his mission was and so do you. We are the only ones who do, and when he sent you the touchdown question it was confirmed for both of us."

"How do you?..."

"We've met once, actually."

"When?"

"At the state championship game where Kars scored the pick six to win the game."

The reference convinced Benz. He did not know this person who talked with him twenty-four years after a football game, and he couldn't remember meeting anyone in particular that night on Ford Field in Detroit, but they knew enough.

"And you scored three touchdowns on runs of 2, 21, and 35 yards."

"I'm heading out right now," Benz said.

"I'll send his route to your Hum."

"Okay. Um what should I call you?"

"V. Hurry."

V told Benz that he would disable the Red Zone monitors when he got close and turn them back on once he was in the clear.

Benz drove the ten hours southeast as fast as the Hum would go. He did not stop for the satellite fly-bys and refused to answer calls from the contract company. He had to stop and cage the signal antenna because they threatened to disable his Hum and leave him stranded in his tracks. Benz drove through the night— bouncing and thrashing at almost sixty miles an hour. The small nuclear reactor in the rear of the Hum produced as much electricity as it was designed for, as Benz's headlights cut through the darkness. The roof-mounted radar made sure he avoided the large Hum-killing rocks. A sandstorm approached from the southern hemisphere which would cut his speed in half when it hit.

Jacked up on the way too many Martian Muds, Benz pulled up next to Kars's shielded Hum an hour after first light. The dust blew, and an occasional lightning flashed near the southern horizon. Most of the dust storms on Mars were a nuisance, but the big ones still grabbed Martians' attention due to the static energy released from the moving particles. Everything needed to be well grounded during those gales.

Benz had arrived more than twenty-four hours after his best friend had gone silent. He knew Kars had, at best, ten to sixteen hours of air left in his Evo. That is why Benz took the thirty minutes to shield and ground his Hum. He tied off one side of the massive Shimmer to the same stakes that Kars had driven into the ground and worked his way around the vehicle. Benz pounded the grounding rod into the regolith and attached the heavy cable to protect the vehicle from lightning strikes. Kars had done the same for his truck. Benz was certain the storm would cover his tracks, and electronically, he had shielded himself with the cage just a few hours after he went rogue. He knew the authorities would be called due to the cage he used to block their signal to disable the Hum. He was protected from getting physically chased into the forbidden area because even the F.P. would never come out there.

"Unless they alerted the Marines," he thought, then reconsidered and dismissed the thought due to the high cost of the operation to track one guy going on a joy ride in a Hum, so he felt pretty safe.

"You got me?" He spoke to text the message to V.

"Copy that. I'll sent the comm code for the drone network. That will give you direct access to our escapee."

"That's a good name for him," Benz smiled as he entered the tunnel, following his friend's footprints.

"Still connected?" V asked.

"Yes. Just passed the second drone."

"I got a map of the area, I'll send it."

"Thanks, but how did you get it?

"You'll be entering the Russian cave."

"The one with the collapse?"

"Yes."

"How did you get it, I thought no one had a map. That the mystery died with the cosmonauts?"

"Let's say I have some knowledge of the events surrounding that operation."

"Oh yeah?"

"Yes."

"So you know how Kady died?"

"Of course. She died in the collapse."

"Right. But how did the word get out? If everyone died, how do we know what happened?"

"I've seen video."

"What? How? Why do you have access to that when no one else does?"

"Others have seen it as well."

"Wait aren't you afraid that our confession session could be intercepted?" Benz's toes rubbed against the inside of his boots as he descended.

"Not possible with LOS laser comm. If anyone tries to hack in the laser connection is broken."

"So, tell me V, how did you get to see the video where my best friend's wife was killed?"

"Ex-wife."

"You're right. Ex-wife."

"All that I can say to you right now is that she was in on the operation."

"Who was in charge of the operation?"

"There are a few different opinions on that."

Kars would like to have this information.

"Yes, I think he is ready to hear what happened. You bring him out alive and I will tell him, and you."

Twelve hours later, Benz had yet to find Kars. He followed the drone network, remapped the system for V, and uploaded it. He found the tube next to the final drone and discovered that it had recently collapsed, covering Kars' bootprints with new debris. Benz tried to dig with his bare hands but couldn't make enough progress himself.

V remotely activated several bots, starting them on a secret journey from Shepard to the accident site. He had used drones to cover the bots with a Shimmer, but the wind played havoc on the operation. They would not arrive before Kars ran out of O2.

Benz grew more frantic with each passing hour and talked incessantly with V. Then V had an idea. He superimposed his new map from the cave, found where the collapsed tube was in relation to the lava mountain, and sent Benz in his Hum north along the base of the cliffs. He sped off without removing the Shimmer blanket, tearing it away from the stakes with the vehicle.

Another hour and they were well into hour thirty-nine of Kars's air. The driving conditions became impossible, with rocks and boulders blocking cliff access. Benz cycled out of the Hum and started off. Then he stopped and returned to grab a spare O2 canister and bounded off toward the towering cliff, grimacing in pain from his leg wound. He knew he had topped off his Evo's atmo while driving, but the running and jumping over rocks would eat up his air supply in just a few hours.

"Should have brought two tanks," he thought.

"Hey Benz, go another 500 meters north and check that area," V texted.

"Okay."

Five minutes later, Benz slowed down to check the crags and boulders for signs of life.

"This is like finding a needle in a stack of needles."

⚙

With the last few minutes of air remaining, Kars crawled through a fissure in the rock face. On the other side of the final tube he could find, Kars sends his ping signal.

"We've got a ping!" V typed.

"I hear it. How much time?"

"We've crossed the forty hour mark five minutes ago."

"Direction?"

"Northeast— fifty meters," V said.

Benz located the outline of an Evo and rushed to Kars's side as He drew his final breath of air. Kars's CO2 converter was out of charge and filled with dust and grime. Benz dug out the front of his suit to find the external port. He used his suit's compressed air function to blow out the connection, attached the canister, and released the pressure. The red lights outside Kars's Evo switched to green, and Benz heard his friend cough and draw in fresh O2.

A rocket lifted off from Mars in the distance over Benz's shoulder.

"Is that a Rocker?" were Kars' first words to Benz in two days while trying to sit up and watch the liftoff.

"Yes, that's a fricken Rocker."

"Thought so."

"Glad you are still suckin' O2, bro."

"Me too." Kars laid back, enjoying the fresh atmo. "Are we comm blocked?"

"Yeah."

"Cool." Kars drew in the fresh atmo with deep breaths.

"I've got water."

"Yeah, good. I'm out."

Benz hooked up the share tube with his friend and Kars drank as fast as he could.

"I found a huge cave system," Kars said, disappointment suppressing his speech.

"Worried that it's still unstable in there?"

"Yeah. I thought it would be perfect, but the people who blocked this area were right."

"No, I don't think they are," Benz said.

"Why? How are any of the caves safe with all of the tremors?"

"Because the cave is untouched. The Russian cave is above it and south. There was zero movement in the cave you labeled Alpha. The tunnels collapsed, not the cave."

"Tunnels could be drilled and reinforced?"

"That's what I'm saying. What does V think?" Benz asked.

"You know about V?"

"We are old buddies now. He thought he would need someone else to do his dirty work because you were smashed into a flat cake."

"I almost was smashed in a secondary cave. I'm sorry I couldn't tell you about him."

"No biggie. It all worked out."

Benz helped Kars to his feet.

"I think the big Alpha cave will hold atmosphere with a bit of work," Kars said.

"No comp?"

"We could bury a reactor near the Russian base and no one will ever bother to look. It's in a red zone."

"That Alpha cave is huge."

"Massive. Ten times or more than the E-Land site they showed me."

"We gotta tell Ally."

"No. Not yet."

"She's your girlfriend."

"No, sh-she's not."

"Yet." Benz says and slaps his buddy's shoulder. Kars smiled and dismissed the thoughts.

"Let's get you to the Hum."

THIRTEEN

12 May 2048 (Sol 7632)
Teapot Key, Florida

"I like the bathing suit! Wonder Woman!"

"Thanks."

"What are you dreaming about?" Nan handed her sister an open can of cold carbonated water.

"Thanks. I wasn't dreaming— just thinking about things."

"I know you."

"I miss him and touching the calm ocean helps me remember." Connie looked at her sister sipping the water.

"Sure is a beautiful day." Nan said beneath her visor. She wore a pink one today. The sisters leaned into each other. "Remember how much he liked to fish."

"That's what I was thinking about."

"He liked it more than Dad."

"I know. We could hardly get him out of the water for the whole time he was down here."

"Yeah, before he went back home he caught fish every day. It was so awesome."

"The fish was delicious."

"We haven't had that much fish since."

"We ate it every day, sometimes twice a day."

"Con, I ate it for every meal."

"That's right. Especially when he started shrimping."

"It was soooo good. Shrimp and grits for breakfast."

"You and your grits. I loved the Snapper tacos for lunch," Con said.

"Yep. That's right."

"Remember the Mahi?"

"The giant ones he used to bring us."

"I think that was his favorite time— living here."

"It was," Nan said.

Silence washed over them as they looked out over the calm teal waters.

"I know we don't talk much about it anymore, but he was hurting and hiding behind all that fishing," Nan said.

"He was."

"But he seemed happy living down here on the beach with that old boat."

"He was happy and sad at the same time," Connie said.

"It seems like yesterday and a thousand years ago."

"It has been so hard knowing I won't ever see him again, on this side of the veil."

"We don't know that!" Nan said, realizing it was too harsh at the moment.

"I know, but most people never come back from where he went."

"Yeah, but he ain't most people." Nan grabbed her sister's arm.

"No, but I know he was still struggling when he went off on that God-forsaken rocket ship."

"It wasn't God forsaken, they made it."

"Yeah, he made it and found out how hard that life really is."

"I bet he misses fishing living up on that dust bowl."

"I know he does."

"I heard he went skiing a few years back, on that big mountain up there."

"Olympus Mons, is what they call it. His Momma told me he had so much fun he almost moved to New Brussels, so he could ski every day."

"He ain't moving there. He hates being told what to do. I'm old, but I do remember that side of him."

They both chuckled at the memories.

"You think God had a hand in all of this?"

"I know he did and I trust him too, but I don't know what it is. He hasn't told me."

"I think Kars is like Joseph."

"Joseph who?"

"From the Bible."

"Oh?"

"I think God sent him ahead for a reason."

"All the hurting is happening down here, so I don't understand."

"Right. Joseph's brothers sold that boy into slavery to get rid of him, but God knew what he was doing all along. He was preparing a place for his people to take shelter."

"Didn't they become slaves for over four hundred years after that?"

"I said like Joseph, not in every way. I still believe God will use that boy."

"He is far from a boy now and it's long past time that he was running away from things."

Connie pulled away from her sister's overheated skin.

"Ladies, you've got a call."

"Call?"

"Yes, on the sat phone."

"Lordy, what now?" Con asked no one in particular. Both women returned to their cabin home.

When they pushed through the door, the television was on, showing a building engulfed in flames.

"What in the world?"

"Church burning has started up again," Dennis said.

"Where now?" Nan asked.

"Virginia had a whole slew of them last night, something like forty or more have gone up in flames," he said

"My goodness. There won't be any arrests either."

"Of course not, they're in on it!" Connie said.

"Who's on the phone?"

"K-26." Dennis handed over the headset to Nan.

"Go ahead."

"QB?"

"Confirmed."

"K-26. Memphis."

"Confirmed. Go ahead."

"There is a new wave forming."

"Western? Northern? Eastern?"

"Yes."

"Confirmed. Tell Momma we love her."

"Will do. Out."

"Out." The phone connection went silent.

"What's going on?" Connie asked while Dennis stepped outside the cabin with his rifle.

"That was K-26."

"I heard that, but I don't know the rotation today," Con said.

"Today, K-26 is M."

"Aww. How did she sound?"

"She sounded strong," Nan said.

"Where was she calling from?"

"Phoenix. She say there's another huge wave forming."

"Oh my. Where are we going to put them? Where is this one coming from?"

"She has intel to support the idea that it will be coming from all three zones."

"Response to the new attacks, I imagine. The western refugees will have to be routed into Texas." Connie sat down.

"I think at least half of the central group will have to be sent there too."

"Where are we going to put all those people from the east, let alone half of the Midwestern states?"

"Free states will have to absorb most of them. Church buildings, basements, camping sites, wherever we can find a spot." Nan looked at the wall map of North America.

"Lord, help us, please."

"Amen. Do you think it is time to split the Quad? Send half to the Midwest?"

"I don't like it, they are still so young."

"Stop it. M will be thirty three in a couple of months. Ry was just thirty one. You keep thinking of them when they were still here."

"That wasn't all that long ago. Plus they came every spring to visit."

"You're losing your noodle!"

"At least I still have a noodle to lose!"

"Con, sit back and take a look. You know we need to do it."

"I know, I just don't like it. I don't have to like it, either."

"I suppose not. Let's ask Dennis to help."

Dennis was summoned into the cabin. The three of them sat at the kitchen table, looking at the map on the wall.

"I don't think we can send them down route three."

"It has become too dangerous. Could we truck them south?"

"Some of them, but there are so many coming."

"Another church just got bombed during a service. It was a early morning mass at a Catholic church in Peoria."

"Oh, my God, please have mercy."

"I hear there are other groups sending some refugees to live on retired oil platforms," Dennis said.

"And many are escaping across into Mexico and taking boats to Cuba, of all places."

"Well, after the Commies were thrown out twenty years ago, Cuba is a viable alternative," Connie said.

"We should look into boats to make runs out of Marathon," Dennis said.

"That would help. We have tons of contacts on the island that are willing to help," Nan said.

"We need a confab with our benefactor." Connie looked at each of them.

"It's time. We need an update on when to open the pipeline," Nan said.

"Let's set it up sooner rather than later," Connie said. "I know he is busy, but this genocide in the making won't wait until we are ready. We have to get prepared faster. Make the call, Dennis."

"Did you see the parade of politicians promising to build a wall on the southern border to keep our citizens home and safe? Creepy has begun." Dennis put his toothpick back into his mouth.

"We knew it was coming. Now, it has arrived," Nan said.

The trio spent a half hour praying for the people they know and for all those they never would meet but who ran for their lives in the face of tyranny.

⸻ ❖ ⸻

12 May 2048 (Sol 7632)

"Up!" Said one guard who kicked the bottom of Bry's barefoot.

"Now," said the other armed guard.

"What?" Bry fought her way out from under Dora's bunk.

"You are bring transferred, Princess."

"Turn around," said the larger man in the light blue uniform.

Bry turned and held her wrists in position to be constrained. The big guard cuffed her and spun her around to leave. Each man took an arm and pushed through the crowd of silent onlookers. "Make a hole or we're gonna bust some heads." The crowd split.

"String the traitor up!" was shouted from the back of the room as the guards marched through the double entry doors onto the porch Bry had slept under. What she did not expect was the group of broadcast media armed with cameras and microphones, along with the print media's horde, using their Comm units to record the event.

They trudged her across the yard, out of the gate, and down a long sidewalk to the facility next door.

"Can you tell us what you think about the ruling in your case?"

"What ruling?" Bry asked.

"You are guilty of treason."

"There wasn't even a trial." Bry knew the state-sponsored media would edit out that comment. They were required to toe the government line, or they would lose their media credentials.

"Do you think they got it right?"

"I never think they get it right. Their whole house is corrupt."

"What are you going to do while you wait your appeal?"

"I'm going to run for president, then I'll toss all you G.U. mouthpieces out of the country."

Bry smirked, knowing none of them would report a single word she said, she kept prodding them, determined to give them nothing printable.

"The G.U. is a criminal enterprise designed to abuse the human rights of people that disagree with them, especially people of faith. They came to power in an illegitimate way, holding onto their power through violence and propaganda. They know none of their governing principals would win the approval of a free people. They are thieves and liars who cannot be trusted."

"Tell us what you really think." All the reporters laughed.

"You are all brainwashed sheep who are being led to the slaughter. Too blind and dumb to see your own destruction crouches outside your door. Worse, you not openly approve of genocide— you celebrate it. One day you will face your depravity, I hope it's not too late when you do. It could be me on the other side of the gun that gets pointed at your head."

"You're gonna be locked up until they hang you, how are you going to point anything?" A reporter with a big microphone asked her.

"They can't lock this up." Bry pointed with her chin toward her heart. "You are already prisoners of your narrow beliefs and your silly little government lapdogs who are licking the face of the G.U. every chance they get. You're all hoping not to get found out that you are not worthy, either. They will cast you all out when they are done with you. Your fate is the same as mine. I just know my sentence is death and you've got no clue!"

"Your appeal will be heard before the Supreme Court."

"When? Twenty years from now? Besides do you think those twenty one jurists will go against the G.U. narrative and side with the truth?"

"What is truth?"

"Well, Pontius." She smiled, bruised lip and all. "I know someone who answered that question quite well. You'd be wise to listen."

"I thought you gave that fantasy up?"

"Because of a little persecution? You don't know history. I gave up on the institutional churches that have been taken over by freaks who are looking for power and have wandered away from Jesus' clear teachings, much to their shame. Whitewashed tombs, shame on them! History will place them next to the churches in Germany that did nothing to stop the Holocaust. I stand with the people who did something— so the world could remember!"

"You are the Terrorist Princess and you are lecturing us?"

"Call me what you want, but your marionette strings are twisted in a knot. You should leave now, and don't forget to take your Soma." Some journalists began searching for the reference, unaware of Aldous Huxley's book, *Brave New World*, from the 1930's.

The guards turned Bry away from the razor wire fence separating her from the reporters and onto a different sidewalk to another building labeled "Maximum Security" on the sign above the steel entry door.

"That is all my friends!" Bry said over her shoulder.

◄O►

After the grainy video was turned off, Nan looked at Connie. "She's still a feisty thing."

"She never been shy, that's for sure."

"What does this all mean?" Dennis wanted to know.

"I'm not certain."

"I think she is mad at us for turning away from her," Nan said.

"She turned from us, not the other way around."

"She's stubborn as the day is long and thinks she's smarter than everyone else."

"Wonder where she got that from?" Connie looked at her sister.

"She's not my granddaughter!!" Nan said.

"She got it from that woman buried in the garden behind the house."

"That's a fact!" Nan agreed their mother was a stubborn woman until the end.

"Remember how much of a hard time she gave us when we first wanted to bring her down here with us?"

"I still have nightmares over those arguments," Connie said.

"We thought we were going to have to drug her and put her on a plane to get her down here."

"That wouldn't have worked due to security, but I was up for lots of Benadryl and a road trip."

"She was glad she came."

"Those were the best years of her life, well the best years after dad died."

"Yeah, they were," Nan admitted.

They thought about their beloved mother for a few moments.

Then Dennis gave them a quizzical look, his palms opening and eyebrows rising.

"I gotta say, Dennis, that video was much different than what the news channels put out. Are we thinking about sending it out over the dark net?"

"Already done, Ma'am."

"Good."

"Now, what do we do? Nan asked. "We can't leave her to rot in prison."

"I know that. I guess we must devise a plan to bust her out," Con said.

"It can't be able to be traced back to us."

"I know."

"That would compromise the entire network."

"You're right." Connie's lifted her hands off the table in a measured surrender of the point.

In the trees, they operated under orders to maintain stealth, but on the ground, several dozen Warriors were gathered near the reporters while they questioned the woman as she was marched past on the other side of the razor-wire fence.

Circling a few hundred meters above the scene, two Reaper squadrons kept an eye on things while trying to determine the actual number of Pluck warriors. They noticed most of the crowd was filled by Prode doing their bidding. There were a few Carne sprinkled in the informal gathering below.

"Sergeant , take a squad of five and break up the circle flying above us, please." Tic spoke to the Angel Warrior in front of him.

"Yes Lieutenant," he snapped a salute and flashed from view. So did five other warriors. Immediately above them, the Reapers broke off and formed into two groups circling. The enemy put a few hundred meters between the rings and awaited an attack.

The entire time the woman's procession took place, the Reapers waited. When the guards escorted the woman inside the facility, nothing made a move toward the Warriors.

Suddenly, the rest of the Warriors on the ground went stealth and disappeared. The Reapers began screaming out with certain expectations of battle. They drew their Scythes and spread out a few more yards so none of them would be close enough to another where one Warrior could efficiently dispatch more than one Reaper at a time. They all screamed and carried on for a few minutes in mental preparation for the fight.

The nonsense died down as the anticipation waned.

The Warriors' stealth was so good that they could reach out and touch the Reaper before they saw them. The first squad split in half, and three

Warriors each pierced through the Reaper circles as the rest of the Warriors came out of stealth, drew their swords, and approachd their enemy.

The Reapers nearly fainted from the display of power from the much larger Warriors. They all turned and fled the scene, shrieking in fear and in every conceivable direction, storing their weapons for maximum speed. Twelve Reapers did not make it a kilometer before they were sliced in half from top to bottom, which made sure of a long trip back to Applyon and an even more extended stint in rehabilitation.

"Gilboa!" Came the rallying cry of the infuriated Angel Warriors, seeking to avenge their brother's passing.

FOURTEEN

Sol 7639 (19 May 2048)
Alpha Cave, Mars

"I'm going to need more Shimmers to cover the containers," Kars said.

"We'll have to do this under the cover of darkness," V said in his text.

"That's the only way this works."

"I'm going to have to screw with a couple satellites to get us a window."

"Won't they send a repair drone?"

"Yes, but they can't see me."

"Doesn't change the fact that we need to get twenty Shimmers here before that happens."

"We've only got a one night window. I have to finish my overwrite program and simulate it. The Revolver is coming and it will unload its cargo on time."

"But you're going to take over a few of them and steer them outside my cave in the middle of the night?"

"Yes, and you are going to hide them until we can get them moved inside."

"Right, but I need the heavy equipment to drill the entry tunnel large enough to fit those containers."

"I hear you."

"Plus, I can't throw all that debris out onto the plain and not have satellites or drones see the plume and the piles of discarded grindings."

"You're going to figure that out. Get some help from Benz. Maybe it's time to bring in the Underground?" V asked.

"Maybe you're right."

"I gotta run. I need some Colombian to keep me awake while I figure out this vampire program."

"You mean while your AI is working, you are going to be drinking fabulous coffee?"

"Details, details, details. Later. Out"

Kars laid back on his bunk. The Hum was dark, but indicator lights glowed a dull green on the side panel across from him, just behind the passenger seat. He knew he would have to set up inside the cave as soon as his detailed fissure mapping project (F-Map) was done. The specialized drone mapped in detail all the cracks in the rocks inside the cave and getting its information by sending sonic pulses deep into the rock. The information would allow the program to predict future damage from quakes by comparing the cavern's integrity to all the seismological activity on the planet. The Tharsis Rise is Mars' most active seismic area due to its settling rocks born from volcanic activity. The program also gave him specific areas where material was most likely to be freed during a quake so he could determine the extent of the excavation and reinforcement efforts.

Much needed to be considered before the structure of the cavern was worth risking people's lives. Kars would have to bring the Underground up to speed soon, leading him to his favorite pastime— Ally. She was the first person he wanted to reach out to. He had to figure out how to get her out here without exposing her to the danger of knowing where this place was located.

Kars was done sleeping for the day. He grabbed his comm, which was connected to Marsweb through his laser connection to V's encrypted virtual private network (VPN). That was the only way to prevent Ridge from tracing his location while maintaining a connection to the rest of his dusty world.

The first message in his mailbox informed him that LIFT had approved his leave of absence. The Hum he occupied was now being leased by a LIFT subsidiary, and he was subcontracted through a shell company under another dead guy's name.

The chat-link connection was still active inside The Legions of Doom Fifth Estate. This was where he and Benz sent and received messages without the prying eyes of the government or Lieutenant Ridge.

To VikingSword44: "Fight now." Kars knew the command would send a ping to Benz's comm.

To GuineaBerserker: "Go." Benz then initiated a private encrypted pop-up chat box between the gamers. V had created the option from one of his dad's old games, which still had people playing from all over the solar system. You had to know where to go and what the code was to enter the portals.

"How goes it?"

"Good. F Map should be done today. Did you get the request for the 20 extra large Shimmers?

"Yes. Working on it. Got a dozen for sure. Those get T-D tomorrow. Don't ask how."

"Same T-D?"

"Yes, but this is the last one for a while on that line. Don't wanna raise suspicions."

"May have to use the rest to move that equipment?"

"Yes, that will be here today."

"Have you talked with her?"

"No, it was someone else. One of the guys who escorted us, I think. I'll meet him today."

"How goes the solar repairs?"

"Been done for a couple of days. Just have to plug in the ones I've already fixed. Those Bots were dumb."

"How are you going to be able to stay on site?"

"You kidding? Marco is begging me to stay on. Says he will double my LIFT salary."

"Wow. Cool. Now you can afford to get your own Cube! JK. My leave came through last night. You could get a mental health leave."

"Yeah, I'm thinking about applying for that."

"Don't wait too long. Send it to my guy," Kars said. "So I could be looking at going the way of Reagan."

"No comp?"

"For real. Not sure how to make this happen otherwise."

"That's last step kinda stuff, Bro. You sure?"

"No. Not sure. Just trying to think it through."

"Don't rush."

"I hear Ridge has been shaking things loose up in Free Port."

"Heard the same thing. People running scared. He wants the head of this bombing case."

"Pretty sure he still thinks we were involved."

"Fact."

"I need a boring machine."

"What? Why? How am I supposed to do that?"

"I need a entryway to slide SD containers in."

"That will leave a horrendous mess that all the satellites will immediately recognize."

"Not if I do it backwards."

"Inside out? How?'

"Got lots of places to store debris. I'll have to run a few access tunnels inside first to get the height I need."

"Genius!"

"Hardly, but it could work."

"I'm going to come out with the farm machines at the end of the week. I'll get a few extra off days."

"Good. I'm going batty looking at caves."

"How many?"

"Seven that are promising. Maybe a handful more that could work."

"That would be like the largest natural cave system on the whole rock."

"Without a doubt. There are more here, too, just all the seismic movement makes them suspect. Alpha is running warm over 7C."

"Wow! Cool. Ceiling still good?"

"Know that for certain today."

"Right."

"I'm gonna tell her soon."

"Figured you'd want her to see it."

"Yeah, for professional reasons."

"Ha!"

"You think she'd come with you on the farm equipment?"

"No way. Then she'd know and not have plausible deniability on the location."

"Yeah. Maybe I'll come back for her and bring her in the Hum?"

"As long as we install the Anti-track," Benz said.

"I made one, but it can only be used at night. Two oscillating blowers on the back of the Hum. Works like a charm."

"Crazy. This Anti-track system is really good and really expensive."

"You didn't buy it."

"No, I'm borrowing it!"

"Yeah, alright!"

"You want me to reach out to her?"

"Yes."

"Done."

"Thanks. Check back in twelve?"

"Yes. Twelve from now. Should find out about the Shimmers by then."

"Cool. Later."

"Sooner, dude."

"Yeah."

⋘◦⋙

"Who's that?" Lieutenant Ridge asked the junior Federal Police officer while pointing at the monitor on the man's desk inside the F.P. headquarters in Free Port.

"That's Ally Briski, but her last name may be an alias. She is suspected of being involved in that Underground movement, The TJU. She is a citizen of Eland.

"No, it's known as TJU. Not THE TJU," Ridge said, pointing out the distinction.

"Yes sir."

"And they are a home grown terrorist organization."

"Technically, they are an alleged terrorist organization, sir," the Federal Police information officer said.

Ridge looked at the man, wondering about his allegiance. The desk jockey realized he had overstepped his boundaries but kept on working to cover his reddened facial features.

"Lieutenant, you'll notice your suspect comes into the scene at the ten second mark."

"Where is this feed from?"

"The arrival platform in Shepard. The Bullet Train from Eland."

"No sign of his side kick?"

"If you mean Kars Dee, no."

They watched the video.

"Play it again, Deputy. This is very suspicious. Almost two weeks since the bombing and all of our leads have dried up, except the two men who were closest to the scene. And now this Ally woman is suddenly hanging around."

"I have no record of Kars on any database for over seven days."

"How is that possible? Does he not live in Free Port anymore? Or Eland, or Shepard? Has he vanished into the dust?" Ridge knew the three cities were independent from one another, but the presence of American intelligence and security operated openly in all three places. Free Port was technically the only incorporated city-state; the other two were wholly owned corporate cities. The American justice system was used for legal issues because both companies were based in the United States, and their security teams worked arm-in-arm with the Feds.

"I don't know, Lieutenant. Maybe the Underground is hiding him?"

"Maybe. We know a lot about the crime, it will only be a matter of time until we figure out the who behind it all."

"Sir."

"How long ago was this surveillance video taken?"

"Half an hour. As soon as he pinged my system I alerted you, per the order."

"Is there anything captured on how Benz got there?"

"Checking."

He began typing on his keyboard in what looked like a frantic manner to Ridge.

"He never entered the terminal."

"Or do you mean his Biomedical ID was never pinged inside the terminal?"

"Correct. There are no electronic indication that he was inside."

"But he knew enough to meet up with this suspected terrorist a half an hour ago just outside the arrival gates?"

"Yes."

"Where did they go once they met up outside of the terminal?"

"Looks like they went into a stairwell and that particular access portal was having problems with its lighting and camera systems."

"Convenient. How long has that portal had those issues?"

"Umm. Searching."

Ridge stood up scrolled through his communicator's screen, and selected a name.

"Need you up here," Ridge said into his comm.

"Lieutenant, that portal has had many issues over the last year or so. Most have been with the lighting and camera." He was speed-reading through the maintenance log.

"Our suspect walks into the air lock along with this girl and cycles through without a Bio-metric reading? How is that possible?"

"I'm not sure. A glitch?"

"That would be a helpful coincidence. No, someone is assisting them."

"I don't have any data to confirm that, Lieutenant. Maybe they've joined forces with the Communists."

"Maybe it's you helping them! Communists." Ridge scoffed. "I want to talk with the person in charge of that portal."

"I'll send the contact to your comm."

"Now, deputy, if not sooner."

"Lieutenant." The man did not bother looking up or saluting. He knew Ridge and his personality, so he hid behind his busyness.

Ridge's comm buzzed, and he picked up as he walked out of the F.P. surveillance lab.

"Ten minutes away. Coming in from the Depot District."

"Wait! You have to go to Shepard. Our friend Benz has shown up on the radar down there. I want you to go get him and bring him in for questioning," Ridge said.

"On it."

"Take the bullet train and your partner."

"Right. You want both of us to go with the budget problems and all?"

"Right. Leave your partner here. You go ASAP." Ridge's hatred for budgetary constraints rose inside his gut.

"Got it."

"I'll alert Captain Somersbey of the BOLO and that you are en route. Bring them both in. I'm sending you the case file."

"Roger. To be clear, you want them brought back to Free Port, sir?"

"Good point. Let me know when you've got them and I'll hop the train down."

"Copy."

When Ridge connected with the head of maintenance for the Shepard train terminal, they spoke at length about the trouble their department had with the portal in question and the lack of funds to replace the airlock. Satisfied with the answers he received, Ridge looked elsewhere for answers on how a suspect in a crime could avoid detection in a modern train terminal Bio-metric airlock. "Of course. He's a LIFT employee and knows the system better than we do." Ridge thought and smiled.

"I have underestimated you two," he said.

"Helek, we are close. One minute," Iggy said.

"Roger. Reroute and report to the train terminal, Hamms has got the FE with the Shiner. She needs cover until we link up."

Captain Helek kept an eye on his charge as Kars's Hum rolled into Shepard's LIFT ground operation depot.

Iggy and his side-kick, Corporal Lu, landed on the transparent roof of the ultra-modern train terminal and spotted Hamms on the top of the parked train, waiting to follow his charge. The entry doors banged shut on the terminal airlock, and atmo was pumped in to fill the void. This was the first station on the planet that allowed the passengers to disembark the train and move into the terminal without using an airlock because the whole portion of the structure was an airlock. Subway connections and exits were made through the pressure-rated rotating doorways which always locked upon train arrivals.

"Captain Hamms, Sergeant Igor and Corporal Lu at your service."

"Roger Iggy. That's quite a ride!"

"Yes, sir. Just rode it last week."

"My mark is on her way. I need cover over at the number 14 airlock."

"Roger that,"

"Yousif is on the FE. We just need a clean egress from the building and out to Heleks mark."

"Electronic cover?" Iggy asked if the Warriors were going to cover the egress in the electronic spectrum and the spiritual side of life."

"Be prepared to offer a screen if the promised shiner cover falls through."

"Roger. This is just a meet and greet?" Iggy wanted to know the nature of the gathering.

"No. We have cover duty for the next few days."

"Roger."

Iggy looked at Lu and shrugged.

"Hey, I'm Benz."

"I'm Ally. Thanks for doing this."

"I'm just the delivery boy. I'm handing you off to a friend in a corridor about a klick from here." The pair began walking together.

"Well, thanks anyway. How is Kars?"

"You two haven't talked?"

"No. I thought the partnership wasn't going to happen and he had moved on. I haven't heard a word from him."

"You will hear from him today, I'm pretty convinced."

"He hasn't been in Free Port."

"No, it's way too hot up there. Ridge and his enforcers, plus the press hounded us, so we left."

"I can only imagine. I'm sorry about your friend, the one who lost his life in the blast."

"Hagus. Yeah, he wasn't much of a friend, but thanks."

"What do you mean?"

"He was so new. You never want to get close to the newbies on the Ground Crews because they are just so stupid— over half of them die within the first year."

"I knew you had a dangerous trade but I didn't think the survival rate was so bad."

"Actually, it's worse than that. Half of the guys who live through the year end up moving on to other professions, so only a quarter of the guys they are bringing in stay in the field longer than a year. We are understaffed by eighty percent right now."

"Interesting."

"Here is A.L.14." Benz pointed.

Air Lock 14 has a rotating pressure door that cycles people into a stairwell. Ally slid on her shorty helmet and gloves to seal herself out.

"You won't need that down here. Everything has atmo, until the end."

"Oh? Okay. What do you call it?"

"What?"

"You said everything has something until the end."

"Atmo?"

"Yeah. That's not a word we use."

"Elanders don't use atmo?"

"You mean air. Breathable air?"

"Pressurized breathable air, survivable atmospheric conditions for humans."

"Must be trade lingo?"

"Maybe. I saw some of the protest got violent up in Eland."

"Free Mars freaks demanding guaranteed income."

"They sound like that M.U. group."

"Mars Utopia?

"Yeah."

"There are so many splinter groups now," Ally said. "All of the stuff they are proposing is for more control over the people not more freedom. They are not who they say they are."

"I thinks they're Commies."

"You're probably right."

After a few more minutes of small talk, the pair arrived at a pressurized glass airlock door, where a step ladder leaned against the inside wall.

"What's this?" Ally asked.

"Your escape. Cameras are off. We'll go inside together and pressurize the tube above. You'll climb the ladder through the access tube. There are ladder rungs above the entry. I'm here to close the port and take the ladder back to its place in the maintenance crib."

"So you are closing me in the access tube?"

"Yes. Then I'll depressurize the air lock and leave."

"How long of a climb?"

"Thirty meters and that's the good news."

"What's the not as good news?"

"Funny. There are no lights and it's a tight climb," Benz said.

"What about my shorty?" Ally referred to her lightweight helmet that deployed a Bubble from the jawline around the neck and provided a few hours of breathable air.

"Tether." Benz held up a two-meter stretch of black cord with hooks on each end.

"Why don't I just wear it?"

"They weren't built for climbing a ladder in an escape tube. Trust me, you don't need it."

"What's at the top?"

"Your ride. You'll come up beneath a Hum and enter through the floor emergency access hatch. Three knocks with this." He held up a box end wrench and handed it to her. "Knock, and the door will be opened to you." Benz thought he was clever with the biblical reference. Still, Ally did not give him any sign that she recognized his humor, which was odd. Benz always knew how to make women laugh, that was his superpower on Mars— it had worked in all the bars he visited.

"Let's do it." Ignoring his attempt to flirt, Ally climbed into the airlock. It was a tight fit for both of them and the ladder. They couldn't open the step ladder. They just held it for one another. First, for Benz to prime and open the hatch. Then Ally climbed to the top of the ladder, dropped her shorty to the end of its cord, and continued up the cold steel rungs of the escape tunnel. Benz opened the step ladder and climbed up.

"Godspeed." Benz closed the hatch, sealed it, removed the ladder, and left.

All the light was removed from the tunnel.

Ally reached down for her shorty, fumbling in the darkness to find the exterior light on the unit. She leaned against the ice-cold rock wall that had been drilled smooth with a vertical boring machine. The LEDs on her helmet weren't bright, but even a hint of light would assuage all of her growing anxiety.

She found the switch, and the light flickered on. Then she had to start her climb. The air was frigid, and she tried to remember to breathe in through her nose to warm the air before it froze in her lungs. Most Martian lungs were not used to breathing air so cold, and Ally tended to have asthma as a result of long exposure to frigid air.

The hole was beyond cold as she tried to climb hand over hand. She pulled the neck of her shirt over her mouth. Fifteen more rungs, and she leaned back against the rock and grabbed her gloves. The steel froze her hands, and she needed the protection.

With three high-pitched bangs on the steel hatch, Ally began to shiver uncontrollably. Then, the wheel on her side of the hatch began to twist on its own, ever so slowly. When the pressure equalized, her ears popped. She looked into the full brightness of a flashlight, while trying to shield her eyes.

"Sorry." Kars lowered the beam. "You look frozen. Come on up. Ally it's me, Kars."

She did not recognize him at first without his Evo and remained in a stunned, icy silence. Kars lifted her by the arms so her feet could stand on the hatch rim.

"Come on. I've got you."

The warm air of the Hum surrounded her. Kars stood, lifting her shivering body under her arms. When she stood on the floor of the Hum, he turned her to face him and noticed that her lips had blued.

"You must be frozen. Benz sent you up the tube without a coat. Sometimes the guy doesn't think." Kars began vigorously rubbing her back with his hands, while Ally threw her arms around him to absorb his heat. Their breath warmed each other. She was six inches shorter and nestled her head into his chest while he kept rubbing her back.

"I'd like to keep this up," he said. "But we have to get out of here before we get noticed."

"Th— th— thank you," is all Ally could say through chattering teeth.

He grabbed a crinkle blanket from one of the bins on the folded Murphy bed beside them.

"Here. I gotta shut these hatches so we can move." He meant the escape tube and the lower Hum emergency hatch, which he had secured in a minute. The retractable hatch interface was stored with a button on the dash of the Hum. Kars sat in the driver seat.

"Let me get off base and then I will make you some coffee."

"You mean Mud?" Ally sat in the passenger seat with the silver blanket wrapped around her shoulders.

"No, I got a surprise."

"Really?" Ally unhooked her shorty tether, removed her gloves, and blew into cupped hands.

"Just arrived last night." Kars steered the Hum through the security gate and off LIFT property, a half mile from the train depot.

Amazingly, the cameras that were down for a maintenance cycle snapped back to life two minutes after a certain Hum left, heading east.

⸺◈⸺

Benz replaced the ladder in the maintenance closet and cycled through the airlock, leading out through the employee construction wing of the cave. He slipped on his Evo helmet, getting ready for egress to his Hum so he could get back to work on the solar field, when one of his favorite people showed up, pointing an E-stol at his face and ordering him to remove the helmet.

⸺◈⸺

Ally and Kars spent the day parked on the eastern edge of the solar field he was supposedly working on. They laughed and talked the day away over lunch and then dinner. Kars wondered a few times where Benz was. He tried sending him a few messages over the comm, pretending they were busy working nearby. However, each attempt was returned with silence.

"Do you think he got picked up?" Ally asked.

"That would make sense."

Kars went silent while thinking about Benz.

"Should we change locations?"

"Um." Kars struggled to think. His fear problem resurfaced when confronted with the idea that his best friend may be locked up, while Ridge continued to look for him, too.

"Kars?"

"Yeah. I'm just thinking."

"We should move, right?"

"Yes. Yes. Let's get our Evo's on, I brought one for you from LIFT. I think it will fit."

"Okay."

"Thanks. Sometimes I struggle and want to shut down when I feel overwhelmed, but I'm working on it."

"I think we all struggle with that."

They retreated back and began getting into their Evos.

"We'll strap a Shimmer over the Hum and drive off the farm."

"What about the dust plume and the tracks?"

"We are going to have to go slow. We will follow the railroad access road so we won't worry about the tracks and slow enough to not make a dust cloud. We only have to make it to nighttime then we can run like the wind."

"How does that work?"

"We've got a low-tech system to cover the tracks. It works good enough the satellites can't pick it up."

"I'm interested in that device, for other projects we've got going," Ally said.

"A couple of oscillating blowers and some cords."

The Shimmer went up in five minutes, with both of them working. Kars grabbed the two blowers out of the passenger storage bin and attached them to both rear corners of the Hum. A pipe with ropes that looked like long dreadlocks was clipped to the rear mounting hooks of the two wenches. In the down position, the ends of the rope dangled on the ground across the width of the Hum.

"Genius," Ally said. Kars smiled inside his suit, lifting the wench enough so the ropes were above the ground. During the day, they traveled on a road with many tire tracks already imprinted into the sand and dust.

————◆◇◆————

Just before sunrise, Kars finished the trip by pulling into his spot near the cliffs. He left the Hum with Ally still sleeping in the bunk, adjusted the Shimmers to cover past the Hum, and installed the grounding rod. When he cycled back through the airlock inside, Ally was still sleeping under a crinkle and his favorite blanket from Earth.

Kars found his special purchase from the LIFT store and brewed a fresh pot of Colombian coffee. His resupply mission was a success— now he needed his friend Benz to be alright.

"That smells amazing." Ally sat up. Her blonde hair looked like an older brother had held her down in a headlock and given her a long, painful noogie. Kars smiled briefly, remembering doing the same thing to his sister. He stood, poured her a cup, and delivered it one step away to her bedside. "Good morning. Sleep well?"

"Amazingly well, thanks. What is this?"

"A gift. I have more if you like it."

Ally sipped at the hot mug. "Oh my gosh. Oh, that is so good!"

"Colombian."

"I've never tried it."

"It's been fourteen years since I've had any. My Gigi is a coffee snob and she always had expensive coffee around. Pops used to say that Gigi would run out of toilet paper before she'd run out of coffee or chocolate."

"It's amazing. Who is Gigi and Pops?"

"My Mom's parents."

"Sounds like you are close."

"Currently about 40 million klicks away from her."

"Pops has passed?"

"Yeah, a long time ago."

Silence weaseled in as they reminisced about their families and sipped at the steamy black concoction, allowing its warmth to invade their bodies.

"You have family?"

"Sure. My mom and I are close. Dad left when I was a kid."

"When did you make the jump?"

"You first," she said, feeling at her hair. Then, she began to comb through it with her fingers.

"Benz and I arrived 13 Earth years ago during the great migration."

"So did I. On what Sol?"

"Sol 3073."

"Sol 3080."

"Wow, you came in that wave too?"

"Yeah. I was so young."

"How young?"

"Are you asking me how old I am, Kars?" She comically feigned her incredulity.

"Sure, why not. My Hum, my rules."

"Well, I never!" They both laughed. "I am thirty-six, unmarried, and without children. It's your turn."

"Okay. Um. I'm forty one, no kids, but I have a dead ex-wife.'

"Ouch. Actually, I knew that about you. We did research on you once you were ID'd."

"Kinda figured that. You have a distinct advantage."

"True. I'm a woman."

"Touche. What was the name of that city you took me too. The one up near Eland."

"Jeru."

"How is it going up there?"

"Good. They are moving people in from all over the planet."

"So people are just disappearing? What will the MGA say about that?"

"I don't think the MGA is very popular. People like their freedom on Mars."

"True, and the Global Union is putting pressure on the cities up here to clamp down."

"That's part of what's at stake in all of this sneaking around."

"I'm glad to have a part in it," Kars said.

Ally only raised her eyebrows in response, afraid of what to say before she saw his surprise.

"Are you ready to see what I have to show you or are you going to lay around in bed all day?"

"So ready. Well, everything but the hair." They both laughed.

Inside the Alpha cavern, Kars had mounted temporary lighting on the ceiling to help with perspective. He took Ally the final few steps up on the rock overlook in the center of the dome and told her to reveal her mask, which took the visor out of dark mode.

"Ah. Um." She turned a complete circle to take it all in. "You've got to be kidding me!"

"What?"

"This is amazing! So, freaking amazing." She hugged him awkwardly with her Evo arms, trying to wrap around his torso. Kars hugged back, and his warmth surged inside.

"We've got seven caverns."

"Seven? Holy Lord!"

"And I know there are more. We have to be careful and will have to reinforce portions of them because of seismic activity. We're bringing out a boring machine so we can drag landing canisters inside for unloading and once we empty them, we'll use them for shelters."

"How?"

"I think we are going to have to get this cave done first. Spray foamed and airlocks on the tunnels."

"I didn't mean that. How are you bringing landing canisters here?"

"Well because we are so close to the Anzacland rail line it isn't impossible either way."

"Either way?"

"Yes, both by TDs and from the Revolvers."

"Wait. What? You plan on dropping landing canisters here from Revolvers?"

"Crazy right? Wasn't my idea, but it's pure genius."

"How is that possible when MGA knows everything when it comes to landing on the planet? And what's a TD?" Ally asked.

"TD is short for Train Drop, we've been using one of the pull over spurs to hijack, I mean, borrow some items."

"Nice, and the MGA?"

"They think they know everything and they also have a margin of acceptable losses. We are just planning to make those acceptable losses happen here first, then we will crash the booster somewhere else. You breathing my air?"

"Yes, and I'm not sure how you are going to accomplish what you are planning."

"I can't do this without you and your team."

Ally had a hundred questions about the cavern system, the quakes, and the supply landers.

"Listen, we have a significant advantage I haven't told you about."

"We do?"

"Several actually."

"Do continue, mystery man."

"You don't know it, but we are in the Red Zone right now."

"Um. How is that an advantage? Aren't we in extreme danger?"

"The danger was manufactured or should I say exaggerated. The Russian cave that collapsed is above our position and south about a half a kilometer. Actually, we could have walked through it to get here except a tunnel filled with debris during a recent quake."

"How recent?"

"It almost killed me, but I'm fine."

Ally studied Kars and his cute smirk and dimples. She decided right then and there that she would marry him one day. "So the danger is real?" She stumbled through the words as her mind caught up with her fluttering heart.

"The danger of collapse is mostly contained inside the lava tubes. They seem to be the weak link in the area. The caves that are secure seem to have survived intact for a very long time. That's why we're driving a boring machine over here from Shepard."

"Because bored tunnels out of rock are stronger than lava tubes?" Ally asked.

"Especially when they are circular reinforced concrete with steel rebar," Kars said.

"The circle is the strongest shape."

"Plus there is zero radioactive leakage here. It is all confined to a collapsed tube up in the Russian cave. Check your meter." Kars pointed at her radiation readout.

"So, all this Red Zone hype has been a lie from the beginning?"

"Exaggerated, yes. Our government tried to save it until they had the infrastructure to take advantage of the extensive cavern system."

"The Russians found it but the Americans wanted to use it even after the collapse."

"Yes."

"We can do it for them!"

"That's exactly what I thought!"

They stared into each other's eyes.

"Kars, you have surprised me."

"In a good way, I hope."

"In the best way you could imagine."

"I have not stopped thinking about you since we met."

"Really? I must admit I didn't think you were interested at all," Ally said.

"Interested in you or the project?"

"Either."

"I was very interested. I am very interested. I wanted to find a way to surprise you, impress you," Kars said.

"You exceeded any expectations I could ever had. Like way above. We can make this work, right?"

"The cave, or us?"

"Yes."

"That's what I want."

"Me, too."

Message to Kars Dee from your secret admirer.

According to a news program pirated by TJU, "Bry has been moved to a maximum security building for her own safety." I thought you should know, V.

Fifteen

Sol 7645 (25 May 2048)
Eland, Mars

"Ally, my dear. Come in, come in. It is good to see you."

"Thanks, Bill. It's good to be seen."

They embraced as friends do. Bill, a man in his late fifties, wore a hoodie and sweatpants as if he had just returned from the gym.

"Welcome back to Eland. Did you sleep well?" Bill took a long drink of water.

"I slept okay. It's nice to sleep in your own bed."

"Something to drink?"

"No, just had some mud." He motioned to the padded chili-red living room-styled chairs. They sat with a glass coffee table between them.

"You look well rested. Tell me about your mission."

Ally relayed the facts of the meeting, from the Benz pick-up to the cold tube insertion into the Hum. Running from Ridge, Benz getting captured, and, in the end, her insertion into the westbound Anzacland to Shepard train while it waited for an east-bounder to pass.

"Where was that?"

"Just south of the Red Zone. I rode it all the way back to Eland."

"Did you get off in Shepard?"

"No. I didn't want any facial recognition shots in the terminal."

"Good. I read a report on your movements and want to hear about your connection with this Kars character."

"You know, going in, I had low expectations. I thought he had given up on getting involved with this mission and I thought I'd be left waiting in Shepard like a lost little girl waiting for her parents, but I was wrong. I had figured he was too timid to get onboard, but it turns out he was already searching."

"Do you mean he was out on his own searching for caves?"

"Yes."

"What did he think he would accomplish by doing that alone?"

"Not sure." She was not completely honest. Knowing Kars was trying to impress her, but Ally left that out of the report— for now.

"We wanted to groom him for the job and bring him up to speed on what works. We need him to do this search with the utmost secrecy and under the proper camouflage."

"I understand."

"I wonder what gave him the idea that we needed him to do anything on his own."

"Not certain."

"You didn't give him any of these thoughts?"

"No, sir."

"Are you certain?"

"Watch the recording, sir. You can hear everything I ever said to Kars Dee."

"I have watched it. Perhaps, I'll take another look."

Ally bit at her lower lip. "He was trying to impress me."

"Impress you?"

"Yes."

"You mean he's attracted to you?"

"Yes."

"Interesting. We can use that to our advantage, Ally. Well done!" He grinned at her.

"Sir, it's much better than you could even imagine."

"What is?"

"What Kars has done. Is doing. His plans and his abilities. The vision he has."

"So you are attracted to him as well?"

"That's beside the point. He has found a cave system like you could only dream of. Ten times bigger than Jeru."

"What? Ten? Ten times bigger?" Bill sat forward, depositing his drink bottle onto the coffee table.

"And there are at least six other caves connected."

Bill shook his head like he cleared out cobwebs, leaning forward even more. "Did he ask about Jeru?"

"Yes. Just how it was going."

"What intel did you share?"

"Only that people were beginning to move there from all over the planet. You know, to get away from the sway of the influence of the Earthies Global Union."

"I wish you would not have done that, Ally."

"He already has visited the site, Bill. He knows about the struggle for freedom everyone is feeling."

"You're right. I don't know him like you do. I'm glad he's on our side."

"Yes. So am I."

"He is on our side?" Bill leaned in ever so slightly.

"It certainly looks like he is. All the evidence suggests he is."

"What about these caves?"

"He calls the main cavern Alpha and is getting a boring machine out to the site soon."

"You've seen it?"

"All of it and more."

"How did he find something everyone else has been searching for decades to find?"

"It's actually hidden in plain sight. Kars has worked on the rails for years. It was right beneath our nose the whole time."

"How so?" Bill asked.

"Because our government has been hiding it until they have more need and resources to take advantage of the situation. Plus, it has been hidden by Mars lore and fear."

"Fear?"

"Yes, we were all told there was a massive radiation leak, so all the ground penetrating drones sent out to search for caves didn't bother to consider the site because it was uninhabitable. Or to be more precise, they believed it was uninhabitable."

"Where is this Alpha, Ally?"

"He blindfolded me on the way in after I had slept through the night, so I cannot point it out on a map. He said he was protecting me."

"Plausible deniability."

"Right. So, I don't know exact longitude and latitude."

"He wasn't sure if he could trust the beautiful woman he was attracted to."

"Yes. Definitely."

"You don't know where it is then?"

"I do."

"How? Where?"

"How is because he told me the general area. Before I say where, Bill, I want you to know that the Evo he got for me had a new Certified Compliant seal, so every system was just checked and certified to be operating nominally."

"Yes, I'm aware of the process."

"The rad level never once got above what we absorb on the surface. Most of the time it recorded a zero radiation level."

"Where, Ally?"

"The Red Zone."

Bill sat in stunned silence. He considered the possibility.

"Bill, it's a perfect cover."

"You're right. Thanks be to God!"

They sat in silent appreciation for God's provision.

"Wait, you said he was bringing a boring machine? How will he make that happen?"

"He is connected to LIFT."

"How connected?"

"To the owner somehow."

"You've got to be kidding?"

"No. There is someone in orbit, too. A secret spacecraft that evades radar. I don't know much about that, other than the ship is able to mess with Revolver landing canisters. He is going to land canisters outside Alpha."

"Could this be the answer we have been praying for?"

•◦•

"Repeat, you said to drive through the sensor field, roger?"

"Affirmative. Proceed through the field."

Fifteen minutes later, when Benz began to breathe again, and the worry dropped off his shoulders. He drove the lumbering boring machine named Dig 21 across the Martian desert southwest of the Tharsis Rise, which bucked like a rodeo bull beneath him from the uneven terrain. Benz had gotten used to the motion in the first few harrowing hours of the journey the night before. He was also delivering the extra Shimmer blankets for the landing canisters while towing the ancient farm equipment in a line resembling the nineteenth-century American West wagon trains, minus the oxen. The boring machine was extremely powerful. Benz joked that if it ever got all its wheels stuck, the planet would spin faster beneath him because of its torque. Dig 21 was equipped with its own high capacity nuclear reactor and plenty enough low-range power to tow more than twenty pieces of equipment clear across the planet, if necessary.

Kars, inside Alpha watched day two of the carbon nano-tube spray-foam application and it's stunning transformation. The specialized bot he had picked up the day before from the Anzacland rail spur was mounted on a scissor lift to reach the high ceiling of the cavern. On the cave floor, loader bots moved the rocks and regolith so the spray bot had a level surface. Two pillar bots installed slip-form steel forms so reinforced concrete columns could be built to strengthen two ceiling areas. One was halfway to its destination, and the other was a quarter of the way up. Both had multiple bots scurrying over the area above the forms, placing and tying rebar vertically and horizontally above the slip form as other bots delivered concrete into the sealed forms. The heat from the chemical reaction forced a stream of steam from a vent on the top.

Due to Ally's report, the Underground had proved to be all-in on the project. They sent the equipment from Shepard on her word, before the leadership made the trip.

"Hey, am I gonna get a ticket for double parking a monster boring machine in front of your store?" Benz approached Kars from behind.

"Only if you're blocking the handicapped spots!"

"Wow. This is awesome, brother!"

"They showed up yesterday. I can't believe how fast they are."

"Which tool?"

"Both the spray bots and the builder bots."

"Amazing."

"Yeah I ran down to the spur to get them."

"How are you doing?" Benz asked his best friend, touching Evo's shoulder.

"Me? I'm fine. How are you? Is the real question? And how did you get out?" Kars struggled to read his face through the Evo's visor.

"Like I told you, it is a long story."

"Yeah? Start at the beginning."

"Ridge's dumb idiots grabbed me in Shepard right after I got Ally in the tube. They took me in for questioning. I told them nothing. Not one word. I knew they were just guessing about things, trying to get me to talk. I demanded a lawyer. They slapped me around a little bit. They told me it would have been worse if I had been up in Free Port. But the Shepard guys thought we were heroes, so they kept checking how things were going. It was funny, actually. Ridge shows up, thinking he is in command. Starts telling the Shepard guys what to do. They are getting ticked but do what Ridge wants, until this captain shows up and calls Ridge out right in front of everyone, me included. He tells him that the F.P. boys are violating my constitutional rights and that the questioning should stop until my lawyer shows up from Free Port. So they put me in a holding room, while Ridge and his guys hunted for evidence. In the middle of the night, this private member of the Shepard security team opens the door and tells me to pack my stuff because I'm getting released.

Apparently, they got an order from some mucky-muck in the corporation who has ties to Free Port saying that they had to let me go."

"No kidding? Ridge must have lost his flipping mind."

"When I'm walking out, I hear Ridge yelling from another room at the kid who let me go. I didn't look back and got out of town to the solar farm."

"And the boring machine?"

"Yeah. It was sitting at the farm, already daisy-chained to the farm equipment. I sent the Hum ahead after I attached the Shimmer to the roof and slow walked it out. It should arrive at your Hum by tonight."

"I can't believe it. Ridge must have gone nuts."

"I never want to see that Nazi again. He's the devil incarnate. To think that the Federal Police, the ones who are supposed to protect our God-given rights are behind the assault on our freedoms just ticks me off."

"He's evil. I'm starving, you wanna eat?"

"Yeah. Protein goo is all I've had for a couple days."

"Gross."

"I kinda smell."

"You always smell."

The men shared lunch in Kars's Hum.

"So you and Ally are a thing now?"

"Yeah. She's awesome. We are making a go of it."

"Go of what?"

"I was gonna marry her, probably soon."

"Congrats, Bro. So, what's wrong? What do you mean, was?"

"I want to. But I've got a huge problem we haven't talked about yet."

"What's that?"

"I don't know how to say it without wrecking your life."

"What? It can't be that bad."

"Yeah, it can. It is."

Benz stopped chewing and stared at his friend.

"Have you seen any news about the fugitive the G.U. authorities caught in Georgia?" Kars asked.

"On Earth? I may have. I can't really remember."

"The Terrorist Princess?"

"Oh yeah, that. Sure, she's wanted in the C.S."

"The Compliant States hired the G.U. to go get her in Georgia."

"That's illegal isn't it?"

"Used to be, but the governor of Georgia, the governor of a free state mind you, said the action strengthened their relationship with the G.U. while catching a known terrorist. He saw it as a win-win. Of course his head is on the chopping block now, they are starting impeachment proceedings on him."

"As they should."

"Yeah, but."

"But what?"

Kars looked into his eyes. "The so called Terrorist Princess was moved to a facility in North Carolina."

"Okay?"

"They found her guilty of treason."

"Treason?"

"Yeah. Now she is facing the death penalty."

"She gets an appeal, right?"

"Yeah."

"I don't understand what this has to do with us?"

"It has to do with me," Kars said.

"How?"

"She is my sister."

"Bry is the Terrorist Princess?"

"Yeah."

Kars passed him his comm that had Bry's picture on the screen.

The hum of the systems inside the vehicle was only heard for a moment.

"I'm sorry, Bro."

"Thanks."

"You heard from Gigi?"

"No. I don't know what to say. I kind of ran away and now she has to deal with all this crap too."

"Maybe they've got a plan?"

"To break her out of a maximum security facility?"

"Why not? It's not like the G.U. has built any state-of-the-art prisons yet. Most of their stuff in the Compliant States is low tech, like work camp kinda stuff."

"So I've heard."

"Reach out man. Back channel it through V or something."

"Maybe."

After five more minutes of silent eating, Kars tells Benz, "I'm going back."

"Back? Where? Free Port?"

"Earth."

"What? Why? How? That's really going back, Kars. Like you can't take it back, going back. They'll only allow you one exit. So, if we leave, it's for good."

"I've got a plan. Part of a plan. Sort of a plan. I'm making up a really good plan."

"Come on, man. I've got nothing back there."

"I know, that's why you're not coming with me."

"What?

"Yeah. This has to be a solo flight."

"Why?"

"Because I need you here," he said, gesturing toward the cave in progress.

"Here?"

"Yeah."

"They're not gonna let you leave for at least a year."

"I know. But they can't stop me from leaving in two weeks."

"TWO WEEKS! How? Who are you?" Benz pushed his plate away.

"What?"

"You were scared out of your spacesuit when the Goons showed up at our door."

"They threw you through our door, is the way I remember it."

"Yeah, my shoulder still hurts. But that's my point. Kars, you were afraid. I saw it in your eyes. But you're not scared now. You're talking about marrying some chick and leaving Mars, why?

During a long silence, the two contemplated the ramifications.

"They've got my sister."

"I know, but up until a few minutes ago I thought she was out of the game or dead." Benz said.

"She was dead to me for a long, long time."

"Why now?"

"Because I think that is what I am supposed to do. Like this whole thing needs to happen. I don't know why— I can't get it out of my head."

"Are you coming back?" Benz meant to Mars.

"I'm gonna try. But I don't know. I haven't thought that far ahead. I just know that I gotta go. I also know this has to be built, and you are the one who can do it. I know you can."

"I don't know, man. Where did all of this come from?"

"Hagus. He died, and a part of me died too. I am sick of being afraid. There is too much at stake. For me. For you. For Ally. For Bry. For the Underground. For freedom. I've got to stop running. I can't expect others to step up and do my part in all of this. This is way bigger than me. Than you."

Benz was lost deep in his own thoughts.

After finishing eating silently, and donned their helmets to check on the bot's progress.

The spray bot had repositioned itself next to a pile of boulders the dozer-bots had pushed up into a mound earlier. The bot deployed its transparent spray dome and sprayed the beige foam onto the rock above it.

"The loader and dozer bots are lagging behind," Kars said.

"I'll go check where they are unloading. They probably have made a mess," Benz said.

"We are filling the old lava tube to the south."

"Roger." Benz trudged away not knowing how to feel.

An hour later, the spray bot repositioned again while Benz returned.

"Get them straightened around?"

"Yeah, they were stuck in competition mode again."

"How full is the tube?"

"They should be caught up with the stacking and be halfway back."

"Okay. We gotta figure out if your boring machine will make it into the Russian cave.

"I think it is going to prove to be too big. We may have to grind it through," Benz said as they headed toward that tube.

Ten minutes later, they flicked on their suit lights to illuminate the tube connecting with the Russian cave.

"This tube was almost filled with rubble when I first came through. Moved it all back into the Russian side."

"How does that work with all the bodies?"

"I had the bots make a road over to bury them. I have plans for a wall to seal the entombed area in, but we need the space to hide the rubble."

"Can that cave ever be made safe?"

"We'd need a lot of time. The spray foam will help, plus a few dozen pillars and a lot of reinforcements.

"I guess that can happen later."

"Yeah, later— like after the people move in here."

At the entrance tube, the connecting point from the leading Russian cavern to the outside world, Kars sent Trippy on a mission to map it. The drone returned in five minutes with all the needed data.

"Looks like it's the antenna array and the roof tanks are the problem," Benz said. As they checked the superimposed picture over the newly made map.

"Can we take them off?"

"I don't think so."

"Then how is this going to work? I need that boring machine to start drilling today. We've got a lot of tunnels to make."

"We may have to wait until tonight. It should be able to grind this tube out in an hour."

"We can't make a dust plume— the satellites will see it."

"Only if they are looking for it, but we can check with V-man."

"Every rock outside would have to go back into its same position," Kars said.

"We will send Trippy out before we start and interface that map with a couple of bots to make the clean up right."

"Okay. Sounds like a plan. You should get your stuff ready to go right after sunset."

"Yes, boss." Benz mocked his friend with a salute as he walked away.

"Don't forget a Shimmer!"

"Yes, boss."

Later that night, when the boring machine was finally inside the Russian cavern, it was programmed to dig a new four hundred-and-eighty-seven-meter-long tunnel to Alpha. The bots loaded the grindings and piled them on the top of the tomb area. A Shimmer blanket loosely hung outside over the entryway into the Russian cave. The clean-up process was scheduled for two hours before dawn to replace every notable rock back in place, so satellites could not distinguish between the original Russian entrance and their new larger canister entrance. Suddenly, an alarm sounded inside both Evo's.

"What is it?"

"A Bugg!"

"Crap!"

"Emergency shut down, now!"

"How far on the Bugg, V?" Kars asked.

"I'm just seeing this too," V said. "Hang on for a..."

The signal to V went dark.

"Laser comm is down," Benz said. "V probably switched it off."

"That Bugg is close."

"Hopefully it's high enough they don't blow the Shimmers apart."

They both knew the Buggs had twelve powerful lift motors that could be manipulated to provide thrust in any direction. The commercial version of the Bugg is used by LIFT People to fly passengers and packages between cities every day. Their nuclear reactors gave them unlimited range, and they are remotely piloted vehicles.

The Federal Police and Marine Buggs use real pilots to fly their machines, and they are almost silent.

"It's got to be Ridge looking for me," Benz texted Kars. They were under radio silence protocol now and sat in the darkness, waiting for Ridge and his men to break through the Shimmer covering the new canister opening.

"We can hide from these pukes for a long time," Kars texted.

"If they come in, they aren't leaving." Benz replied.

***

25 May 2048

Teapot Key, Florida

The morning had been filled with tension for the sisters. They had been trying to get reports on Bry's condition for several days but had been met with silence. Their nerves were frazzled, so they called for anyone on the Key to join them for a prayer session on the beach. Someone brought a guitar, so the praying morphed into praising that stirred every soul, even the Angel Warriors circling above them.

An hour into celebrating God's goodness, a high-speed drone streaked in from the northeast, circled to reduce speed, and landed on the picnic table closest to the cabin. This was the visual confirmation that the message was from Larry. Dennis grabbed the drone, removed the flash drive from the storage compartment, and handed it to Nan. He gave the unit to one of the guys to drive it up to the charging station at the main house and keeping it on standby in case they needed to return a message.

Nan handed the drive to Connie, who plugged it into the laptop's cord.

"You got an encrypted message this morning from the dark angel," revealed onto the screen the sisters hovered over.

"Let's take this inside," Nan said.

"You keep on praying," Connie told the gathering of eight people.

The sisters hurried indoors so they could see the screen more clearly.

"Okay. Play it." It contained an audio file.

"Gigi and Nan, I've been wondering about plans for Three. If you need something from me, just let me know. Right now I can make the crossing in 88 days."

Gigi's eyes glistened with fresh tears as Nan hugged her around her neck.

"Larry wouldn't have passed this along if he had any doubts, right?"

"I'm certain you can trust it."

⸺⊰◦⊱⸺

"All clear," Kars said through his Evo comm to Benz.

"Any word from above?" Benz asked.

"Just got a ping on the system; we're reconnected. He's trying to eavesdrop on some F.P. conversations to find out what they are doing flying a Bugg over the Rise.

"Alright. I've been thinking," Benz said.

"Do you need to lay down?"

Benz didn't respond to the joke but he stopped in front of his friend so they could see each other through their helmet visors. "You asked me to finish this cave," he said.

"Yeah. I know it's a huge ask."

"If I do this then I would have to die," Benz said. "I could never just walk around in any city on the planet as me, ever again. I have to fake my death and then only travel when some terrorist organization lets me travel— and then it will be under a dead guy's alias."

"They aren't terrorist. If you won't do this, they will take over and do whatever they want. We'd have no say in how this plays out!"

"Who says I want a say?"

"I guess no one, Benz. I thought living for something bigger was something to keep us going in the face of what Ridge is plotting for us!"

"You are asking me to die."

"We all have to one day or another, brother."

"And you are saying this to me? Have you been taking drugs or something?"

"I never have been so convicted about something in my whole life."

"But you're talking like a crazy man! What about Ally?"

"I don't know. It feels like I am being asked to sacrifice my relationship with her for the greater good. I don't want to give her up. Those freaks intend to kill my sister!"

Benz was angry that he would ask him for such a huge sacrifice.

"I don't know. You feel like you have to go, but I feel like I am the one giving up everything."

"I'm sorry, Benz. I know— this is a lot to ask."

"I'm out." Benz turned away and left.

Sixteen

27 May 2048 (Sol 7647)
Teapot Key, Florida

The Bees' cabin on the beach has a steep roof covered in synthetic grass, which looks like a thatched roof found in Pacific rim communities. There is a large vent at the peak which allows hot air to naturally rise through the house, escaping through a duct and drawing cool ocean air in through the windows. During the calm days the Florida sun can get too hot for this system to keep up. Fans were installed a few years back so the old sisters could comfortably bear the heat. They still refused to have air conditioning and did not like to use electric lights, often falling asleep right after sundown. It was rare for the two to gather around a map on their kitchen table with Larry and Dennis at sun set.

"How many people would we need in that plan, Larry?" Nan asked.

"At least twenty. Plus we need the rig to have armor to punch through the fences."

"We'd have a follow up vehicle behind the, what did you call it?"

"The Ramrod."

"Right. So, the Ramrod breaks through the two barriers, followed by two Humvees with the troopers who lay down smoke and take out the two towers."

"And the second half of the team fights their way into the Maximum security building where she is being held."

"How many people get killed in this scenario?"

"I've run the numbers ten times and at least half will be casualties."

They all paused and pondered.

"That's too many men to sacrifice," Connie said. "We need to think different."

"How can we knock out their radar so they can't see us coming?"

"If you do that, they will know you are coming."

"Is there something we could do for a couple weeks in a row, then hit them?"

"Maybe," Dennis said.

"When were these pictures taken?" Nan asked Dennis.

"The ones of the front gate are from a week ago."

"We can't screw this up. If we fail they will move her."

"You're right. If they are convinced that we are coming for her. What if we plan to free everyone? Then, if the mission fails, they may just increase security."

"How many of these facilities are there now?"

"At least fifteen in Virginia, Kentucky, Tennessee, and North Carolina."

"We could hit a few other facilities at the same time as a distraction from our real target.

"Great idea, as long as it doesn't cost lives," Nan said.

"We can't guarantee that. Either we fight to get these people released, including your granddaughter, or we negotiate. We know they don't want to negotiate with us because they think we're terrorists."

"We need to use their perception of us against them."

"Agreed. What's the most effective way to do that?"

"I think it's the direct assault," Larry said. "That would show we are not intimidated to operate against their criminal incursion and the ongoing genocide."

"We need to pray about this whole mess," Connie said.

"Before we do that, our meeting with LIFT is a go," Larry said.

"Okay, we'll include safe passage for our meeting as a petition, too," Con said.

⸻ ◆ ⸻

"Ah, the famed Terrorist Princess. I am Doctor Phan." The Doctor read Bry's chart.

She said nothing, refusing to look at the man.

"Today I am here to evaluate your oral health. You know the mouth tells us so much about our overall health and wellbeing." Phan set the file on the table in front of his prisoner.

Bry's eyes shot flaming darts at the infamous torture artist as her heart cried out to God.

"Now let's have a look to see what your mouth is telling me. My assistants are going to lay you back and put on this bite collar. We don't want you repeating your mistakes that you had with my colleague." He dangled the leather mask in front of her face.

Bry didn't move.

"We know you have information of the Underground both here and on Mars. I think you would like to share that information with me. More than you want to have dental work."

⸻ ◆ ⸻

"Hey, I've got an idea."

"What do you know about that! You can think!"

"Silence, skinny man!"

"What are you thinking now?"

"So much. I need to get back to Earth but I can't do it through the traditional means."

"In case you want to come back to Mars?" V asked.

"Yes, plus I don't want anyone to know I'm visiting home because my plan is to get Bry out."

"How are you going to do that?"

"Before I can run I need to crawl. The crawling part is getting off this rock. The running part is busting her out."

"One thing at a time, then?"

"Yes."

"What are you thinking?"

"I want to use a Rocker to escape. They auto-connect with their Revolver for sample return missions."

"They also boost at about nine G."

"Right, so I'll need a containment tube to help with that, lying flat on the floor of the ship."

"That will help. We will have to get you a booster suit for takeoff. They squeeze in response to the G-force being applied to keep most of your blood in your brain."

"Great idea."

"What next?"

"I'll need enough food, water, and atmo for the trip. How long is the revolution right now?"

"Today is about eighty nine days. You are catching it at the right time."

"Then I plan to spend most of the transit time inside the Rocker which I empty out."

"You can't just throw everything out before launch. They are configured to a specific weight and trajectory. You will need to remove the same amount of weight you are adding."

"Yeah, I get that. But after launch I could toss everything I don't need to give me enough margin."

"There is plenty of margin built into the system. You could be off twenty percent and still connect."

"Ah. Okay. That makes things easier."

"But there is a bigger issue for you. You would have to overwrite the launch program without the ship contacting the Revolver. If something goes really wrong during the flight, the crew on the Revolver will take control of the ship and self destruct it if they can't."

"I'm counting on that, V."

"Another problem is that ninety five percent of the Rockers unload at the refinery, then are reloaded with materials meant for Earth use. You could be weeks waiting to cycle through their system up there.'

"Crap."

"You'd have to find and hijack a scientific auto launcher."

"Yes. That could work. Right?"

"It would have to be one with a specific mission to connect to a Revolver."

"Do you know of any that fit this criteria?"

"Look at you sounding all scientific."

"You know me. I am science."

"Hahaha. What was that guy's name? He was an idiot."

They both laughed at the memory from their childhood.

"Okay. Looks like we have three coming up for the next Revolver flyby in fifteen days."

"Only three?"

"Don't sound so pessimistic."

"I was hoping to choose my seat and have in flight movie options to binge for a couple of months."

"Make sure you order the fake lobster, it's always so realistic and yummy."

"Yeah, no."

"Okay, actually this one is your best bet."

"Where?"

"Well, sir, I can book you a flight on Rocker N-42. We have a window seat available on this transport, but unfortunately it's in economy class."

"Where does it launch from?"

"North of the Argyre Basin. It's a Canadian flight. They may get upset once they realize you have thrown out some of their precious cargo."

"Canadian. They owe me anyway. We'll just call it even."

"Why do they owe you?"

"Got picked up by the Canadian Coast Guard one time while fishing and they charged me a thousand bucks to tow my disabled boat across the St Clair River. I'm glad it's a Canadian vessel, payback time."

"It's technically not their vessel, they just bought the flight from LIFT Science."

"Cool— it's a LIFT Rocker."

"Yes. Oh yeah, let me guess, you are certified on those systems too?"

"Every LIFT system, V. I can't help it."

"I know, you've had too much alone time."

"Look who's talking?"

"Yeah, I'm starting to go batty." V used his index finger to flutter his lips while making crazy man sounds.

"Starting? I think we've arrived!"

"Funny."

"What else is that Revolver picking up?"

V yawned as his fingers glided over his upright keyboard. "Searching."

"Lift says every docking bay will be occupied on this return trip. So, it's a complete turnaround."

"That will be a mess to navigate."

"Yeah, they need a full load of fuel too."

"Is that four Fuelers?"

"Yes."

"Will the Fuelers be in the way if I show up late to the party?"

"They've got Canadian Aerospace Flight on Rocker N-42 scheduled for bay 27. Yeah that will be an issue if you get there late. Looks like Fueler 177 will be docked above that bay unloading Methane, Liquid O2 and a crew pallet."

"I just have to be on time."

"That will work. N-42, your flight, is supposed to dock ten minutes before the Fueler."

"How long to unload?"

"Fueling should take ten minutes, then they take the long loop back around to the gas station."

"You said a crew pallet?"

"Yes. Lemme look. It's food and medical supplies. Plus there is a crew member's laptop and incidentals."

"Okay. This is my plan. I've got fifteen days until lift off."

"You're nuts," V said.

"You're sworn to secrecy," Kars said.

"What about Ally?"

"I'm telling her tonight."

<hr>

"Hey, Kars!" Butterflies danced inside Ally's stomach.

"You made it back!"

"Yes. This is Bill. He's with us and he may or may not run a few things."

"Your boss? Hi Bill. Welcome to Alpha."

"Kars. It's so good to meet you. I can't believe my eyes. What did we walk through back there?"

"That's a five hundred meter long air lock, sir. Or will be, once it's done," Kars was proud of the accomplishment.

"Incredible. Why so big?"

"It's designed to allow us to roll landing canisters inside the cave for processing."

"You're talking about the massive Revolver canisters?"

"Those are the ones."

"That's never been done. They usually empty them and then take the cargo inside."

"It's nothing new on the tech side. We just needed a couple more pressurizers to pull it off. Then we're going to use a canister to hold the atmo during the downside of the vacuum cycle. The real benefit will be the individual pieces of cargo won't have to be packed in vacuum rated sub-containers. We' 'll save a ton of weigh with less packaging."

"You mean that you'll save weight in future flights, right?"

"Yes. More pounds of actual supplies can be launched if the ship delivering them has less packaging mass to haul."

"True. Where did you come up with a couple more pressurizers?"

"I've got some connections that are proving to be fruitful."

"Aren't people going to miss those parts?"

"Yes, but their replacements will be available to purchase in a few months."

"With a higher price tag, I imagine."

"I'm not in control of any of that."

"I heard you brought in a boring rig?"

"Yes. Benz drove it here daisy chained to the farm equipment."

"Where is it now?" Bill asked.

"We just turned it loose on the far side of the cave digging a line north for a klick. That tunnel will connect with another cavern and we will then turn southwest to connect a third and the final part of that circuit will bring it back here."

"How long do you expect that to take?"

"About a month, depending on drill health. We need a few more cutting edges and hope to source them somewhere on the planet."

"We have some contacts in Brahman, maybe I can help."

"That's great. I can send you the model number."

Bill turned his attention to the ongoing spray foam project.

"You've made a lot of progress on the foam." Bill glanced up.

"It's about thirty eight percent complete. Only need another train car of chemicals to finish it, before we are sealed up."

"I just can't get over the scope of this project, Kars. Even the largest corporations would hesitate to take on a project of this scale."

"Thanks. Corporate guys get caught up in the dollars without knowing how these things come together. It has been something to watch."

"Well, if all you did was watch, none of this stuff would get done. How do you do it?"

"Spent lots of time working with bots on the rails."

"You haven't accomplished all of this by yourself."

"Nope. The bots are a work multiplier that never need a bathroom break."

"How many are running around here now?"

"Don't know off the top of my head. Twenty or thirty."

"I've had lots of help and encouragement." Kars looked at Ally, who watched him. "So, what do you see as your role in this community, Bill?"

"Are you planning on living here, Kars."

"I wasn't sure until yesterday."

"What changed?"

"Something you don't know about me, well maybe you do, is that I love to fish. I've missed fishing the big lakes for Walleye and Salmon. I'm originally from Michigan. Anyway, I've had a pipe dream about finding a cave where I could create a lake and stock it with fish, so I could hook one on Mars sometime before I die."

"Quite a dream."

"Not too different than downhill skiing on Olympus Mons."

"Touche."

"Anyway, the tunnel we are digging right now will connect with a cavern that drips with water. It evaporates before it hits the ground but the humidity is off the charts. When we mapped it we identified several fissures the water flows from and can estimate more than enough water for a 40 acre reservoir fifty feet deep."

"Your certain of this?"

"We are in the middle of confirming the theory with ground penetrating radar, but we're optimistic."

The men conversed for over an hour. Kars showed them the map he had taped together and pointed out everything he knew at this point. He explained the Russian cave situation, arguing that for a claim to be valid on

Mars, you have to occupy the plot of ground for ten years of continuous habitation. "Now, it's just a memorial graveyard to maintain," Kars said. "Their dead will be remembered and honored."

Bill tried to take it all in.

"Bill, I am sorry, but I need to take this woman on a date. Can we continue this conversation in the morning?"

"I understand. May I explore?"

"Anywhere you'd like. Keep an eye out for the bots; you can't always trust that their sensors haven't been covered in dust." Kars watched Bill stride off.

"Hey you. Will you meet me in my Hum in fifteen minutes?"

"Maybe... Of course."

Kars knew she was smiling just by the tone of her voice.

Inside the Hum Kars washed up and changed clothes after getting out of his Evo and locking the smelly suit up in its case in the back, then slapped his face with some aftershave.

The airlock cycled just as he turned down the interior lights. A real candle flickered on the table as Ally strolled in. Her helmet popped free with a hiss. She smiled at the scene.

"You had some help, right?"

"I don't know what you are talking about."

"Candles, silk flowers, chocolate, hot food, and you cleaned up, all in fifteen minutes!"

"I've been busy."

"I'll say." She wiggled out of her Evo in the rear of the Hum and plugged it in to charge while Kars arranged food on the table.

"So, this is a date, huh?"

"I hope so."

"You could have asked me first."

"What would you have said? You know, the you, before seeing this spread."

"I would have said that I needed to check my calendar."

"Oh yeah?" Kars stood right before her, handing her the silk red rose.

"Thank you. This is amazing, you are amazing."

Kars reached for her and hugged her for a long moment. "I really like you, Ally."

She blushed, averted her eyes, and buried her face into his shirt to breathe in his scent.

"We better eat," he said. "You know, before it gets cold."

They spent the next hour talking, laughing, and sharing the pasta dinner Kars had picked up in Shepard with his resupply. Even the bread was pretty decent. The bottle of wine was terrible as far as wine goes, but great on the Martian scale of wine quality.

"This is nice. Thank you."

"I'm glad you're here."

"I am too."

"Bill seems like an intense guy."

"He is focused. I think right now he's a little beside himself."

"What do you mean?"

"He had no idea about the scope of this project."

"He approves?"

"Of the project? Yes."

"Of me?" Kars asked.

"He has done more digging into your past."

"Great."

"It's all good. It doesn't matter anymore."

"To him? Or you?"

"Both of us."

"What does that mean?" Kars's fear monster woke up in an instant, nudging to speak to his heart again.

"We both know that you are an answer to many years of prayer. It's like God has been preparing us for this project and at the right moment he provided in a most unexpected way— you."

"I don't think..."

"You don't think that God could use you?"

"True. I have spent many years running from him, hiding."

"And now?"

"Now, I see him working everywhere I turn, including in my heart. I've been getting emotional just thinking about it all."

"I believe that God prepared you for this over the last thirteen years."

Kars didn't know how to respond.

"I think God has been preparing us for this, as well."

"For what?"

"For all of it."

"All? Including the us part of us?"

"Yes."

Kars leaned in and kissed Ally's warm, soft lips for the first time. Ally lifted her hands to both sides of his rough face and kissed him back.

"You know, living here, we don't know how much time we have until we get stuck outside the airlock." Kars quoted the familiar Martian phrase.

"Yes, death is everywhere."

"It's everywhere on Earth too, we just can distract ourselves with every-thing else."

"True."

"I want you in my life. I want to spend my life with you, Ally, but I can't ask you to marry me."

"I'm really confused."

"I know I can do that to people. I have to go away for a while."

"What?"

"I'm going back, Ally."

"To Earth?"

"Yes."

"Why?"

"I think that God wants me to find my sister."

"Find your sister? I'm supposed to believe that you love me now but you have to do something that any one of ten billion people could do?"

"I know, it sounds crazy."

"Explain it to me, Kars."

"Okay. You guys have done your research on me and that's fine. But you are not able to access some of my real history."

"Like what?"

"Who I'm related to."

"What?"

"I changed my name before I rode the wagon and had creative people make another identity for myself."

"So, you lied about who you were?"

"I was hiding. I didn't want to be connected to my past."

"Why?"

"I was afraid."

"Of what?"

"I was afraid of the expectations. I was afraid of the cost. I was afraid of everything!"

"What are you talking about?"

"The Terrorist Princess."

"What?"

"The Terrorist Princess."

"What about her?"

"You know who she is, right?"

"I only know her reputation in the Underground."

"Do you know what's happening to her now?"

"She got caught up in a bogus conviction for treason or something. She's on my prayer list. Why? What does this have to do with you?"

"Bry is my sister."

Ally felt dizzy and leaned back, her head spinning with the new information.

"I've been living in denial. Trying to run from who I am and, and, I need to stop," Kars said.

"I need to think, Kars. I'm going to Bill's Hum. I'll talk to you later." She rose up and donned her Evo before he knew what to do or say.

"Listen, I'm glad you told me. I will see you in the morning, alright?"

Kars tried to smile. No words came out— they were stuck inside his head like another dam had been built.

Ally clamped her helmet, cycled through the lock, and fled.

⸺◆⸺

The four Leech had finally caught up to her as she slept in the back room of Bill's huge Hum.

"Listen let's get moving!" said One.

"I smell fear," said Two.

"And that fear needs a new home," One said while shaking his butt from side to side.

"You look ridiculous!" said Two.

"We are trying to get two anchors set tonight, boys. Fear in front and shame around the corner. We'll have to put a few turns on the anger anchor while we are in town," said Four, the apparent leader.

"Don't forget insecurity!" Three said. They all had a good belly laugh as they climbed inside Ally's heart.

———◦———

Sol 7648 (28 May 2048)

Alpha, Mars

"Can I come in?" Ally texted, wondering if she would have to bang on the side of the Hum to wake Kars.

"Yes."

Ally cycled through the lock, which felt like the process took an exuberant amount of time.

Kars stood, not knowing what to expect when she stepped inside. Ally could not get her helmet off fast enough before grabbing Kars's face and pulling his lips into hers. The fresh peppermint tingled on his lips. He thanked God that he was awake enough to have brushed his teeth. He could not help but laugh in the middle of the kiss.

"I'm sorry," he said.

"That's not the response I was hoping for."

"I prayed while kissing you. I thanked God that I was awake enough to have brushed my teeth."

"Yeah, I took a gamble that I was moving into bad breath territory. But I was willing. I am willing."

They resumed kissing.

"Get out of the suit will ya?" Kars asked.

"Help me." Ally wiggled in all the right places as Kars lifted her up into a full-frontal hug. When Ally tried to push her foot down on the inside leg, she tripped, and they both fell over, laughing. She finished kicking the suit off and returned to meet his mouth while lying on top of him. Their breathing deepened as he tried to pull her through his own body.

"You taste so good," she whispered and kissed his neck.

"Okay. Okay. Okay. This is going to end with one thing happening."

"I know. I'm standing up right now."

"I want it to end that way or begin that way."

"So do I." Ally sat up, unable to conceal her excitement from the kissing session. She rolled off and grabbed at his hand.

"Does this mean you are breaking up with me?" Kars laughed at his own joke.

"Yes. Definitely." As Ally laid her head on his stomach, and he draped his arms over her.

"I'm sorry for dumping that all on you last night. I didn't know how else to tell you."

"I get it. There's not really an easy way to say that you are the brother of the Terrorist Princess."

"Yeah, well. I guess I am guilty."

"You are incredibly brave for wanting to rescue her."

"It's insane really."

"Yeah. And I want you to know that I will be waiting for you here, and if you can't get back to me then I will come to you. I love you Kars."

"I love you too, Ally. I want to marry you and spend the rest of our lives together no matter where we live."

"Yes."

The kissing resumed with a new tenderness that could not be helped or stopped.

"Wait. Wait. Is Bill a house church leader?"

"Yes, why?"

"Is he awake?"

"Yes, he was having a mud when I left."

"Let's get married right now. He can do the ceremony and Benz can be the witness."

"I thought he wasn't talking to you?"

"He's my brother, he would do anything for me. Well— almost anything."

An hour later, Bill and Benz met them at the emergency Atmo shelter inside Alpha, and they had themselves a Martian wedding. This first marriage in Alpha City was performed with four people in Evos, their helmets off, and not a dry eye was found.

"Thanks, guys. We are heading out to the Hum to celebrate. We aren't available for a few hours," Kars said.

"Days. A few days." Ally said. Everyone laughed.

The newlyweds cycled through the lock and ran to the Hum outside the cavern. They turned off their comms and proceeded to consummate their marriage vows— several times. Only sleep and hunger interrupted their tender intimacy until the harsh reality of someone banging on the side of the Hum startled them both out of their dream-like state.

SEVENTEEN

28 May 2048 (Sol 7648)
Teapot Key, Florida

"I can't believe how quiet this boat is," Connie whispered to her sister.

"It's a hydrofoil, not a boat," Nan said with just enough snark to make her point.

"We are heading across an ocean without sinking or swimming while sitting in a hull. I call that a boat!" Connie gave it right back.

They all laughed.

The sisters, Larry Shields, and a pilot named Merle sailed southwest from Teapot Key at fifty miles an hour, with nothing more than a hum from the electric motors just beneath the surface of the calm teal-green waters of Florida Bay. Their minuscule wake was not distinguishable twenty feet behind the craft. The transparent hull was elevated from the water during this race to Marathon Key— with the two hydrofoils cutting through the sea. The Shimmer blanket fastened to the canopy masked their movement from the peering eyes of satellites, but it rattled in the wind, sounding like an open bag of potato chips in front of a window fan.

"Been a long time since we've got together with Daphne." Nan tightened her visor to fight against the wind.

"I thought the same thing," Con told her sister. "They didn't have any graduation parties for the kids, so I don't even remember how long it's been."

"Wasn't it at mom's wake?"

"We've seen them since then, right?"

"I don't think so," Nan insisted.

"We are going to swing south under the Seven Mile bridge to get to Boot Key," the pilot, a bearded man in his twenties, told Larry.

"I thought we got picked up in Marathon?"

"It's just off Marathon Key. South— secluded and away from the houses."

"Down by the old radio station?"

"Exactly. That station is still operating."

"No kidding?"

"That's what I hear," Merle said.

As the boat raced beneath the Seven Mile Bridge, the sisters huddled against the cool early morning air. Larry noticed and asked the pilot for a blanket. Merle pointed with his chin as he kept the boat from hitting the bridge and Larry retrieved a large beach towel from the storage area below a seat and covered the girls' backs.

"Thanks, Larry." Connie said. They both smiled.

"Should only be another few minutes," Merle told them.

The new dock on the southwest side of Boot Key would have been easy to miss if Merle did not know of its existence. As they approached the dock, the transparent hull of the boat lowered itself into the water while the four legs of the hydrofoil rose from the floor. Merle set the auto dock feature, reached forward, and looped a rope from the bow around the mooring post on the dock while Larry wrangled the post at the stern.

Larry placed the step, helped the ladies out of the boat, and handed them a special umbrella for both of them to hide beneath.

"Follow the path to the first trail on your right. They will meet you there in about five minutes." Merle checked his analog watch.

"Thanks. We will see you up in Duck."

"Yes sir."

"Be safe."

The blue and beige camouflaged dock led away from the water to a stone path. It snaked through some palms and scrub brush, then turned right revealing a long, straight section of a partially shaded trail made up of white coral sand. Larry led the way beneath his Shimmer hat, his hand on his sidearm. A couple minutes later, after another trail shunted off to the right, their path wound them around to the Helo pad. Before the sisters could sit on the bench to wait in the shade, something wrinkled the sky above the concrete, bringing a terrific wind. Sand lashed at their legs and inverted their umbrella, nearly ripping it out of their hands. This was all done by the powerful motors of the LIFT vehicle. The motors switched off as soon as it set down, and everything stopped moving.

The side compartment door opened, falling toward the ground and revealing a set of stairs built inside the door. An elegant woman rushed from the vehicle, almost running toward the sisters.

Larry was about to intervene by intercepting the unarmed running woman.

"Sophie!" Both Nan and Con squealed as the three hugged in one lump.

"What a nice surprise! No one told us that you'd be in town."

"I just found out you two were coming and I wanted to meet you! How have you been?"

"Good for an old woman," Nan said.

"You're not old," Sophie said.

"I know, I was talking about your aunt Connie!"

"No. She's not old either."

"You don't tell persuasive lies," Con told Sophie.

"Where's Brad?"

"Oh he's buried up to his neck in engineering things with LIFT."

"At the cape?"

"No, on Raccoon Cay."

"Is he joining us after work?"

"I don't know when he'll be finished today."

The trio linked arms and headed toward the aircraft.

"How are you doing?"

"Great."

"How are the kids?"

"Both in college. Olivia is a junior and Oliver a freshman."

"Where are they attending? I used to know, but it slips my mind."

"Hillsdale. The southern campus in South Carolina."

"Not too far then?"

"Not at all. We go up to visit about once a month."

They boarded their LIFT, which appeared to be the color of the sky. The outer skin was covered with a new chameleon overlay, which could transform colors to match the surrounding conditions. Right after boarding, the door was raised, and everyone was told to strap in. The seats faced the center of the luxurious craft in an elongated circle. There were low tables in front of both halves of the circle, divided by a serving aisle.

"What does your dad have you doing these days?" Nan asked.

"I am running the Wellness Center for LIFT employees. Lots of support group type stuff. The employees are far from home and need time to adjust to the climate and work environment. Every job here is super stressful so they need a place to vent."

"Do you like it?" Nan asked.

"It's rewarding work, it really is."

"How's the church going?" Connie grabbed a water bottle from the table.

"That's been great. We are hooked in and doing mission in Duncan Town once a month.'

"That's awesome. What needs are you guys targeting?" Connie sipped the water.

"We do lots of basic nutrition training, proper sanitation habits, food distribution, and occasionally we fix up a dilapidated house or two."

"Things are bad In Duncan Town?"

"Yeah, the town has exploded since LIFT arrived. That has brought both good things and hard things with it. Drugs, gambling, and prostitutes have followed the money."

"Isn't that on a different Cay than the launch facilities?"

"Yes, but the ferry runs twenty-four hours. There are manufacturing facilities on the northern Cays too, so more folks work here than ever."

"Prepare for take off." The pilot's voice came through the speaker above them.

The twelve turbo blades swung into action, lifting the craft up at an alarming rate. The sisters laughed in response to the butterflies in their stomachs.

"Woo-hoo!" Connie grabbed for her sister.

The high-end luxury transport aircraft rotated a hundred and eighty degrees while the rear-mounted motors began to reposition to provide forward thrust. Off they went, leveling off fifty feet above the ocean. Small wings extended from beneath the craft to help provide lift, which allowed more motors to provide thrust. Within a minute, the craft sailed along at three hundred twenty-five miles an hour to the southeast.

"Ladies and gentlemen, we have a one hour and thirty-five minute flight to our destination. The crew will be serving a delicious breakfast this morning. Our weather is blue skies and butterflies all the way to our destination south of Crooked Island. Everyone up front, along with those serving in the cabin, want to thank you for flying with LIFT People. At LIFT everyone is our kind of people! Crew clear for meal service."

"That's so nice," Nan said.

"The chef from the boat made this breakfast. It's amazing." Sophie whispered leaning forword.

For the chatty ladies, time seemed to pass as quickly as the aircraft flew. Larry still tried to figure out which woman Sophie was related to calling them "aunt." He listened carefully to the conversations. Finally, he picked up on the fact that the guy who owns LIFT was married to the Bee's younger sister, Daphne, and Sophie was their daughter.

The aircraft banked starboard, then withdrew its wings. It gained altitude with a rush from the motors repositioned to lift and slowed the forward motion so much that the seat belts automatically tightened around the passengers.

"Sorry about that, fighting against an unexpected head wind. Touchdown in five seconds."

The nimble craft set down gently on the upper platform of a chameleon-skinned yacht. Before they exited the helo, a canopy automatically deployed around the aircraft, concealing it from peering eyes.

Daphne waited as her sisters slowly exited the Helo.

"Aww look at you guys! You look so tan!"

"Hi Daphne. You look great! Did you have work done?" Nan asked about her perky breasts beneath her bathing suit top, pointing with her eyes.

"I'll never tell!" She struck her chest out, turning to profile them, showing off. They all laughed, sauntered off together to the reception area inside the glass door. "We flew the plastic surgeon in a couple months ago. He did the operation on the boat."

"That cost a fortune!" Nan said, Daphne smiled.

"Hey Doc!" Connie hugged the man in the wheelchair.

"Hey Con, Welcome! How are you? You look fantastic. That sun and ocean is treating you well."

"We love our little Key, that's the truth."

"Hi Nan," they hugged.

"Thanks for having us aboard."

"It's our pleasure. We'd love to have you anytime."

"We know you are one of the busiest men in the world right now."

"It does keep me going."

"So how did you get away?" Nan asked.

"I'm the boss. They probably get along better without me breathing over their shoulders."

Nan was impressed with Doc's self-awareness.

"How was the flight?" Doc asked.

"Those things are quiet," Nan said.

"And fast," Con said. "I just heard that they call them Buggs on Mars. Do they have a nickname here too?"

"It depends on who you ask," Sophie said. "The black ones are still called Nighthawks in a lot of places."

"That's a holdover from that other company, right?" Nan asked Doc.

"Yes. They developed the tech, we just improved it."

"Craig's cousin worked there," Connie said as they gathered inside.

"He worked for us for a few years, too," Doc said. "He's retired now."

"Sit. Sit. So, what brings you here, ladies?" Doc asked.

"We wanted to see our sister," Con said. "And we need to talk with you about our growing problem."

"She's been excited ever since she heard you were coming. Got her hair done and a manny-peddy. Trimmed and plucked all day long. Got some saggy things fixed up a couple months ago."

"I had to look good for my girls." Daphne flashed her million-dollar smile.

"I haven't been called a girl for decades," Connie said.

They all had a good laugh. A server came in with a tray of fruity drinks and sophisticated looking hors d'oeuvres.

"What growing problem are we speaking of?" Doc bit into a cracker topped with a dollop of ornate cheese.

"Our people problem."

"Yes. I'm aware of what's going on up north. We are involved in getting the people out who need to leave."

"You know the type of folks coming out, right?" Nan tested his knowledge.

"Yes. Jews and Christians are both being pressured," Doc said.

"The Jews who have helped hide folks are really being targeted," Daphne said.

"Yes, New York has the worst record of human rights abuse in the world right now. Mao would be so proud," Connie said.

"Mao and Adolph," Doc said.

"Yes."

"What are you thinking?" Doc asked the Bees, wiping his hands on a napkin.

"I think the Underground is working like crazy to get people out of the Compliant States and moved into the Free States, but our churches and centers are already overwhelmed," Connie said. "We need more places to put people. Cuba has been allowing some persecuted people to find asylum. The Bahamas are doing a tremendous job. We've got some South American destinations that could pan out. But we've heard talk about getting the younger ones off the planet. We wanted to know what we could do to help make that happen. Could we help by sorting out the proper candidates ahead of time?"

"You are right in saying there has been talk, more than just talk. We are planning details now. There already has been a lot of building as well as training."

"What does that look like?" Nan asked.

"It means we are building and testing specialized containers for use on Revolvers. They are experimental landing canisters that allow people to be shuttled from Earth to Mars without detection. They won't need space suits because they will travel from point to point inside the pressurized containment system.

"Sounds like what is needed," Nan said.

"We will be able to take them from here all the way to a new Martian city for processing and assimilation into Martian culture. The self-contained canisters hold up to two hundred and fifty people during the transit."

"How are you going to do this?" Connie asked for details.

"Well, that is the part we are still perfecting, but we are confident the results we receive from our current testing program will provide the solutions we are looking for."

"How is this possible?" Connie asked. "I thought that all the food, water, atmosphere, and waste control has made this type of travel impossible because the weight required for each person is just too much to make a difference, which takes the cost out of reach," Conned asked.

"And I thought the space-faring nations all had to provide a manifest to the MGA to verify everything shipped to the planet," Nan said.

"Not to mention the current planet-wide immigration restrictions imposed by the MGA a couple weeks back," Connie said.

"Ladies, relax. This new technology puts people in a state of hibernation for the crossing. They are ensconced in a living gel. It allows just enough calories to be absorbed to maintain their weight, while slowing their metabolism and brain function down to the lowest common denominator. We have a canister coming to the end of its live testing phase as we speak."

"I thought those units were too heavy?"

"Those individual units were too heavy. I mean those old systems are much too heavy to use for two hundred fifty separate units. This is a new design where all the passengers are put to sleep en masse by one specialized unit."

"One unit controls two hundred fifty people at the same time?"

"Yes. It uses a generalized standard across the human genetic spectrum."

"Some may die during transit as a result?" Nan said.

"All will die in the north if we don't do something!" Doc snapped at her.

"It's been weighing heavy on him." Daphne reached around her husband's shoulders.

"How many of these canisters can be snuck onto Mars?" Connie asked.

Doc took a deep breath, trying to remember the ladies asked so many questions because they cared. "Virtually as many as we want. We control the launch and landing cadence for the entire planet, not everything is ours, of course, but we are the traffic controllers of the world, so we direct the chaos. With that kind of scheduling power we are free to insert landings wherever necessary and manufacture the paper trail to cover ourselves."

"That's amazing," Connie said.

"Things are beginning to come online. I don't know if you have heard yet, a major discovery has been found on Mars. It must stay in this room until it is time to reveal it." Doc leaned in toward them.

"What's that?" Nan asked.

"The largest cave system ever to be discovered. It's at least seven caves and one of them is producing running water," Doc said.

"How is this possible?" Larry asked. "I've not heard of such a thing and I listen to news from Mars every single day."

"It's the Underground. They are keeping an air tight lid on it. It's still early but we are ready to start dropping supplies within a few days."

"I thought you said it was just discovered. With a three month crossing time, that means you've known about it for a while, Right?" Nan asked.

"No. We are in the process of redirecting supplies meant for other cities to the new cavern they are calling Alpha."

"Won't your customers miss their shipments?"

"Not when they think they unexpectedly crashed into the Tharsis Rise."

"Oh."

"After landing we will blast the landing portion of the vehicle into inaccessible mountainside near Shepard. They will get their orders fulfilled, it will just be a few months later than they had hoped. But Martians already live with this mindset every day. They are a patient people."

"Out of necessity," Larry agreed.

⸻◆⸻

"Colonel Amadan, Ready Squad three reporting as ordered."

"Major, your team is to deploy over the northern edge of Crooked Island. Stealth on the deck watching for low and slows."

"Roger, Colonel."

Amadan directed all the security forces around the confab on the yacht. A hundred Angel Warriors surrounded the secret gathering. Underwater units to guarded against an attack from the sea.

After lunch, Larry and Sophie toured the ship while the rest of the family continued talking.

"The Underground Railway needs to be up and running sooner than we thought, but now the question is, where will we store the people until the special Containers are ready?"

"We are within a few weeks of having enough containers built to cycle all we can through the system on Mars," Doc said.

"This is all moving so fast." Connie shook her head.

"I thought we'd have more time," Nan said.

"The G.U. getting involved is forcing our hand," Doc said.

"So where can we separate the candidates and house them until we can send them?" Connie asked as a loud rocket blasted off over her shoulder from the LIFT complex on Raccoon Cay.

"I'll never get tired of seeing that," Nan said. They all turned to watch the monstrous rocket thunder upward.

"That's the new GL-2 rocket. Our most powerful rocket ever built. Quite a sight," Doc said. "We've got seven being used and seven more being built this year."

"Impressive. Did you ever think you'd be running rockets to Mars? It's so crazy that it must be a work of God."

"It is," Doc said. "There is no other explanation. I feel like I was born for such a time as this." He paraphrased the verse from the book of Ruth in the Old Testament.

"What if we used cruise ships?" Daphne said.

"Hmmm," Doc pondered.

"It would have to operate like a legitimate business and appear that people paying for a cruise," Nan said.

"Could we run them out of Port Canaveral?"

"I don't see why not," Doc said.

"In the meantime we can begin testing the canisters in real-world test," Nan said.

"Like sending a few of them to Mars?" Connie asked.

"Yes, just as soon as they are ready up there to receive them," Nan said.

"We can't wait until they are ready before we send them— we need to send them now with the hope and faith that they will be ready in three months," Doc said. That silenced everyone to consider the ramifications of this decision.

"We may be sending whole canisters to their death."

"We are still working out some kinks..." Doc trailed off.

"Kinks? That would be the lead story of every news outlet in the solar system. LIFT transports 250 dead bodies to Mars for burial!" Nan's intonation was meant to get underneath Doc's skin.

Instantly mad, Doc yelled, "I can't have that!"

"We know, Doc. We'd have to keep the lid on it somehow," Connie, the peacemaker, said.

"We have to inform the passengers of the risk ahead of time and only take those willing to sign off on it," Daphne said.

"What about the forced sterilizations? Are we going to enforce that rule too?" Nan asked.

"We don't have time, not to mention the immoral aspect," Connie said.

"There is a lot to think about." Doc wheeled himself out of the room.

Eighteen

Sol 7653 (2 June 2048)
Free Port, Mars

"Lieutenant Ridge, can you explain to me why you authorized the deployment of ground piercing radar Buggs over the Red Zone? Either you are too stupid to know that is against Martian Law, or you think you know better than everyone else who has come before you and you believe that you can operate with a general disregard for your superior officers and the law?"

"Captain, if I can."

"No. You cannot. I am speaking and you will listen. Do you realize the shit storm you have brought upon this office? The leadership in Shepard wants your head for your unauthorized operations within their city and now are demanding your head on a pike!"

"But."

"Ridge, you had no authority to spend the funds you have used and have depleted our resources to go after the real criminals. What do you have to say for yourself and these actions?"

"May I answer?"

"I asked you a question!"

"Sir, I know that one of our trains was bombed and there was tragic loss of nine lives. I was pursuing leads on the two men who I believe were involved in the attacks. I saw video evidence that they deployed some kind of energy shield to protect themselves from the blast so they could appear as modern day heroes. I think they are involved in the Underground and are currently hiding in or near the Red Zone. There is evidence leading me to believe that they are leaders in a criminal operation to steal and defraud the government of the United States."

"You told me about the video, have you been able to recover it?"

"No sir."

"You had one of the suspects in custody in Shepard and lost him? Have you apprehended him and brought him in for questioning?"

"No, sir. That was why we used the Buggs, sir."

"Over the Red Zone when there has been no indication that the Red Zone has been violated?"

"We believe." Ridge sat up and changed his approach. "I believe, these two criminals would not care about the restrictions, and I know they worked the rails just to the south of the zone when this section of track was laid, giving rise to the suspicion they would know the weaknesses of the archaic system."

"These two guys who work the rails for years, are suddenly criminal masterminds who have the ability to violate the most recognized and monitored area on the planet, make videos on Federal Police hard drives disappear, deploy an advanced technology in a bombing— all to look good? This doesn't add up, Ridge."

"Respectfully, sir. Why have the two men, these everyday heroes, disappeared?"

"Perhaps we are looking at the wrong suspects? You may have developed a confirmation bias against them and have lost sight of the whole picture."

"I do not believe that is true. My team and I have been following where the facts lead, sir."

"You and your heavy handed Goons are leaving a trail of destruction and chaos without regard for the Bill of Rights or my budget!"

"I should have asked for permission to use the Buggs, sir. I got caught up in the heat of the chase."

"You had better go back and rework this whole case with a fresh set of eyes. Last chance, Lieutenant. Do I make myself clear?"

"Yes, sir."

"Now get out of my sight. I've got to make a call to my cohort in Shepard to explain that my hyperactive and over-exuberant Lieutenant's actions were done out of a blind zeal to catch criminals."

"Sir." Ridge saluted and left with his Federal Police hat in his hand.

Sol 7653 (2 June 2048)

Alpha City, Mars

"Father, we thank you for this day and for this meal that you have provided."

"And I thank you for my brave husband and these last few days you have given us together to celebrate our marriage. Watch over us as we live, plan, and follow you."

"Amen," they both said, letting go of each other's hand.

"This looks good. Thanks for cooking." He leaned in and kissed Ally with chapped lips.

Kars smiled. He was truly happy. The last four days had been the highlight of his life. The most beautiful woman on Mars had married him, and they had locked themselves into a Hum to celebrate. His love and admiration for her continued to grow as he got to know her. She was everything he could have hoped for in a wife, more in fact. But even with this new reality inside his heart, there was a budding anxiety. His fear level grew when he realized he only had one week before leaving for the bright blue marble in the sky. He had begun this day with an uncertain feeling about his future.

He questioned his sanity concerning the upcoming mission to rescue his sister.

Only one hope might stop him from proceeding— that the Underground on Earth could pull off the rescue before he had to leave. Kars hoped something would happen in the North Carolina wilderness. Still, internally, he knew God had called him to step in and lead the rescue of the Terrorist Princess. Ten days ago, he heard and believed that calling was an easy decision. He had not intended on leaving his wife behind to worry about him. Part of this growing anxiety was he had promised to give her all of the details of his plan during breakfast.

"V, this is Ally. We got married the other day."

"That's why I've been ignoring you this week," Kars said.

"Benz filled me in," V said. "Hi, Ally. Welcome to the family."

"It's nice to meet you," Ally said to the blank screen.

"We've been working around the honeymoon and congratulations are in order," V said.

"Thanks. It was an unplanned matrimony," Kars said but Ally knew it was all going as planned.

"So, Ally and I are going over our plan. I wanted to bring you in just in case she had questions."

"Gotcha. So I'm serving as an argument arbitrator between you newlyweds?"

"Ha!"

"We haven't been married long enough to argue, V." Ally laughed and touched her husband.

"Right." V asked, "What do you need to know, Ally?"

"I think I have a good overview of the plan, but I do have some concerns."

"Join the party. I think he's nuts."

That quip certainly wasn't encouraging news to Ally.

Kars interrupted. "Which Revolver am I hitching a ride on, V?"

"That would be good old number Nine."

"The dreaded number Nine?" Ally winced.

Nine is considered the unluckiest of all the Revolver Fleet because of several accidents with its drop ships and landing canisters over the years. One particular episode killed more than one hundred Norwegians in a mining camp near the equator. Martians always say, "Cover your head— 'cause number Nine is near," whenever they learn the Revolver Nine is approaching Mars.

"Listen Ally, I'm going to give it to you straight. The way I see it, Kars hooking up with a Revolver is the fastest possible connection back. Their flight time is the quickest of any current transport ship, making the voyage in just under 90 Sols. The problem is the faster the ship, the more precise the launches up to the Revolver orbit have to be. Most Rockers connect with the foundry on the Mars Orbital Station first, then are boosted up to Revolver speed to get aboard. It gives them a speed advantage gained in the orbit of Mars. With new boosters and filled propellant tanks there is a lot more room for errors."

"If he misses the connection?" she asked.

"Missing your connection with a Revolver means you would languish for years in the icy cold of space. The only hope for Rockers that misfire is the fleet of robot tugs, but they only net the strays and then take the slow boat to Earth or back into Mars orbit. Depending on both of the planet's rotations, it can take years. It gets bad. Right now, the planets are not in a favorable position with each other to miss orbital insertion. They are so close the window for error narrows."

"Which means if Kars' Rocker misses its connection, there is no hope for him to live through it," Ally said, casting her eyes at her husband, who looked at the floor.

"He will freeze to death or more likely starve to death first— then freeze. Either way, failure means death," V confirmed.

"You're such an encouragement!" Kars said.

"I knew this was a difficult mission, but I didn't know the specifics."

"We still need to talk about slowing down enough to reenter Earth's orbit. There has to be a series of perfectly timed burns to enter Earth's orbit, or you could skip off the atmosphere and end up heading out on the fast train to Venus.

"Great. Just great. I knew speed would be an issue falling into the gravity well of the inner planets, but ships do it every day, right?"

"Yes, ships designed for orbital insertion do it all the time. But a Revolver is a bus that doesn't stop for bus stops, it throws its passengers off and uses the planet's gravity to sling shot it around and back out toward Mars, while picking up new passengers along the way."

"So how are you going to make this happen?" Ally asked.

"Well." He paused to gather his thoughts. "Instead of Kars's Rocker going to one of the orbiting space stations around the planet to unload its goods and then be reloaded for another Revolver mission, we are going to break it free from the Revolver sooner, that way we can turn it around and use its filled up propellant tanks to ease it into orbit through a series of insertions burns and the final burn to slow it into a safe landing approach and emergency parachutes to finish its journey."

"The refilling the propellant for the boosters, installing parachutes, and surviving ninety days in space is all on Kars to do?" Ally asked.

"And God, I would say— mostly God, in fact," V said.

"This is crazy, Kars."

"Agreed," V said.

"Agreed," Kars said.

"This news cannot be shared up or down the Underground. Only four people know what is about to happen. Well, maybe five," V said.

"If this happens," Ally said.

Ally felt like she had the wind knocked out of her and began to cry.

"I didn't sign up to watch my husband commit suicide!"

———◄O►———

"Listen, we have got to pray for what's going on up there. I can sense something is not right and we need the situation to be getting better, not worse," Connie said. Inside her heart, she was getting nervous about the upcoming launch of the first experimental passenger canister. This landing canister was inside a new rocket on a LIFT pad on Raccoon Cay. The people they had just approved should be offloaded from the cruise ship for transport to Mars at any minute, which she could not mention in an open prayer session on the beach.

"Father, we pray for our brothers and sisters all over this world and all over the solar system. Have mercy on us, dear Lord. Make a way for us to live at peace wherever possible. Protect those fleeing persecution. Assist those helping with this effort. Preserve for yourself a remnant of faithful followers wherever they are in your creation. Lord we cannot know your ways because they are higher than our ways. But we know you and trust you during these darkening days."

"We pray, Lord, for those being tortured right now, Father, that you would fill them with your Holy Spirit and give them the right words to say at the proper time. Give them grace, oh God."

The prayer and praise continued until the sun went down, and then most of them made their way back to their homes on the island.

"Nan, have we heard anything more from North Carolina?" Connie filled up a tortilla with roasted meat and beans.

"Got a text during the prayer meeting that things are worse inside the facility. Guards are withholding food now to punish the prisoners for things the Underground is being accused of doing. They are going along with their G.U. overlords who are releasing the same propaganda all over the globe."

"How is she doing?"

"I haven't heard. She is locked up twenty four hours a day. I can't imagine it's good."

❖

The text message on Benz's visor read, "The toys are falling out of Santa's sleigh."

"Heading out," he replied.

"Twenty two minutes. Stay near the face, not sure how this new program is going to act."

Benz cycled through the new inner tunnel lock. The massive doors the bots built from poured concrete were now upright and had secondary airlocks attached. When canisters were not cycling through the long airlock, people could still use one door or another, depending on which was open to the planet's one percent atmosphere.

Benz hiked through the old Russian cave next to the tremendous pile of grindings on top of the tomb section. He climbed into the access tunnel where he had stored the specialized canister retrieval bots. After powering them up, he wandered down the rest of the tunnel and out into the cold, dark night. The stars shone bright, as was the orange orbital foundry. Benz pulled his arms inside his Evo and rubbed his face to wake himself for the long night ahead. He sent a message to the honeymoon Hum. He hoped Kars wasn't preoccupied or tired from the previous evening's strenuous activities.

Benz did not want to know. He was so filled with conflicting feelings and emotions that he did not know what to think. He wanted to be on this project and seeing the daily progress gave him a real sense of purpose. He also resented his friend for asking him to make such a massive sacrifice of his life to the Underground and also to people who immigrated illegally from Earth. He also knew why they had to leave their lands and ride the wagon up here— he never had to face that kind of persecution. He admired their faith and, at the same time, resented the fact that they would have to come here. He had always believed that Mars should be occupied by people who wanted to preserve and promote the planet, not just people who ran away— even though he knew of so many folks who had immigrated legally had done so to escape to Mars for one reason or another. He was more convinced than ever that people could not outrun their problems and needed to face the harsh things.

Now, this whole God thing came up again. He had lived through the God stuff when Kars lived with his Gigi on the island, and Benz spent the summers there. He was intrigued until Kars decided to run from it all. Benz just put it on the back shelf of his life and went on living the way he wanted. Now, with the persecution happening all over the home planet, he had to reconsider what it all meant. Was this God the Christians worshiped real or a figment of their imaginations? But how could a collective distortion exist across the entire planet or solar system? He had read about mass psychosis in people groups around the world who had been duped by different charismatic leaders all throughout Earth's history, but this would be the first mass hypnotic event involving different people groups from all over the world, who represent every tribe on the planet. Plus, the Christians he knew were ordinary people struggling with life no matter where they were. They just had faith, to one degree or another, that trusted in Jesus and his saving work. Maybe he was not as confused as he thought.

"Hey, thanks for the message," Kars said. "Try this." He held out a thermos with a feeding tube attached. Benz shoved his arms back into his sleeves, hooked the hose to his port, and enjoyed the hot Colombian coffee.

"Wow! That's gonna keep me up all night! It's really good."

"You've had it before, I take it?"

"Yeah that girl I dated who worked at the bar in Eland. She had it all of the time."

"She got it from her other boyfriends, if I remember right." Kars smiled to himself.

"That guy was a turd," Benz said.

"Hey guys," Ally said.

"What brings you outside on such a beautiful night, Mrs. Dee?" Benz asked.

"I'm just here to help. I'm not trying to butt in to your bro-time."

"No bro time happening here, just waiting for Santa to drop some goodies off his sleigh."

Sonic booms shook the cliff, and canisters streaked out of the dark sky coming over the Tharsis Rise behind them. All six canister landers were in a full-breaking burn. The sky sizzled with the ignition and burning fuel. This was the most vulnerable part of V's plan. Sensitive seismometers would record the seismic echoes from the sonic booms along with the hard landing of the massive machines dropping onto the plain next to the Rise.

Two landers touched down first, then another, and the final three in quick succession. Their rocket engines all shut down while dust clouds formed around each of them. They were all within a square kilometer or less from the cliff face.

"You've got to get going now. Thirty-one minutes until a sat," V urged them in their Evo's speakers. Bill had just joined the trio when the booms sounded.

Each person had a bot tethered with them, and two more followed, one near Benz and the other next to Kars, as the four of them bounded off toward the dust plumes.

Inside the dark ship surrounded by Angel Warriors, V smiled with each subsequent crash of the landers in the foothills of Moe— northwest of Shepard. He managed to capture all the seismological data and change its source-code to make it appear to happen a couple hours after it actually had, and just as the group of landers crashed. V knew he could only confuse the satellite network remotely for so long before they could adjust and track the landings to the Red Zone.

"Hopefully it will be long enough." His highest priority was to supply the growing underground city.

V chuckled with a passing thought of Robin of the Hood, "I'm Robin the Hood!" V's old English accent was horrible, but he laughed anyway.

The canisters began their lay-down procedure while the team ran out to the landing zones. The four arms extended down and out from the circular body of the canister. The two longer arms were pushed away from the side of the canister, rolling on wheels on the ground and drawing the top of the canister over. The faring for the connection joint slid upward, revealing the large ball joint that allowed the canister to rotate horizontally as the top legs compressed and drew it further down. The stubby legs on the ground pushed down to take the pressure off the joint. Then, the auto-release mechanism set the lander free to roll out from beneath the canister connection. The front of the canister was designed to be coupled with the bots the team guided out.

When they arrived at each site, all the canisters had been brought to horizontal position. Kars and Benz each used their two bots to hold corners of the Shimmer blankets they had to drape over and secure to the ground with stakes. They were done in fifteen minutes and hiked off to retrieve their next canister. Ally and Bill headed to the rail spur in front of the expanded entrance tunnel with their bots towing one canister each. The bots were specialized to pull the fifty-meter canister and lower it onto the rail cradle, which was connected to the tug that pulled it on the rails into the entry tunnel and slid them into the massive airlock. The first two bots cleared out of the way, and were pointed toward the last two canisters, which hid beneath their Shimmer blankets.

All six canisters fit inside the Alpha airlock tunnel, with room for three more. They were left to warm throughout the night before being opened on the other side. After the canisters were all cleared off the landing zones, the landers powered up and zipped off to crash into a mountain on the northwestern side of Shepard.

The ground team headed out to clean up the landing zones and erase the tracks leading back to the entryway rail system before the sun rose, revealing Santa's naughty nighttime activities.

Nineteen

Sol 7662 (11 June 2048)
Argyre Basin, Mars

"I can't believe how calm you are under pressure," Ally smiled at her husband, while holding his arm with both her hands. Kars drove his repaired Hum the final fifty kilometers to Rocker N-42.

"You seem calm too. You're all smiles, considering what is happening today," Kars said sheepishly.

"I know. It's crazy. I've been praying so much about God's will and his protection over you, I think He used my prayers to calm me down too."

"You know I'm going to miss you every single second?"

"I know, but I'm going to miss you more."

"Is that even possible?"

"Yes. Absolutely." Ally squeezed his arm tighter.

"If we hurry, we'll have time for a proper goodbye." Kars kissed her head and smiled.

"I can't do goodbye, how about, a proper 'until I see you again?' Wait, how much longer do we have?" Ally knew the repairs to the Hum had cost them five hours. The breakdown could have been much longer and that would have led to disaster if Kars had missed his flight. Bill was the unsuspecting hero when he flew out a drone with the new part and saved

255

their butts. Now, the old coil and the drone were strapped down to the roof, under the Shimmer.

"At our current speed, Kars cycled through the readouts, "fifty two minutes."

"Does that get us there with enough time to do everything?"

"Yes. Should be plenty of time."

"Is that as fast as you can go?" Ally knew the answer; she toyed with the boy inside Kars's heart.

"Nope. Top speed gets me there in under forty two minutes."

"Well, what would we ever do with ten whole extra minutes, Kars Dee?"

"I've got a few ideas."

"I'll go back and get comfortable so you can concentrate on driving and thinking about those ten minutes."

"I could just put it on auto pilot and come back and join you right now."

"You could do that?" Ally asked.

"No, you can not put it on autopilot." V interrupted over the Hum's speaker system. "You won't have enough time to unload and reload everything before the pre-launch stage when all of Rocker's systems go hot for startup."

"You're such a buzz kill, V," Kars said.

"Just thinking about the mission, Kars, and only the mission."

"How do I turn you off from listening to us?" Kars asked.

"You can't."

"Well, then be forewarned. There will be some marriage type activities happening inside this Hum in forty one minutes or less. Put on some headphones, go make dinner, run on your treadmill, or do something else, cause it's gonna get rowdy up in here!"

"Yee-Haw!" Ally yelled from the Murphy bed and threw her shirt at her husband. She hit him in the back of the head. "He can't see us!" she whispered.

"I can see you if I had the camera turned on," V said.

"No, you can't— because I put tape over all four of them, for privacy reasons."

"You can't stop the woman from changing out of her dirty work clothes on Mars, V. You don't have the power to stop her from dancing while she does it either." Kars turned up an old Kane Brown country song as Ally yelled and yipped in the background, as the Hum danced over the dusty terrain.

"Eww! Overshare!" V went silent.

The final fifty clicks morphed into Kars' all-time favorite drive— on any planet.

⸎

The dirty Hum sitting just off the eastern edge of the solar farm was leased to Benz. When the fire ignited, it billowed black smoke throughout the interior. An explosion tore through the vehicle, and a black cloud billowing upward, followed closely by the nuclear reactor melting down. The fire died immediately after the oxygen tanks blew due to the ninety-eight percent carbon dioxide atmosphere, but the damage had already been done. The black mushroom cloud rose slowly above the wreck as the sun broke the horizon.

An emergency drone circled high overhead, taking radiation readings far outpacing the legal Martian safety limits. Commands were sent for the drone to sacrifice itself to investigate whether anyone was in the Hum when it blew. It found human DNA in the vapor cloud, and Benz was the only LIFT employee who had operated the vehicle over the last few weeks. His bio-metric signal gave off its emergency pulses from a melted Evo, indicating his life had come to an abrupt and violent end. The interior near the suit was splattered with dark brown frozen blood. The Federal Police officer on duty made the decision, in conjunction with a consultation with Shepard's medical examiner. They both concluded that Benz had died in the unfortunate accident. His next of kin on Earth would receive the notice within forty-eight hours and the insurance money sometime shortly thereafter. With the massive radiation leakage from the Hum's reactor, recovering the body wouldn't happen for a generation.

"Bet you've never watched yourself die before, huh?" V asked.

"No. That's a first. What do we have on the agenda for today, according to your estimation, V?"

"Well let me see, the bots completed the spray foam in Alpha last night, which means the cave needs a pressurized inspection to verify it's atmo tight. The temporary wall on the new airlock to Lake City needs to be removed after the airlock tests are completed this morning. We have to get ready to do a blade switch-out on the boring machine once it breaks into the Bluville cavern, which means a couple of bots will need to be pro-grammed for that job. The river canals need their initial drainage diagram imputed into the drill bots so they can be sent off to work on those."

"What am I going to do after lunch?" Benz laughed then the realization hit him.

"I already know what you're going to be doing," V said.

"Yeah, so do I." He remembered his buddy out on the Argyre Basin.

※

"While I get this hatch opened can you fill the air lock with the O2 bottles?"

"Yes," Ally said. "I know you're saying O2 and meaning atmo, right?"

"Yes. Sorry. No one uses straight O2 since the Apollo fire a hundred years ago."

"It was only eighty."

"Okay, smarty pants."

"I put them back on, the smart ones I mean." Ally laughed.

"You're smart with or without pants."

"Aww, you say the nicest things!"

"Can't help myself."

Kars smiled while using a piece of steel pipe to leverage the steel latch on the Rocker's hatch and had great difficulty getting it to move. He hooked his boots through the roof rail on the Hum, pulled down on the bar, and felt some movement but realized the latch bent instead of rotating. He slammed the pipe into the side of the latch and watched a plume of dust fall onto the roof of the Hum. They parked the Hum beneath Rocker N-42 to allow Kars to access the hatch without a ladder. A couple more smacks with the pipe, and the latch began to move. The steel broke free from its rusty restraints with one lunge. Kars deployed a Shimmer umbrella above the portal and moved inside the Rocker's storage bay to inspect what he had to move.

The ship's cargo was stored in color-coded and numbered bins tied down to the floor with adjustable ratchet straps. Kars hopped back through the hatch and landed on top of the Hum. With one more bounce, he was on the ground and cycling the airlock. He tossed the twenty bottles of Atmo onto the roof with the cases of supplies. "The Air lock is empty, Ally."

"I've got a couple more containers," she said.

Kars stuffed the supplies into the Rocker and climbed in, then had Ally pull the Hum forward. He emptied bins through the hatch, dropping their contents onto the barren, dusty ground below. Kars kept the bins inside until he knew how many he would need. He was also aware that he was ruining scientific studies and destroying premium Martian rock and mineral samples. Kars noticed some samples were labeled for the University of Toronto, a government lab in Halifax, Nova Scotia, and UBC-Vancouver.

"Sorry, eh?" Kars tried not to laugh. He knew this sabotage was only funny now and only to him. Some poor scientist would lose their lifelong dream of studying genuine Martian samples.

"How's it going?" Ally asked over her comm from inside the Hum.

"Almost got as much cleared out as I need."

"Let me know."

"Roger. Two minutes."

"One more package in the airlock that Benz told me to tell you that you must have with you."

"Okay." Kars was sweating, and his Evo worked extra hard to remove the condensation. "And the battery packs? Did we get those?"

"Yes, in the blue bin in the air lock."

Kars had Ally back the Hum under the Rocker again, then jumped down and emptied the airlock onto the roof. When he hopped back on top of the Hum, he detached the G-Tube they had carried out to the site and shoved it into the hatch, along with the rest of the equipment. The final package was a soft-sided duffel bag three feet long and two feet wide, marked "Experimental," with red block letters on the side and a screen-printed picture of a flying squirrel beneath the word.

"Ally, you've got to go. This thing is starting to wake up. I'm hearing pump heaters activate."

"I'm gonna miss you!" Ally said.

"I love you." Kars watched the Hum move away. The anti-tracking blowers activated, erasing the Hum's presence at the launch site.

"I love you, too. I'll see you soon." Ally turned off her mic so she could cry.

"Ally, you've got to go as fast as you can. Don't worry about covering your tracks— punch it!" V said.

"Kars you've got to hurry," V said. "This Rocker was updated with the improved heaters and you've got four minutes until launch or less. What is the temp at the launch site?"

"Outside it was minus four."

"You may only have three minutes. When the pumps pressure up, you've got two minutes."

"Get Ally clear, NOW!" Kars yelled.

"She's driving as fast as she can. I told her to forget about the anti-tracking protocol. She'll make it out past the boulder field."

"Crap! The pumps just pressured up!"

"That was fast!" V began researching another question he had.

<hr>

Lieutenant Ridge rested comfortably on his bed after his busy evening. When he opened his eyes in the morning, for a brief flash, the silky black reflection of his personal Reaper leaked out of his eyes, covering his Sclera. "What do we have planned today, my lord?" He remembered his prize from the night before and rolled over.

Fifteen minutes later, while he was in his shower, the Reaper inside him drove him out to his computer, still dripping wet. He dried his hands on the towel he had grabbed and brought the wall unit to life. Ridge watched the lead stories splash across his feed as he dried his hair.

"What am I supposed to see, Oh great leader?" he thought.

"Lieutenant Ridge, sorry sir! You gave me permission to enter." His aide was mortified and turned around at the sight.

"What are you afraid of?"

"You aren't in uniform, sir."

"What do you want?" Ridge covered himself with his towel. At this precise moment, Ridge's evening prize tiptoed out through the opened door while his aide tried to ignore her departure.

"Sir, when you gave the order for us to watch all avenues of escape from the planet, the AI flagged an anomaly out on the Argyre Basin."

"The Argyre Basin? This better be good." Ridge was immediately reminded to pay attention by his Reaper commander living inside him.

"Sir, the AI came up with an unlikely scenario in which an Automated Launch Vehicle could be used to transport items off the planet."

"Items on a Rocker?"

"Yes, sir. Contraband which could give us evidence to follow."

"Okay. When is the next Revolver due?"

"It's almost here. The AI suggests that all launches be inspected before liftoff to insure all illegal activities are contained."

"Can't we do that with drones?"

"Yes, but I need a signature on the authorization."

"Done. When are the launches?"

"Today. There are three from the Argyre Basis. One direct to Revolver Nine, the others to the Orbital foundry facility. Of course there are plenty of Rockers already lined up from the foundry that will be loading onto Revolver Nine after it makes its drops. Which could include contraband."

"Inspect the direct flight first. Can you get the drone there before it launches?"

"That will be close."

"What does the manifest say is on that Rocker?"

"It's a LIFT flight containing Canadian scientific materials. Looks like rock and mineral samples."

"See if we can get a delay from LIFT."

"We don't have a warrant."

"I know. Ask nicely. Talk to Brady and tell him it's my personal request. And I want Revolver Nine's cargo manifest and where those things are headed."

Ten minutes later, the long-range drone, number 7448, zipped off on its way to inspect Rocker N-42. A Reaper squadron shadowed the black drone out into the Martian desert.

⚬

"You've got to get out of your Evo, they aren't meant for the deep space. Your spacesuit is in bin number three."

"I don't have time, V!"

"Your Evo could be compromised, plus I know you don't have the proper G-force clamps for launch."

"What do you want me to do? If I deploy a Bubble inside this launcher and we take off before I am suited up, I'm screwed."

"Why?"

"Because I don't have everything put away yet. The O2 bottles have got to go in bins or I could be in trouble."

"Yes— get them stowed now. Then we'll see where we are with time. GO!" V said.

Kars picked up as many stainless steel canisters as possible and stuffed them into an empty rock bin. Benz's unique duffel bag with the flying squirrel was at his feet, so he stuck it in a different bin. He then grabbed six more O2s before he got a sixty-second countdown clock displayed on his visor. The final O2 bottles were stored, and the three bins got ratcheted down with twenty-nine seconds left until lift off.

"The Hatch!" V texted. "It needs to be tightened to hold down the safety sensor."

"Can you override?"

"Negative. Critical safety check is cycling through right now and it will abort the launch."

Kars tried to tighten the hatch from the inside, but he had bent the steel handle and there was a small gap in the seal which wouldn't hold the safety sensor in it's closed position for launch.

"Now what? It's bent!" Kars voice texted V.

"I'm trying to override... Nope can't do it from here. Can you take the sensor off and connect the wires together?"

"MY tool bag is strapped in already."

"Five seconds!"

Kars took a deep breath and pushed hard to hold the hatch tight against the seal.

"Green! Green light. You are go for launch, Kars!"

⸻◦⸻

The pictures the drone transmitted back to Federal Police Headquarters showed a typical Martian landscape racing beneath the flight path. The drone pilot knew he would not have enough power to return the drone to the station due to the constant camera usage and uploading of the live video feed over the satellite network. He knew he'd have to fly another long-range drone to retrieve it.

Lieutenant Ridge strode into the room and watched over the pilot's shoulder.

"How's it going, pilot?"

"Good, sir. Should be just one more rise before we get a look at the Rocker."

Ridge said nothing as he ran his fingers through his hair. His Reaper smiled like a child at the sight of his own birthday cake.

———◆◇◆———

The five Reapers trailing the drone received orders from Ridge's master to disable the Rocker as it blasted off.

———◆◇◆———

"Bigs, go transparent up one over the Rocker. An inbound Reaper squad just blipped active on my screen."

"On it! This leaves Ally vulnerable, Captain Helek." Bigs said while pumping his wings with all his might.

"I am aware. Nothing I can do right now. Ready Squad is making the shift."

———◆◇◆———

"Ten."

Kars jumped over and grabbed a screwdriver out of the side pocket of his LIFT tool kit, and jumped back to the hatch. He stuffed the flat blade between the latch and the bent metal catch and drove the plastic end in as hard as he could with his hand.

"Six."

Kars hooked one of his carabiner's to a strap connected to a tie-down hook, and then he tried to lie down flat with his back on the floor. Not all of the bins were strapped down, but his time was up.

------◄O►------

The Reaper Squad dove with a single focus toward Rocker N-42. The weather in the area was calm except for the tiny plume of dust from a retreating Hum off in the distance. The Squad leader knew they only had to nudge the Rocker over and, at the same time, strike the guidance system with a jolt of energy. Then, the ship would turn over and crash into the flat, dusty basin terrain. The crash would be written off by LIFT, and the Canadian science team would chalk it up to the cost of doing research a whole world away.

------◄O►------

"Dusted three of them, two are headed to you, Cap!"

Captain Helek wedged his way out of the interior of the Rocker through the metal skin exiting on the south side of the ship to intercept the remaining enemy. Reaper screams above him, piercing the thin Martian air made the hair on the back of his neck stand in attention. He drew his sword as his eyes flashed red, then jumped toward the inbound pair. Bigs was above the Reapers descending on them but knew it would not be enough to stop them before they got to the Rocker.

------◄O►------

"Four."

"You got this," V said. "Praying for you."

"Four seconds, Ally," V said. Ally swung the Hum hard to the left so she could watch her husband lift off.

—◆◇◆—

The high-speed drone cleared the rise and sent back a video feed of a normal Rocker off-gassing propellant in preparation for launch.

"What is all that crap underneath the ship? Can you zoom in?" Ridge asked.

"No zoom feature on the live feed— but I can get close," the pilot said.

"What the heck is that?"

—◆◇◆—

Captain Helek was not the fastest Angel Warrior with the sword. He misjudged the speed of the closest incoming Reaper and swung hard but behind the streaking devil. Bigs caught the lead Reaper by the foot as it reached for the tip of the Rocker. The Reaper nudged the ship as planned, just a few feet up in the air, then was bisected by Bigs. The dead Reaper crashed into the ground, followed immediately by Bigs, who snapped his left wing in two with the impact and rolled away from the rocket blast. Helek moved his sword and dusted the final Reaper just as it sent out the electrical charge to kill the Rocker's guidance computer. The high-voltage electrical charge was absorbed by Helek's sword, causing it to glow bright yellow and become as hot as the sun, burning the Angel Warrior's hand and causing the sword to drop to the ground.

—◆◇◆—

The picture from the drone was grainy as the rotating blades kicked up dust and covered the very things Ridge tried to see.

"Do we know when this thing is supposed to take off?" Ridge asked as the rocket motors came alive, driving the drone into the ground. The feed went dead as the drone melted in the heat of the rocket exhaust. Then, to put an exclamation point on the end of the drone's life, an electrified Angel Warrior sword crossed into the physical realm and slammed through the top of the drone, piercing the melting vehicle clear through and pinning it to the ground.

———◄O►———

As the Rocker's engines burst to life, they pushed two giant plumes of dust away from the ship. The vessel shimmed and wobbled a couple meters off the ground. Still, the guidance computer adjusted the gimbal vector control on the port motor, momentarily redirecting the thrust to alleviate any further distortion.

Inside N-42, Kars was slammed hard against the floor with the roar of rockets. His Evo detected the extreme thrust and sent the command to tighten the bags around his legs to the maximum— in an attempt to hold his blood up in his torso. His abs bags inflated in the next split second in response to the sudden G-force pinning him motionless to the floor. The Rocker shook violently as Kars lost consciousness, his body unmovable against the nine-G ride.

His suit did its best to keep his blood in his torso and brain, but the acceleration was too much. An alarm sounded off in the distance— just beyond Kars' consciousness. His primal thoughts were stirred against its maniacal screeching. "Stop," he said inside his head to no one.

With the second command, "Stop!" Kars was awake. His body felt like it weighed ten thousand pounds. Everything continued to shake, but the noise level inside the hold had fallen off. He didn't know how long he was out until "93 seconds" scrolled across the inside of his visor, followed by, "Get up!" that V had typed.

All calculations about weight removal from the Rocker before launch and its corresponding replacement weight had been a guessing game at best. Kars activated his visor's controls to show projected telemetry while he activated a few buttons with his eyes.

"Shit! I'm not going to make the Revolver!"

"I can help you. I can intercept with your position in thirty minutes," V texted.

"No! You've got to save the cave! Save the cave, V! That's your prime objective! I am expendable. Ally needs the cave." Kars said in his voice-to-text mode.

"What am I supposed to tell Ally?"

"Tell her I love her."

Kars' head swirled as the G-forces began to drop off.

"You can make Fueler 177," V texted. "I can redirect with retro burns. But you will have to do an EVA. You will need to grapple the Rocker to the Fueler for the final leg of the trip to Revolver Nine."

Seven minutes later, Kars pulled his trusty screwdriver from the latch and yanked himself through the hatch. He fastened his umbilical cord to the Rocker's docking railing as the pale red of Mars filled his rearward camera view. Kars turned to check whether the Fueler raced past the image of the planet behind him. He figured the only way to connect with Fueler 177 would be to hook onto one of the docking rails of the robot spaceship.

"I can't see it."

He could not abandon the Rocker— he had to secure it to the Fueler and then use that ship to give him a lift to Revolver Nine. The only cable he found was fifty meters long, with hooks and a snap latch. V informed him that his Fueler moved six feet a second faster than he was, so he had one chance to hook on. Kars attached his carabiner to the cable he needed to throw it onto the Fueler. The other end had to loop around the Rocker's docking rail back onto the cable. All of the Revolver mated ships in the fleet had four universal docking rails running the length of each vessel, equidistant from each other. Those rails enabled speedy egress and access to the transport ships.

"There it is!" Kars said when the white and red floating tank came into view from the heart of the Martian equator. It seemed to head right for him.

"It looks like it's going to hit me, V!"

"Nope, but it will end up dangerously close to your port side."

"Crap." Kars pushed off to round the Rocker but was yanked back by his umbilical cord connected to the rail of the Rocker. He disconnected his safety cord and headed to port. Before he could reconnect to the Rocker, the Fueler loomed large. Grunting, he tossed the cable, and the hook clanked off the side of the Fueler. Kars yanked it back and retried his toss, focusing on the docking rail that ran the length of the massive tanker. The hook missed the rail and hit the tank, but with a quick tug on the cable, the hook snapped around the rail and pulled the cable across Kars's suit gloves with a buzz. He reached down and hooked his umbilical to the cable. Kars then looked at the cable's hook, unsure if it would hold up against the sudden yank of tension from the much larger craft. Kars jammed his boots beneath the railing of his Rocker and began pulling on the end connected to the Fueler— trying desperately to increase the speed of his own little ship before the cable pulled taunt as the cable slipped through his gloves. He had five seconds to make a difference.

The sudden crash of the tightened cable shook Kars off the Rocker. His umbilical cord connection to the cable allowed him to grab onto the steel rope as he is flipped around. He would have been thrown off the Rocker if he had failed to connect his cord. The Rocker's rail bent toward the Fueler, ripping several mounting brackets off. Other bolts and clamps securing the railing sheered off and flew into space. However, the railing absorbed the impact— even though it was a twisted mess. The Fueler's railing was also bent outward and back toward the stern. Its trajectory was altered by the sudden gain in mass from the Rocker. The Fueler's thrusters automatically ignited to adjust its course and reconnect its laser sighting system to the invisible Revolver Nine, which was thousands of miles ahead. When the thrusters burned, they tightened the cable line with the Rocker, and the forward tug slammed the Rocker into the side of the Fueler's hull. More thruster burns and more banging and rattling reverberate through both ships.

Kars jumped into action, sliding down the cable toward the stern of the Rocker, which was against the starboard tank. He used a ratchet strap he brought from the vehicle's hold to bind the two ships together around undamaged sections of railing. Kars retrieved a second strap and finished the tie-down process, then allowed himself to breathe a sigh of relief.

"V, Rocker is tied down."

"Awesome. We were holding our breath!"

"And praying something fierce!" Ally texted.

"Well, I sure appreciate the prayers," Kars said.

"I was busy sending good vibes." V also sent a laughing emoji.

"Good vibes, the essence of doing virtually nothing and making yourself feel better for it, somebody somewhere said that," Kars added.

"I think I'd just rather ask the King of the Universe for help," Ally said.

"Hey, if I borrow a couple of solar panels from this Fueler, it's not gonna matter, right?" Kars asked.

"Should be fine while it's burning toward the Revolver. Plus if you are only talking two panels they won't even notice a voltage difference. I think. What do you want them for?"

"I've got a slight issue with my suit. I'm going to grab a couple and then go back inside N-42 to repair my Evo."

"You've got enough time to change out suits."

"No. I've only got a couple of minutes of power left." Kars's communication went dead.

"N-42 report."

No reply.

"N-42 report," V said.

Twenty

12 June 2048 (SOL 7663)
Teapot Key, Florida

"We have visual confirmation that a new cave system has been discovered. We have some footage sent to the secondary account. Of course there are crazy rumors all over the underground network about caves with rivers and lakes," Bill said over the secure satellite link connected through V's spaceship

"And roads paved with gold, no doubt." Nan winked at Connie.

"Yes, the largest cavern is called Alpha, and it is the most massive cave found to date on Mars. It has S/F and Atmo and airlocks."

"Is it still beneath the radar?"

"Yes. As far as we can tell."

"Good news. I think Santa will be in favor."

Of course, the Bees had known about the discovery for almost two weeks from their meeting with Doc. The update on the spray foam, atmosphere, and airlocks being up and running was such welcomed news. The girls were also aware that the first three canisters of refugees were packed in gel and sleeping through their first twelve days on their ride up on Rocker Twelve. They would arrive in a little over three months because the ever-changing cycle of orbits pulled the planets further from one another, each subsequent Revolver trip would take longer than the previous— for the next year.

"I'm afraid we've got some bad news. Benz has been killed in a Hum accident. An apparent reactor melt down."

"That's horrible. I know a few people who will take this news hard."

"The Gestapo is putting eyes all over for him and his sidekick, who is currently missing."

"Missing?" Connie stood up.

"Yes, ma'am. As of now, he has been absent for several days. We should have news soon. His Hum is scheduled to RTB tomorrow," Bill said.

"And is it returning?"

"They're OFS."

"Roger." Connie was aware of the Return To Base acronym but not the other, and she looked to Larry, who whispered, "Operating at Full Stealth."

"So, we are a go with toys?"

"Yes. Full go."

After the meeting, Connie sauntered toward the ocean, Nan followed with their special umbrella, which covered both sisters. This particular Shimmer umbrella also scrambled audio signals, so nothing could be recorded from a long-distance mic deployed on any government drone submarine offshore or one high in the sky.

"Father, we lift up the folks making the crossing right now. We pray that you'd lead them home in safety and the security of knowing you. I pray for Benz's family, that you in your mercy would bring them comfort in their trial. Surround them with your angels, fill them with your Spirit, and whisper peace into their hurting souls right now."

"Amen. And the one we are hurting for, Lord. We know you have plans for him and we chose to trust you right now, even without knowing what you are doing," Nan prayed.

"Hang on, kid. Hang on." Connie wiped at her new tears.

"Amen. Let's go look at the new cave pictures, while God does his whole ruling the universe thing."

"Yeah, I'll be giving up my control of the galaxy for a few minutes."

"Good." Nan pressed in close to her sister.

"Did they say how they found the cave, or who made the discovery?"

"Not that I know of."

⸻◆⸻

The gurgling, choking, and coughing were dead giveaways to the agony taking place. The grainy video feed was dark except for the white emaciated body tied to a bench. The body convulsed in response to an ice water bath. The bruises and cuts all over her torso spoke to the torture she had endured beyond the immediate waterboarding session.

"You know what is happening on Mars. You have all of the connections. You are the famous Terrorist Princess! This pain can stop anytime you want. We will get you a warm bed and three hot meals if you cooperate. You are the only reason these lessons have taken so long." The Global Union Major was just off-camera.

"I don't know anything, and not telling me was done on purpose, so you couldn't drag anything out of me."

"But you can make some interesting assumptions that could help us."

"Not helping, yo... you. You are evil and I would rather di... die." Bry's body convulsed to create some warmth.

"You will die very slowly after you tell us everything you know."

"You're going to kill me, so why would I tell a peace-loving Global Union Major anything?"

The Major became unhinged and kicked the bench over with a primal scream. The video feed recorded the crash. The sickening sound of Bry's humerus bone snapping in two echoed off the slimy basement walls.

<hr>

Kars clambered through the hatch of Rocker N-42. He replaced his screwdriver to seal the door with a bang and deployed a Bubble completely over his Evo. The tricky part was forcing the Bubble to slide down his legs and enclose his boots before sealing. He parked his tool bag on top of his feet so he would have access. His suit was damaged, a direct short in a sub-system, draining the batteries fast. When he removed his helmet to the freezing atmo of the Bubble, he tried to repair it by sliding the top of his Evo down to inspect for the damage. His systems check told him it was located on the left, toward the back. With his shoulders out of the helmet hole, he attempted to spin the suit and check through the bunched-up materials.

There it was, a rip in the outer fabric twelve centimeters long. Several wires were frayed and glowing hot from the short circuit.

While Kars worked the repair, the rear end of Fueler 117 spun on its central axis to regulate the temperatures of the four gigantic fuel tanks. This action brought the Rocker in and out of direct exposure to the sun every couple of minutes. So Kars's spaceship went from freezing at minus two hundred degrees Celsius to plus two hundred degrees Celsius during every rotation. His Rocker had enough insulation to handle the temperature fluctuation, but its metal skin protested the cycle. With the hatch closed, the Bubble's atmosphere began to warm up— reaching a toasty one hundred below zero.

After every minute that passed, Kars shoved his hands inside his suit to get the blood flowing again. Making precise electrical repairs in this situation was next to impossible. His suit ran out of power and flashed its shut-down lights. Kars grabbed his headlamp, blew on his hands, and slapped them together before flooding his Bubble with white light. He cut the wires and clamped them with Martian-rated connectors. It was a stopgap until he could get into his new suit in bin number something. He decided to worry about that when he owned a few more minutes in this life.

The electrical tape and cold glue for his suit resealed the components into a lump of vacuum-rated rubber sealant.

"Thanks LIFT."

His hands began to freeze so he took a minute to held his fingers inside his mouth.

Ice formed from condensation inside the Bubble. He had no idea how long that could go on without causing depressurization.

The battery pack inside his tool bag was brand new. The old unit, still warm from the sudden loss of power due to the short, felt good on his fingers. The new battery was stone cold and would not have much charge, so Kars strapped it together with the warm battery, and stuck it down his pants to warm the exposed side. He nearly froze some skin on his belly in the process. While he waited for the battery pack to warm, he attached an electrical connection port and let it dangle outside his suit. He reached in and rubbed the battery pack. He needed enough power to start his suit systems. The atmo was the primary system and needed a five percent charge to reach start-up mode.

He shivered against the cold, knowing he was running out of time to control his body, even with the Bubble. He tried to slide the pack into position but missed the compartment. The pack dropped onto the floor of the Rocker. He was afraid it would rip the thin skin of the Bubble. He could not reach the ground without falling over on his helmet, which was on top of his tool bag on top of his feet.

"This is so stupid!"

Kars stretched for his pliers in the side pocket of his tool bag, then tried to hold them steady enough to grab the wire assembly from the battery pack. On his third attempt, he snatched the plastic clip end of the wire and pulled the pack up to his hand. He guided the next effort into the battery compartment and snapped the connection wire together. He stuffed the pliers in his outside elastic holder on his thigh, pulled his suit over his shoulders, and stuck his hands down the sleeves while releasing the hands-free catch. Kars began his dust-clearing ritual when he realized he was in outer space without the ever-present curse of Martian dust and sealed it shut. A few seconds later he latched his helmet.

His suit hesitated after pushing the initial internal power button with his chin against his shoulder.

"Okay, Lord, I need you right now to help me in this mess. Please."

His prayer was answered with silence for the next two seconds, before his visor monitor came to life while the computers ran their system diagnostic programs. His display indicated a seven percent charge with his brand-new battery pack. When ripped through his Bubble with his great grandfather's K-Bar the atmo popped inside the hull of the Rocker with a dull thud.

The solar panels he had gleaned off the Fueler stood behind him. A few zip ties later, he connected them to make two daisy-chained ropes, which he would use to hang the panels from his shoulders like an old-style bi-folded sandwich board sign. He needed a few more ties to get his big helmet through, then cinched the sides as tight as he could. It would have to do until he could charge his suit. Kars plugged in the electrical connection to the external plug he had wired up a few minutes before.

Kars opened the hatch and carefully guided his new charging system through the portal, then activated his mag boots so he could stand facing the sun. However, he quickly found out he would have to continue circumnavigating the spaceship to remain in the sun for the full effect of the photovoltaic panel, which converted distant sunlight into electrical energy to charge his battery.

After twenty revolutions, Kars's suit comm returned online.

"Control, copy?"

No reply.

"Control, do you copy?"

"Copy! Yeah, I copy. Welcome back! This is great news," V said.

"You won't believe me when I tell you what I had to do."

"At this point, it doesn't matter, I'm glad your back!"

Kars used the camera on the back of his hand to take a shot of himself clumping around the Rocker before stepping over onto the Fueler again to stay in the light.

"What is that?"

"That's what happens when you short out your Evo battery."

"No way! Oh my gosh! Classic Kars!"

"What are you saying?"

"You wreck stuff. Always have."

"I've been known to wreck a few things, but now I can fix them too."

"So glad we didn't lose you, buddy."

"Copy that."

"Hey, for real, I intercepted something you need to see."

Kars watched the clip of his sister enduring another torture session. He turned off his mic and screamed as loud as he could. He stood still for three rotations before he began walking again. He needed his batteries fully charged.

"Now!"

When Kars's helmet speaker crackled to life with a single word, he shoved off as hard as he could from the Fueler. He held onto Rocker's docking rail as his ship separated from its ride. The Fueler was on final approach to Revolver Nine. Kars attempted to make it appear that his Rocker had powered up next to the gigantic Revolver in the shadow of the Fueler. Rocker N-42 sent out its anticipated electronic docking ping to the Revolver's computer guidance system, startling the officer in charge so much that he spilled his coffee on his uniform.

"What the hell? Where did that Rocker come from?" he asked his underling.

"No clue, sir."

"Who is it?"

"The ping IDs it as Rocker N-42."

"Why's it so late?"

"Not sure, sir."

"Better take a look."

The loadmaster brought the cameras out of their sleep to visually inspect the arriving ship.

"She seems fine..., whoa! Check that railing!" For a second it looked as if a dark figure moved out of camera range around the far side of the Rocker. The loadmaster could not verbalize that fear out loud— his boss would assume he'd been hitting the sauce again. It must have been a weird shadow cast through the mangled railing.

"The hull has been slammed around too, Lieutenant."

"Run an inspection drone around her before we grab on."

"Roger." He gave the command to launch the inspection drone from its bay on the opposite side of the ship to have a close look for any fuel leakage before the massive transport ship committed to taking her aboard. If there was leakage in the propulsion system, safety protocols would not allow the Rocker to be loaded. She would be left for a salvage crew to figure out its issues before sending it Earthbound or back to Mars.

The drone quickly worked on the Rocker and found no fuel leaks.

"She's banged up, but no real trouble here, sir. It appears it got tangled up with the Fueler en route."

"What leads you to that conclusion?"

"The Fueler has a mangled railing and dents on one of her tanks."

"There are no leaks on the Fueler, right?" Knowing how devastating that situation could be, the officer's fear kicked in.

"None, sir."

"Good. Put the Rocker to bed so we can get the fuel transferred."

"On it."

"The seal was on the hatch of the Rocker, right?"

"Yes, I saw it shining in the darkness." He lied but quickly rewound the video feed to make sure he remembered what he thought he saw. He also checked to see if something or someone had dashed into the shadows.

"Get it stowed away. I'm going to change my shirt."

"Aye." The master of Revolver Nine loading operations sent the capture command to the mobile crane. It slid down the exoskeleton of the Revolver, grabbed onto the Rocker, and placed it in storage bin 27E, where the docking clamps secured the load by locking themselves around two good rails for the long ride to Earth. The mangled railing was left mindlessly waving its goodbye to the bleakness of deep space.

Inside the beat-up LIFT, Kars held his breath and hung on as he heard the inspection drone hook on for a systems check. He thanked God he had remembered to re-hook the load seal onto the arm of the latch. Even though it wasn't actually hooked through both sides of the locking mechanism, he was certain it would pass an initial eye test.

The crane tossed the ship around and put it to bed, with docking clamps securing it for the ride. The Fueler clanked into place a couple seconds later, casting its long shadow over N-42 while filling Revolver Nine's fuel tanks
.

As he strapped his Evo in for the night, Kars could hardly believe how his day had turned out. He pulled his arms inside, expanded the torso, and searched for something to eat in the food pocket, which held a meal bag from the storage bin. The food pocket could be accessed by both the exterior and interior of the suit. While in expanded mode, it exposed a small airlock access for supplies to be pulled inside the suit. The interior lights and music he played allowed him to escape from reality, except for his sweaty body stink wafting up from his gross neither regions. Despite the smell, Kars was incredibly grateful to God and asked Him to protect his wife, sister, Gigi, and friends as he munched some food, then drifted off to sleep.

⏤◆⏤

"Everyone calls him Foot."

"I don't care what they call him, hunt him down and bring him in for questioning." Ridge's face was bright red.

"Sir, what legal authority do we have?"

"Someone blew up a damn train and I want answers!"

"The duty officer here in Shepard says he needs a warrant to bring his employee off the job just to answer questions that should have already been asked."

"Let me talk to him!"

"He said he can call you back, Lieutenant."

Ten minutes later, Ridge's comm came to life.

"Ridge."

"Lieutenant, what do you need?" the annoyed duty officer asked.

"I want to talk to Foot."

"This was the guy who was wounded on the train blast and now all of a sudden you need to talk to him again?" said the man.

"Listen, I am coming down there with an arrest warrant for you for obstruction of a Federal Police investigation unless you get Foot into an interview room right now!

"Okay. Okay. We'll bring him in."

Ridge slammed his comm onto his desk.

"Any clues on Mr. Dees whereabouts?" Ridge asked his aide.

"Like a fart in the wind, Lieutenant."

"It's like he ceased to exist. I wonder if somebody offed him because he knew something?" Ridge said.

"That's the only thing that makes sense to me. His eyes got so big when we slapped him around a little bit, we knew he wasn't going anywhere."

"We may have underestimated him."

"I don't know, I thought he would wet his pants."

"Get this Foot character in the room and keep your eyes open," Ridge demanded.

━━━━◄O►━━━━

SOL 7664 (13 June 2048)

Revolver Nine's 13th Cycle, down-bound to Earth.

In the morning, Kars had a copy of the ship's manifest on his helmet display, which included the contents of every vehicle Revolver Nine carried back to Earth. The bin numbers were indicated, making his hunting excursions much more targeted.

Kars read up on the crew rotations with all their details down to the berths each member was assigned. Half the crew would be put into their hibernation pods in another couple of days, leaving six team members to run the entire ship, which was four hundred eighty-seven meters long. Only two people were on duty in the central Control Module (or CM), leaving the remaining four to live in the rotating Crew Pod (or CP). The two-person teams served a twenty-four-hour shift and forty-eight hours of time off. The ship piloted itself on its programmed course, established before every rotation to Mars. Each Control Modules (CM) was its own spaceship which was docked onto the much larger CP. The Control Modules were the ships that rotated out Revolver command teams. Most of those teams held younger members since the retirement qualification for LIFT Revolver crews was ten cycles. If you could endure ten trips to and from Mars, you earned yourself a house in a Bahamian beach resort for the rest of your life. A few people tried to double up to get full pay on top of the house, but that required twenty trips— a feat yet to be accomplished.

Kars needed the ability to travel up and down the ship's spine to hunt for supplies without worry. All ships being carried back to Earth had electrical and information connections to the Revolver; some had air lock-enabled connections into the spine. Kars opened a video from V about Revolver Nine.

"If you remove all of the stuff off a Revolver, they are a simple ship. A fifteen hundred foot spine with a Quad Ion Pulse Drive engines on the back, the CP stuck on the front end with a CM docked out front of the CP," V's recording said. "Everything else is clamped onto the rails of the spine including the access shaft up the center. That shaft has air locks every hundred yards but those locks are controlled in the CM. Of course they can be overridden but the computer alerts the crew to the activity. The best access points for you will be the six ships that have external air locks you can cycle in without triggering an alarm. They could get the information but no one would ever expect to be boarded in such a manner."

The video continued, "After half the crew goes to bed for their long nap, you are going to have to disable some of the video feeds to get around. Each crane has cameras to aide in the loading and unloading process and these are not in use during transit. But there are cameras on the elbows of the crane that give a good perspective down the ship and these are left on in sleep mode but they respond to movement. There are Cameras up and down the spine that can be controlled remotely from the CM if there is a need. They are part of an instrument cluster on every airlock. You'll need your cold weather sleeve for your Evo in bin number two to wear. It's black and will help you hide. You will have to figure out how to disable the cameras. They will send out crew members to fix or replace them because the crews are mandated to keep watch over their load. A Floater does a visual inspection once a week walking the spine and are required to check every clamp, electrical connection, and airlock."

The video stopped. Kars already had an idea from his rail working days, plus Ally used it in the Hum. Duct tape. The stuff covered lenses but still allowed the other sensors to function normally. Since it blacked the camera out, the lens had no movement to stir the motion detectors. At the same time, the cluster could still measure radiation, monitor for fuel leaks, and measure rattle factors for loose loads.

Kars pulled up the map image on his monitor and began making mental notes of where he wanted to explore. He tried to comprehend ninety days in his Evo, and quickly, he decided to find his new suit and try to figure out how he could change out of his already smelly Evo in a ship without atmo.

SOL 7664 (13 June 2048)

Alpha, Mars

"Hey Benz, how goes the building?" Bill asked.

"The printers are doing great, they are over-performing. Like I've already said a hundred times, we need more supplies."

"Yep. It's our highest priority right now. We've got some coming from Brahman tomorrow but we have to transfer it to a Tram first."

Benz knew that method all too well. Unloading the chemicals from a train car with a pump to a tram-towing tanker and driving it twenty clicks north from the railway had to happen during daylight so there would not be any freezing issues with the load.

"What about the Chinese?"

"We are trying, they always want to keep everything above board on the financial side of things."

"The money is real, right?"

"Of course."

"I don't understand the problem."

"I think it's a cultural thing. They don't even want the appearance of impropriety."

"There's a lot of impropriety in Xing," Benz said.

"True. How is the progress?" Bill asked.

"We are entering the final stages on ten temporary shelters in the central section. You can see the bots are busy building the mezzanines on both sides of the main avenue. Those structures will need human workers to finish them out. The architect is finalizing designs for the cubes inside those areas. The drill bots will finish the water line from Trippy City so the pond can begin to get filled tomorrow," Benz said.

"I thought that was a lake?"

"It is, I just call it the pond after seeing what's happening up in Lake City."

"Yeah, that is going to be incredible. Kars will love it when he gets back. We have to figure out how to get some fish up here."

"That would be awesome."

"I can't believe he's out looking for more caves," Bill said.

"That's his personality, he likes discovering things and leave the details to the rest of us."

"Strange."

Benz almost spilled the beans on his best buddy and chastised himself for the slip.

"When is the atmo test complete?" Bill asked.

"Looks like less than an hour," Benz said. "We could be walking around without our suits by noon."

"That's what we all want."

"It's what we all need. That and a bath in that pond!"

"Now you're talking!"

"I'm really looking forward for the pipe to start delivering water to the river and watching it run downhill to the pond."

"Yes, and walking bare foot in the sand." Bill paused to consider the dream.

"I appreciate all the hard work you are pouring into this place, Benz. Everyone does."

"I need some more bodies."

"I know. We are vetting some more today in Eland. Maybe in the next few days."

"I've got canisters stacked up in the Russian section and more are to arrive tonight with nowhere to put them."

"There are so many people on the way now."

"It's that now— but not yet thing, the pastor talked about on Sunday."

"Kinda just like it."

"Everyone is praying."

Ally told me the bombing investigation is getting intense," Benz said.

"Yeah, Ridge is trampling over everyone's civil rights trying to find someone to blame."

"That guy is evil. I think Ally is going to stay here while Kars is off cave hunting."

"Yeah, she is."

"Can't blame her for avoiding the Ridge rage."

"He's gunning for us."

Twenty-One

Sol 7748 (4 September 2048)
Revolver Nine's 13th cycle, near Earth's moon.

Kars was exhausted. He had broken into the CP again the night before. Wearing his black space suit skin for this break-in. He had managed to close the outer door of the airlock and pressurize it, which began its rotation to match the CP. This nearly made Kars puke the first time he engaged it, feeling like he'd tumbled in a clothes dryer. But when he focused on removing panel twelve with his tools, he finished the process without getting sick. So he was able to shimmy through the maintenance tube. Panel twelve was a maintenance-rated panel designed to allow people to troubleshoot the airlock from a pressurized side, whether or not the lock held pressure— which meant the panel was built to close from the inside. The airlock storage tanks, pumps, and filters were only accessible from inside the portal. The trick was getting the inner panel door to align with the access tunnel once the dryer was up to speed with the CP. Kars replaced the screws with twisting snap clips, which meant he now had quick access to the panel and the area beyond.

Behind the airlock equipment was a standard connection ramp to the crew hibernation hardware. The hum of the individual cryogenic pumps and the dim green indicator lights made the space feel claustrophobic for Kars. This had been a growing feeling for a couple of weeks. He knew it was an internal check in his psyche, which rebelled against the loneliness of long-distance space travel confined inside his space suit. He almost lost his mind before he could finally change out of his Evo. The septic system in that suit had frozen up, and the stench from just from wearing it gagged him.

In a dream, he used a bottle of atmo to pressurize the specialized heated Rocker transporting temperature-sensitive cargo back to Earth.

The following day, Kars broke in and released the pressure of an atmo bottle into the hold. Its contents pressurized the area to thirty percent atmosphere. It worked— enough. Kars slimmed out of his Evo to take a sponge bath. He unplugged his sewage system on the old suit, nearly puking. After dressing in clean clothes for the first time since leaving Mars, he fell asleep on the floor. Hours later, he was startled back to reality by an O2 alarm sounding, which forced him out of his vacation and inside his new suit. The bath and clean smell of his new digs reinvigorated him. He dragged the corpse of his old Evo back to his Rocker, where he told himself he would finish working on it later. He dropped it on the floor behind the pallets. The new burst of energy was short-lived. He longed to stay in his new heated space to sleep, but he needed to find a CO2 scrubber to live long-term in that new Rocker.

Early on, Kars made a calendar on the inside of the hull of his original Rocker, marking it off each day just before falling asleep. That worked against him psychologically because he became fixated on how long he had left to go, which depressed him. In time, he realized that once a week was a good rate to mark off and not go crazy with anticipation.

Another factor in his psychological slide was the fact he had only received an email from V when he could locate a direct link to his ship, and V had to forward mail from Ally. V's rocket was still in a geosynchronous orbit above Alpha. Most days, Kars had no access to a line-of-sight laser connection and had even gone as long as twelve days between communications. This mission had become more complicated than he could have imagined. His heart ached for his wife, and he found himself reminiscing and looking at her picture for hours while he was supposed to be sleeping. The only thing keeping him from turning himself into the commander of Revolver Nine was the life sentence for piracy he was sure to receive and the punishment he would have to serve out in the Lunar Prison colony, slaving in a mine locked away from everyone. That, plus his continual watching of his sister's torture video, kept him on the secret side of this mission, hiding behind thin walls and sneaking into each of the ships that were tied off to Revolver Nine.

Kars also tried to keep his sanity by messing with the crew during the flight. So much so that they referred to his aberration as the Phantom in off hour conversations in the CP. Kars spent a lot of time listening to people from behind the panels. Of course, he thought he would pass out the first time he experienced the gravitational pull of the CP, which was seventy percent Earth. Thirteen years away from his home world made it hard to adjust back to the gravity he grew up in. Even at seven-tenths of actual, it was almost twice the rate of Mars.

Kars did not take long to figure out how to raid the food stores inside the ship, stealing food from the storage bins in the hold behind the kitchen. He disconnected the bins, took what he wanted, and then reconnected them. They were none the wiser because the computer only counted the food that was processed through the distribution machine. He located the spare microwave oven and lugged it to his commandeered Rocker, number A27— the one with heat, to warm up his contraband food.

After installing a spare CO2 scrubber, he spent most of his hours awake living in the new Rocker, hoping no one would look at the power consumption for his heated home away from home. He had also spliced his way into the video feed from the access tunnel in the spine, so he was aware when crew members ventured outside to do their weekly checks.

During those days, just getting out of his suit became his goal for every minute of his day. His skin began healing from the sores he had developed from his dirty Evo life. He covered the glass portal from the inside with black plastic. The window allowed people to see directly into the Rocker from the connection tube in the spine. He placed the plastic in the Rocker's airlock door. Kars attached remote-controlled magnetic locks to the inside of the airlock to keep unwanted visitors from breaking in for a few minutes. He had quick access to the outer airlock on the opposite side of the Rocker, where he always kept the inner door open and his suit ready.

On many lonely nights, he found himself outside, walking up the long line of loaded ships and making his way to the CP. During those late-night ventures, he always stole a look at the beautiful growing blue marble beyond the ship or the shrinking red dot behind it. But, he could not look for too long, or his loneliness would soar to unbearable levels. While on the Revolver, his coping mechanism had become one of avoiding thinking about what he had left on Mars or what he was moving toward on Earth. He tried hard to stay present and keep a disciplined, mission-minded attitude. Still, sometimes, usually at night, he got tired of the grind. Remembering what was at stake for his sister and millions of others trapped behind the lie of the Global Union focused him and brought him into a better mindset.

The four ships docked next to the CP airlock were loaded with supplies for the crew during the trip. He accessed the outer airlock on supply ship three. Then he held a black blanket in front of himself, holding it over the access tunnel camera as he crept past and into the lock of the CP. Breaking in had become too easy with the complacent crew, but the sheer excitement for Kars was addictive.

Having figured out the shortcut behind panel twelve, Kars discovered that no one entered the Hibernation room where the pods were kept. The crew viewed this as an unlucky invasion of privacy, plus their vital signs were on a monitor outside the door. Kars crawled through the access panel below the beds, but he could only manage it without his space suit. So, he regularly left his suit in the maintenance section behind the airlock and hibernation pod, then slithered through the panel so he could listen through the door for the people who may be talking close by.

Kars spent time studying the people in the pods. Four men and two women were the sleeping part of the crew, held in a perpetual dream-like state. He was fascinated with the regular body activity inside the pods. Hands flexed and moved against their restraints. Lips moved against the ventilator. Eyes rotated below their lids. Whiskers grew, as did finger and toenails. Facial muscles moved in response to dream-induced impulses meant to reduce the recovery time after a stint in the pod. The same was true in the arms, legs, and feet. Kars found himself wondering who these people were and what their lives were like outside of their plastic prison.

⬥

Sol 7748 (4 September 2048)

Alpha, Mars

Ally Dees sat next to the New River in Alpha. This narrow, slow-moving trail of water that was no more significant than a ditch on Earth. She had been trying to read her devotions but was continuously distracted by the magical sound of water flowing over rocks. The upper pool, located where the supply pipe stuck through the western cave wall, had been filled. When it overflowed a couple of days ago, water poured down its carved course, creating what the folks call the New River, which empties out into Big Lake, the name given to the pond in Alpha's central park.

Several people stopped by during her time there, watching the river wash over the rocks and then leaving in wonder, often with eyes full of tears. Moving water acts differently on Mars due to the reduced gravity. Still, it has been the single cavern feature that reminded people of Earth. Of course, the level of Big Lake was shallow and would need another month of steady filling before it could spill over into the Last River.

The Last River is the fitting name for the final tributary of the Seven Caves water system, which originates in Lake City. The path for the Last River cut through the floor of Alpha Cave. A bridge was being built over the river for Straight Street to allow the water to flow to its final pool in Alpha on the northeastern side of the cavern. When the river exited through those buried pipes, it would run through the Farmland cave and end at the Last Lake cavern. From there, the new water processing facility would pump it back up to the beginning in Lake City. The master plan, after the city is revealed to the rest of the planet and the water system is filled over capacity, is to bottle and sell purified Martian water under the Alpha name. Some say it would be more precious than rocket fuel.

"Hey Ally, I saw you sitting over here and wanted to say hello," Benz said. He felt naked and small walking around without his Evo and rubbed his left arm with his right hand.

Ally stood from her seat on the rock and hugged him.

"It's good to see you out of your suit."

"Crazy, right?"

"Where have you been for the last month and a half?" Ally asked.

"Spending time in the northern caves, trying to make some progress with spray foam while we have the materials. Just doing my part."

"I gotta hand it to you, this place is really taking shape."

"The transformation is amazing. All of the cubes being built on the East Mezzanine is mind-blowing."

"We are about to get much busier in a few days."

"It feels like the place is ready to come alive."

"Those canisters are coming. We will have hundreds of people walking around in a few days."

"I thought some were going to be taken to Jeru until more Cubes can be built?"

"I heard that too."

"How goes the farming?" Benz asked.

"Now that we have temperature and humidity stabilized it's going much better."

"Yeah, getting that reactor online was a huge step." Benz remembered the process took him months of long nights and splitting headaches to accomplish.

Ally smiled. "Any idea on the sky?" Ally asked about the artificial sky program being set up by a few guys from Eland. It was supposed to simulate the sun, complete with dramatic sunrise, sunset, and clouds. Of course, it was all going to be projected on the spray foam ceiling of the cave, which had been painted a light blue hue.

"I don't have any idea. That's all your buddy, Bill's doing."

"I heard he wanted it up and working when the first canisters arrive."

They both looked skyward.

"I think those people are going to arrive in this city and be underwhelmed."

"Underwhelmed? What? Why? This place is the most amazing place on the planet." Alli unconsciously placed her hands on her hips.

"It is, but it doesn't compare to even average places on Earth where they are coming from."

"Maybe after they get over their hibernation hangover they will be excited?" Ally said.

"I think we should consider having a month long adjustment and training period out on the surface, then bring them in here to live, otherwise they will take it for granted."

"I hope you are wrong, Benz."

"Me too, but I'm not."

Ally laughed.

"Any word from our mutual friend?" Benz said.

Ally checked around to make sure they were alone. "Not a peep. V says he's having trouble finding the correct coordinates to connect his communication laser the further away he gets."

"I can't imagine what it would be like facing the whole trip awake instead of a long nap in between launch and landing. Doing it alone must be killing him." Benz realized his error. "Sorry."

Ally smiled as she looked down, nudging a rock with her shoe.

"I keep reminding myself that he likes being alone, but I agree, this has to be very hard on him."

"I'm sorry you're going through this." Benz touched her arm. To Ally, the whole touching situation had been an incredible part of living in the new shirt-sleeve version of Alpha. With everyone living outside their space suits, people had been using physical touch to reconnect and shake off the Evo isolation of the last few months.

"Thanks. I have my days, but I know he is right where he is supposed to be."

"I'm still struggling with that one."

"That's okay, Benz. I don't judge you for that."

"I know. I miss him and I'm certain you do, too."

"Yes."

"Are you going stir crazy yet?" Benz asked.

"A little. Going to Shepard tonight. We need some new seed strains for the wheat and sorghum for the Farmall fields when they are ready.

"Those fields are getting close to coming online, finally," Benz said.

"You've had a lot of trouble up there," Ally said.

"Yeah, that cave has been a nightmare. Every time I go, there is another issue." The thought of that cavern made his stomach turn, so rubbing his hair he changed the subject. "So, you are making a trip to Shepard? What does old Bill think about that?"

"It's fine. He's fine. I need some time away from the cave Kars spent so much time in."

"I understand. Be careful. You're not going alone right?"

"Nope. I've got a couple travel buddies from Eland. And we should be in and out."

"Good. Ridge has been on another rampage. Keep your head on a swivel."

"Will do."

"All right, I'll see you when you get back," Benz said.

"Take care."

<hr>

"I'm right here!"

Silence.

"No wonder this planet is named after Nergal the Babylonian god of death and pestilence. Even her moons are cursed. Phobos wears the curse of Fear, and Deimos is cloaked with Terror," Lieutenant Hamms said. "Both are bathed in lies, being named from the children of the false gods of Aros and Aphrodite. I cry out to the Living God!" He announced his passion to the Reaper squadron circling above the Shimmer-covered entryway into the Russian cavern. His zeal to speak the truth of his God to the pagans above him overruled the professional decorum Angelic Warriors were required to uphold. It was obvious Mars was getting under his skin. "I need a vacation."

At the time the Reaper squadron noted their position and sent a direct message to their commander, who was holed up in Lieutenant Ridge's body. This discovery could change things for the Lieutenant and his demonic host.

⸺⬦⸺

4 September 2048 (Sol 7748)

Teapot Key, Florida

Connie knelt beside her bed. "Father, we lift up our Bry before you, Lord. We know she is being tortured by evil men carrying out their immoral plans. Please give her the strength to carry on. Please, Father, give her the peace that passes all understanding. Bless her with your Holy Spirit and surround her with your angels. Preserve her life. We cannot accomplish any of these things, Lord. Even though we would have if we could, you can," she prayed. "Remind her, right now, of her favorite verse from Joshua, "Have I not commanded you? Be strong and courageous. Do not be frightened and dismayed, for the Lord your God is with you wherever you go."

⸺⬦⸺

An Angel whispered to Bry. "You're not alone, child. He's right here holding you. Don't give up! I know this is hard, and it's not His plan. It's the brokenness of this world ruling at this moment, sweetheart. Don't give up. You are loved, my child. Remember his promise to you— "You are a hiding place for me, you preserve me from trouble; you surround me with shouts of deliverance," the angel reminded her about the ancient Psalm while holding her head on her lap. She brushed Bry's matted hair between her fingers as her life hung in the balance. The angel also prayed on her behalf with moans and shouts no one in this world could understand. She began to sing an angelic lullaby to Bry.

Then, through the slot in the door of her isolation pod fell a piece of bread and a plastic zipper bag of water. The attending angel's face shone with gratitude.

"Bry, wake up. Someone has given you a gift."

As Bry nibbled the bread, another gift arrived in the form of a memory, along with an answer to an old woman's prayer: "Have I not commanded you? Be strong and courageous. Do not be frightened, and do not be dismayed, for the Lord your God is with you wherever you go." She repeated the encouraging verse over and over again.

⊷◆⊶

Sol 7749 (5 September 2048)

Revolver Nine, approaching Earth intercept

"I don't understand!"

Kar's helmet was shoved inside an outer panel next to his Rocker in the loading bay. He had been following the electronic control cables for the docking clamps. He could not isolate the lines he needed to trigger the clamps for his ship.

"I've got to get these clamps to move! V, do you have any more ideas? I tried everything you suggested." He sent the mail. If he was lucky, he would only wait forty minutes for a reply.

Now that he came down to the last days before causing Rocker N-42 to disembark from Revolver Nine without having access to the command module for the docking clamps. The default setting for the clamps was in the locked position. If anything happened, the Revolver would hang onto its cargo— so cutting the lines was out of the question, not to mention all of the attention he would get from the crew as final preparations were underway for Earth intercept.

All the ships attached to the Revolver would detach and head off to rendezvous with their intended targets. Most were destined for orbiting outposts around the globe to be unloaded and processed for final descent to Earth. Even the Command Module (CM) was leaving for the LIFT command central space station, so a new crew could take over for the next outbound journey to Mars. The new CM was due to pull up alongside Revolver Nine to begin the exchange protocol. After the switch of Command Modules, the old crew rode alongside until all the cargo ships were set free for the final safety check of their command.

A stressed out Kars thought about using the vacuum-rated torches to cut the rail, but the heat sensors would immediately pick up on it. Unable to solve the mystery of the clamps, he moved his solar-paneled self back inside the heated Rocker A27 through its outer airlock. He had brought the duffel bag from Benz with the flying squirrel on the side in order to finish his preparations for atmospheric insertion.

The duffel held two experimental Squirrel Suits, a large and a medium. Kars had heard of them but had never seen one up close. The suits were made from a chained carbon nanotube fiber and morphed into a flying wing. In its natural state, the cloth appeared to be nothing more than a specialized fabric— but when powered up, it became a hardened shell. That shell, in theory, allowed humans to survive a catastrophic orbital event and glide down through the Martian atmosphere in wide back-and-forth 'S' moves, used to decelerate and come to a soft landing on the planet.

Several successful tests using bots as guinea pigs had been conducted. Still, human tests had not been completed before he left the planet. The real problem for Kars was that the design of his Squirrel Suit was meant for orbital insertion into the Martian atmosphere. Kars was not going to Mars. Earth's atmosphere was much more dense and rose further above the surface than Mars, which would create more heat to be created when entering. "With two suits of different sizes you could put one inside the other, ride the one out until it was fried and then energize the next suit to finish the descent. You're welcome! Benz." His handwritten note inside the bag explained his logic.

Kars had no idea how Benz got his hands on the suits. He held one up to inspect, noticing ahead to the wall of the Rocker. He focused on the Rocker's panels, aware of the high-temperature insulation behind each of them. He began to remove as much of it as he could to stuff into the larger Squirrel suit. Half an hour later, the suit bulged with bright pink fibrous insulation.

"This ain't fitting back in the duffel bag." when he held up his creation, fear gripped his throat.

"God, I don't know how this is going to work. It's not like I have lots of options here. I'm afraid. Please help me. I am sure that I am supposed to try this for you, for her. I've been over this a thousand times and I can't see another way, or any way right now. And how am I supposed to get those clamps off?"

The answer came in the form of a verse from the book of Joshua which echoed into his heart.

TWENTY-TWO

Sol 7750 (6 September 2048)
Shepard City, Mars

Ally lived in Eland since coming to Mars, but she often frequented Shepard City. She was contracted and spent a few months helping engineers bring a couple of farms online five MY ago. She fell in love with the food at a taco stand on the southern edge of town during her time in Shepard. Even thinking about it now caused her mouth to salivate. She told her cohorts that if they would take their new seed to the Hum, she would buy the tacos and meet them there with lunch.

The aroma of meat grilling wafted through that section of the city, drawing in hungry people all afternoon. The smoke from the grills, the strings of lights above the tables, and the yellow umbrellas all welcomed Ally back— like a hug from an old friend.

Lieutenant Ridge and his two favorite enforcers were eating lunch at Maria's Mexicano when Ally ordered three lunch specials to go. From his perch at the round wire mesh table, Ridge immediately recognized the wanted woman. He smiled a broad and satisfying smile as he bent his neck to take the final bite of his grilled chicken taco without removing his eyes from his beautiful target. He did not to waste the view or the good money he had spent at the only place in Shepard that sold genuine grilled chicken instead of imitation plant-based meat byproducts. Enjoying every last bite he licked his fingers and pointed out the visitor to his two brain-dead friends.

"We are going to need to ask that gorgeous woman a few important questions." Ridge pointed her out.

"Okay, boss," the larger Goon said before taking another bite of his taco.

"Now, you idiot!" Ridge said.

The two men dropped their food, stood quickly, and rushed to grab Ally's arms from behind. Ridge picked up one of his Goon's half-eaten tacos and took a final, satisfying bite before joining them.

"I am Lieutenant Ridge." He wiped his mouth as he flashed his Federal Police badge. Ally went pale with fright. "We need to talk, young lady."

Unfortunately for Ally, Ridge and his guys returned her to Free Port for a long and detailed discussion. Ridge grilled her for hours at a clandestine site in an obscure tunnel far beneath the city. His black opp site was notorious for getting people to confess to things they had never done, just to make the pain stop.

Ally was not able to stand up to the torture for very long before she buckled and spilled out everything she knew about Kars. Her lover had kept her in the dark about specifics to protect her, but Ridge pressed her to make educated guesses.

"I'm not sure which Rocker," she said. "He wouldn't let me see the Rocker's call number and kept me blindfolded during transport. I don't even know what day he left. I was put to sleep before and after transport and auto-driven back to the city." Ally was in tears. If she caved in on some less important things, she could protect the real important stuff. She never revealed their marriage or the Underground connections, claiming they spent their time looking for caves throughout the Tharsis Rise.

"A good Christian girl like you spent several weeks roaming around in a Hum with a single man? That's scandalous and very naughty, young lady."

Ally said nothing but felt a heavy darkness descend into the dimly lit room.

"Ah, but you know the before and the after dates, now don't you my pretty little thing?" Ridge stood. Her hands were tied above her head suspended from the ceiling, and her feet were secured with cable ties.

The ten-day window helped narrow his search and perhaps warn the Revolver Kars boarded if he made it. For all Ridge knew, the guy was a human Popsicle floating around the solar system.

"We will be making an arrest or two with all this help you have given us today, my love. If you like to join me for dinner, I would gladly pay for a chicken taco or two." Ridge ran his index finger up the side of Ally's face while lusting after her.

Then the Goons doused her with two buckets of cold water before they, along with Ridge, left her in total darkness. She was glad they had washed Ridge's stink off her face.

"Even the darkness is not dark to you; the night is bright as the day, for darkness is as light with you." Ally whispered the ancient Psalm.

⸺◈⸺

Kars's Visor began his programmed sixty-minute countdown. He sat outside Rocker N-42, staring at one of the locks holding his ship onto Revolver Nine. Then it hit him like a ton of bricks.

"The bolts! All that I have to do is remove the bolts on the rails! Why didn't I see this sooner?"

Kars rushed inside the beat-up lander through the hatch he had left open. The bolts for the rails were a standard 18mm, eight on each clamp. Five were accessible, two in a painful location, and one hidden entirely. Using his power driver, he zipped the easy twenty vibration-resistant nuts off within five minutes. Knocking the bolts through their holes with a hammer sent them drifting off, flipping head over heels into space. Soon, they would become long-burning streaks of light in the Earth's sky. Kars wondered if some shards of high tinsel carbon steel could survive the trip through the atmosphere and actually crash into the planet.

Twenty minutes later, only four bolts remained on the two captured rails of the extended external docking mechanisms. But even with only one bolt in place, each of the four rail clamps was more than capable of holding on to the Revolver's docking pins. Ten minutes later, Kars still struggled to turn the nut past the last few threads. While he sweat inside his suit, his environmental system worked overtime to clear humidity from inside his visor. He could not get his fingers past the flange.

"You're not gonna make it!" He panicked.

"Think. Think! God, I need some help getting these bolts out of these holes, please."

Then it hit him to use a strap. He fed it up and over the bolt, then pull on one side like a belt. It worked much faster. He left one turn on each nut until there were a couple of minutes left in his personal countdown.

⸻◆⸻

"Helek, where are you?" Sergeant Iggy asked into his comm. Iggy, Lu, and Junior had just shifted to Rocker N-42 at Captain Helek's order.

"Over in the loading bay, on the other side of the ship," Helek said.

The three Warriors flew over and joined him.

"What are you watching, sir," Lu asked.

"Those bolts." He pointed. Everyone followed his finger's direction without understanding the implications.

"If this kid can't get these last few bolts dislodged, we may have to help him."

"Do we have clearance to do that?" Iggy asked.

"Not yet. I'm waiting on command to give us the green light."

"When we shifted we were spotted by a Reaper squadron," Iggy said.

"I figured," Helek said. "But I need your help, so it doesn't matter. Just be ready, this kid may be in for the ride of his life."

***

Earth dominated Kars's visor. The slight atmospheric contact caused the Revolver to rattle and shake. Now, with the rail clamps unbolted by 99%, his Rocker shook freely on the loosened bolts. The latch on his hatch was secured for his kamikaze trip down to the surface, but his growing fear was the vibrations would be felt throughout the Revolver. The crew would notice the vibrations and do something to lock down his Rocker.

Kars's soul churned. He prayed out loud for God's protection, while self-doubt pounded against his heart. When his suit countdown clock hit two minutes, he removed the two lower nuts, then the uppers. The Rocker dropped a couple of inches as the bolts all shifted off-center with the gravity draw of the Blue Planet. The Rocker remained connected to the Revolver's docking pins and was now shook more violently.

Kars tried shaking against the outer walls and slamming himself against the wall that held the hatch.

"I've gotta go out!" He floated toward the portal. There was no room for error; the Rocker had to be dislodged from Revolver 9 within forty-five seconds.

***

In the harsh conditions of space, a squad of Reapers tried to hold the Rocker in place and managed to keep it hung upon its own bolts. Captain Helek's squad popped out from transparent and sliced eight Reapers with one swing of their swords. Sparks flew in every direction from the strikes. It appeared to the crew that a micro-meteor had hit Rocker N-42.

◆◇◆

"What is going on out there?" Captain Conley shouted at the monitor. "Get the crane down there and latch onto that vibrating piece of crap!"

"Sir!" Private Pete Timmons sat down in the crane command chair. Timmons powered up the starboard crane, stretched open the claw, and began trundling the crane toward the dented and abused Rocker N-42.

Timmons watched his camera intently for the correct Rocker when another flash whitened his screen. He wanted to ignore it, but Conley peered over his shoulder.

"What the hell was that?"

"I don't know sir. It looked like a direct sun reflection into the crane camera."

"Not the flash, the movement."

Right before their eyes, the Phantom of Revolver Nine materialized. A human in an Evo covered in two solar panels flipped out from a hatch and up onto the top of N-42. In one smooth motion, the human pushed off across the side toward the docking pins and momentarily out of view of the crane camera.

"We've got an EVA on the Rocker," Conley said.

"It's the Phantom!" Timmons shrieked with fear. He pointed at the monitor, covered his mouth with his other hand.

"Can you grab that ship before it gets damaged?" Conley asked Lieutenant Jacobs, pointing.

"Who is this guy?" Jacobs asked.

Throughout the Control Module, faces smashed against windows and screens to catch a glimpse of their Phantom. It was the most excitement they'd had in three months.

"I'm trundling as fast as I can sir."

"He's shaking that Rocker!" Conley said.

"I think he trying to dislodge it!" Jacobs said.

Revolver 9 lost operational control over Rocker N-42 as the last threads of the four remaining bolts lost their ability to hold against the tension gripping the rail clamps. The man in the black photo-cell-covered space suit dislodged the spaceship from its berth. The Phantom leaped off of Revolver 9 and onto the Rocker, which began to rotate and tumble away.

In a final desperate attempt at control, Timmons brought the robotic arm into play, causing it to lunge to grab onto the dislodged ship. But the remote-controlled arm only bumped the rail farther away instead. The spaceman hung on during the impact with the crane's arm but immediately launched himself to the rail on the opposite side of the craft. His boots swung wide over his head like a gymnast on the high bar. Kars, the Martian Phantom of Revolver Nine, disappeared from view.

———◆O◆———

The Command Module, flying parallel to the Revolver and waiting to take command of good old number Nine, swung wide around the ship, trying to pursue the dislodged Rocker so it did not cause damage to the mother ship or the cargo. The detached CM came into Kars's view as he tumbled feet-first through the hatch. Inside the now independent Rocker

N-42, Kars locked the hatch with his trusty screwdriver and a bang of his palm. He used the interface inside his suit to control the ship by plugging in the direct hardwire he had rigged up months before, locking into the flight command center, isolating everyone else from remotely controlling the craft.

With a quick stabilizer burn, he dipped away from Revolver 9, underneath the stunned crews in both Command Modules.

Unbeknownst to him, Kars Dee had just become a Martian legend— the superhero space-walking phantom Pirate of Rocker N-42. He opened his comm and offered a long stress-relieving, guttural war cry, cementing his legendary status into space folklore for generations.

As he started his deceleration burn Kars's computer confirmed that his telemetry was nominal. He rotated the Rocker, held on, and initiated a full powered twenty-minute burn. To counter the renewed thrust, he needed to pull on his first Squirrel Suit as soon as possible. That proved much more difficult with the violent shaking caused by the ignited rocket engines and the atmosphere. Trying to step inside the smaller suit, his knife sheath hooked the material. When he fell over he worried about damaging the chained carbon nanotube. Upon standing, he realized he no longer needed his phantom solar cells and removed them. Inside the suit, Kars had to connect the interface to his own suit. The Squirrel Suit software booted up on the left side of his visor with an animation of a red flying squirrel who swooped in, landed on red dirt, and then waved with both hands.

"Cute."

The more difficult maneuver was getting the suit he now occupied inside the second one which was stuffed with pink high-temperature insulation. He had practiced it several times earlier but his Rocker was not diving into the Earth's atmosphere at the time. The rattling and shaking intensified with each passing moment. With the growing gravity he bounced to pack his smaller suit inside the larger Squirrel. He thought to unzip and slide his glove out to connect the second umbilical electrical cord and work the titanium zipper closed, but his visor began to rattle against his jaw, shaking his teeth.

"Father, protect me. Surround me with your Holy Angels and if it is your will, guide me safely to the ground. Help me, Lord to help my sister escape the evil ones. In Jesus' name. Amen."

Revolver 9 made all the necessary calls up the chain of command as the stolen Rocker descended into a fireball streaking across the blue sky below. Every nation turned its satellites and radar installations toward the fireball, trying to determine the nature of the threat and where it was heading.

The interior of N-42 heated up. The skin on the nose of the craft began to glow even through Kars's suit visor plus two Squirrel Suit portals. The ship's nose pointed down after the burns, taking all of the heat built up from the speed friction against the growing density of air. Kars called for a stabilizer burn to spin it around on its axis, but he over-compensated and the ship began wobbling like a top, losing momentum and throwing him around inside. The automatic gyroscope controls kicked in to settle the ship as the rocket engine nozzles began to take the brunt of the descent, which allowed the nose to cool enough to stop the red glow.

An alarm rang inside Kars's suit, warning him of the overheating engines. He rotated the ship back to nose down and dumped what remained in the fuel tanks, which sent a tremendous hundred-foot-long fireball stretching out behind the ship. The nose glowed more, so he spun the ship back around to let the nozzles take the heat.

Thirty seconds later, he pointed the ship nose-down as it was buffeted by the thickening thermosphere. The titanium skin glowed and shook.

"Come on!" Kars yelled. He burned the stabilizer, rotated the ship around to cool off the nose cone. Beneath the rocket nozzles, the aft of the ship was flat, absorbing the reentry friction. The outer edge began to glow. Kars knew he was getting perilously close to losing control of the Rocker. He commanded the nose back around, pointing it down into the gravity well. The hatch handle glowed red hot. His trusty screwdriver's handle melted, streaking the glowing hatch with black plastic. The skin of the ship snapped and popped with the radical temperature changes. He had to get the hatch open— but not too soon.

Kars felt steel rip and tear as the docking rails melted off and bounded away. He ducked in next to the loaded pallets, noticing the temperature on his suit fans was topped out on his gauge. They fought to circulate air, but he was inside the two Squirrel Suits. With a double blink, he manually reduced the internal cooling command to save the fans from frying and reduce battery usage. At least his borrowed suit smelled new, not like months of human sweat mixed with all kinds of nasty.

Buried deep inside two Squirrel Suits with an extra layer of insulation, he was not yet feeling the heat generated from the friction of reentry.

He pinned himself under the straps of the pallet as sections of the outer skin melted away. The bow thruster support beam melted and bent in half. As it was ripped off, the compressed Hydrazine bottles exploded, tearing through parts of the hull. The nose cone began to melt, sending shards of molten titanium splashing against the tops of the pallets. The plastic containers on the pallets were filled with stacked 3-D printed aluminum automotive parts. The plastic packaging caught fire, and the smoke jetted out behind him as the tail section of the Rocker broke away. Individual parts caught fire, melted, and blew out. The ship was encapsulated in flames as it fell toward its end.

"I guess I don't need to open the hatch anymore."

The Squirrel Suit was constructed from chained carbon nanotubes designed to stiffen with an electrical current. A switch activated the internal power source and brought the fibers to life, deploying the suit, making the skin stronger than titanium. The major problem for Kars was these suits were designed to make an emergency space jump from crippled ships through the Martian atmosphere, which is one percent as dense as Earth's. They had only recently been tested and never with a live human. About half of the dummies survived the descent while the others melted into fireballs of one kind or another, making impact failure craters on the surface.

"Send your angels, Lord!"

—◇—

"Shift ten percent," Helek commanded his Warriors, hanging onto the remnants of Rocker N-42. The shift allowed the Warrior's wings to absorb some heat generated with reentry. Four Angelic Warriors were out on the ship's skin, deflecting debris and heat along the way— their wing tips glowing red.

"Let's surround him!" Helek yelled above the chaos.

"Hold together, boys." The four warriors held on to each other while surrounding their unaware Shiner as they punched a hole into Earth's atmosphere.

—◇—

Kars had to use the mass of the pallet of aluminum parts as a shield as long as he could. As he held the straps holding the tubs of parts, they melted and gave way. Kars ducked behind, pushing against the growing weight of the pallet. Due to energy use and battery capacity, Squirrel Suits can only remain deployed for about fifteen minutes. Kars had to wait as long as possible before engaging the outer suit. The thermal readout from the outer suit was still within range, so he held out as long as possible.

The violent shaking of the Rocker breaking apart around him caused him to yell out, to burn off some of the building stress so as not to mentally snap. He had never been inside a fireball before. When the O2 canister straps burned off, the bottles bounced around and fell off the side of the former spacecraft. Terrible explosions followed behind him as they were blasted from the ship. From the long-distance cameras on the CM, it looked as if the ship had blown itself apart.

Kars was forced to deploy his exterior suit as the last parts of the pallet broke apart around him. Kars flipped over and pushed off the floor as it ripped away, energizing the Flying Squirrel as he jumped.

Emerging from the center of the fireball, the black flying wing began its descent behind what used to be a spaceship. Kars began making "S" turns to spread the heat along the nose of his suit while trying to stay behind the expanding debris field. His Rocker's disassembly was almost complete. Back and forth, Kars zig-zagged like a downhill skier, using the interface to command the steering flaps on his suit. He restricted his movement inside the growing cone of falling debris. He could not turn too much or he would lose control and begin tumbling. He would also lose the thermal protection offered by the pieces of the Rocker that were still ahead of him.

Gravity became a growing problem. He was used to .38 gravity on Mars for thirteen years, but he had lived in zero-G for three months, which had cost him strength and stamina. Even the time he spent sneaking around in the seventy percent gravity of the CP did little to help him. Kars tried to relax and let the suit do its job as he hurtled down the maelstrom.

Kar's heat indicator alarm sounded. The gauge was off the chart. A burn hole appeared through the nose cone of the outer suit. The insulation helped, but it would fry in a few moments. He tried to energize the second suit, but it could not fully extend inside the other suit against the insulation. "I gotta get the outer suit off!" He screamed and prayed simultaneously.

"Papa's knife!"

Kars yanked the knife out of its sheath. Using his left hand to unzip the inner suit, he poked the other into the outer suit. He wrapped some insulation around his glove and cut off the outer Squirrel Suit. He sawed through the electrical connection, severing the outer Flying Squirrel's power. He hacked away for a few seconds, pulling the material toward himself. Kars pulled his smoldering glove back inside the second Squirrel Suit and activated its power cycle. It snapped into action, becoming more durable than titanium in a millisecond.

What Kars did not know was that his progress was being filmed by a long-range, high-speed camera on the new Command Module for Revolver 9. Crewmen onboard recorded his actions and fed them live to the web, which garnered instant internet response wherever humans lived.

"Who is this fire-riding Martian? Hero or Pirate?" The lead sentence scrolled across news banners on monitors around the solar system. The corresponding video showed the elevated knife sparking and glowing against the atmosphere, slashing off lower portions of the first suit. The glowing knife disappeared, and the second Squirrel Suit snapped into its flying wing form. The front of the second suit was still covered by a large segment of the first Squirrel Suit and some bright pink insulation— both flapping violently in the wind as they worked to deflect some of the massive heat transfer. A split second later, the Squirrel Suit began weaving back and forth behind the growing debris field like an Olympic slalom skier racing against the clock and the gates.

———◆◇◆———

Corporal Lu's entire right wing became engulfed in flames as his compatriots held onto each other, all with their heads bent low in the melee, surrounding their human.

"Help him pull the bottom of that suit off!" Helek said.

The angels pulled on the fabric, which allowed Kars's knife to slice through the material instead of bunching it up.

"I can't..." Corporal Lu was ripped from the group of four warriors. His wings torn off, he tumbled away from the burning fireball.

"Get out in front of this one." Helek commanded his two guys to deflect more heat away from the front of the final suit.

———◆◇◆———

"Emergency! All personnel report to command center. All personnel report to command center!"

Benz had just left the command tent a minute before the alarm sounded. What could be so important?

"What do you need Bill?" Benz pushed through the door.

"You've got to see this!"

316

Bill stood and spun his desk monitor around so Benz could see the picture of a glowing knife.

"What the ... ?" Benz tried to make sense of the images. "Where is this?"

"Someone is trying to enter Earth's atmosphere riding a Rocker."

"It'll never make it. They weren't designed for Earth reentry."

"There are some that are."

"Start this from the beginning." Benz sent off a text to V.

"Are you watching?"

"Yes. Everyone in the universe is watching," V texted back.

"How much time delay?

"Twenty minutes or so."

More people arrived in the tent.

"Here's the video from the start." Bill clicked play.

"Nan! Come in here!" Larry waved to the boss.

"Who is this fire riding Martian? Hero or Pirate?"

He started the video over for the three people inside the Bees' cabin.

Inside the dank cell, a comm unit was placed on the food slot at the door of Bry's isolation pod. A young guard bent over and whispered into the slot, "Hey, get up. You need to see this."

Twenty-Three

Sol 7750 (6 September 2048)
Somewhere over North America

The temperature gauge could no longer measure the heat on the skin of the Squirrel Suit as it dove toward the ground.

"I've got to slow down!" Kars drove his flying wing out from behind the glowing, burning debris field, making wide turns against gravity. He knew he would either burn up or bleed off some speed. Gravity became a more significant issue, pulling on him and wearing on his resolve to continue.

"Come on!" He screamed and banked right.

Sweat dripped down his face, soaking all of his clothes. With another turn, he witnessed the complete dismantling of his former ride. Rocker N-42, that beat-up piece of space crap that had managed to get him halfway across the solar system and so close to Earth he could smell it, was now engulfed in a fireball, but there was no time for Kars to wax nostalgic.

He tried to access his Evo GPS system, but the icon spun in circles like it was searching for a signal. He checked his antenna's status. It indicated that there was no damage, but the GPS icon would not stop spinning. In time, he was far-off from his busted old ride as it melted and burned, streaking the sky with ever-widening fingers of smoke.

When the stealth black flying wing swung out from behind the melting spaceship, the long-distance camera on Revolver Nine's new command ship tried to keep the image in the center of its viewfinder. As the Squirrel suit danced like a skier during its descent, the image shook its way outside of the camera's range, then was gone.

Far off in the unseen distance, a pair of gray Global Union fighter jets, fresh off their Chinese assembly line, raced off the tarmac from the Canadian Union base in Petawawa, their noses pointed to the heavens. Their radar could not pick up the expanding debris field a hundred miles ahead. The twin planes ran full throttle with their afterburners engaged as the pilots endured a constant command stream from an anxious General into their ears. That G.U. officer attempted, through sheer determination, to will the planes faster than their sixth-generation design allowed. At a mile a second were over two minutes away from intercepting the growing inferno. When radar monitors began showing pieces within the wreckage, the pilots started to search for an aircraft maintaining controlled flight among the debris or in the vicinity of the falling, burning mass. Both men energized two air-to-air missiles inside their underbelly weapons suite, sliding their fingers into firing position.

⸺◆◇◆⸺

Streaking through the thickened atmosphere, Kars bent his frame to the right, and his memories flashing back to learning how to ski. His grandfather had taught him just after his thirteenth birthday. Half of that first day was spent on his butt or walking down the slopes to pick up his skis after another "yard sale" fall.

"Take the pressure off of one ski by pushing down a little on the other," his Papa had told him. "Lean toward the ski that you are lifting. This will turn you back and forth, and you will be able to control your speed. When you learn to control your speed, then you can relax and enjoy yourself." Kars smiled at the memory, and a glint of hope grabbed at his heart.

"Where am I?" he asked no one in particular. When he clicked on the map option, map of Mars came up, then he knew. The GPS icon spun, searching mindlessly for the Martian system. He was definitely not on Mars anymore. The green, blues, and whites of this world seemed so vibrant. The dull, rusty red was gone, maybe forever. The view through his visor and then through the Squirrel Suit window was very restrictive, making him feel claustrophobic with the peripheral views of the cameras on his helmet only showing the inside of the dark suit as he streaked below a pair of fighter airplanes.

An alarm sounded, and a red indicator flashed at his suit temperature. The gauge was pegged past the upper limit. As he glanced from the window, he noticed the outer walls of the Squirrel Suit glowed red. His gloves began to smolder, causing him to yank them from touching the sides of his suit.

Kars began calling out to God in desperate prayers. His time was running out.

Then he saw the answer. How could he have missed the obvious solution? The cloud formation off to his starboard was a billowing tower of moisture waiting to cool his little ship, so he leaned into the glowing wing again and forced it to the left. Within twenty seconds, his wing hissed, popped, and steamed from connection with the water vapor he streaked through. The glow faded on his personal plane, causing him to break harder. He had to reduce his speed, or nothing would be left of him except a small impact crater.

Now soaring, he whooped and hollered, beginning to believe he could make a landing. Kars noticed large bodies of water outside his craft, and when he turned his head, he recognized the Great Lakes. His approach was from the northeast, so he pointed his craft south and hunted for more clouds.

Minutes later, far behind him, he could not see his Rocker impact the ground in a wooded area in western Pennsylvania. A significant impact crater and fireball from the sudden kinetic energy absorption instantly ignited trees on the hills surrounding the crash site.

⸺◆○◆⸺

Following the wide band of burning spacecraft, the fighter pilots gave the descending destruction a wide berth. One pointed to a streak of steam punching through clouds below their position. They both rolled their planes over into a dive and raced off in pursuit of the end of the line of steam.

⸺◆○◆⸺

Helek, Iggy, and Junior were scorched and singed from holding onto the flying wing. When heard Kars's prayers of desperation, their hearts were stirred to hang on even tighter with each sentence, mingling their requests with his. The ten percent shift to the flesh side of existence had bled enough heat off the hull of the Squirrel Suit to save the man inside. Those actions would also later give the inventors of the technology a false sense of security when they tested newer iterations of the device. In essence, Helek knew they exchanged Kars's life for the lives of a few test pilots in the future. He hoped his superiors would approve of his unauthorized move to save the Shiner they held onto.

When the remaining trio hit the cloud formations, flying seven thousand miles an hour, ten percent of their angelic bodies began to steam and smoke, leaving a line across the sky that, unfortunately, pointed directly to their position. Two fighter jets dove to catch the black point at the end of the white line in the heavens, knowing that was their target.

With the temperatures lowering on his wing, Kars had to bleed off more speed. Without GPS, he had no idea how fast he was traveling. He began maneuvers to gain altitude, then went back into the wide turns: Pull up to gain altitude, then push hard into wide turns. The sky painting was no longer a straight line, and the jets made considerable progress in their pursuit of the flying suit.

"Iggy, we've got two G.U. fighter jets approaching from the north," Helek said.

"Sir?"

"Fall back and intercept them."

"ROE?"

"I would love for you to blind them from seeing this wing. But do whatever it takes to stop them from shooting him down."

"Roger." With that word, Iggy fell off the flying wing. He held himself straight as an arrow while he shifting entirely out of the flesh side of life. This was so he would not rip his wings clean off when he slowed to match speeds with approaching planes. He had no such limitations without an atmosphere to hold him back.

"Too much speed!" Kars pulled up hard to absorb the momentum. While flying, he used voice commands in his suit to access an old file that held a global map for Earth. The image appeared on his visor screen, but by the time he fumbled through the controls, he had gone another three hundred miles. He was surrounded by green below and blue above. He needed to pinpoint the camp where his sister was being held in, so he could get close.

He noticed in the Squirrel interface an altimeter icon and a star-finder application. He made both active, and a map with his position and altitude popped up on the right side of his visor.

"Brison City, North Carolina," he said to the search function.

"Yes! 300 miles southwest!" Kars gained some altitude, then streaked off toward his sister.

"There you are," Iggy thought. "Contact," he said into his comm.

"Copy," Helek said.

Iggy slipped up behind the pair of fighters from above them. He grabbed the right stabilizer and used his sword to cut the hydraulic line, sending a fluid spray into the wind and bringing a red warning light to life on the pilot's heads-up display. Iggy shot over to his partner and pulled the same maneuver on that airplane. That would certainly send a bunch of Chinese scientists and engineers back to the drawing board. Or they might face a firing squad for gross incompetence. Within seconds, both planes lost their directional ability and were foced to use manual overrides to find a course back to base.

"Zoomie's RTB," Iggy said. Helek knew the two jets and their pilots had returned to base.

Upon hearing of his two new jets' mechanical troubles, the Global Union General swore in Mandarin, then ordered a base in Virginia to prepare two swarms of DB-5 Hunter-Killer drones to intercept the flying wing as soon as the AI could best determine where the craft would land.

The First State Church of Brison City, North Carolina, was holding a celebration after their Sunday service. It was Labor Day weekend, and the Compliant state government suggested that all churches in the state should offer special worker celebrations in conjunction with the holiday. A few weeks before the event, a priest requested parishioners to provide food, drink, games, and party supplies for the celebration. The congregation's response was unconventionally positive. A large celebration would be held on the church lawn, with the entire community invited.

People who would never darken the door of the communist-controlled church came out in force with smiles plastered all over their faces. Leah Thompson and her fifth-grade class raised money to buy balloons and rent a helium tank for the special occasion. They set up their work area inside a large tent and inflated thousands of red balloons. The entire class participated, except Bryce, because he had an allergic reaction to a bee sting and had to go home.

When it was time to sing the people's pledge to the working class, everyone gathered outside the tent and belted out the communist song with gusto. The Priest and Global Union church coordinator beamed with pride and recording the event live on TicTok.

Near the end of the song, just before the balloons were released, Leah Thompson's dad started the song again, encouraging the people in the football field-sized circle to give it all they had.

Several thousand red balloons were unleashed to the applause of the happy crowd. The cloud of balloons floated skyward.

The church was on Slope Street, just a few blocks north of the Fontana River. The wind that day was light and variable from the southwest, blowing a few thousand balloons over the area formerly known as the Swain Country Recreational Park. Two years earlier, the park and the burnt-out hulk of First Baptist Church were replaced by the Western North Carolina Global Union Regional Development Center. Its doubled fences topped by coils of gleaming razor wire welcomed everyone who stayed as their guest.

◆◇◆

The image of Jesus stared down on the rows of bunk beds. The facility's warden, a short man of Chinese descent, possessed a sour temperament toward his guests along with the picture of Jesus. He ordered the image painted over four times. Still, Jesus bled through with his piercing eyes and punctured hands, calming the tortured souls in the facility. The warden ranted and raved against the picture, but he could not destroy it. His budget had no room for a wall hanging of that size. He just stopped entering the maximum security building because he did not want to be confronted with his failure to stamp out the wall-painted Jesus.

The scuttlebutt among the rebel leaders in and around the facility was that an attack was imminent. Six other facilities had been victims of physical attacks, with truck bombs, rockets, and machine gun fire being the main source of that aggression. Rebels had received word to watch and wait for a sign.

"Come on, girl." Ashley stood fixing her shirt. She reached down to shake her bunkmate's shoulder. The young woman had a homemade cast on her left arm and shadows of bruises all over her body and face.

"Come on. Let's take you outside for a walk today," Ashley said.

"I'm up." Bry groaned swinging her legs off the other side of the bed.

The duo shared a lower, twin-sized bunk bed. Two more ladies were still slept above them when Ashley helped Bry out of the sleeping area. They smiled at the wall Jesus as they tiptoed past out the double door to the yard. Bry had been moved out of isolation after the last bit of torture. She figured they let her heal so they could repeat it.

"Looks like a nice Sunday morning today." Ashley smiled. Bry's bruises glowed purple in the sun as the two began a circuit of the track, which used to be the old ball field. After strolling halfway around, Bry let go of her human crutch and wobbled under her own strength.

"Look at you!"

"Almost feel normal. Almost," Bry smiled, revealing her missing front tooth courtesy of her G.U. dentist. Her left eye swelling had gone down to the point that she could see out of it again, and she was hopeful her arm had almost healed. Bry anticipated the healing, not the renewed torture, and prayed while she walked.

From the other direction, two men approached the women. As they moved over to pass, they whispered, "Be ready today."

After their lunch of one ladle of soup, Bry returned outside and sat with her face to the sun leaning on her dormitory building. While staring off to the south, she noticed a dark and foreboding cloud rising from the southwest. Prisoners began talking and pointing at the unusual formation.

The massive launching of red balloons to celebrate a communist holiday floated toward the prison.

"I think this is our sign." Bry smiled.

As the objects approached, they changed from a dark presence to a sign of hope. The prison population discussed the sight when the lockdown alarm went off, causing goose bumps on Bry's arms and neck. She joined the file into the dorm under the watchful eye of G.U. soldiers dressed in riot gear. Under normal circumstances they were all too happy to swing their leaded clubs to motivate the stragglers or talkers in the group, but now, Bry could see fear in their eyes.

Just before she was to step onto the porch, a swarm of a hundred drones shot over the roof of her building and began engaging the balloons. They used their blades to pop them, mowing large swaths through the widening formation. One drone got several ripped balloons tangled in its blades, stalled, and slammed into the ground just beyond the fences. The prisoners who cheered were severely beaten.

"Did you get a cage?" one woman asked Bry.

"Nope."

The overweight woman pulled what looked like a knitted mitten from beneath her shirt and pressed it into Bry's free hand. Bry tucked it in her cast, then decided to shove it down her pants while watching for guards.

※

"Now what!" Kars yelled inside his Evo as the interactive map function quit on the Squirrel portion of his visor. The little doofus of an icon stood and looked at him with its hands spread open and shoulders shrugged.

The power setting on Kars's Evo, still showed more than forty percent charge. But the Squirrel Suit's power had dipped to less than five percent.

Kars wondered how long he had until he turned into another piece of space junk dropping from orbit and crashing into the side of a mountain. He was still invisible to radar while he had the suit deployed in its flying function, but he had no clue after that. "I guess it really doesn't matter much," he said. "You know what you are doing," he said to God. "I gotta park this thing."

The mountains below him were closer than they appeared through the lenses of both suits. Cruising over a peak, a fire tower raced into view, so he was forced to roll over to miss hitting its grounding antenna.

"Wow!" He dipped low, following the contour of the land. A large lake opened up below him. With its jagged shoreline, he knew that the lake was a byproduct of a hydroelectric dam.

"That's gotta be Fontana Lake." He immediately pulled into a sharp speed-killing curve. He blasted past the far shore, his momentum carrying him inland for several miles. A massive sonic boom followed him across the lake, through the woods, and then through a field of rising red balloons. The boom shook the buildings below and rattled windows throughout the town. The swarm of DB-5 drones were immediately redirected to follow the streaking black wing southeast, but they could not keep up even as Kars slowed dramatically.

He circled out and dropped just above the treetops, searching for the lake he had flown past. When he descended over a peak, the dark blue waters stood before him. He circled out over the dam and around the outer perimeter of the shoreline once again. As he banked, he saw the sand and one speed boat racing the other way across the water. Kars pulled harder into his turn, coming in behind the racing boat. The four people on board hung onto their hats and whooping it up on the holiday weekend. Kars managed to swoop low. So low, in fact, he was afraid he would hit the water and flip over and break his neck right at the finish line. As he slowed, his

Squirrel Suit bounced like a kite in low wind, undulating up and down for a few seconds, nearly stalling. When it hit the water in the center of the speed boat's wake, Kars was knocked unconscious. The suit's power holding it rigid ran out, and he sank like a rock.

—◆○◆—

Same Day

Teapot Key, Florida

"The signal balloons are away!" Larry watched his real-time feed from the Free Florida Brigade. The militia army was positioned to attack the prison camp in North Carolina.

"So what's next?" Nan asked. Connie lifted her head from praying. She asked God to intervene and protect the men and women during the attack.

"It depends on what the drones do," Larry said.

"Boom!" The sonic boom could be heard through the laptop speakers. The Bees thought some sort of bombing had occurred.

"What's blowing up?"

"I don't know!" Larry sent a text.

"It was a sonic boom, maybe from the G.U. Jets chasing that thing dropping out of the sky?" the text from the rebels' leader at the prison read.

"It was a sonic boom of unknown origin," Larry reported.

The feed showed a black streak flash through the frame.

"It's that Martian Pirate!"

Larry, who had been told by V to wait to reveal Kars' plan to the Bees until he had made it down, could not hold it in any longer.

"Listen ladies, sometimes in the fog of war you have to, as a leader, I mean, make some decisions that don't make much sense when you are planning. Like how goals could ever intersect. I mean, it was impossible. Impossible."

"What's impossible?" Nan was completely confused. Connie glanced at their security chief, who tried not to say what he obviously wanted to say.

"Spit it out, Larry. We don't have many more days to live," Connie said to lighten the mood.

"It looks like you swallowed some bad frog legs, Larry," Nan said.

"Alright, listen, I." He reached both hands in front of him, palms down. "I was sworn to secrecy because the likelihood of the plan working was almost zero. Zero. Also, I didn't know about it until it was already underway. I had nothing to do with the decision to make it happen."

"Larry, what in the world is going on?" Connie stood.

"I don't know how to say it."

"Just spit it out for goodness sake!"

"Okay."

"Now, please," Nan said.

Larry took a deep breath, looking directly at Connie. "Kars is the Martian Pirate."

"What?"

"The Martian Pirate. The kid riding the burning rocket down to Earth."

"Yeah? What about him?"

"It's Kars. Your grandson."

<hr>

"Helek we're gonna need a ready squad!" Iggy said when he saw the swarms of drones flying over the prison.

"You don't need a Ready Squad, Sergeant. You've got us!" Amadan appeared next to the singed Angel Warrior.

"Colonel! Praise be to you, Lord God Almighty, you provide for your servants!"

"Amen. God be praised! Now we got an attack to carry out, soldier! Rejoin your comrades in protecting that shiner."

"Yes, sir!"

"And Sergeant, well done. Welcome back to Earth," Amadan said.

"Sir."

⸻◆○◆⸻

The weight of the water above him pressed Kars awake at the bottom of the lake. Initially he could not lift his arms which caused him to panic. The water shoved the deflated Squirrel Suit against the murky lakebed, trapping him below. He noticed that he had plenty of air in his tank. Miraculously, his space suit had not been compromised by all of the chaos of the day.

"I gotta get out of this Squirrel." But how to make it happen? He had to unzip the Squirrel Suit but discovered that the zipper had been welded shut. The de-energized material adhered to his suit like a plastic bag in water is making it difficult to cut through. Kars managed to grab his trusty K-Bar out of his leg holster and began sawing away. Fifteen minutes later, he was exhausted but done. He slithered out of his chained-carbon-nano-tube flying wing like a butterfly from its chrysalis, then used his wobbly legs to stand on the bottom of the lake. The gravity and water pressure were almost too much to bear. He was unstable but began to shuffle-walk out of the depths. After five steps he stopped to take a break and fell over. Kars was forced to crawl a few feet and then rest. Crawl a few more feet, then stop for a break.

He asked his map program if he had enough air to finish his journey across the bottom of the lake. The program seemed to go to work. He prayed its icon was a reliable measurement of its internal calculations.

"We lost him, sir."

"Keep looking. He's going to run out of air," Larry said into his comm, knowing if the kid was knocked out and ran out of atmosphere, he would suffocate whether he was on land or in the lake.

"No word?" Connie asked.

"Not yet. We lost him after he went supersonic over the prison. The leader up there is a good man. He's got a sizeable contingent searching as we speak.

"Okay. I believe we will find him." Connie returned to praying for her grandson.

"I'm sure you are right." Larry struggled to believe how it would happen.

"I know they've got teams out under Shimmers searching without giving away their position." Nan looked up from a laptop.

"Yeah, this group is the best trained battalion we have," Larry said.

"He's in the lake." Connie did not lift her head and immediately returned to praying.

"Helek, you copy?" Amadan said into his comm.

"Sir."

"How are you guys holding up?"

"Top notch."

"How are you deployed?"

"Stealth ascending stagger."

"Roger. Danger close," Amadan said.

"Copy that. Danger close."

Amadan had half of his Angel Warriors deployed undercover around the lake, coordinating the Pirate concealment operation, while the other half of his force was a couple miles away with the rebel army in positions near the prison.

They were particularly interested in the Reaper Squadrons popping into the theater without warning. Drone activity was extremely high throughout the area, hovering and darting around the quadrant.

Amadan knew the Reapers were also searching for the Martian Pirate at the bottom of the lake.

◆

"I understand. Thank you." Larry set his comm down. Two ladies looked at him, waiting to consider his new information.

"The G.U. has dispatched a QRF from southern Virginia to come to the area to aid in the search and to protect the camp," Larry reported as calmly as he could, knowing their entire plan was now in jeopardy.

"Is the 120E in play?" Nan asked.

"Yes we've got ten of those surprises to drop on them." Larry smiled.

"This QRF is fog of war kind of stuff, right?" Nan asked.

"Yes. You always expect the fight to go a different way than you plan, but you still want to have as many advantages as you can," Larry said.

The new 120E was an electromagnetic pulse weapon based in a mortar round. It was designed to destroy all electronic circuit boards within about a mile of the mid-air explosion. It sends out a high-energy wave at light speed to melt circuits and ruin electronics. Because it was based on a mortar round, it was highly maneuverable and could be operated by a small crew.

"So, will the drones be toast?" Connie asked.

"Drones, vehicles, power plants laptops, comms. Anything not in a protected Faraday cage gets zapped," Larry said.

"So what if we used them on the QRF too?" Nan asked.

Larry began texting.

—◆○◆—

"Helek, don't speak, just listen. What if you shift one of your guys twenty five percent in case our friend needs help?"

Amadan's comm clicked once. He knew one Warrior shifted to the physical, which was not a direct disobedience of the Rules of Engagement against going to the physical side of creation during the fight because the battle had not yet begun. The Colonel knew this operation could be a bloodbath for his battalion. A direct assault on the prison and getting two marks out from the enemy pressure was a daunting assignment. Still, the hundred Angel Warriors assigned to the mission were the finest soldiers he could muster. He needed the kid to get out of the lake so the attack could commence before the QRF would show up with reinforcements of both kinds.

"Iggy, go twenty five percent and make some waves to rinse our guy off."

"Roger."

TWENTY-FOUR

Sol 7750 (6 September 2048)
Alpha, Mars

"Bill, you're going to want to hear this," Benz said into his comm. The seven caves comm system was being tested, and there were still many dark spots within the Alpha network where signals were lost or impossible to acquire. The installers from Anzacland assured the leadership team that they were only a few days away from having the system up and running.

"Benz, I'm in Lake City and..." Benz's comm went blank, so he tried the text option instead. "I'm in Alpha in the command center. Come as soon as you can."

"911?" Bill responded to the text with his own.

"Yes. Two of them."

"Fifteen minutes."

"We've got hostiles approaching and I'm not authorized to signal the alert."

"Where did you get your info?"

"V."

"The canisters are inbound, too!"

"Yeah, that's a problem," Benz said.

Within five seconds, the red alarm rang in Alpha, bringing all the people working in the cavern to the command center.

"What's the second 911?"

"The F.P. took Ally."

"They used her to find us!"

———◆———

"Don't you worry. I won't let anyone harm a single hair on your pretty little head," Ridge said to Ally just before placing his Evo helmet on, covering his sardonic smile. His squad of Federal Police soldiers geared up for their assault on Alpha as a harbor for illegal immigrants. This was the spin Ridge used to keep the assault in the realm of legal issues rather than a military invasion. The two Federal Police Buggs flew over the Tharsis Rise, getting close to their destination.

After getting Ally's confession, he was able to locate the entrance to the cave system using the old Russian maps and then plot the attack from the air. Once his commandos landed, finding the new habitat that Ally disclosed the Underground was busy building wouldn't be too hard. He was sure he would find his disappeared LIFT employee, along with a slew of undesirables, in the search. This would be an epic day for his career.

———◆———

The rogue wave unexpectedly knocked Kars head over heels, leaving him grasping for something solid to hang onto.

"I must be getting close to shore," he thought. As he righted himself, he crawled over loose rocks and soft muck, leaving a plume in his wake. The sun was nearly down while he crawled on until he ran into a wall.

"Now what?" Kars was exhausted, and his temper was short. He needed a snack and glanced at his air gauge before expanding his Evo to access his food. Five percent power made him nervous, but he figured he must be close to the shore. After the expansion and pulling in his arms, he could rub at his face and get some circulation moving below his beard.

When he forced a protein bar open, he had the sudden idea of inflating the gravity bags wrapped around him to protect him from excessive G-forces, thinking it could give him more ballast to float. If he left the Evo expanded and upped his internal pressure, he thought he'd pop to the surface and paddle to shore.

"Nothing has been easy. Why should this be any different?" he asked himself and pushed his head back up into his helmet. The tubes inflated, and the pressure pushed against his ears, and he felt his feet leave the bottom of the lake. He shoved his arms back into the sleeves and released the lock, reaching forward into the darkness like he was going on a blind midnight adventure to find the bathroom.

When he touched the rock face of the underwater cliff, he forced himself back down so he could push off with his legs and pull up with his arms simultaneously.

⋅⬦⋅

"What's he doing?" Helek asked Iggy over their comm.

"It looks like he is trying to inflate his suit."

"Why?"

"To float I would guess."

"We're running out of time and daylight." Helek said frustration growing inside him.

"Colonel, are your guys close?"

"Roger."

When Kars emerged from the bottom he was only in eight feet of water. His combination of newfound buoyancy and push-pull effort plopped him out of the water like a fishing bobber suddenly getting released from a snag.

Iggy flipped his wings beneath the water's surface, sending a wave to push the inflated Evo toward shore. That action flipped Kars head over heels again. He could not stop the follow-through momentum from smacking his head on the hard beach of stone. After the move, Iggy returned to one hundred percent stealth.

⁜

"Got him!" said a soldier from the Florida Brigade after witnessing the scorched Evo pop out of the water and flip over, hitting its helmet on the rock.

Two soldiers rushed to the Evo but were uncertain how to proceed.

Kars was unconscious, and his atmo expired. The internal alarm sounded, but Kars thought it was an alarm clock from a dream. He just wanted to sleep. Another CO_2 alarm sounded. It did nothing to rouse him.

"What do we do?" one soldier whispered to the other.

"I don't know."

The first soldier, known as Andy, knocked on the helmet glass. He pulled his knife and used the blade to gently tap on the visor.

"I think he's out cold from the fall."

"Yeah. I don't know how to get his helmet off, do you?"

"No idea."

"Lets pull him onto shore."

They grabbed under the Evo's arms and pulled as hard as they could against the weight of the space suit.

"Holy crap this is heavy!" Private Andy said to his comrade.

"I hear an alarm going off inside the suit."

The second soldier leaned in to listen and pulled back in disgust. "This thing stinks!"

Andy caught a whiff, too, just as two more militia members came to help.

"Let's get this into the trees and covered with a Shimmer," the voice came from a Sergeant of the Brigade.

Each man took a corner, and together, they carried the Evo ten yards underneath the canopy of trees.

"Sarge, do you know how to open an Evo from this side?"

"Why?"

"We've been hearing alarms going off inside the thing."

"We got to flip him over."

Inside the suit, Kars felt cold and his body started sweating against the high temperature. When the Evo is flipped over, the visor, having been set in "flee and allude" mode, became opaque to hide the occupant's identity. The Evo looked like a dirty, burnt balloon with legs and short arms.

Andy went back to tapping on the helmet's polymer shell. The team maintained silence during this operation as a precaution, so the tapping was extremely quiet.

"There's a lever on the front, but I can't see it with all of this sand and dirt. Dip some water in your helmet and wash this off," the sergeant said to soldier Andy.

Sergeant Schiffler texted his Lieutenant to seek instruction on the Evo helmet informing him the alarms sounded inside the unit, but the occupant was unresponsive.

Andy retrieved water several times, dumping the contents and returning to the lake for more.

"Don't open that Evo!" His Lieutenant text back. "We don't know about contaminants coming from Mars!"

Sergeant Shiffler realized that decision was wrong and looked around for a medic.

"Pass it down the line— we need a medic," he told his guys, then put his ear to the Evo. The alarms had stopped. He could not hear anything other than the noise coming through the walls of the suit. He shook the suit back and forth and told Andy to set a ping for a medic.

"That's gonna give us up, Sarge."

"This guy is gonna die if we don't do something," Sergeant Shiffler said.

"What about the release in front?"

"What?"

"You said the Evo had a release."

"Yeah it's a long lever, should be steel. Let me have that knife."

Sergeant used the tool to probe the remaining dirt on the Evo helmet. "Get more water." Andy ran off and returned, dumping the water on the face plate.

"We got a medic coming Sarge," someone said behind him.

"Tell him to hurry!"

Kars pulled air into his lungs, and there was no oxygen left to feed his blood. His dream world grew dark and discombobulated. The sleep was a welcome friend. "*I am so tired,*" he thought, snuggling under an imaginary blanket.

———◆———

"Lieutenant Ridge!"

"Ridge here."

"Sir, we've got an air lock without windows."

Ridge was busy examining the front of the Russian entrance where the rock had been recently ground off smooth on two sides and the ceiling. "Is it green?"

"Affirmative."

"Go through it! What else are you going to do, invite them out to play?"

"Yes sir. Sending half the squad."

"No, send them all!"

"Sir, that's not proper protocol."

"Do what I said, Sergeant!"

"Sir."

The five advanced team members cycled together through the tunnel airlock from the Russian cave, entering into a space filled with thick darkness. The tunnel had rails on the ground that gleamed when the team turned on their lights with their e-stools aimed into the blackness.

"We are through. The railroad tracks continue on this side of the lock, sir."

"They must have built a giant airlock for train cars before these tracks were connected to the Anzacland spur?" Ridge questioned the logic of his own thought.

"Unknown, sir."

"Follow those tracks, and we will cycle through behind you." Ridge regretting leaving Ally in the Bug. Of course, she didn't have an Evo, so she was not going anywhere.

"Roger."

What Ridge and his crew didn't know was they were being watched from the command tent by Benz and Bill. They had sent the rest of the contingent to Lake City to hide in the cliffs on the north side of the lake with Evo's and weapons. All the lights had been shut down in Alpha, but the atmo was left on. They hoped to entice Ridge to order his soldiers remove their helmets.

"What if I reprogram some Bots to help us?" Benz whispered to Bill.

"Do it!"

<hr>

"Too easy, Ridge, you big dope," V said to his monitor. He finished deciphering the encryption of the two Buggs that sat in front of the Russian Cave. The F.P. had used a scrambler to hide their advance on the cavern, which V had not seen before. They snuck their Buggs under the radar to gain entry to Alpha.

"I know you got Ally." V fought for footage from the F.P. base in Free Port. Twelve men and one woman was all the V needed to see loaded into the two Buggs from the base.

He rewound the feed from the Russian cave and counted twelve black Evos sneaking inside.

"You should ask to come inside my house, fool!" V laughed while his fingers danced on his upright keyboard in a flurry of movement powered by adrenaline.

"Let's do a little weight trial on them, Buggs." Each Bugg powered up and lifted off the ground by a foot, then settled again and turned the motors off.

"Well, Ally is certainly in the second Bug." V opened communications into the vehicle.

"Ally, are you busy?"

"V?"

"Yep. It's your favorite dark angel in the sky!"

"I wouldn't say favorite, but you're definitely in my top ten now!"

"Wew. I was worried."

"Uhh, can you get me out of here?"

"I'm working on it. I had to figure out where you were before I blew up a Bugg."

"That makes me happy."

"How is Ridge doing?"

"That guy is an animal."

With that thought, the Bugg without Ally had an unfortunate accident with a Hum parked less than a mile away. The Hum ripped the side of the Bugg open and broke off half of its lifting motors.

"I think I see an F.P. insurance claim in the near future," V announced.

"Hope their rates go through the roof."

"That's not the only thing going through the roof."

"What do you mean?"

"Hang on. Oh, by the way, Kars landed in a lake in North Carolina. Just got word. I don't have any more details."

"What the heck?"

Ally's Bugg lifted off and landed on the Hum that had disemboweled the other flying machine.

"Hang on. I'm connecting you with your ride." Seconds later, the hatch at the bottom of the Bugg revealed the airlock tunnel through the Hum roof. "You need to go now, Ally."

She sat on the Bugg's floor with the information about Kars landing on Earth.

"Ally. NOW!"

Ally slid over to the hatch and shimmied herself through the umbilical connection to the Hum below. V closed the hatches, retracted the tunnel, then blasted the Bugg off to the top of the Tharsis Rise.

Ally sat in stunned silence, praying and crying at the news about her husband. When the Hum started leaving the area, she jumped up to check for any information on the web about his landing or crossing during the last couple of days. But a sudden urge to kneel and pray for him became overwhelming.

Same Time

Teapot Key

"He's down. They've got him and are sending a medic to his position." Larry pumped his fist.

"Oh thank you, Jesus!" Nan proclaimed.

"Did the coded message come through?" Connie asked.

"My contact notified me that he was down," Larry said.

"But without the coded message from the contact confirming that he is alive, they could just have recovered his suit!"

"You're right. Let me check." Larry sat back down in front of his computer.

Same time

Jeru, Mars

V sent a message, "Send an urgent notice to the entire Underground network to stop and pray for the Pirate!"

"Helek, you've got to do something. He has run out of air!" Amadan said calmly into his comm.

"QRF is ten minutes out. What are the orders?

"HOLD. EVERYONE HOLD!"

After reading through his communications with his Lieutenant, Larry sent a direct message to Sergeant Schiffer.

"Kars. Kars, Gigi sent us to help you." Schiffer whispered into the suit, repeating Commander Larry Shields's text.

In his twisted thinking, Kars managed to stand when he heard his name. He staggered over to an imaginary door, pushed it open, and scouted the area. There was smoke in the distance. A pillar of thick black smoke like someone was burning tires. The cloud hanging over the pillar swept over and began to choke Kars as he stood in the doorway to his imagination. He toppled over, coughing with the stench. It felt like hands were grabbing around his neck, squeezing like a Boa constrictor. He felt his face go cold, scratching at the skin of the snake devil wrapped around his throat. Kars coughed and spit as his face changed to a fire-red color, while his eyes bulged against the torture. In a rush of adrenaline and clarity, Kars's eyes shot open and he could see the North Carolina countryside. He gave the command to open his helmet.

With the pop and hiss of the helmet in front of him, Sergeant Schiffer forced the steel lever wide open. He grabbed the helmet, twisting it free from the rest of the suit. Out rushed a foul stench that nearly knocked him over. Kars began trying to pull himself out of his own suit— like he had done thousands of times on Mars, but he did not have the strength to make it happen. Instead, he smelled the humid air, the lake, and the trees, all in one long breath, and began to sob. His emotions spilled out of his rancid Evo before he was pulled clear. After Kars slithered out of his nest, the men helped him sit up as the sun retreated over the mountains. While his eyes adjusted to the unfiltered scene before him, more raw emotions boiled over.

"Welcome back, sir." Schiffer touched the crying man's back.

"What a ride," Kars managed to say between blubbering. Andy showed up with another helmet full of water.

"Sir?"

Kars grabbed the helmet and dumped it over his own head, amazed at the refreshing feeling.

"We've got to go now."

Kars was placed on a stretcher, and his Evo was strapped to another. The band of merry men marched off into the forest, blending into the evening. The four unfortunate souls carrying the Evo nearly gagged with every step.

"The nesting birds are beautiful this time of year," was the message that went out all over the underground network. It was also a command for the attack to commence. Within a minute, ten 120E mortar rounds were sent flying into the North Carolina evening.

⸺◆⸺

"Everyone is here, Lieutenant. Now what?"

Ridge assessed the situation. They could not see their own hand in front of their face without their suit lights, and he knew their lights would give their position away.

"Turn off your suit lights," Ridge commanded. "Use the NVG's."

"There is no ambient light to amplify, Commander. But my sensors tell me that there is Atmo."

"This cave has Atmo? Can anyone else confirm?" All the other men confirmed that a breathable atmosphere existed.

"Remove the helmets," Ridge commanded.

The hiss of excess helmet pressure being bled off echoed through their tunnel.

In front of their position, a bot used its loading bucket to drag a long, slow, and ominous sound across the rocks on the tunnel road into the cavern. The twelve Federal Police officers felt the hair on their necks rise in fear.

"Send two men forward with their infrared suit lights on," Ridge ordered. The other ten men formed a perimeter in the vast sea of utter darkness.

◆○◆

Two hours later, Kars slept in the back of an ambulance as it crossed into Georgia. The governor of the Peach State was made aware of the attack on the G.U. prison camp a few miles into North Carolina. He mobilized National Guard units north of Atlanta to defend the border against all Global Union intrusions as well as five old F-22s to defend their sky.

When Kars's ambulance sped its way south, it was stopped by a military vehicle carrying wounded from a nearby attack. One stretcher was loaded onboard, before the vehicle raced off ahead of the growing convoy of Florida Brigade Forces heading home.

Kars stirred, checking the person lying within inches of his head. It was dark inside the ambulance but he could make out an IV dangling its long tentacle from a half-empty bag of liquid to the wrist and another to the left arm. Beside him the other person drew deep, rhythmic breaths.

Kars felt the wall above his head, for a switch. When he flipped it on a string of LEDs lit up the inside of the emergency vehicle. The person beside him stirred, folding arm over her eye. Her other arm was covered by a filthy homemade cast.

"What?" Bry asked from beneath a stupor of medication and exhaustion.

"I came to rescue you." Kars wept. He touched her bruised cheek, tucking her thinned hair behind her ear, and pausing his hand on her warm face to take it in.

"Kars, is it really you?"

"Yes. I'm here now."

"Oh, thank you, God! My prayers have been answered. Are we in heaven?" Bry mumbled into her dream. They both fell off the cliff of consciousness while holding each other's hand.

⊷◉⊶

"Helek. Sitrep."

"Colonel, target secured, headed south."

"Out of danger?"

"Affirmative."

"We need you back in North Carolina. All hands on deck. This battle is getting out of hand."

⊷◉⊶

As cheers echoed off of the cavern walls of Jeru in celebration of the Martian Pirate surviving his fiery descent to Earth— three experimental canisters filled to capacity with seven hundred and fifty sleeping refugees streaked across the Martian sky headed to their destiny. They were supposed to land outside Alpha, the cave city that had just been plunged into the heart of darkness.

The End.

Also by Craig Matthews

Other exciting books from Craig Matthews

Available Everywhere and
www.craigmatthewsmedia.com

Other exciting books from Craig Matthews

Available Everywhere and
www.craigmatthewsmedia.com

INVERTED

Other exciting books from Craig Matthews

Available Everywhere and
www.craigmatthewsmedia.com

Other exciting books from Craig Matthews

Available Everywhere and
www.craigmatthewsmedia.com